T0146982

A NOVEL

Refiner's FIRE

LAURA OTIS

REFINER'S FIRE
A NOVEL

iUniverse books may be ordered through booksellers or by contacting:

iUniverse
1663 Liberty Drive
Bloomington, IN 47403
www.iuniverse.com
1-800-Authors (1-800-288-4677)

ISBN: 978-1-5320-7529-2 (sc)
ISBN: 978-1-5320-7528-5 (e)

Library of Congress Control Number: 2019908960

Print information available on the last page.

iUniverse rev. date: 08/30/2019

For Antje Radeck (1963–2018),
loving mother, generous friend

1

Changed in
a Moment

Julia drew a deep breath and filled her lungs with wet air. A smooth arpeggio flowed from her core, its warmth engulfing the faucet's hiss. With water bubbling over her fingers, she scrubbed a carrot raw and marked the time with rhythmic strokes. Smiling, she savored the easy openness of a low A.

Clack!

In the living room, a flat block hit the floor. From the sound, it must have been a puzzle piece, maybe a yellow star escaping its pointed bed. Julia turned off the water and broke the flow of her voice.

"Bettina?" she called.

"Ja, Mama!"

A gay clatter followed a soft thud, and a small fist gripped the door frame. By degrees, Bettina revealed her grinning face: red curls, a brown eye, a puffed chin. Her pink shirt had a long tomato stain that trailed a string of cast-off islands. In her free hand, she was swinging the empty puzzle frame.

"Assi," she pleaded.

"Not now. I'm making dinner," Julia said.

She knocked four potatoes into the sink. They bumped the metal in a tenor burst and rolled to a quivering halt. Bettina glowered and tapped the puzzle back against the kitchen door. Several times a day, Julia held Bettina's warm sides as she called through the window to their neighbor Astrid. Their shouted conversations about food and dreck cheered the willful two-year-old as much as their housebound friend.

"Aren't you hungry? Don't you want to eat?" Julia asked. "After dinner we can talk to Assi. Why don't you stick those puzzle pieces in their holes, and when you're done, there'll be something yummy."

A quick smile split Bettina's scowl, and she thumped back to the adjacent room. Clacks and scrapes gave way to thrashes as she kicked the couch's sprigged blanket into a pleasing shape.

Julia dragged a forearm across her brow and breathed wet vegetables and pungent sweat. The June heat had invaded Berlin like an avenging army until each household threw open its windows in surrender. In her fifth-floor apartment, the air had stopped moving, though her plants under the living room window begged it to flow. At least the kitchen steam was nourishing her voice. She let the water rush and sent another arpeggio into its twisting stream.

Tonight she had assigned herself two measures that eluded her: the steepest slide in Handel's "Refiner's Fire." One of the toughest pieces ever written for an alto, this aria from *Messiah* conveyed the wrath of God. Racing along in skewed, uneven steps, it moved as unpredictably as flames. In her years of singing, Julia had never found anything so hard, but Arno swore her voice was made for its leaps and falls.

Julia stared into the stream until its bulges took the form of Arno's hands. Since her first audition in a dank church basement, his insistent fingers had been shaping her sound. As Arno charted the currents of her voice, "Refiner's Fire" had become his obsession. But in the past two years, she had disappointed him.

Julia caught her breath. Palm up, thick fingers tense, Arno's hand trembled before her, as though he were holding an iron ball.

"Fi—"

Julia's high D ruled the moist air, but she slipped on the tricky B-natural. In the aria that spun from F-major to D-minor, the B lay like a bright, forgotten marble waiting to trip a singer up. If only she could hit those first four notes. She closed her eyes and tried to envision their shape. Julia attacked arias by dividing them up, picturing the one living thing as many. Each four-note turn formed a unique figure that she named for its personality. "Motherfucker," she called the wild descent that she had chosen for tonight. Its downward rush deceived every instinct, and Handel seemed to have written it just to taunt her.

Julia let loose another soaring D, but it floated too easily. She reached across a puddle for her tuning fork. Yes, the note was flying heavy, lacking the brilliance to shoot her down the right path. Smiling, she thought of how Arno could pull a D like a gold coin out of empty air. She tried the run again from the proper height, pausing each step of the way down. D, C, B-natural, A. Then the next four: G-sharp, F-sharp, E, D. The notes made no sense, and when she closed her eyes, she could see only dust spinning in grayness.

"No!" A bright voice cut into the swirl.

"Bettina," she called, "*Was ist?*"

Three puzzle pieces clacked in a dotted rhythm, and Bettina reappeared with her matted bear.

"Knuti won't put the pieces in. He wanna talk Assi."

Bettina's dark-brown eyes had a determined look as she kneaded Knuti's arm. Smiling, Julia wiped her hands on her thighs. In the golden light, Bettina's skin glowed like the curve of an untouched fruit. Julia wiggled her fingers into her daughter's hair and savored its maple smell.

"Mama!"

Bettina darted for her nest on the couch. On the living room floor lay circles, squares, and stars that might have dropped from a magician's robe. The lumpy couch sat under its blue-flowered quilt like a despairing cat with rumpled fur. Across from this uneasy resting place, a small TV and stereo stood on improvised shelves. Shiny knickknacks winked from bookcases anchored by musical scores down below. A faint gleam drew Julia's eye to the table under the window, where she raised violets, philodendrons, and spider plants.

Drinking light, the silent leaves stood so still that the open window above them didn't seem real. It hung over them like a painting, admitting no air or sound. Julia stooped to gather the puzzle pieces, which clung to her hands like sliced cheese. Bettina held the puzzle back as a waiting tray, and Julia dropped them onto it. Two heads bent over the pile of shapes, one hot and auburn, the other fuzzy and gray. Knuti the bear had accompanied Bettina since the day of her birth, yielding silently to her kicks and cuffs.

"Tell him he can't get up till all the pieces are in," Julia said. "Watch him. Make sure he does it right."

"Ja, Mama," Bettina murmured. She pushed Knuti's nose into the heap.

A boiling pot clattered on the stove, and Julia rushed to peel the freckled potatoes.

"Fi—"

She shot into an A minor arpeggio and froze, gripping the knife. That dark, easy bound lay just past Motherfucker like some rich, chocolate reward. Without thinking, she must have sung every note right, like a gymnast whose first leap makes her next moves effortless. The notes lost their strangeness, and for the first time, Julia heard the phrase as a whole. How could Handel have written it any other way? Tears filled her eyes, but she blinked them back and tried the run again faster. If she could just get into it from the start of the section ...

"For he is like—"

The piece sounded thin, as though an instrument in the orchestra had dropped away. Under Julia's floating voice, the faucet hissed, and the pot lid rattled. From the living room came only silence.

"Bettina?" she called.

Was that a rustle of the blanket? With Knuti for company, Bettina must still be sorting her shapes. Julia sang through the pummeling arpeggios, alternating between playful A7 and rich D minor. She had to find Motherfucker from the longer approach to reach that calm, dark water past the rapids.

A high-pitched noise cut the faucet's continuo. Something must be happening outside. With a grimace, Julia turned off the water, and the sound sharpened to a scream. Inside Julia, something exploded.

Three bounds took her to the living room. Under the open window, two plants had vomited black dirt onto the floor. Knuti lay nose down on the couch, but Bettina had disappeared. Julia kicked a plant aside and leaned out the window. Ten yards away in her own window, Astrid was rocking, the heels of her hands over her eyes. She cried out with each forward motion, her fingers lost in her hair.

Down in the courtyard, a small pink heap broke the ground near the yellow recycling bin. Scraggly bushes stretched thirsty feelers toward a glassy puddle of red. Astrid's son, Basti, stood with his phone to his ear, his straight, broad shoulders tense as metal. A shriek burst out of Julia's belly, blasting the music from her throat.

2

Thou Shalt
Break Them

Against the table's hard edge, Julia's chest swelled and shrank in a rapid beat. Her black drawstring pants bit her belly with each breath, and her tight bra held her breasts like a trap. A gathering stream of sweat tickled her chest, and she crushed it with an absent fist. The June heat had broken, but the interview room preserved last week's tropical air.

Julia's fingers caught the poppy-red silk of the scarf over her rising breast. The policewoman's eyes burned with a spotlight's glare, and Julia's hands sought cover in the loose mesh. Astrid had warned Julia to dress herself up, but this cheap scarf had been the best she could do. She had bought it last year at the Christmas market, where she had pulled its red from a shimmering rainbow.

The *Kommissarin* stared with a deep blue look that drank more than it conveyed. Her eyes might have been sympathetic, but their unwavering light revealed only a desire to know. The blond ponytail that her hand kept seeking hung like a relic from another time. Bobbing cheerfully behind her hardened face, it made her look like a Janus head that grinned on one side and frowned on the other.

"Can't we do this at the hospital?" Julia asked. "Please. I need to see Bettina."

Since the ambulance doors had boomed shut, she had barely left her daughter. Bettina had landed on bushes, the police said, those scraggly brambles that formed clean white berries in winter and drooped in summer. Somehow, the stalks confusedly embracing the recycling bins had caught Bettina on her way down. They had formed a loose network under her head, so that she had struck something more like a basket than hard ground. Aside from some painful cuts on her arms, at first she had seemed fine.

Then she'd faded. Yesterday morning, a neurologist had called to say that Bettina seemed groggy. Her shrill cries diminished to gurgles until she couldn't be roused from murky sleep. When he reexamined her closely, he found the trouble: a small fracture near the top of her skull. A tiny spear of bone had pierced a vessel, and a lake of blood was crushing her brain. He operated immediately and expected a good recovery, but a pulse in his voice betrayed some doubt. There could be brain damage, or Bettina might not reawaken. If and when she did, she would be pinioned, alone, and terrified.

"Please." Julia leaned forward. She breathed from her belly and tried to straighten her voice. "Please. She's all alone. If she wakes up … she—" Her voice heaved.

The Kommissarin massaged the bridge of her nose, using her thumb and finger as a pincher. "No, we need to talk here. We're recording this. We have regulations."

Julia folded her arms and met the Kommissarin's weary eyes. They had the tense, swollen look of a woman due to get her period any moment.

"We could do it another time," Julia said. "After she wakes up. Or ... I—I just have to be with her. She needs me." Her voice sounded dull as a half-filled jar.

The blonde Kommissarin returned her gaze. "No, we need to do this now."

"For God's sake!" Julia's voice broke out. "We could do this anytime! I need to be with her! Don't you see? You got kids?" The Kommissarin's hand crept toward her ponytail. "*Ja,*" she murmured.

She closed her eyes, and Julia sensed the policewoman picturing her apartment's layout. That would be the keynote in their tense duet: why Julia had left a two-year-old alone next to an open window. The authorities needed to learn whether Julia had violated Bettina's right to care—first in this police investigation, then in a longer ordeal with the child welfare office. If they found Julia guilty, they could fine her, jail her, or remove Bettina from her care. But what did it matter if ... Julia's breath caught, and her nails bit her palms.

"She's in good hands," the Kommissarin said. "Let's hope for the best."

No light shone in her gray eyes.

"Who else is responsible for this child's care?" she asked. "You have any family helping you? Any friends?"

"*Ja.*" Julia twisted her back. "My neighbors watch Bettina sometimes. Astrid Kunz. And her son, Basti Kunz."

"Uh-huh." The policewoman scratched a note, even though an unseen device was listening.

"What about Bettina's father?"

The question jolted Julia like a botched chord.

"Are you in touch with her father?" asked the Kommissarin.

"*Ja.*" Julia's voice was exhaled breath. Erik revealed himself, puffy, earnest, and red.

"Erik Kiepert is the father?" The policewoman lifted a page as though she were separating layers of pastry. "Would you say that you have a good relationship with him?"

Julia raised her chin. "*Ja*. We understand each other."

"He's declared paternity." The Kommissarin wiggled the suspended page. "But he lives in Frankfurt. Can you explain that?"

Julia smoothed the poppy-red scarf, but it caught on some rough skin. "He wants to be in Bettina's life, but he's got a good job down there."

"So why don't you move down there? If he wants to help?" The Kommissarin's questions flew at Julia.

"I—I need to be here. I'm a singer," she murmured.

The Kommissarin puffed out her thin lower lip. "So—Frankfurt—there's got to be music there. You're a professional singer, right? You sing opera?"

Even on the policewoman's immovable face, the word *opera* spread a glow. In Berlin, few people listened to opera, but everyone revered it. In some minds, its arias lay like hidden jewels waiting to inspire with emerald flashes.

"I haven't sung in any operas yet," said Julia. "I sing cantatas—oratorios. I've applied to the opera companies here—and a professional chorus."

The Kommissarin's hand slipped under the table, and Julia suspected she was massaging her belly. The policewoman closed her eyes and released her breath.

"Is there another relationship keeping you here?" she asked. "Is that why you won't leave Berlin?"

Julia clutched fistfuls of red silk. "No. It's the music."

The Kommissarin studied Julia's face, and her gray eyes softened to dense clouds.

"What about your neighbor Basti? He seems to care about you and Bettina."

Julia swallowed. In a metal bed, Bettina might be opening her eyes to see only a scrubbed wall.

"He's twenty-two," said Julia. "Ten years younger than me. He's got a girlfriend—Birgit. He's just kind. He likes to help people. He—" Julia's voice twisted, and the Kommissarin tilted her head.

"And your conductor—" The policewoman glanced at her sheaf of papers. "Arno … Weber? Are you close with him too?"

A hot, wet ball burst in Julia's chest. "What does it matter?" she cried. "Why are you asking me this? I don't sleep with him! Let me get back to Bettina!"

The Kommissarin exhaled with satisfaction. "Take it easy," she said. "I just want to get a sense of your support network. I don't know if you know this, but there's another claim on Bettina."

"What?" Julia released the sweaty scarf, and its red hills softly sank.

"Erik's mother, Renate Kiepert, is suing for custody. Did you know that?"

Julia's stomach clenched. The mention of Renate tautened the air until it seemed ready to produce lightning. Julia could picture Erik's mother gazing at Bettina with flat black eyes. Since the day of Bettina's birth, Renate had been extending sticky tendrils toward a child she saw as rightfully hers.

"She can't do that, can she?" asked Julia.

"Well, she can file the suit," said the Kommissarin. "She can make the claim. Bettina almost died in your care."

Julia sensed the soft puff of Bettina's sigh as she paused between waves of sleep. Her little daughter mustn't wake up alone.

"Julia?" The policewoman's alto cut in. "I need to know about your support network. You work at Dorrie's Donuts, right?"

"*Ja.*" Julia pressed her feet against the gray floor.

"And Bettina goes to day care while you work. What do you do with her when you're singing?"

"I have babysitters—friends who help me." Julia's voice floated.

"I don't understand why you reject the Kieperts' help." The Kommissarin pressed her. "It sounds like you need it. Are they harming Bettina in some way? Is she at risk with them?"

Julia raised her eyes. The woman's face masked curiosity more hot than professional.

"I don't like Bettina to be with them," said Julia. "They care about culture. They don't care about people."

The Kommissarin nodded, and her ponytail bobbed. "What about your own family?"

"My parents are dead." The phrase sliced Julia's memories. Her mother giggled uneasily, and her father laughed in a deep, red roar. Julia's words passed through their sounds like a silver blade through a ghost.

"What you're telling me," said the Kommissarin, "is if you raise Bettina, there are going to be times when she's unsupervised— like the other night."

Julia summoned her deepest tones. "That won't happen again. I'll move downstairs. I'll watch her every minute. I won't leave her."

"How did it happen?" asked the policewoman. "You must have known she could climb. Why did you leave that table under the window? Frau Kiepert says she moved it away in April, 'cause she was worried about something just like this, but you must have moved it back."

"*Ja.*" Julia's breath ran short. "I grow plants on that table. It's the only place where there's enough light."

Basti had found the mahogany table a few years ago and had restored it to life with loving hands. The chocolate flowers around its rim glowed with the warmth of another time.

"So she did make you move it—but you moved it back?"

"She didn't *make* me move it."

Julia bristled. How long was this woman going to grill her?

"Why did Frau Kiepert move the table?" The Kommissarin pushed her.

"Because she was afraid—" Julia's belly wouldn't support the waiting words.

"She was afraid Bettina would climb up on the table. But you weren't?" As though cued by a conductor, the Kommissarin's voice quickened.

"No—she never gets up on that table." Julia faltered.

"Why not?" asked the Kommissarin.

"Because—" Julia closed her eyes. Smiling proudly, Bettina offered her a bouquet of leaves. The smack, the scream ... The heat when her palm struck flesh ...

"Have you ever hit your child?" A clear, calm alto stream.

Julia gasped. "No!"

"You have never hit Bettina."

"No!"

"But she knows you don't want her up on that table. She always do everything you want?" The woman's gray eyes begged Julia to reveal herself.

"No. Of course not," she muttered.

"If I told my kids not to get on a table, they'd be break-dancin' on it thirty seconds after I left the room."

Julia refused to smile. "Bettina's not like that."

The glow in the policewoman's eyes faded. "So this sounds pretty rough," she said. "You've got two jobs. Neither one of 'em pays much." Her eyes sought Julia's. "Your family's gone. You got any brothers or sisters?"

Julia shook her head.

"So no family of your own. You don't like your guy's family—"

"He's not my guy," said Julia.

The alto wave crept on like a black tsunami. "You ever think maybe you just made a mistake? Maybe you shouldn't have had her?"

"No!" cried Julia. "I've never thought that!"

The policewoman's fingers twitched.

"Fuck this!" yelled Julia. "Let me go back to my daughter! Would you be asking me about my support network if I made a hundred thousand a year?"

"I'm asking you about your support network 'cause your daughter fell out a fifth-story window," said the Kommissarin.

Julia froze, her hands sculpting empty air. Blood thumped in her ears, and she fell back against cool metal. The policewoman's gaze had deepened in color, as though a violin line had melted into a cello solo. Something in Julia's cries had summoned a look that was disturbingly familiar. With darkening eyes, the Kommissarin was staring at her the way people used to look at her mother.

3

Every Valley

Henningsthal lay on the Siegen-Giessen line, a town of twenty thousand that was slowly shrinking. Badly damaged in the war, it had been rebuilt to look as people thought it once did, its steep-roofed houses creeping up the slopes of the Westerwald. If you ever took time to walk through its streets, the town's fairy-tale look dissolved. Near the market square, half-timbered houses stood like slabs of stale gingerbread, but most homes had been rebuilt with modern practicality. On the plain beige facades, the windows swung out from the top or the side, so that they were easy to clean.

When passengers from Siegen to Giessen felt their trains slow, they looked up from their papers with exasperation. *My God*, they thought, peering out at the dingy station. *Are we stopping again? Why are we stopping* here?

Next to the station stood an improvised shack with one glass wall and a plaster facade. Some embedded planks gave it a medieval look, and a gothic sign over the window said "Imbiss." At the *Imbiss am Bahnhof,* you could buy roast chicken, *Bouletten*, and fries; it also sold bratwurst, potato salad, and beer. Around train time, it did very brisk business, and for years, the big, brown-haired girl in the window was the one thing in Henningsthal that caught people's eyes.

Since Julia had been born, her family had lived off the Henningsthal snack bar. Her mother, a thin, quiet woman, worked from six until three; her father, from one until midnight, so that they overlapped at midday, when the place was busiest. As long as Julia could remember, she had worked and played there—there was always so much to do.

In the mornings, her mother mopped up the filth the town's bums had left. She wiped down tables, stowed bulging bags of rolls, and fired up the coffee machine and rotisserie. If she got up at five, she could catch the Giessen commuters, who wanted warm sweet rolls and coffee. She smiled faintly when the first rays warmed the grimy glass, brightening the cascade of plants that she kept. Julia paused sometimes to watch her soft brown hair glow, but there was no time to lose. Between customers, her mother skewered chickens, slapped together Bouletten, and tried to fill the coffee machine faster than people could empty it. No matter how hard she worked, there was always a customer shifting his weight from foot to foot.

Julia caught on quickly, and by the time she was five, she could unload bottles of juice from the crates. In the refrigerator, she aligned them like cool, clinking statues. At fifteen, she was carrying crates from the trucks, joking with the drivers about how strong she was. Julia had always looked like her father, a heavy, dark-haired man with coarse skin and thick brows. Even now, she smiled with his fun-loving smile, and her voice echoed his cadences.

"Julchen," he called her. "Julchen, *meine kleine Prinzessin*."

Most afternoons he blustered in around one, speaking gruffly and breathing hard. He brightened as the day wore on and rocked the customers with his belly laugh. By eight, Julia's parents made sure she went home since the Imbiss was different at night. As it got later, they sold more beer than coffee. In the dark chill, when commuters were safe in their homes, her father served sixteen-year-olds with shaved heads and drunks who threw up on the sidewalk.

Her mother didn't know it, but Julia often awoke at night when her father came in. Under the covers, she would smile in the dark as he bumped and brushed against things. Sometimes he sang with a rich, warm voice, and she would creep to the door to hear him. Her father only sang at night, when his face was red and he was happy.

"Sh!" her mother would say. "You'll wake her up!"

Then there would be more bumps, and her mother would giggle.

Most of the time, Julia's mother was sad. In the afternoons, her shoulders drooped as she sat at her desk and stared at piles of papers. Even as a girl, Julia knew what they meant: bills for the drinks, the meat, the electricity. Her parents schemed to pay taxes, and insurance, and rent. Working seven days a week, they barely saw each other, so that her father's noise and her mother's stillness became separate worlds. Julia watched her mother's hushed despair, and as Julia got bigger, she tried to help.

Of one thing, her parents made sure. Each week Julia took a music lesson with Frau Glintenkamp. Bills or no bills, her father said, no girl of his was going to grow up without culture. In Germany, any child whose parents could afford it learned to play a musical instrument. Rich or poor, people felt that music nourished fine thought, and its cadences led to higher truths. In the opening cascades of Bach's *Christmas Oratorio* rang a promise that life meant more than scrubbing sidewalks. For Julia's lessons, her parents spent money they didn't have, since it soon became clear she had talent.

When Julia was ten, a music teacher noticed her voice: clear, clean tones that held the others on pitch. The sturdy, brown-haired girl had an unflinching quality, and she took people's gazes with calm serenity. Julia liked being heard, even enjoyed being seen.

"Give that girl lessons. She's gifted," said the teacher.

At Frau Glintenkamp's, Julia blew air through her lips and laughed at their fat, loose tickle. Her fingers tasted the cool smoothness of the curved piano. When Julia sang, the old woman's eyes changed from guarded to peaceful, as though she were seeing something far away. Frau Glintenkamp told Julia to breathe from her belly and pressed hard to make sure she did.

"You've got a lot of weight on you for someone your age," she said. "You must have a healthy appetite."

Julia stared back at the soft-haired lady whose skin hung in spotted folds. She couldn't imagine Frau Glintenkamp enjoying any food, but the boy who came in after her loved to eat. No matter how much homework Julia had, she stayed to hear Erik play piano. She liked the friendly boy with the orange hair and goofy red face. Erik laughed as though everything were silly, but he made the notes blend like a well-trained choir. He touched the keys in a soft, sensitive way, as though they were his friends and he wanted to hear how they got along.

Erik rarely came to his lesson alone. He appeared with his mother, who spoke to Frau Glintenkamp as she did to Erik and Julia. Frau Kiepert had the same snub nose and wide-set eyes as Erik, but with her dark, loose hair, she looked more like a monkey.

"He practiced every day this week," said Frau Kiepert. "He's stopped curling that middle finger. Don't you think he's ready for Chopin?"

When Frau Glintenkamp paired Erik with Julia in recitals, Erik's mother approved, but Julia was glad Frau Kiepert couldn't hear their lessons. She had a different way of listening than Frau Glintenkamp—as though she wanted you to make mistakes, so she could tell you how to fix them. When Julia sang and Erik played, Frau Kiepert's eyes settled the way most people's did when they ate good food. After a while, she let Erik go home with Julia, except that they didn't go home.

Erik loved to work at the Imbiss, and Julia's father beamed when Erik and Julia walked in. As though sniffing their scent, her father raised his broad nose, and his grin welcomed them. "Hey, young people! How's the music world? How's Chopin?"

While Erik's mother thought he was studying math, he was restocking the refrigerator, devouring bratwurst, and listening transfixed as Julia's father described skinheads' brawls. During the slow period from three to five, Erik and Julia studied, sprawled out on the floor in the plants' soft breath. Erik helped Julia with English, which piqued her ear like the whine of a hungry dog. Erik had flown to Florida, and he laughed at the Americans' mushy accent. The way Erik spoke English, even Julia understood it—it sounded like the words of a song.

Erik had planned out his life like a clean gray ribbon of autobahn. He would study music and education and become a teacher since nothing mattered more than shaping young people's minds. He didn't want to be an elementary school teacher like his mother. In high school, people decided how they would spend their lives, and that was when you could do the most good. Erik wanted to be a *Gymnasiumlehrer*, a teacher in one of Germany's top high schools. Julia had to help him calculate percentages since he wasn't so good in math.

When Julia turned fourteen, people began to look differently at her mother. She remembered because that was also the time when Erik stopped coming to the snack bar. After his lesson, he would blink, smile sunnily, and say that he had to go home and study. Julia stopped hearing him play since her mother needed her at work. Her father had begun rumbling in later and later, and if Julia didn't take charge, her mother couldn't do the books. When her father arrived, he was angry and sick, and Julia's mother groaned about his messes.

Late at night now, his sounds had a different tone. Thuds shook the walls, followed by hissed curses. Instead of laughing, Julia's mother cried on a high-pitched note. Julia got up at six, walked to school, and when classes ended, she headed straight for the snack bar. She opened her books on a white plastic table, and between pouring coffee and frying potatoes, she fished with the old man in the sea.

As Julia's father put it, she was filling out. The men who came by loved to joke with her, a bantering that grew more pointed after dark. Julia's father rarely appeared now before six, sometimes not until seven or eight. After a fourteen-hour shift, her mother's eyes were red and her mouth shut tight.

"If it's after eight and he's still not there, just close. It's not worth it," her mother said, but Julia knew they needed the money. At night, the place was going to hell. Her mother would come in at six to find it half-plundered.

One night her father didn't come home alone. Instead, two policemen brought him. In her frayed red bathrobe, Julia stood beside her mother and flushed as the older cop said her father had been urinating in public. The younger policeman didn't say much, just stared with bright eyes at Julia's chest. When the police left, she and her mother wrapped her father's limp arms around their shoulders and carried him to bed. His body felt soft and floppy, and his smoky breath tainted her hair.

The next day, while Julia was helping her mother, those heavy, gray looks began. Not from the men, who ordered bratwurst and beer, but from the women, who took chicken sandwiches and coffee. "*Guten Tag*, Frau Martens," they would say with that look, pitying her for a disease they were too smart to catch.

For a while Julia and her mother spun like twin motors, Julia running the shop from three until eight. If she could have closed then, everything would have been fine, but sensing that he wasn't trusted, her father appeared out of spite—and he brought his friends with him.

"Hey, Julchen! Hey, *Mädel*!" they shouted.

They crushed her with smoky hugs and pierced her face with pointed whiskers.

"Hey, hey, that's my daughter!" laughed her father, but Julia fought herself free with her own strength.

Her mother described what she found in the mornings: the door open, the refrigerator empty, the floor crusted. Julia's family had no more money, and her music lessons stopped. Julia barely saw Erik since he was taking *Gymnasium* classes, preparing himself for college.

"How are your parents?" he asked with troubled eyes.

"Fine," answered Julia.

She couldn't tell Erik what it felt like to peel cold, wet underwear off her father. More and more now, her mother let her unwrap him when he was delivered home like a filthy gift.

Lately, it wasn't her father who worried her. A week ago, her mother had seen a doctor about the lump in her breast. He had ushered her hurriedly into his office, and his shocked, angry look had said it all. Exhausted and desperate, her mother had swallowed her angst until the lump was visibly large. The doctor ordered an immediate mastectomy, and Julia took her to the hospital in Giessen, leaving the snack bar in her father's hands.

After the surgery, her mother needed rest. Julia got up at five, unloaded the deliveries, and closed the Imbiss while she went to school. She reopened at three to catch the evening commuters and left when her father arrived. In the mornings, she now mopped the sidewalk, dissolving its crusty messages in steaming water. If her father failed to appear, she served customers until blackness drove them back to their homes.

When the police learned that Julia worked alone at night, they began to check in regularly. Good-hearted customers sometimes lent a hand, claiming they had nothing better to do. The men complimented Julia's rounded body but kept things to a certain level. If one of them got out of line, his *Kumpels* restrained him with gentle touches. Sometimes Erik came by for a bratwurst and fries. His broad face had erupted in pimples, but his eyes glowed with fondness. He helped Julia take inventory and clean the refrigerators, which were becoming pocked with mold. He told her he had decided to study in Cologne, the best place for a combined degree in education and music.

From Giessen, the news was not good. The cancer had reappeared in her mother's right breast. She needed a second operation and chemotherapy, and someone had to run the Imbiss. With one year left, Julia dropped out of school. She took her mother to Giessen and left her there. Erik helped, though by now his mother treated any attempt to see Julia as a knife jabbed into her side. Julia got up at four and checked on her father, freeing him from his stiff clothes if he needed it. She fired up the coffee machine and caught the clinking crates of drinks the drivers handed her.

"Hey, Mädel," they said and nodded respectfully.

From two until five Julia took a break—for *Mittagspause,* she wrote on the bleak "closed" sign. But really, she ate her lunch quickly and used the time to handle the books. Her father had left them like a dusty keyboard, and she learned how much to pay the bakery to keep the bags of rolls coming. Julia opened again from five until ten and called the police if mutters turned to sharp shouts. They rarely did, since the workingmen kept an eye on her. On her way home, she searched for her father, but a new look in her eye kept his Kumpels away.

White-faced and drawn, Julia's mother returned to the Imbiss. Knowing that Julia had left school made her sicker than the treatments. Erik left for Cologne, but he called Julia often and described the crazy people he was meeting. Several men asked Julia out on dates, and sometimes she went with them to dusky bars. They grumbled when she refused to drink, and their touch stirred her will to fight. At the Imbiss, she kept the radio playing and sang along with the Spice Girls. Her mother rallied, and her father floundered. When the police brought him home, he would vow to quit drinking and for a while would come to work each day. Eventually, Julia would find him red-faced and laughing in one of the nearby bars.

Erik talked about a girl who studied business and music, a flutist who had worked as an au pair in Scarsdale. Her host family had two awful kids who had rooted through her desk, but she had stopped them by mastering their computers. When Erik talked about Johanna, his laughter rushed like water through a rocky bed.

"They couldn't tell their parents!" He laughed. If the vicious brats did, Johanna let them know that they would never play another online game. Erik reveled in Johanna's imaginative toughness, her strategies so unlike his own.

With Julia's mother failing and her father asleep, she cooked, cleaned, unloaded, and argued. The Imbiss passed a surprise health inspection on the condition that she disinfect the refrigerators. Julia kept the crates of drinks rolling in, although she owed the distributor a thousand marks. When she thought about breathing from her belly, she laughed. Imagine paying money to learn how to breathe!

Her mother hovered in the Imbiss like a wistful spirit, her regrown hair darker than it had once been. Hesitating, she struggled to remember people's orders and paused with her finger under her chin. As she studied the pale, heart-shaped leaves of her resilient plants, she rubbed her temples, since she had been getting headaches. Julia found her one afternoon crying over a pile of mail.

"I can't read it anymore," she said.

This time Julia made her father come to Giessen. Big and heavy, she summoned the voice she used with the suppliers. A slim female doctor looked at Julia pityingly, but Julia folded her arms and glowered. She hated it when people felt sorry for her, and under the force of her gaze, the doctor reverted to scientific tones. A malignant tumor was pressing her mother's brain in a hollow surrounded by vital centers. They could try to operate, or they could medicate her so that her last days would be hushed and dim. The doctor looked from one to the other until her eyes rested on Julia.

"Operate," she said.

Her mother died before they reached the tumor.

Erik and his mother came to the funeral, where Julia's father was none too steady. So did old Frau Glintenkamp, who had developed a strange bob to her head.

"What a terrible thing for you," she said. "But now, maybe ..." Her teacher's blue eyes softened with the look Julia's singing had once brought—that vision of a place far away. With a trembling hand, Frau Glintenkamp extended a red plastic spoon toward a bowl of creamy potato salad. Something soft brushed Julia's shoulder.

"I brought you some food," said Erik. "You haven't had anything to eat."

He offered her a plate of glistening Bouletten, which blurred as Julia's eyes swelled. Warm, moist, and round, they looked so much juicier than the dense meat patties her mother had shaped. Erik set the plate awkwardly on a nearby table and wrapped his arms around her. He stroked her hair fondly as she cried into his shirt. Her mother would never make any more Bouletten. Erik didn't say a word, just held her until the sobs stopped coming.

"I can't believe she's gone," whispered Julia. "I mean, I knew, but I can't believe it."

"She was a lovely person," said Erik. "And she's not gone. The best of her is in you."

"Oh, come on!" Julia laughed. She was sure she had heard this line in a movie, with exactly the same rhythm.

"Why don't you sit down?" Erik urged her. "Here. Why don't you try some food?"

Julia hadn't thought she was hungry, but the pungent Bouletten smelled as comforting as Erik's hug. He smiled encouragingly and pushed the plate toward her.

"There are so many people here," he murmured. "She must have had a lot of friends."

"Some of 'em are my father's friends." Julia frowned.

She glanced across the room to where he sat, drinking quietly with his Kumpels in the far corner. One of them rested a hand on her father's shoulder as he gazed down at his weak thighs. His thick brown hair softened his reddish skin, and his gray suit gave him a serious air. He sat very still, as though remembering something, but like cheap fireworks, he could go off at any moment. Erik seemed to follow Julia's thoughts.

"How has he been? How has he been taking it?"

Julia grimaced. "How's he gonna take it? He's a drunk."

Erik nodded sadly. "Can't you help him?" he asked. "Some kind of clinic? They have such good programs now ..."

Julia shrugged. "He's been through a bunch of 'em. He stops for a while, but he always starts again. He misses his friends. He doesn't know what to do when he's not drinking. Thing is—he *likes* it. The programs can't do anything about that."

Erik sighed. "It's such a waste. And it's so hard on you. What are you going to do now?"

Julia searched for Frau Glintenkamp's gray head. "I don't know," she said. "I want to study."

Erik's warm brown eyes radiated sympathy. "Why don't you go somewhere?" he asked. "You have a right to study. Let your father run the Imbiss."

Julia scrunched up her mouth. "Who's gonna run him?" she asked. "He'll just kill it. After all those years she worked."

"So why don't you sell it?" asked Erik. "Somebody else might do a good job with it."

Julia glanced at her father, whose heavy features drooped. Until now, selling the Imbiss had never occurred to her. It had ruled their lives since before she was born.

Seeing her hesitate, Erik persisted. "Come on. You could go anywhere. You could do anything. Why stay here?"

Julia's father seemed to feel her gaze, and for an instant their eyes met. Startled, he tried to give her a smile, but fear nibbled its edges. Ironically, he raised his glass, and Julia turned away.

"You want me to sell him too?" she muttered.

Erik hesitated. "I—I'm sorry. I didn't mean to offend you," he said.

"Oh, that's okay." Julia sighed. "It's not such a bad idea."

She scanned the guests, round, grayish people in stiff clothes. All alone, Frau Glintenkamp stared out at a tree branch whose leaves were dancing in the wind. On the end tables, greasy plates lay waiting to be stacked. A flowered blue dish at a table's rim held shiny circles of scallion. Julia felt her mother touch her elbow and whisper that it was time to clean up.

"Are you okay?" Erik asked, shifting his weight.

Julia followed his eyes. Near the window, his mother was studying them closely. Julia looked at her with the same expressionless stare she used when guys asked her if she gave good head.

"How's Johanna?" she asked.

Erik smiled sheepishly. "Oh, she's mad at me because I applied to study abroad without asking her."

"Yeah, you gotta watch out for that." Julia smiled sardonically.

Erik glanced across the room, and she tracked his thought. She was echoing her father's cadences.

A week later, Julia put the Imbiss up for sale. Her father fulminated, but she convinced him that the shack caused more trouble than it was worth. He signed the papers, which left them 10,000 marks after all the debts were paid. A Turkish family bought the Imbiss, scoured every surface, and installed a vertical spit to make *Döner*. In Julia's old window, Izzet smiled into the morning breeze, his chin resting on his fist. People grumbled at first, but they soon got to like the eager man with his cheerful ways. Julia wished he had kept the plants in the east window, the ones her mother had loved.

Legally, the 10,000 marks belonged to her father. Julia took a thousand. With the cash in a neck pouch, she left for Berlin, where she used half for the security deposit on her apartment. With her work experience, she soon found a job in a restaurant but later moved to Dorrie's Donuts since men troubled her less on day shifts. She stayed in touch with Erik, who married Johanna several years later, as soon as they had earned their degrees.

In Berlin, signs for concerts brightened each wall. Choirs were singing Bach, Beethoven, Handel, and Mozart. At the package store Getränke Gillmann, a handwritten sign on a bulletin board caught Julia's attention one day as two juice bottles clinked in her canvas bag. The sign was written in bold black strokes, the numbers crowding the strips she was supposed to tear. It said that a choir was looking for singers, and the rehearsals were Mondays in the Friedrichskirche. Anyone with a voice was welcome to try out, regardless of singing experience.

The night of her audition, Julia fueled herself with two bratwurst, then sucked on mints to mask their taste. At the piano in the Friedrichskirche basement, she found a broad-chested man whose blond hair shone in a hundred different shades. With his thick arms, he reminded her of the truck drivers who handed her fifty-pound crates. He looked her up and down, and his eyes paused over her breasts. He tried a few chords, as though forgetting she was there. Then he played up to a fifth and back down again.

"Can you sing that?" he asked.

He had a resonant, low voice, rushed by a strange intensity. Usually, people with voices that deep didn't talk so fast.

Julia sang the notes, and her throat opened like a flower. The conductor led her higher, and his body relaxed; his impatient look melted. With brilliant blue eyes, he gazed at her as though seeing her for the first time.

"That's good," he said. "Now let's try this a little lower."

As she sang, Julia's body awoke like a lonely creature starved for sound. The notes came from her center, resounding in her wide-open throat, and her mouth shaped them lovingly. As the blond man played faster, she matched his pace and smiled as her voice emerged.

4

Good Tidings to Zion

The phone's bright, dissonant chord sliced Julia's thoughts, and her watering can wobbled. Jewels of water appeared on her hand-finished table, and she ran to the kitchen for a towel. She glanced at the window where her apartment's warmth met the cold outside. Ten Berlin winters had failed to impress her, but the biting December air promised months of frigid days. The chord pierced again as she wiped the drops. Damn it, who could that be? Anyone who wanted her would have to wait. From her machine rolled a musical voice, playful but with unaccustomed anxiety.

"Julia? Listen, I need you, Mädel. Please tell me you're there … Julia? If you're on the toilet, girl, wipe your ass and get out here!"

Only one voice sounded like that, rich and resonant in its haste. Julia leaped for the phone.

"Arno?"

"Oh, thank God."

She could almost smell his exhaled smoke.

"Arno? What is it?"

A drop of water broke free from a clinging leaf and moistened a spot she'd just wiped.

"Oh, thank God. Julia—listen."

"Yeah. What's going on? What's happening?"

Arno drew in his breath. A flash pulled Julia's eyes to Astrid's window, which framed her neighbor reading at her kitchen table. The big blonde woman dug in her ear, then reached for a cup without moving her eyes from her paper.

"How's your voice, Mädel?"

"Good—better lately. Wha—"

"*Geil!*" Julia could feel Arno's grin. "Listen, I've got a job for you. How would you like to sing the alto solo in the *Christmas Oratorio* tomorrow night?"

"What? Sascha Neumann's—"

"Sascha Neumann has the flu. I just got off the phone with her."

Only the pace of Arno's voice betrayed what he must be feeling.

"She just called you *now?*" Julia gasped. The downbeat was in thirty hours.

"Yeah, stupid cow," he growled. "Says she wasn't sure until now. Been wheezing for days, and she doesn't call me. You're it, girl. You're the only other pair of lungs in Berlin that can do justice to these arias."

Julia reached for the wall and pressed her palm against the bumpy paper.

"Arno, I—"

"I've heard you do it."

"Yeah, in the Johanneskirche here in Charlottenburg." Julia frowned as her father's cynical tones emerged.

Each year, every town in Germany performed Bach's *Christmas Oratorio*, with varying degrees of competence. The rich, joyous piece was so well loved that the humblest church choirs took it on. In a land where music marked the seasons, Christmas without the

Oratorio was unthinkable. With a dubious choir, Julia had made it happen here in Charlottenburg. Her father's wisecracks stuck like burrs to her memory of the performance.

"You were great in the Johanneskirche," insisted Arno. "You rocked the place. You sang the best 'Schlafe, mein Liebster' I've ever heard."

Julia laughed low in her throat.

"That's it!" he cried. "That's the sound I want! No one else makes that sound! Tell me you'll do it."

Julia bent her fingers, then stretched them as far as they could reach.

"Tell me you'll do it, or in five seconds I'm calling Dagmar Schleifer."

Julia's laugh warmed her belly. "Even though I'm the only one who can sing it."

"Sure you are, but I need an alto tomorrow by six. If you won't do it ..."

In her nearby window, Astrid waved, pointed to her paper, and mouthed something. The twist of her lips unsettled Julia. She waved back and cut in, "But don't—"

"Look." Arno's voice lost its playfulness. "I've been hearing you for years now. You're ready. If you don't know it, you can go on singing in the Johanneskirche."

"I'll do it," said Julia, low and flat.

"You'll do it." She could feel Arno's grin. "That's my girl. I knew you'd do it. Okay. So the dress rehearsal's tonight at six, and I work with the orchestra from three to five. I've got to hear you first—just to be sure. What are you doing now? Can you get down here right now?"

Julia thought quickly. They wouldn't need her at Dorrie's Donuts until the early shift on Sunday. She could cancel the voice lessons she was giving this afternoon.

"Yeah, I could do it in …" She glanced at her wrist against the wall. "Half an hour. I could be there in half an hour."

"Okay. Okay." Julia sensed Arno reckoning. "Call me when you're outside the church. We can work until the orchestra comes. If you sound okay, you can stay for the rehearsal. Then we can work some more. Thank God. I'm glad Sascha can't breathe. I'm sick of her fucking vibrato."

———————————■———————————

When Arno introduced Julia to the Bartholdy Choir, their murmurs spread in a soft wave. He had handpicked these singers, many of whom were music students or teachers. They had been touring together for the past few years, and like Arno, they were becoming internationally known. All of them knew what it meant to lose one of the best altos in Germany the day before the performance. Some looked at Julia gratefully, and Rudi Mertschenk, with whom Julia had sung many concerts, gave her a thumbs-up sign from the tenor section. The greasy first violin nodded and smiled respectfully, but most of their eyes broadcast doubt. An alto who could come on a few hours' notice, who wasn't booked two weeks before Christmas? They applauded Julia because Arno demanded it, but they clearly feared for the concert they had been preparing for two months.

Julia faced them with absolute calm, although her looks must have magnified their mistrust. She had run out the door in a gray sweat suit that made her curves look like lumpy bulges. She had pulled back her bushy brown hair in a ponytail, so that the lights were blasting her rough features. She had never been pretty, but she liked having a face that made people look twice. She raised her chin and made sure that her eyes showed no trace of fear.

"This is Julia Martens—from Berlin," said Arno. He locked eyes with anyone who showed skepticism. "She'll be replacing Sascha Neumann, who's"—he grinned—"home fighting phlegm." The singers laughed, but a soprano with glasses exhaled with her lower lip puffed out so that her scanty bangs fluttered. The choir's doubts couldn't quench Julia's air. As they wound through the three-hour oratorio, her voice only gained strength; it was the choir's sound that needed nourishing. Fuming, Arno demanded that they stay when he dismissed the orchestra at nine. The weary singers shifted their weight and tried to relieve their sore backs.

When the sopranos interwove a chorale tune with a bass solo, their high E sagged pitifully. The old continuo player shook his head, wagging his billy goat beard reproachfully. Exasperated, Arno pushed through the empty seats until his ear hung inches from the front-row singers. He nodded to the Russian mathematician, her eyes bulging, her mouth wide open, but glared at the woman with glasses.

"Heike! It's higher!" he yelled and jabbed his thick finger up.

Heike glowered, her jaw clenched.

"That's not an E," he spluttered. "It's—it's sagging like a pregnant dachshund! Oh—excuse me, Carola." He nodded to a red-haired alto whose belly was stretching her green sweater.

"Oh, no problem. I've always been partial to dachshunds," she said calmly.

The singers burst out laughing while Arno, bright red, ran his fingers through his rough blond hair. Burly and muscular, Arno Weber seemed made for a different business. To Julia, he looked more like a Henningsthal teamster than a fine-fibered Berlin musician. Although he wasn't tall, his thick neck and powerful build made him look like someone used to lifting. Even more than his strength, his energy gave you pause. Maybe because he directed a hundred people at once, his full attention reduced most people to stammers. When his gaze focused on you, the force of his eyes was overwhelming.

"Look," he told Heike. "Just sing the note."

"And that note would be …" said the soprano. She folded her thin arms.

Arno looked up thoughtfully and in a piercing falsetto sang a clear, penetrating E. The continuo player nodded.

"Ja?" Arno smiled mischievously. He extended his hand, palm up, fingers outstretched, and commanded the sopranos to sing.

"Ja!" he cried. "Ja-*wohl*! Ja-*wohl*!"

The singers applauded as he returned to the podium. "That's it! That's what I want! Now sing it that way tomorrow night."

At ten he released the fading choir, then led Julia down to a practice room. For another hour, she sang while he played and guided her with his hoarse voice.

"You've got the best part in the piece," he said. "The whole feel of it—it's got to come from you."

As Bach emerged from Julia's core, Arno kept his eyes on hers and listened with unaccustomed calm. Tired as he was, he would have jumped at any false turn, and it pleased her that her notes relaxed him.

"Yeah," he murmured. "Yeah, just like that. Watch me there … I'm going to bring you in."

When Julia had sung each aria twice, Arno gazed at her for a long time. "You were right about your voice," he said. "It's better than it was last summer. More open. More liquid. You'll ace this. I'm just wondering what to do with you next."

He enfolded her in a tired hug, then ordered her to go home and sleep. In the night, the melodies turned inside her, curving softly as the light came. After waking, all day long Julia found herself counting the hours until the notes could emerge in their supple shapes.

———————— ■ ————————

As Julia climbed the U-Bahn steps, she inhaled deeply, and cold, moist air filled her lungs. The Christmas market's spice drove off the tunnel's reek, and she savored the heavy scent of sugared almonds. She could reach the Remembrance Church only by crossing the market, so she joined the slow-moving throng. At three thirty it was already almost dark, but brilliant lights warmed the pushing crowd. She passed the crepe man in his white chef's hat, so fat he must have been poured into his booth. Quietly Julia tested her voice: "*Berei*—" Yes, wide open. She smiled again. The dampness frizzing her thick brown hair had revived her voice after last night's battering. There had been a new richness to it lately, an insistent, living warmth.

Julia tried another entrance, enjoying the note that emerged from her belly. "*Eile, Ei*—" An old man in front of her turned and nodded, a glow warming his timid blue eyes. A crescent-shaped stain marred his back, and she wondered how that dark new moon had appeared on his dingy coat.

Pork and onions sizzled in a pan beside her, so close that the heat warmed her face. On her other side, a boy tossed rings onto green bottles, trying to win a stuffed polar bear. Julia smiled at a display of ceramic houses whose candles turned their windows to yellow gems. In the Palestinian booth, brass tureens shone, and red-and-blue plates flashed brilliantly. Light glinted off the cellophane wrappings of gingerbread hearts that said, "Ich habe dich lieb." Below them lay pans of sticky almonds, which a red-faced man shoveled into paper cones. Their dusky sweetness called her, but she couldn't risk a rattle. One piece of almond could break her voice like a jagged rock in a stream.

Anyway, she still felt full from the rolled beef and red cabbage she had eaten at Karstadt. Julia had always had a healthy appetite, and lately it had increased. A few days ago, the queasiness that had been bothering her for the past few months had suddenly died away. She cleared her throat and tried her voice again. *"Berei—"*

Its flow reassured her, but as she approached the church door, doubts began to swirl. Was she really going to sing *here*, with the Bartholdy Choir, one of the best choirs in Berlin?

From the mat under her feet came a sickening smell. Someone had peed against the church door, and the grooved carpet was airing its angry memory. If the stoop had been asphalt, she could have scrubbed it in seconds, but these plush mats held on to their sufferings. For a moment she hesitated before the heavy bronze door and pictured the swaying man who must have sprayed it.

Here on Breitscheidplatz, there were many such men. Bombed in the war, the broken tower of the Remembrance Church ruled a concrete island in West Berlin's busiest district. Since the ruin couldn't house services, a thinner tower and octagon had been built beside it. The irreverent Berliners called these concrete beehives the Lipstick and Powder Box. Visible from the Bahnhof Zoo train station, the Remembrance Church attracted people with nowhere to go: weary tourists, street kids with puppies, red-faced alcoholics, and lonely old women. Every night around six, some of them lined up behind the Powder Box for a free meal. Those who could afford it would hear Julia sing tonight.

Quick steps behind her made her turn, and Rudi Mertschenk danced up, his thin face topped by a blue cap.

"Na?" He grinned. "All ready?"

"Yeah." She sighed.

Julia had known Rudi as long as she had known Arno, ever since she had come to Berlin. Ten years ago, they had both landed in the choir Arno was conducting, before he had become nationally known. With his reedy voice, Rudi would never sing solos, but Arno kept him close for his clean singing and organizational skills.

"Nervous, huh?" Rudi nudged her. "Don't worry. You sing better than Sascha Neumann any day."

Rudi pulled the door open with a wiry arm and guided Julia into the foyer. She followed him down a circular staircase that trembled under their feet. Since there was little heat, she kept her coat on while she sought a room to warm up her voice.

She spotted Arno through the windows of his office, but her wave froze in midair. With his lips moving, his eyes burning into the score, Arno stood conducting music only he could hear. Except for quick snaps of his wrists, he was barely moving, but every cell in his body registered the music. He grimaced as he hit a stretch that worried him and rested one hand on his head while the other stopped and started his imaginary orchestra. Which movement was he conducting? With her eyes on his lips, Julia tried to see. Arno seemed to be singing all the parts at once, jumping from one instrument to the next. Much as she longed to hear his voice, Julia doubted that she could reach him. After several minutes in which he failed to notice her, she left to stretch out her voice.

In her brown wool coat, Julia ran through her range. She touched the high A and turned like a swimmer reclaiming a familiar pool. She sipped some water, wondering when she would have access to a bathroom, then tried the coloratura of "Bereite dich, Zion." The aria emerged clean and full, resounding in every cranny of her head and breast. At four, she climbed up the quivering stairs to sing the final rehearsal.

On the risers, the singers were negotiating for space. The orchestra was testing and tuning. Julia took her place in the audience's front row between the round, cheerful tenor and the soprano soloist, a tall blonde American in black satin. In increasing numbers, Americans had been invading Berlin, wide-eyed singers drawn by the wall's collapse. Arno liked them since they were pretty well trained and so awestruck by the land of Bach that they did whatever he wanted. Last night he had ordered the soloists to come in full dress, and light danced in the ripples of the soprano's skirt.

"Take off your coat and stay awhile," whispered the tenor, his red-brown beard catching points of light. Playfully, Julia shook her head. She clutched her brown fur collar and savored its warmth.

When she took off the coat for her first recitative, the front-row musicians gasped. The second violin reddened and squinted at a descending run in his score. For the concert, Julia had pulled on her only good gown, a maroon velvet dress from a secondhand store. Luckily, the velvet stretched, since she had been putting on weight, especially in her already large breasts. At school they used to call her Double-D, and she often hid herself under cloud-like sweatshirts. But the wine-colored gown offered her breasts like loaves. Arno caught her eye and grinned naughtily, his teeth biting his lower lip. He cued the oboe and continuo.

"Nun wird mein liebster Bräutigam," sang Julia. "Now, will my dearest bridegroom …" Her voice spiraled into the darkest corners. The gray continuo player accompanied her with the tranquility of an Egyptian cat.

"Ja!" Satisfied, Arno cut her off and called for the tenor.

Inches shorter than Julia but equally round, he brushed against her as he passed. Confidently, he nodded to the orchestra and met Arno's eyes. He began his first aria. "Frohe Hirten, eilt, ach eilet"—"Happy shepherds, hurry, oh hurry."

For an hour Arno tested the weakest links in the chain that connected soloists, Evangelist, orchestra, and chorus. As the Evangelist telling the story, the tenor would play a double role, narrating in his recitatives and cavorting in his arias. Arno led the musicians through a tedious string of starts and stops and kept his commanding voice low. Most of the time he looked pleased, and when he wasn't, he betrayed it only through a hardening of his lips.

"Okay." At 4:55, Arno tapped the podium and addressed the whole ensemble. "Okay. You sound good. You sound good. When you play this thing tonight"—he glanced at the chorus—"when you sing it, I want you to feel the pulse. This thing can come to life, or it can move mechanically. What's going to happen is up to you."

As he spoke, his eyes caught each musician in turn, issuing a personal appeal. Rudi nodded supportively. "It's more than Bach," said Arno. "It's more than just notes. This thing is life. It's black out there. That's what he was doing—bringing life, bringing …"

Next to Julia, the soprano soloist stared with parted lips. Whether or not she understood, she was drinking Arno's passion. Knowing how much trouble he had expressing himself in words, Julia met his eyes and smiled sympathetically. It was a quality they shared. Deep and powerful, Arno's voice stopped most people in their tracks, but in its headlong rush, it could falter. As he hesitated, Julia sensed that something was distracting him. Normally he hid his uneven command of words, but tonight his rhythm was off.

Arno paused. "You know what they say about Bach—it's perfect, it's math, it's mechanics. Well, it's not. It's about birth and death—pulsing, breathing …"

Arno's voice dissolved, and for a moment there was unbroken silence. He lowered his eyes to the podium, where he rested the fingertips of each hand. The soprano leaned forward.

"*Na ja ...*" He grinned huskily. "You sound good. You sound good. Just play it—sing it—like you mean it. The thing starts at six."

The rehearsal dissolved into a scraping of chairs as the singers and players rushed for the basement. In the minutes before the three-hour performance, they ate black-bread sandwiches from plastic containers and drank tea from steaming silver thermoses. Julia joined the line for the bathroom and watched the women squirm three deep before the mirror.

"You sound beautiful," said the flutist, a young woman with a crown of soft braids. "Would you like to go ahead of me?"

"Thanks." Julia blushed.

She found herself behind Carola, the pregnant alto, who was shifting her weight from leg to leg. Turning, she eyed Julia's bare bosom, then her middle.

"That's a beautiful dress," she said. "Is it vintage?" She reached out to stroke the rich velvet.

"Yeah, I think it's pretty old," answered Julia. "Must have belonged to some old lady who never wore it."

"It's gorgeous," said the flutist, cocking her head until a pin flashed in her crescent of brown braids.

In a wavering gap between women, Julia watched herself in the mirror, her lips moist, her brown hair free and full. She was wearing almost no makeup, but the warmth of nearby bodies brightened her face. Under heavy brows, her dark eyes glinted, more amused than scared. She took her turn at the toilet, then reentered the crush.

"*Na?* All ready?" Rudi jostled her elbow. "You sound great. You look ..." He nuzzled his pointed face into her hair. "Long way from the Friedrichskirche, hey?"

Rudi grinned eagerly and quivered like a hungry rabbit. Self-conscious about his teeth, he dampened most smiles into curves, but tonight his inhibitions had dissolved. Julia pushed him off but took an herb bonbon, which he was offering the singers from yellow cans.

"Line up! Line up!" called Heike. "Line *up*! Ten minutes!"

"Aren't you dressed?" gasped Rudi as Arno rushed by in his jeans.

"Julia! Hold that last C before the da capo!" Arno called.

Sucking spicy sweetness, Julia followed the bossy soprano while Rudi ran off after Arno. Shivering in the draft, Julia took her place beside the soprano soloist, whom she suspected spoke little German.

"Here, take this," whispered an older singer, handing Julia a soft black shawl. Julia offered it to the American, whose shoulders were trembling, but the soprano indicated they should share it. With her arm pressed against the thin soloist's, Julia huddled until Arno stalked up in his black suit.

The soprano drew in her breath. Even for Julia, who had followed Arno through countless concerts, the sight of him in black was overwhelming. Tightly focused, his energy seemed to shoot out through his hands, and his blond hair shone brilliantly against his dark jacket. Despite all the years she had known him, Julia felt her face flush. Arno's was also burning with color.

"Now, here's a nice present." He grinned, unwrapping the women. "Ready, Mädels?" He kissed their cheeks. In the quick brush, his rough skin scratched Julia.

"Hold on to that C!" he hissed in Julia's ear.

"Ready, Manfred? Ready, Jörg?" he asked the tenor and bass. They nodded.

"Dann los geht's," he whispered.

Arno led them up the stairs and down the main aisle. Every seat in the church was filled, so that the way forward was half-choked. Julia followed the soprano's slim hips, which were dodging the angled chairs. As Julia swam toward the glowing orchestra, she nearly sank into the dark, breathing throng. A gleam of color raised her eyes to one of the church's eight walls. She was crossing a hive of blue glass panels, no two of which were alike. In the faint light, some panes burned with spots of red, while others shone with indigo and turquoise. Over the chorus, which stood waiting behind the orchestra, a great bronze Jesus looked as though he were being propelled into heaven on a jetpack.

From every seat came appreciative applause, and those on the aisles smiled up as Julia passed. Since there was no stage, the soloists sat in the audience's front row, facing the orchestra and chorus. Julia settled between the soprano and tenor as Arno mounted the podium. When the clapping died, he turned to face the audience.

"Before we begin, I need to announce a change in the program." Arno's voice rang out resonant and sure, with no trace of his earlier emotion.

The audience rustled behind Julia, then froze with sudden stillness.

"Sascha Neumann has fallen ill and will not be singing tonight. The alto solo will be sung by Julia Martens. We appreciate her willingness to step in and sing for us this evening. We hope that you enjoy the performance."

A groan rolled through the church as Arno turned to the orchestra.

"Don't worry—they don't know anything," whispered Manfred.

The soprano squeezed Julia's hand with icy fingers.

An instant later Arno started the oratorio. Julia hadn't been watching, and the descending fourth in the timpani struck her like a fist. Manfred caught her hand to steady her, but her heart was rioting. She could smell the searing disinfectant back in Henningsthal.

In a dizzying cascade, the music flowed downward, and Julia felt as though she were falling. She tried to slow her breathing and crush the urge to pee. In front of her, Arno's back straightened, and he raised his hands.

"Jauchzet, frohlokket!" exploded the choir. "Shout, rejoice!"

The first violin smiled as his arm shot back and forth, and the flute swayed with the musical swirl. In joyful 3/8 rhythm, the choir brought Bach pulsing to life, their mouths round and their eyebrows raised. It wouldn't be long now. Julia drew in air and tried to force her breath down to her toes. As the choir repeated the first section, jewels of sweat appeared on Manfred's forehead. With their eyes locked on Arno, the musicians slowed and relished their final chord.

In the brief pause between movements, a baby squealed, and Julia imagined Arno's wrath. Above all else, he hated children whose random cries pierced his music. In the parents who brought them he saw not just stupidity but malice. The silences formed part of a living whole, and a baby's scream was a murderous stab. Luckily, this child made no more noise, but it was early. Who would bring a baby to a three-hour concert?

Manfred strode to a spot they had marked with tape, where Arno could see the soloist without turning his gaze from the orchestra. Ten feet in front of Julia, the tenor smiled majestically and filled his belly with air.

"Es begab sich aber zu der Zeit …" he began. "But it happened, at that time …"

It was almost time. Ice-cold, breathing far too fast, Julia listened to Manfred tell how Joseph and his pregnant wife reached Bethlehem. As the Evangelist, he linked the movements with glowing words, much as the Christmas lights joined the brilliant booths outside. With his good-natured smile and determined stance, Manfred inspired confidence. What had Arno said? The spirit had to come from her? Why not from the Evangelist? Wasn't he the one holding the piece together? "Dass sie gebären sollte," finished Manfred. "That she should give birth." Oh, God. Julia felt herself rising. Manfred smiled encouragingly as he passed on the way back to his front-row seat. Julia straddled the tape and looked up at Arno. Already his face was streaming with sweat. He cued the oboes, and as their first chord sounded, he extended his hand to her with absolute trust, so there was nothing she could do but sing. On the raw night, her voice filled the church like warm liquid.

"Nun wird mein liebster Bräutigam …" she sang. "Now, will my dearest bridegroom …"

Julia felt her body opening. Emerging from her core, the notes resonated in every cell. Effortlessly, she touched the high E: "Now, will the hero of Da-vid's line!" Arno glanced from Julia to the oboes, and his hands created spaces for her to fill. Subtly, he guided her through the phrases, steadying her but trusting her instincts. As the first violin joined the oboe, she felt a new power, a living presence. To announce the birth, Bach had brought back the 3/8 rhythm, and her blood pulsed with his love song.

Arno cued her, and she sang to the audience: "Bereite dich, Zion, mit zärtlichen Trieben …"—"Prepare yourself, Zion, with tender feelings …"

From her womb to her lips, she was a wide-open pipe, and the melody emerged, rich and full: "Den Schönsten, den Liebsten bald bei dir zu sehn"—"To see the most beautiful, the most beloved with you soon."

So this was what Arno had meant. These three hours of music celebrated a woman's belly, and only an alto could convey that sound. Playfully, Julia spun her B: "Eile!"—"Hurry! Hurry to love the bridegroom most eagerly!"

Arno's eyes flickered with amusement. Only on her last C did he issue a command, compelling her to hold the note until the da capo. When the time came, the fermata felt so natural that Julia barely noticed him guiding her. With perfect tranquility, she repeated the first two-thirds of the aria, caressing the turns and savoring each note. Arno exhaled and met her eyes with a triumphant smile. Then he cued the choir for their next chorale.

"Beautiful!" whispered the soprano.

Manfred nodded admiringly and wiped his brow with a wadded white handkerchief. It was almost time for his first aria.

Ready to show what his voice could do, the tenor held his score a little higher. In this movement about happy shepherds visiting the Christ child, he was accompanied only by flute and continuo. Beaming, Manfred leaped to a G, and the flute answered gleefully. He enjoyed his runs as a bicyclist loves a downhill rush, but Julia knew how hard he must have worked on them. With his round face distended, his mouth agape, Manfred glided through seamless measures. The flute responded in a lighter tone and echoed his cascade while he breathed. Arno extended his hand, and three chords of the continuo sounded. In her stomach, Julia felt an icy pinch. She shouldn't have been able to hear the continuo.

With her breath crushed, she looked wildly at Manfred. Somehow, he had missed his cue and lost his place. Panic-stricken, he was scanning the score while the flute and organ continued without him. Arno's back held its posture, but the singers' faces reflected his fury. Measures later, the tenor line reemerged, but it wasn't coming from Manfred.

"Geht, die Freude heisst zu schön …" the voice sang. "Go, the joy calls too beautifully …"

All the tenors' mouths were closed. The voice crept along duskily and clarified on a high A. Manfred wasn't singing, but the voice matched his so closely it might have been his echo. Guided by the ghost, Manfred slipped back in: "Sucht die Anmut zu gewinnen!"—"Try to find grace!"

A flicker pulled Julia's eyes to the flutist, who was swaying to the rhythm again. Her liquid notes had never ceased, but she had been standing stock-still. As she began to dance again, Julia slowly released her breath. Manfred wound through his final run, then sang that the babe could be found in swaddling clothes, lying in a manger. He sank down heavily next to Julia, and she and Jörg rubbed his damp back. He murmured appreciatively but kept his eyes on the score, no doubt wondering how to survive his next movement.

When Julia stood for her lullaby aria, Arno still looked tense. He smiled as he cued the orchestra. Watching his hands sculpt the music, Julia again felt the truth of his words: the oratorio depended on her. Manfred might have been telling the story, but she was living it. She was the mother's voice. For her first note, she opened her throat all the way and flooded the church with her sound. Busy with the orchestra, Arno let her sing, his motions fluid and relaxed. The audience sat still and drank the melody. Many closed their eyes, their faces soft with peace.

"Labe die Brust, empfinde die Lust," Julia sang, pulsing on each sixteenth. "Drink from the breast, feel the delight."

In her last phrases, even the continuo fell silent, so that only the flute paralleled her warm voice. Arno's eyes glistened, and he closed the movement with unaccustomed gentleness.

Part 3 opened with a blast of trumpets, and Julia found herself watching Rudi. As the 3/8 pulse beat toward the tenors' entrance, Rudi kept his gaze fixed on Arno. Well before the crucial moment, he spread his lips wide, as though preparing himself for an immense task.

"Herrscher des Himmels!"—"Ruler of heaven!"

Julia could almost hear Rudi's precise, thin tone. How sad that someone who loved music so much could make so little sound.

The fine-boned soprano, on the other hand, amazed everyone with the clarity of her voice. Smiling with pleasure, she glanced teasingly from Arno to Jörg, her partner in her first duet.

"Tröstet uns und macht uns frei," she pleaded, effortlessly tossing her high A. "Comfort us and make us free."

The light danced over her soft blond hair, and her black satin gleamed with each breath. Her voice was pure lightness, pure energy, one of the most exquisite Julia had ever heard. How had Arno found a soprano this good in this season of high demand?

In Julia's next aria, "Schliesse, mein Herze" ("Hold, My Heart"), she realized how different her style was from the soprano's. Standing motionless, she looked through Arno's fingers to the blackness in back of the church. Rich and powerful, her voice throbbed in the darkness, praising the miracle of birth. Again she sensed a living force in her, so that she let the sounds emerge rather than actively shaping them. The slick-haired first violin accompanied her serenely, his eyes sliding from Arno to his score. As Arno slowed Julia in her last descent, she lost all sense of herself. On her final low B, she was a living instrument, guided by the music within and Arno's hands without.

Soon after her aria, the third part ended. The audience applauded hazily, awakened from its trance. Arno led the soloists out the back, where they retreated to the basement, followed by the choir and orchestra. Hot and exhausted, the singers rushed for their water bottles. Most choirs sang only three parts of the oratorio, seeing six movements as too great a feat. But Arno's philosophy was "Wenn schon, denn schon"—or as he put it, "Are we going to sing the motherfucker, or aren't we?"

During intermission, the musicians rested in designated spaces divided by glass panels. The orchestra occupied the central chamber; the choir, a smaller room down the hall. Arno had his own office, and the soloists shared a tiny practice area. Julia pitied the choral singers, who didn't have enough chairs. One woman sat on the floor with her legs extended, her black skirt spread like spilled ink. Not everyone respected the boundaries, and Rudi had penetrated Arno's space. His upraised arm caught Julia's eye as he gesticulated and pleaded. The soprano soloist touched Julia's shoulder.

"I—I wish I could speak better German," she said in English. "Do you understand me?"

"Yes," Julia answered nervously. She wished she were better at foreign languages.

"Your voice is extraordinary—I've never heard anything like it. You sing ... as if you could see eternity. Do you understand?"

Julia studied the woman's brittle features and wondered how such a high-strung person could make such lovely sounds. The soprano's close-spaced eyes burned with the need to communicate, and the intense effort was making her tremble.

"Yes, I understand," murmured Julia, her face glowing. "Thank you. I like your voice too."

In the glassed-in practice room, Manfred sat still except for his lips, which were forming the shapes of future words. His eyes scanned the score like a relentless beam determined to capture each jot. Jörg followed Manfred's example and pulled out his music, and Julia smiled at the contrast between them. They looked like two monks praying, one calm and the other ravished by doubt.

Rudi stuck in his head and beckoned, and Julia followed him out into the hall. He wrapped his thin arms around her and hugged her tightly. Julia relaxed into him, enjoying the energy of his lean body.

"You're a goddess," he murmured. "I've never heard you sing like this. You were good before, but not like this."

"Oh, come on." Julia laughed.

"No, really. You've … advanced to a whole new level."

A laugh rippled through her. Rudi nurtured the technology in a physics lab at the Freie Universität and was known for his artless nerd style. Rumor had it he had once asked a bass if he liked to go out at "frequent intervals." Tonight Rudi's open smile pleased her, since his dark eyes were so often shaded.

"How's Arno?" she asked. "How's he doing?"

"Well, I think I've convinced him not to kill Manfred before he can sing the second half."

"Geez, the poor guy," whispered Julia. "What happened?"

Rudi shrugged, and his thin face tightened. "He screwed up. Started listening to the music and forgot to sing."

Julia looked through the glass at Manfred, who was mouthing an aria. "So who …?"

"That was Arno."

"No way!"

"Yes way!" Rudi shook his head in her face so that their noses almost touched. "I couldn't believe it either, but I saw it."

"He can sing an A?" gasped Julia. "He's been smoking forever. How—"

"I guess you're not the only one who's inspired tonight. He was mad at me. Wanted to know why I didn't do it." Rudi's dark eyes shone with mischief, as often happened when he talked about Arno.

"You've got to be kidding me."

Rudi scraped the bottom of his voice to recreate Arno's growl. "Well, somebody had to sing it, and I didn't hear it coming from you."

Julia laughed in her lowest tones and enjoyed the warmth in her face.

"Well, at least he has you Mädels to comfort him." Rudi sighed.

"Yeah!" whispered Julia. "Where did he find that soprano? She's incredible!"

"*You're* incredible." He smiled and laid his hands on her shoulders.

"No, seriously."

"Oh, Linda? Uh ..." Rudi rolled his eyes toward Arno's office.

"Oh ..."

"Get your mind out of the gutter." He laughed. "Probably everyone's saying the same thing about you."

Julia grabbed for his ribs to tickle him, but Rudi leaped aside with a whoop. Heike put a finger to her lips as she pushed by.

Rudi stifled his laughter and asked Julia, "Hey, you're coming to Löwenstein's, right?" She sensed stillness under his good cheer.

"Oh, I don't know ..." She hesitated. "I have to work tomorrow morning."

"Oh, come on. You've got to," he pleaded. "It won't be the same without you."

"Even for someone who goes out at frequent intervals?"

Rudi dug into her sides, and she bubbled with giggles.

Heike, who was trying to round up the singers, looked archly at Rudi and Julia. "Well, I see why our artists need their private space. Ready for ninety more minutes, Herr Mertschenk? Frau Martens?"

"*Jawohl!*" Rudi grinned. He ran off to join the tenors, but Julia lingered in the hall.

In the orchestra room, Arno was giving last-minute instructions. The flutist blushed as he patted her shoulder. He talked earnestly with the oboes and pointed to the score while Udo, the first violin, passed Arno's directions to the strings. Udo's few strands of oily black hair trembled as he used gestures to show the players what he wanted. By seeing how to move the bow, they could produce the sounds that he needed.

Arno visited the choir room briefly, then moved on to the soloists. Manfred and Jörg stood when he entered, and instinctively, the two women backed toward the wall. His tense movements warned of a searing explosion.

"Stay with me," he said, pointing a thick finger at Manfred. "I'll give you each entrance. Stay with me."

Julia drew in her breath at the staccato rhythm.

"I will." The tenor gulped. "I—I'm so sorry. Thank you! I don't know—"

"Just watch me!" Arno held his hand rigid. Julia froze.

Arno's shoulders relaxed, and he turned to the women. "Well done, Mädels. My God, what a pair!" His eyes sparkled as he looked from one to the other, seeming to enjoy the contrast in their forms.

He frowned and glanced at his watch. "Okay, let's go. Let's finish this thing." He led them back up the trembling staircase toward the radiant lights far ahead.

During the opening chorus of part 4, Julia watched Manfred scan Arno's broad back. The tenor sang his first recitative perfectly, telling of Christ's circumcision. Although he savored his high As, he lingered on the notes more out of obligation than pleasure. Seeking shelter, he had withdrawn into the music and was no longer singing to the audience.

The listeners stirred restlessly as the air grew hotter, and the baby squawked again. This time its cry sounded less good-natured. In the pause before Linda and Jörg's duet, the mother crept through the shadows toward the foyer. Thank God. The echo aria was coming, and if the kid got any noisier, it could wreck the best moments in the piece.

The playful exchange between the soprano and her echo was a river of pure delight. Linda sang her line lovingly, with a flirtatious air. For her echo, Arno had passed over Anja, known for her clean intonation. He had instead chosen a first-year music student whose voice mimicked Linda's like that of a determined little sister. According to Rudi, he had rehearsed the girl relentlessly, until her fine-edged voice had dissolved to despairing breath. In the balcony now, she echoed Linda so perfectly it sounded as though her voice had really bounced off the back wall.

"*Ja, ja!*" Linda's notes spun into the darkness.

"*Ja, ja!*" answered the student, fainter but with the same clarity.

Julia closed her eyes.

"Ma!"

Oh, fuck.

"Maaaa!"

Longing to hear the aria, the mother must have stepped back into the church, and her baby wanted to join the fun. Linda's smile broadened, and she looked ready to laugh. She and the oboe wound on without faltering, but the audience's titters clouded the music. Unable to resist, Julia turned and saw the mother push the baby's head against her breast. The woman looked so ashamed that Julia almost pitied her. She spent the rest of the concert in the foyer, and her baby made no more noise.

By the time the brass and timpani opened part 6, the cool air had turned to sludge. Manfred held his handkerchief in a tight fist and alternately rubbed his neck and forehead. He sang his last aria defiantly, challenging his enemies, confident in his Christian faith. With his eyes fixed on Arno, he seemed to have forgotten the audience as he told of Herod's search and the family's flight. When his last recitative ended, he sank down with his chin on his chest. He didn't move again until an explosion blasted the final chord.

After three hours of silence, the audience relished their chance to make noise. Their applause tore loose with a whiplash crack. Under the high-pitched clapping, a wave of voices rolled. Arno grinned tiredly and pointed to the soloists, and the rumble mounted to a roar. In the orchestra, he acknowledged the first violin, oboes, and flute. When he waved toward the choir, the clamor increased. People rose to their feet and cried "*Bravo!*" A soprano handed Julia a bouquet of roses, exquisite under glinting cellophane. Julia's throat tightened, and the audience blurred. Until now, she'd had no idea how much people had loved her music.

Arno led the soloists offstage, but the clamor only grew. Smiling at Julia, he brought them back for another bow. The choir began to clap, and the orchestra lowered their instruments to applaud. Jörg bent for a bow, but Arno stopped him.

"Nein! Die Mädels!" he hissed.

With a courtier's gesture, he offered the audience the two women, and the church ignited.

"*Brava! Brav-a!*"

Linda embraced her, a strange muddle of cellophane and stiff satin. Then the soprano stepped back, extended a thin arm, and the audience clapped for Julia alone. Tears filled Julia's eyes, and she raised her hand to her mouth. Could this be for her? Had they loved her this much?

"*Brav-a!*" came cries from the choir, echoed in the balcony and far corners.

Linda took Arno's hand and led him forward, and the audience shouted. Beaming, he embraced his soloists, kissing the women and hugging the men. He went on acknowledging each musician until the audience wore itself out. Like a plant in November, the applause died hard, rising each time Julia thought it was done. Suddenly people remembered their dinners, and the clapping ended as abruptly as it had begun.

Many of the singers headed to Löwenstein's, a restaurant in the shadows near Bahnhof Zoo. Julia hesitated, knowing she had to be up at six, but she wanted to share the fun. First she helped to dismantle the risers to make way for the morning service. Wilted but determined, Rudi directed the operation, his white sleeves rolled up to his elbows. Julia hiked up her dress and joined Anja, who was showing sopranos how to loosen bolts. When a step came free, Julia grabbed hold of it and nodded to the hovering echo girl. It weighed thirty pounds, but together they lifted it easily. Julia relished the burning pull in her muscles.

At Löwenstein's, the singers drank and laughed uproariously, creating a giddy atmosphere. About twenty had come, and they had dragged tables into an L shape so that they could maintain their vibrant bonds. Julia settled into the bend with Rudi and Arno, the last to arrive. Suddenly ravenous, she filled herself with bratwurst and fries, savoring the squirt of juice as she bit a perfectly browned sausage. She made sure to sip her beer slowly, so that no one would put another down in front of her. The singers joked about Manfred's mishap, then kidded Arno about Linda. How was he going to lure her back for the *St. Matthew Passion* on Good Friday? Was walking Linda to her hotel just now part of the plan? Red-faced, Arno swore that Linda had been attracted purely by the choir. The singers responded with a bright chord of jeers.

As laughter rushed around her, Julia felt like a rock in a stream, part of the whole yet made of different stuff. At first, she regretted coming, but by midnight she was shouting with the rest, speculating about Manfred's love life and suggesting names for Carola's baby. Julia knew she had to be at work in six hours, but she felt no desire to leave. Her sleepiness lay like thin foam on a heady drink, and her insides quivered with excitement. Smelling of sweat and smoke, Rudi and Arno warmed her sides, one lean and passionate, the other strong and ironic. Julia leaned forward and rested her breasts on the table, luxuriating in the unreality of 1:00 a.m.

When Löwenstein's closed, the last singers scattered, and Arno draped his arm around Julia. Glowing with energy, he squeezed her tightly. "Let's go for a drink. I'm not tired. Are you?"

"I'm beyond tired." She laughed.

"Rudi, *komm*," ordered Arno.

"But I've got to get home to Norbert," he pleaded. "Please. I promised. He's going to be so mad." His fine gray hair stuck up in tufts until he sheltered it under his blue cap.

"So call him," said Arno.

"What, *now*?"

"Yeah, sure, if he's waiting."

With a trembling hand, Rudi pulled out a small gray phone and pressed a single button. Norbert answered with a squawk, and Arno and Julia stifled their laughter.

"Yeah, yeah, I know," said Rudi miserably. He walked a few steps away, then raised his voice.

Julia looked up at Arno, who was watching her closely.

"I'll go with you," she said, "but I've got to be at work at seven. Dorrie's Donuts. On Wilmersdorferstrasse."

"Dorrie's Donuts!" exclaimed Arno. "Dorrie's Donuts? You went to the Hans Breithaus Academy!"

Julia bristled. For almost ten years, she had worked for the American chain that had invaded Berlin so effortlessly. The food was good, and the customers treated her well, but mainly she liked her coworker, Marga. So many people hated their *Mitarbeiter* or had men pawing them and couldn't complain. Selling people their breakfasts seemed like decent work, and it riled her when people laughed about it.

"I know I went to the Hans Breithaus Academy!" she cried. "I worked my way through there with doughnuts. I sing everywhere I can. I teach anyone who'll let me. I've got to make rent!"

"Hey, take it easy." Arno hugged her until their breaths found the same slow pulse. Far away, Rudi yammered out a tense, uneven solo.

"I should have paid more attention," said Arno. "I should have followed up, once you left the Friedrichskirche—once I left it. I've been so busy with the Bartholdy Choir …" He pushed Julia back to study her at arm's length, but his eyes didn't focus.

"But I've got you now, okay?" He smiled. "Now you're my girl. I'm going to do great things with you." He wrapped his arm around her, and they exhaled together.

In spite of the cold, Julia felt warm and peaceful. On the cellophane protecting her roses, icy drops were forming tiny stars. Rudi approached, his narrow face drawn.

"*Na?*" asked Arno. "You in deep shit?"

Rudi nodded. "One drink, I said. Where are we going, the Onion?"

"Yeah," answered Arno. He draped his free arm around Rudi. No one had ever seen Arno drunk, but he hung on Rudi so heavily that Julia wondered. With a slow turn of his chin, he directed her eyes outward.

"Isn't it beautiful?" he asked. "Just look at that. There's nothing more beautiful than a city at 2:00 a.m."

A fine mist filled the air, punctuated by icy grains, and the sidewalk glistened. The turrets of the Remembrance Church glowed yellow, its broken tower jutting into the black sky. Next to it, a thousand indigo panels of the Powder Box shone magically. A BSR sanitation crew in fluorescent orange was cleaning the market, shouting as they scoured in the darkness. From a billboard over the Zoo Palace Theater, Tom Cruise looked down on a runway of lights that led into a salsa club. Under a brilliant lamp, tiny drops of moisture floated softly downward. Arno leaned back and looked straight up into the light.

"*Geil*," he murmured as wetness covered his face.

"Come *on*," Rudi urged, pulling them forward.

Clinging together, they made their way toward the black ribs of Bahnhof Zoo. At this hour, the station appeared as a hole in the neon lights around it. In the blackness, its glowing sign, "Bahnhof Zoologischer Garten," hung like a message from the dead. They worked their way down Joachimsthalerstrasse and breathed the snack bars' rancid fumes. Turning to a relentless salsa beat, one rotating spit had been stripped to a shaggy stem. Rudi steered them around some drunken kids while Arno drove them on like a motor. He slowed only at Planet Eros to gawk at a lattice of black leather over a round behind.

"*Um Gottes Willen!*" exclaimed Rudi as Arno grinned, unashamed. His ice-crusted hair brushed Rudi's cap, and Julia realized that Rudi was taller.

Under the tracks, a group of bundled men were sharing a bottle of wine. One caught Julia's eye, and he leered and held out his flask. His blue eyes laughed in his pitted, red face. Gurgling, he started toward her, and she caught her breath.

"What's wrong?" asked Rudi.

"Oh, nothing," she murmured and glanced back at the drunk. He stared after her with a hurt scowl and twirled his bottle as though reassured by its slosh.

Ahead of her, an ad for the electric company pointed forward like a gigantic sail. Arno slowed before the Theater des Westens to study two sculptures of large-breasted women. One was balancing a model of the building and looked about ready to drop it. Arno tilted his head sideways, and Rudi followed his movement, leaning his head on Arno's shoulder.

This time Julia pulled them forward, but she paused at the Delphi Theater. Overhead, a painted billboard of Keira Knightley was shimmering. Surrounded by shadows, the actress's enormous dark eyes looked out anxiously over hollow cheeks.

"Beautiful," murmured Rudi.

"You think so?" asked Julia. "She looks kind of sick to me. Kind of sad."

"Yeah, she looks like she could use a good meal." Arno squeezed Julia's waist.

West of Uhlandstrasse, designer furniture stores displayed floodlit beds. A creamy sheet glowed like a slab of white chocolate, with brick-red pillows like cinnamon cakes.

"When was the last time you were in one of those?" asked Rudi.

Arno rubbed his face. "Not last night. Night before last, maybe ..."

In all the years Julia had known Arno, he had never been able to sleep before a performance. Pulsing with the next day's music, he could walk for hours. In Rostock, he had once followed seagulls to the docks in the summer sunlight of 4:00 a.m. There was no knowing what he had been up to last night.

Rudi's eyes glinted with mischief. "What do you say we kick in this window and try it out?"

Arno shot him an impatient look, but Julia smiled. What a delicious thought, her head resting on an enormous red pillow, clutching Rudi in front of her, warmed by Arno behind.

"I would do it," she said, "but I have to be at work in five hours."

Arno kicked the sidewalk, laughing and shaking his head. He raised his eyes to Rudi. "I'm not getting in bed with you," he said. "What would Norbert say?"

Rudi grinned, seeming to relish the image of Norbert's wrath. "Oh, it was just a thought. Just wanted to keep things interesting. Come on. Let's go."

But Rudi stopped in front of a hardware store to admire a display of clamps. Freshly molded, with pristine screws, they lay waiting to grasp anything that was offered.

"Man, that's just the kind of clamp I need," Rudi muttered. "I've got to get back to this place."

He glanced at the opening times, but before he had a chance to memorize them, Arno pulled him away. Julia was glad, since the cold was creeping up under her dress. The stores had given way to shrubbery, so she hurried with Arno and Rudi down Bleibtreustrasse. With relief she welcomed the warm, smoky coziness of the Onion.

Famous for never closing, the Onion attracted drinkers from all over Berlin. On past nights, she had seen young people arguing about art next to old men with newspapers and tourists with maps. Tonight, the dark wainscoting looked especially comforting. Above the rich wood, shelves displayed heavy blue-and-white crockery and dim photographs of Berlin streets in 1910.

At two in the morning, nearly every table was filled, but Rudi found a booth by sheer luck. With a sigh, Julia slid onto the bench and stuffed her coat into the corner beside her. The men laid theirs on top of hers, and Julia added her wrapped roses, still sparkling with tiny drops.

For a moment she felt faint and heard the men talk as though from a great distance. They were arguing about what to order, and Arno was seeking his cigarettes. Julia emerged from her dream when a foamy beer hit the table in front of her.

"Oh, no," she said. "I can't drink this."

"Why?" asked Arno. He took a deep swallow.

"I ... I really don't drink ..." Julia faltered.

"Why?" he asked again.

"Why *not*?" demanded Rudi.

Arno laughed, but the hollow sound revealed that his mind had floated off. He tapped his pack of Lucky Strikes against the table, but nothing emerged.

"Shit. They've got a machine here, right?"

"Yeah." Rudi sighed. "Left at the end of the bar, across from the bathrooms."

"Okay." Arno dug out his wallet and left abruptly.

Rudi smiled sadly over his untouched beer. Julia had thought his eyes were almost black, but the soft light revealed flecks of green.

"Was Norbert really mad?" she asked.

"Yeah." Rudi sighed softly. "He doesn't mind my singing—the concerts, the rehearsals. He likes that I sing. He would have been here if his mother hadn't called. He just doesn't—"

"Is his mother sick?"

"Oh, she has these crises. She thinks that she's dying, and he believes her. We try so hard to spend time together. Weeknights we work, him preparing classes, me fixing these physicists' messes. We try to keep weekends for ourselves, but things keep happening."

"So why don't you leave? Why not go home right now?" asked Julia.

Rudi looked at their damp coats and shook his head.

"No, seriously. Why not, if he's mad at you?"

"He gets mad when I'm with Arno," murmured Rudi. "He doesn't like me to be with him. He calmed down a bit when I said we were with you."

"Oh, that's good."

Rudi raised his eyes and smiled faintly, and Julia looked back reassuringly.

"So Linda's really doing the *St. Matthew Passion?*" she asked. "That's incredible. How did he get her to do that?"

Rudi's eyes darkened as he sought for words. "She has conditions," he said. "She says she'll only do it if we lose Manfred—and if you sing alto."

"Me?" asked Julia. "Me, sing alto? She's big leagues—didn't Heike say she's singing in New York tomorrow night?"

"Tonight," corrected Rudi, checking his watch. "Apparently she thinks you're big leagues too."

He looked at her silently and reached for her hands. One corner of his mouth twitched, and his smile spread slowly.

"*Na?* What am I interrupting?" Arno slid back onto the bench and pushed Rudi aside.

"Oof," he complained.

"*Na ja.*" Arno patted his arm. He tore open the fresh pack of Lucky Strikes, lit one, and inhaled deeply.

"We were talking about Linda," said Rudi, and Arno brightened, blowing smoke at the ceiling.

"Yeah," he said, reflecting. "She's gonna come back." He smiled wickedly at the far wall, reviewing scenes that only he could see.

"And she really said she'd only come without Manfred?" asked Julia. The woman had seemed so fragile. Where had she hidden a strong will like that?

"Yeah." Arno nodded. "And she's right. That's the last time he sings for me."

Poor Manfred had recovered so well, but Julia knew better than to defend him. In music, you didn't get a second chance. Angrily, Arno drew on his cigarette, and Julia tracked his thoughts. As a conductor, you couldn't control what people did, but you got blamed when they screwed up.

"The guy has no balls," Arno muttered. "That flute player has bigger balls than he does. Did you get a load of her? Didn't miss a beat."

Rudi nodded cautiously, unsure where Arno's thoughts were heading. Julia sensed they had settled on something that was about to emerge.

"And that baby!" Arno blew smoke at the table and killed the candle flame in its red glass. "Who the fuck brings a baby to a three-hour concert? Who let her in?"

Julia rubbed her belly and frowned at the ruby cup, which had been glowing so prettily. Anger always made her stomach clench, and all that bratwurst wasn't sitting well. She remembered the mother's frightened, guilty look as she'd slipped back into the foyer. Probably her babysitter hadn't come, but Arno wouldn't care about her excuses. He leaned forward, his fast-moving thoughts having already abandoned the baby.

"Listen," he said. The light in his eyes showed that he was ready to talk. He rested his arms on the table, tense as before a first downbeat. "Listen," he repeated. "I know what I'm going to do." He stared possessively at Julia. "You're going to sing the *St. Matthew Passion* in March—and all the cantatas I can get you between now and then. I'm going to get you an audition for the RBB Choir—"

"The RBB Choir!" Rudi gasped. "You can't do that! Somebody practically has to die!"

Arno smiled wryly. "Oh, I can arrange for that. She can't spend her life at Dorrie's Donuts! Jesus! What are you, thirty?"

"Yeah," murmured Julia, her face hot. She tried a sip of beer.

"You're too good!" cried Arno, his eyes burning into her. "You're too good! You always were, but something's happened since last summer—a new dimension to your voice. You've got power—and precision. You know how few singers have that? Sascha's strong, but her coloratura's all over the road. Letting her sing Bach is like letting some drunk drive a Porsche."

"And Bach's not mechanical," said Rudi.

"Aw ..." Arno waved his hand, too excited to reply. He kept his eyes fixed on Julia. "I want you for Handel. I want you for *Messiah*. If they can do it in New York, we can do it in London. I want you for 'Refiner's Fire.'"

"'Refiner's Fire,'" Julia whispered.

She hadn't been sure what Arno was planning, but now that she knew, she wasn't surprised. She had wanted to sing "Refiner's Fire" ever since she had first heard it at the Breithaus Academy. Her last year, a big British alto had demonstrated the runs that derailed most soloists. Through her daunting arpeggios, Julia had sat transfixed, wondering what the woman's lithe voice would do next. Unmoved by the wrath the notes conveyed, Julia had pictured them as forms in space. She had sensed that they belonged in her throat and that her body had been made to sing them.

Rudi still sounded skeptical. "In London? Are you nuts? Handel's their guy."

"Yeah." Arno grinned.

"A bunch of Germans go to London and sing Handel? Who would come?"

Arno tapped the ash off his cigarette. "Everybody would come. It's Handel! With Julia, with Linda ..."

"Yeah." Rudi nodded slowly. "Yeah. It would get incredible coverage, but it's risky. How would we book it? How would we—"

Arno shifted his eyes to Rudi. Their intense blaze settled to a glow.

"Oh, no ..." murmured Rudi. He reached for his beer. "Oh, no. I just did the Vienna tour. Do you have any—"

"Messiah!" Arno breathed. "'Refiner's Fire'! Shit, her voice is made for that! I can't believe I didn't think of it sooner! We'll get Jörg, and I want that flute player ..."

Julia laughed giddily as Arno withdrew into the music. His broad fingers played chords on the table as his mind leaped from movement to movement.

"Look, I've really got to—" Rudi's voice focused to a penetrating point.

Arno seized his arm. "You've got to do this," he said. "Come on, how long since you sang those fugues?" Huskily, he began "He Trusted in God," and Rudi joined him, unable to resist.

Julia leaned back against the pile of coats, feeling silly and dreamy. Smiling, she watched the two men in white shirtsleeves as each one tried to conduct the other. Her eyelids closed, and she welcomed the darkness. The men's voices faded. Something nudged her shoulder.

"Sh—let her sleep," said a gentle voice.

"Yeah, shit, in two hours she's gonna be serving coffee," growled a deeper one.

In the darkness, the voices rose and fell, singing, arguing, commanding.

"No!" said the higher one, a round *O* spinning in blackness.

Something soft touched her cheek.

"Julia."

Arno was gazing down tenderly. Her eyes felt sticky at the corners, and she moved her hand to her hair.

"Don't worry—you look beautiful," he murmured.

Across from her, Rudi frowned at a paper he had filled with notes. Julia breathed in sweetness and saw that her beer had been replaced by coffee. Steaming black, it quivered in its thick white cup, its surface shining in oily flashes.

"Mmm." She sat up and blinked her eyes to clear the stickiness.

"Have some coffee, Mädel. It's almost time."

"So December 10, December 11, about a year from now," said Rudi. "Seventy people, plus or minus five. First choice St. John's, Smith Square if we can get it, and we stay at the Meridian."

"Yeah, the Meridian—the Baylor House sucks."

In the bathroom, Julia brushed out her hair. She washed her face with a paper towel and dabbed her eyes with cold water. While she sat on the toilet, she stared at the tiles until their edges dissolved. Her eyes closed, but she forced them back open. In the mirror, her face looked puffy, and her body seemed to have swollen to a new size. She turned sideways, trying to see whether she had gotten any fatter since yesterday.

At the table, Rudi pulled on his coat, and Arno offered twenty euros to the waiter.

"Julia, *komm*! Drink up! *Es geht gleich los!*" Arno held out a sturdy cup.

She noticed with horror that a clock on the wall said ten to seven.

On the street, the soft wetness had crystallized to a hard freeze. The chill crushed all desire to talk, and they hurried down Kantstrasse past windows of cowboy boots. As they waited for the light at Leibnizstrasse, Arno dug an elbow into Rudi's ribs.

"*Na?*" He glanced at some life-size photos of muscular men naked to the waist.

"Ugh." Rudi shook his head, too tired to reply.

Julia spotted the pink Dorrie's Donuts sign and felt a pang of sadness. Through the one bright window on Wilmersdorferstrasse, Marga's slender form could be seen arranging doughnuts in slanted wire baskets. Her scruffy black hair gave her an angry look, and with a silver stud in her nose and red pimples on her forehead, she wasn't pretty. The tautness of her body suggested a short temper, but she might just have been cold. Marga turned as they entered, and under her brown shirt, her nipples stood out as two tense points. When she saw Julia with the two men in evening clothes, her boyish face lit up.

"Brought some help?" she asked, grinning at Arno. "Any of you sober enough to make coffee?"

"Oh, we'll leave that to the *Profis*," said Arno, eying the doughnuts.
"Mm, those look good."

"Help yourself." Marga laughed. She opened one of the flat cartons she had just unloaded from the truck. Arno stared transfixed at the doughnuts, which stood in shiny brown and white rows.

"We have chocolate glazed," said Marga, "Black Forest cherry, apple cinnamon, maple frosted—"

"What's that?" demanded Arno, pointing to a row of white rounds with red and green stripes.

"Oh, that's our Christmas special."

"No shit?" Arno removed one carefully while Rudi shook his head. "All right, Mädels! We'll leave you to your work."

Rudi gave Julia a tired hug. Arno kissed her cheeks slowly, then lingered over Marga's, seeming to savor the taste of her cool skin. "Mmm." He bit into his doughnut. "*Komm*, Rudi! I'm taking you home to Norbert."

"Oh, thank God," moaned Rudi.

With her eyes, Julia followed the men all the way to the U-Bahn. At a quarter past seven, it was still pitch black, and the lamplight shone on Arno's hair. Rudi encircled Arno's waist, and Arno slung an arm over Rudi's shoulders. Doughnut in hand, Arno raised his free arm, as though cuing in the new day.

5

Comfort Ye

"Who was *that?*"

Marga's voice cut Julia's dream like a blade, and she realized that she had faded out. Her forehead felt damp and chilled from resting against the cold window.

"Hey, you okay? Should you have been out drinking all night?" Marga's fingers dug into Julia's arm. For such a thin person, she had a strong grip.

"Yeah, I'm okay." Julia turned and smiled. "I barely drank anything. We were singing."

"That guy's a *singer?* He doesn't look like a singer."

"Which one?"

Marga scrunched up her face as only she could do, so that one eyebrow rose and the other one sank.

"Oh—Arno. He's the conductor."

"No way! You went out drinking with the *conductor?*"

Marga regarded Bach as alien, but she respected every kind of music. Her awed expression deepened Julia's smile.

"No, not really," said Julia. "There were a whole bunch of people—we were just the last ones left."

Marga frowned skeptically. "Oh, yeah? So who was that other guy?"

"Oh, Rudi."

"Gay, huh?"

The corner of Marga's mouth twisted so that a crusty pimple stood out.

"Yeah. Well … uh … yeah."

"Oh." Marga grimaced.

She went back to transferring doughnuts from cardboard cartons to labeled baskets.

"So you had a gig? Wish I had one."

Marga lifted the chocolate-cream doughnuts one at a time so as not to crush their rippled puffs. Fighting the urge to close her eyes, Julia followed Marga's quick rhythm. The restless girl was a formidable worker, and in their years of shifts, Marga had never once failed to show. Like Julia, she sang, but to a different pulse. With her band Ultraviolet, she performed at clubs in the shadowed alleys of Berlin. Some mornings she rushed in hoarse and exhilarated, straight from a gig. Julia had heard her sing, and Marga's rough, low voice carried in emotion what it lacked in power. As the only girl in the band, she did most of the singing, but her real passion was songwriting. They had spent many shifts searching for words and laughing at Marga's raunchy lyrics.

This morning they didn't hurry, since it might be some time before the first customer arrived. Sunday mornings they drew a trickle of people on their way to the S-Bahn. Together, she and Marga poured coffee for weary workers, old ladies visiting family, and kids who had been partying all night. Julia often wondered why they opened before noon on Sundays and suspected that the foreign managers were making a statement. So what if they paid her and Marga seven euros an hour and sold only half that much? For those who worked and partied hard, Dorrie's Donuts was there. Anyone who came in would spread the word.

"So you feeling well enough to work?" asked Marga.

"Yeah, sorry," Julia muttered. "I'll do the coffee."

In a pattern they had worked out long ago, Julia ran the coffee machine while Marga took orders and snatched up doughnuts. In mind and body, Marga moved at a higher speed and could juggle six orders while racing between the baskets and toaster. Julia followed a slower rhythm, but from her Henningsthal days, she could coax the coffee machine to work even when all it would do was spit gray water.

Today Marga eyed her dubiously. "Seriously, I can do this if you want to sit down. You still feeling queasy?"

Julia pushed herself to her feet. "No, I'm okay. It's the funniest thing. All of a sudden, I feel fine. It just suddenly stopped."

Marga froze. "It stopped? What do you mean, it stopped? How long have you been feeling sick?"

Julia tore open a silvery packet and breathed the rich sweetness of coffee. "September—mid-September, I guess. Yeah. It happened in early September."

Marga counted on plastic-covered fingers. "Shit! That's twelve weeks! That's almost too late!"

Without answering, Julia carried two large metal canisters to the sink. Marga abandoned the doughnuts and followed.

"You're not still thinking of having it, are you?"

As the canisters filled, Julia watched the stream of water shift and bulge. The sink faded to a blur.

"Hey! Hey!" Marga gripped her upper arm, and Julia turned to face her with stinging eyes.

"You can't have this baby."

Julia looked into a face that was pure determination, thin lips, pinched nose, black hair going every which way.

"Why not? Don't I have a right to?"

Marga reached around her and turned off the water. "Because it'll ruin your life. You don't know it yet, but it will. You won't know until it's too late."

Julia faced her unflinchingly. "What if everyone did that?" she demanded. "What if nobody had kids, because it would wreck her life? I mean, that's what's happening, isn't it? That's all you hear—more people dying than being born, more people taking out than paying in. Who do you know who has kids?"

"My sister!" cried Marga. "She's got three of 'em—eight, four, and one. Or two. I forget. Know what her life is like? She can't take a shower without asking her husband first. She can barely leave her house. And that's *with* a guy. The S-Bahn drivers are gonna strike 'cause they want shorter shifts. No union in the world would put up with what she does."

Marga burned with lyric rage, and in spite of herself, Julia laughed.

"Oh, yeah, like it's funny," Marga growled. "Here."

She grabbed one of the canisters, climbed onto a stool, and emptied it into the coffee machine. With her arms tense, the points of her breasts stood out against her brown shirt.

"Look, nobody's saying anything about three kids," said Julia. "Just one. That's all I want. I'm thirty. I want to have this child."

With her jaw set, Marga motioned for the other canister. "You don't know what you're saying. You're a singer. How're you gonna sing with a kid?"

"I can do it," insisted Julia. "I'll get *Kindergeld*, a hundred and fifty-four euros a month. That'll more than cover the day care."

"Shit!" Marga spilled some water on the counter. "Day care's eight to five! You sing at night! Who's gonna watch your kid then? What're you gonna do with no guy to help?"

Julia mopped the puddle hurriedly. "Lots of women do it," she said. "Around here, most of 'em, far as I can see."

"Yeah, they do it." Marga sighed. "But that's *all* they do. You just ask any woman in this neighborhood what she wanted to do *before*."

Julia looked around to see what other tasks needed doing. Her roses were wilting in their cellophane wrapper, so she freed them and stuck them in one of the canisters. On the counter next to the coffee machine, the flowers looked around hopefully, like a dozen faces sniffing the air. Julia took off her coat and hung it in her locker but couldn't bear to pull a brown jersey over her wine-red gown. When she walked back out, Marga had almost finished filling the baskets.

"Jesus!" she gasped. "No wonder the conductor took you out drinking! You're gorgeous!"

"It's getting too tight," Julia said, rubbing her belly. Warm from her coat, the velvet felt delicious, and she spread her fingers wide.

"Turn sideways—you starting to show yet?" asked Marga. "Nah. Maybe—maybe a little. Mainly you just look hot."

"Yeah, right." Julia smiled and pulled on some gloves. "So what else have we got left here?"

"The muffins. Do the muffins."

Julia opened a box of forty chocolate chip muffins, speckled hills in an endless desert. Their outlines shimmered in a rippling wave until the whole store joined in the dance.

"Shit." Julia held on tight to the counter.

"Hey, come on." Marga's wiry arms steadied her and led her to a chair. Marga sat down across from Julia and rested her elbows on the table, supporting her chin on small fists.

"Look. Look what it's doing to you already. How're you gonna sing? Shit, just look at you!"

"I don't know," murmured Julia. "I'll figure something out."

"Go to a clinic!" pleaded Marga. "It'll be so easy! Tell 'em it was in October. How'll they know?"

Julia shook her head. "Oh, they can tell, I'm sure. Ultrasound. Probably half the women going in there lie."

"And is that so bad?" Marga fixed her with fierce hazel eyes. "Compared to the shit women pull when they don't want their kids but they already have them?"

In quick, low voices, they cut in and out, partners in a fast-paced duet.

"Yeah," answered Julia, "like that one who strangled those nine babies and buried them in her flower box."

"Oh, that was just some crazy drunk."

Julia swallowed.

"No." Marga reflected. "I'm thinking more like that one who left those two boys alone for two weeks in summer—"

"Oh, yeah," interrupted Julia. "With two candy bars and two juice boxes—I couldn't believe that. They said they found bites on the older one's legs. He died first, and the younger one was trying to suck his blood."

"Yeah, friggin' little brothers," Marga said with a grimace. "And how about that one in Moabit, just a couple of weeks ago?"

"Yeah, that one who left the three kids in bed and came home drunk at twelve forty-five the next day."

Marga looked at Julia meaningfully and squeezed a pimple over her left eyebrow. "She just wanted to go out. She'd been trapped in there for months with those kids. She just wanted to live again. Reason women are so pissed off at her is she actually did what they all want to do. You hear anyone pissed off at the fathers of those kids who never even watched them for one day?"

"No." Julia sighed.

"Know the difference between her and us? One condom."

"Three condoms." Julia laughed.

"Whatever."

On the fake wooden tabletop, the brown lines rippled as though stirred by Julia's breaths. "Oh, wow," she murmured. "I need a doughnut."

Marga jumped up. "I'll open the register."

"Here." Julia looked around for her purse, then remembered it was in her locker. "Give me a strawberry cream—and a Christmas special. And let me pay for that one that Arno ate."

"Eating for three, huh?"

The register came humming to life. Julia stared at the box of muffins, seeking the strength to stand. Marga returned with the doughnuts.

"Look—I wouldn't do that," said Julia. "I wouldn't leave a baby. I bet you wouldn't either."

"Oh, no?" Marga grimaced. "You gonna tell me that if that conductor guy calls and says he's got some fabulous gig, and he wants to meet you for a drink, and you can't find a babysitter, and your kid's asleep—"

Julia shook her head, and Marga exhaled so that her cheeks puffed out.

"Look. It all comes down to who's backing you. Nobody does this alone. Nobody. Either the guy's gotta help you, or your family, or his. Have you even told him yet?"

Julia frowned. Until now, it had been like a dream that dissolved as soon as she focused upon it. For three months she had been hiding it, unable to find words. Any phrase that emerged made it seem like someone else's experience. No way of telling it made sense.

With effort, she met Marga's intense gaze. "No," she said. "I haven't told him."

Rather than cutting her, Marga's voice softened. "Look, you've gotta do it," she said. "Are you scared? I mean, what's he gonna do? He can't hurt you."

Julia poked at her Christmas doughnut, white and sticky on its wax paper sled. A wave of icy air rushed over her, and three workers walked in, a cleaning crew on their way to the S-Bahn.

"Hey, Mädels!" called a red-haired man. "The *Kaffeeklatsch* comes later! Get to work! You have starving men here!"

With scarred fingers, he brushed auburn strands from his brown eyes, which followed Julia as she poured coffee. Marga dropped doughnuts into pink-and-white bags, directed by the men's pointing fingers.

"That the new uniform you're wearin' here now?" called the jokester. "We've gotta come here more often."

"Whatever floats your boat," Julia muttered, fighting a smile.

"Hey, how much for a dozen o' those, Mädel?" asked an older man whose eyes hadn't left Julia's breasts.

"Ask your wife," snapped Marga and shoved their bags toward them.

"Ooh, *Mädchen*, ease up! You have a rough night?" asked the redhead. Under his stained brown coat, his belly swelled his blue overalls. He winked at Julia as he reached for his bag. Laughing, the cleaning crew walked out with their breakfast, leaving the change for the girls.

Marga sat back down with Julia. "So you can't count on this guy?" she asked.

"No."

"Fuckin' pigs." On Marga's mobile face, the mouth slid left. "They're all the same. They fuck you; then they throw you away like garbage. You know what finally happened with Nils, that guitar player I was tellin' you about? Last Friday, at two in the morning, he tells me he's going back to Cologne, 'cause he doesn't feel close to anyone here."

"No way!"

Marga paused. One eye flickered as a memory stabbed. Her voice held steady, unwavering in its disgust. "Yeah. Five minutes after he was inside my body. So I tell him what I think about that, and he tells me to leave. At two in the morning. In Neukölln."

"Shit …"

"So I tell him I'm not going. 'If you want me outa here, you're gonna have to throw me out,' I say. So you know what he does?"

Julia had never seen Marga cry, and this strange swelling of her features must have been her way of crying. No tears emerged, but her voice softened as the words rushed out.

"He grabs me by the feet, drags me across the floor, opens the door, and dumps me out in the hall. Five minutes later, he opens the door, puts all my stuff down next to me, and closes it again. That was the last time I saw him. I got dressed in the hallway, and I stayed there till it got light."

"Wow, that's horrible," breathed Julia.

"And they wonder why the abortion clinics are doing such good business."

"But not all guys are like that." Julia shifted her weight.

"You don't think so, huh? What's your guy like?" Marga leaned forward, as though hungry for an image.

"Well, he—" The shadow of someone passing pulled Julia's eyes to the window.

"He's married, isn't he?"

"Yeah."

Marga snorted. "That's a whole 'nother story. So you can't count on him?"

Julia groped for words. "No. No ... and ... I don't want to either. I don't want to live with him. He's not someone I want in my life."

Marga smiled. "You're holding out for that conductor guy, aren't you?"

"No—no—" Julia's eyes returned to Marga, whose mouth twitched with amusement.

"You think he's gonna want you with a baby?"

"No! He just wants to help me sing!"

"You won't be able to sing!" Marga's voice sharpened. "God! Why don't you see that? With kids, it's them or you. No more singing, no more conductor guy, just twenty years of cleaning up shit."

"I don't believe that!" cried Julia.

"Nobody does! If anyone knew beforehand what it's like to have kids, nobody would ever do it!"

Julia looked past Marga to the gray light of Wilmersdorferstrasse, where a crow was stalking over the frozen street.

"Go tomorrow!" said Marga. "Go to a clinic tomorrow, and tell 'em it was in October. Go tomorrow! This may be your last chance."

Despite Marga's fierceness, Julia felt an inner calm, the weight of an immovable ocean.

"I can't kill it," she said. "I can feel it in me. I've felt it in there from the beginning. I don't care who the father is. I feel it living in me. It's helping me sing."

———— ■ ————

At ten after one, Julia stepped out into the gray light of Wilmersdorferstrasse, carrying her roses, a duffel bag, and a box of doughnuts. Even though the temperature was well below freezing, the air was misty, and she breathed in playful dragon puffs. On this second Sunday in Advent, people filled the streets, since the stores would be open until six. Families streamed into the new Wilmersdorfer Arcades, where they could admire shop windows out of the cold. In the pedestrian zone, merchants had improvised a Christmas market out of flimsy wooden shacks. A thin woman sat behind glowing Advent stars and drew grimly on her cigarette. Local kids were enjoying the miniature rides, and Julia watched two girls circle on a toy train. She passed a booth selling a rainbow of hard candy and another offering yellow Chinese noodles. In red-and-white paper boats, the noodles quivered enticingly, flecked with shiny bits of vegetable.

As she crossed Bismarckstrasse, Julia gazed at the Deutsche Oper, a giant fish tank with a pebbly facade. Despite her efforts, she still hadn't sung there, not even in an opera chorus. *Maybe now*, she thought wearily. *Maybe now, if Arno ...* But many people disliked Arno, and she wasn't sure how far his connections reached.

North of Bismarckstrasse, the feverish shopping street exhaled with a sigh. Bright windows with skinny mannequins gave way to bins of socks and racks of T-shirts for five euros. The gourmet shop Rogacki did a good business, but most people preferred the Turkish fruit store. Next to its river of oranges, a man was chanting, "*Two* kilos for three euros, *two* kilos for three euros!"

Julia dodged a pair of women in headscarves and turned left onto Zillestrasse. She passed a parking lot, then a vacant lot full of weeds, and gazed at an odd structure ahead. The yellow-brick building had a steeply sloped roof and a Germanic cross over the door. Decorated with inset rows of red brick, it looked like a dry gingerbread house left too long in a shop window. Somehow this orphaned parish house had survived the bombs that had blasted the neighborhood around it. In the refurbished building, the city had created a clinic for unwed mothers. A sign near the door said in German and Turkish that it was open Monday to Friday from

9:00 a.m. to 1:00 p.m. Marga was right. She would have to go. She couldn't put it off any longer.

Julia freed some hair caught under her duffel bag strap and crossed a park that cut a diagonal swath between buildings. When she reached Schlossstrasse, she stopped to watch the Charlottenburg Palace shimmer in the mist. At the end of the gray boulevard, the yellow palace of Prussian kings floated like a hallucination. Its round tower had the grace of another time, and in the working-class district, it sat like a lemon cake in a hardware store.

Julia's own building lay just across the street. Unlike the haphazard neighborhood she had crossed, hers was tightly knit and well bounded. With a small-town feel, it had conducted its business for decades, unmoved by the East's secession and return. Extending from the palace on the north to Bismarckstrasse on the south, from Schlossstrasse on the east to the autobahn on the west, the streets of Julia's *Kiez* ran like tunnels between prewar buildings. One of the first West Berlin neighborhoods restored after the war, the Charlottenburg district had been patched together with minimal luxury. Facades where angels had once hovered had been blasted flat, and without the greenery adorning their balconies in summer, the buildings had little color. Julia's Kiez boasted a *Ziegenhof*, where a herd of goats bleated, and a management association that ran block parties. Another office, which Julia had visited herself, advised those who had fallen behind in their rent. On the streets, short, red-faced couples passed groups of Turkish boys who spoke German as if they had a bad cold. On Hildemannstrasse, the youth center had been turned to a mosque. It was a Kiez for anyone and everyone.

Getränke Gillmann, where Hildemannstrasse crossed Mehringstrasse, was its geographic and social heart. Here residents gossiped as they bought cases of beer and read messages tacked to the boards. Each Sunday morning, property changed hands at the Charlottenplatz flea market. Once a year, on a day chosen by the Kiez management association, the streets rumbled as Getränke Gillmann lent out its dollies and people wheeled their old furniture to Charlottenplatz to be sold. Wobbly tables and wardrobes with bad hinges left one apartment to appear in another, only to resurface at Charlottenplatz the next year. In some ways, this Charlottenburg Kiez reminded Julia of Henningsthal, and she had stayed despite ribbing at the Hans Breithaus Academy. It would have been hard to find a cheaper place anywhere in Berlin—at least, any place safe to walk around at night.

Today in the murky air, the row of heavy houses seemed to lean inward. Julia passed through a green gate and entered her courtyard, the end of a long strip between buildings. Built in pieces, her house had an improvised look. Except for the scaly paint around the windows, the white *Vorderhaus* on the street had little in common with the yellow *Hinterhaus* behind it. The buildings' five floors didn't align, and a white annex jutted out of the Vorderhaus as though the proud structure on the street were turning its back on the rear building. In its own way, the courtyard reinforced this division. Behind the blue and yellow recycling bins, scraggly bushes reached up with hopeful arms, separating the dirt path to the Vorderhaus from the nest of bicycles behind them. Near the stairs to the Hinterhaus basement, a brown-haired boy and girl were struggling with a gigantic wardrobe, and Julia ran to help them.

"Basti!" she cried. She waved her flowers since she had no free hand.

Broad-shouldered and tall, Sebastian Kunz looked built to handle whatever life gave him. His high cheekbones and angular face made him seem older than his twenty years. Over his crooked nose, his dark eyes gazed out cynically, but they warmed as they settled on Julia. He motioned to the girl to put down her end, which she seemed more than happy to do.

"Hey!" he cried as the cabinet's curved top hit the cement walkway.

"Sorry, Basti." His friend giggled.

Frowning, he stooped to see whether the wood had split. He ran a broad finger along the gleaming rim and relaxed when he found it unmarred.

"*Na, Raubtier*, what have you got this time?" Julia laughed.

Basti looked up with a shy smile. "Those flowers for me?"

"Could be. You been good?"

Basti grinned as his helper checked her nails for damage. Like Julia, Birgit Schicke had a round face and brown hair, but her eyes were cornflower blue. Between her low-slung jeans and white jacket, blue lace nibbled her pink flesh. In the past year, her passion for Basti had become a house joke, with bets riding on how long it would take her to nail her man.

Birgit and her mother lived on top of the Vorderhaus, and rumors flew about how they paid the premium rent. Born two years after the wall came down, Birgit was still known as an *Ossi* since her mother, a beautician, had brought her to Berlin from the East. In her Hinterhaus apartment, wistful Frau Riemann swore that Frau Schicke had money from the Stasis, the East German secret police. Basti's mother, Astrid, said that was *Quatsch*. More likely, the curvy beautician was satisfying some lonely husband, who paid out his gratitude in monthly checks.

"Who gave you the flowers?" asked Birgit.

"Oh, nobody. I was singing."

"Singing? Why didn't you tell me?" asked Basti. "I woulda been there."

"Oh, that's okay," said Julia. "I didn't know myself until Friday. The *Christmas Oratorio*. In the Remembrance Church."

Basti whistled.

"Wow, that's great," Birgit breathed.

"So did you go straight from there to work?" asked Basti, eyeing Julia's pink doughnut box.

"Yeah. We went out afterward, and after a while it seemed like there was no point ..."

Basti nodded, studying Julia carefully.

"You want a doughnut?"

Julia opened her box, and they helped themselves. Birgit smiled self-consciously as she sank her teeth into chocolate frosting. Basti ate in large bites, his eyes drifting back to the wardrobe he had wheeled in from Charlottenplatz.

With a passion to fix things, Basti picked up broken furniture all over Berlin. In the basement where their *Hausmeister* had once worked, he refinished doors, repaired legs, and replaced hinges. For years he had dreamed of running a carpentry shop, where he could restore antiques and build custom furniture. But like many young craftsmen, he had failed to find an apprenticeship. Uninspired by school, he had received poor grades, and despite his talent, he couldn't find a carpenter to train him. Without an apprenticeship letter, he couldn't run his own shop, a fact that had barely slowed him down.

With a web of connections all over the city, Basti rescued furniture from flea markets, estate agents, and trash heaps. The BSR hadn't collected oversized trash in years, and rather than paying for its removal, most Berliners simply dumped it. Many of Basti's sources lay in the East, where fast-paced renovations unearthed prewar furniture. He paid boys to call when good-looking pieces turned up, and the ring of his *Handy* had interrupted many conversations with Julia. "Corner of Bahnhofstrasse and where?" he would ask. "A really nice chair, like a rich lady sits on? How rich? Like a rich lady today or a rich lady a long time ago?"

Herr Seidemann, a neighborhood drunk who had once been a carpenter, offered helpful advice. By now, most of his tools had made their way to the Mehringstrasse basement, and Basti earned good money by selling restored pieces to antique dealers. With the extra income, he and his mother lived better than they could have on her disability and his unemployment check. Still, Basti went regularly to the job center to seek apprenticeships. When Julia saw him with a fistful of applications, he would say disgustedly that he was earning his €281 a month, but she knew he longed to be a master carpenter.

The wardrobe he had found today would need every bit of his skill. It was hardwood, probably fir, with a deep brown finish and a grooved scroll pattern along the top. With its glowing curves, it looked like a giant contrabass that could open to accommodate clothes. On each door, a flowery rim framed the inlaid panel, but the doors wouldn't close, and they were badly scratched.

Basti caught Julia's eye. "Nice piece, huh? Got it for a hundred euros this morning. New hinges, a little patchwork here and there, and it'll be worth a thousand."

"That's a lot of work," Julia murmured, awed by the size of it. It was as wide as the stairway and over six feet tall.

"So what else am I gonna do with myself?" asked Basti, crinkling the corner of his mouth. "C'mon. Gimme a hand here, and we'll get this thing downstairs."

He directed the women to take charge of the top. Birgit tried to keep the rich wood away from the railing while Julia tilted the wardrobe so that it cleared the stairs. With powerful arms, Basti lifted the lower end, supporting most of the weight.

"Okay!" he gasped, and one step at a time, they made their way down to his shop.

Julia breathed deeply and savored the scent of varnish, sawdust, and sweat. On the walls and shelves, Basti had arranged his tools like a surgeon, sorting them by function but placing them so that they were easy to grab. At one time or another, Julia had seen him use most of the handsaws, jigsaws, chisels, and planers.

"Thanks, you two," said Basti. "I owe you. I'll get you somethin' nice when I sell this."

Birgit beamed. "Would you get me some flowers like she got?"

"Nah," said Basti. "Don't you want somethin' that'll last?"

"Lemme think about it, okay?" Birgit smiled.

"Yeah, you do that," growled Basti in a voice as low as Arno's.

"And you." He turned to Julia. "I want you to tell me next time you're gonna sing. I'll be there."

"Me too!" said Birgit.

"Okay, everybody out." Basti grinned. "I gotta work."

But as Julia walked up the steps, she felt Basti's eyes follow her.

Instead of going to her own apartment, Julia visited Astrid, whom she kept supplied with doughnuts. Each day after work, she brought a box of leftovers, which she could buy at half price. What Astrid didn't eat, she sold to her neighbors. Her favorites were chocolate cream and chocolate glazed.

Eight years older than Julia, Basti's mother looked somewhat the worse for wear. Her light-blond hair was maintained by frequent trips to the beauty parlor, and heavy smoking had dried out her skin. Although she no longer got up at five, gray rings tugged at her brown eyes. Like Julia, she was full bodied, but her breasts hung more loosely and were boosted by push-up bras. When she smiled, her teeth dug into her lower lip, suggesting a love of fun.

Astrid opened her door eagerly. "Where you been?" she asked. "I been trying to call you."

Only then did the image return, the wave from the nearby window. That's right—Astrid had been trying to tell her something.

"Oh, I'm sorry. I've been singing," said Julia.

"Singing, huh? They pay you good money? Mm!" Astrid bit into a chocolate-glazed doughnut. Her maroon bathrobe opened as she shifted her weight to reveal soft, folding flesh.

"Well—a hundred twenty-five euros."

"A hundred twenty-five euros! Wow!" Astrid's rough features warmed. Like Basti's, her skin had a brownish tone, so that she never looked pale in winter.

"So with gigs like that, you gonna quit Dorrie's Donuts?"

"Nah, not yet." Julia sighed. "Maybe soon. I just never know when they're gonna want me to sing, and I need the money."

"Yeah." Astrid nodded. "I know what you mean. Hey, listen! I wanted to tell you something. You know what I read yesterday— no, no, Friday?"

"What?"

Astrid's concentrated frown told Julia she must have unearthed some new conspiracy. Her ramshackle stories sometimes had a solid foundation, and Julia listened with interest.

"Well, he wasn't drunk!" exclaimed Astrid. "The guy wasn't drunk!"

"What guy?" asked Julia.

"That guy, her limo driver. He wasn't drunk."

"What, Princess Di's?"

"Yeah, yeah. They did some kind of test. He wasn't drunk. It was Charles—or that old witch. They always wanted her dead. They must have done something to the car."

"Gee, you really think that they had her killed?"

"Sure." Astrid nodded. "She was carrying Dodi's baby. A divorce, an Arab baby? They took her out."

"Shit," murmured Julia. She slumped down on a kitchen chair and unbuttoned her coat.

"Wow!" Astrid gasped. "You sang in *that*? They shoulda paid you a couple hundred."

Astrid reached for a second doughnut, and Julia took a chocolate glazed.

"Hey, I need your opinion on something," said Astrid between bites. "I have an appointment tomorrow, and ..."

"Yeah, sure," said Julia. "Show me."

"Yeah?" Astrid's brow wrinkled. "I've gotta put somethin' on that shows him the difference between a real woman and that skinny bitch at the front desk."

"Yeah, yeah, sure," said Julia.

She ate her doughnut in soft bites and watched Astrid model three sweaters. Each time she offered a rounded profile, then flipped the bright wool upward to reveal a lace bra.

"He puts his stethoscope here." Astrid pointed. "And then he just sort of ... lingers. I think he liked that black one, the one with the loops. Last time I was there, he kept circling like a ten-year-old too scared to touch."

Julia wondered how Dr. Kowalski could hear Astrid's heart under those huge dumplings of flesh. But on a regular basis, he filled out certificates saying that her aortic valve stenosis made her unfit for housecleaning. With no high school diploma, Astrid was unlikely to find other work. The cardiologist's pretty young wife managed his office and answered his phones. Despite her presence, or maybe because of it, Astrid believed that he was unfulfilled and needed the love of a full-grown woman.

Laughing giddily, Julia voted for a black lace bra and a soft, clinging pink sweater. There was no denying it—Astrid's figure put little Frau Dr. Kowalski to shame.

"I bet he thinks about me when he's with her." Astrid grinned, her teeth biting her lower lip. Musing, she stared out at the Vorderhaus until her smile faded.

"So what about you?" she asked. "How've you been feeling?"

"I've stopped feeling sick," said Julia.

Astrid frowned and pulled out her cigarettes. "You must be pretty far along, then. You been to the clinic? Have they checked you out? You should let 'em check you out, make sure everything's okay."

Her lighter snapped.

"Yeah." Julia sighed. "I'm going tomorrow."

"Good." Astrid drew in smoke and exhaled with pleasure. She watched Julia silently and waited for her to go on.

"I haven't told him yet," said Julia. "It's gonna be hard. I know he's gonna freak out."

"He's married, right?" Astrid blew smoke at the ceiling.

"Yeah."

"Yeah," muttered Astrid. "They always are."

Julia shook her head. "He's gonna freak out. He's gonna tell me to get rid of it."

"So fuck him." Astrid shrugged her shoulders. "He can't make you if you don't want to. You've got that feeling, haven't you?"

Julia nodded.

"I can see it all over you. You can feel it in there. I remember what that was like. Once I had that feeling, no one in the world could make me kill it."

Julia smiled, but her lips trembled.

"Aw, honey." Astrid grinned. "A baby's nice. Don't let him kill it. Why don't you call him right now? I'd love to hear him freak out."

6

Behold, a Virgin Shall Conceive

Erik called on a September night whose sweetness promised a last spurt of summer. Until then, he had telephoned rarely, and his singsong tenor delighted Julia. Johanna was in New York, and his students were doing a project, so he had little homework to grade. Hearing a Chopin prelude, he had felt an urge to see Julia. What was she doing this weekend? Could he come up?

"Sure," said Julia, feeling a little strange.

Until then, she had always tried to keep her Berlin and Henningsthal worlds apart. The Breithaus Academy singers knew she was from the Westerwald but not that her parents had run a snack bar. Of her musical friends, only Arno understood her origins, and it wasn't because he'd been told. Rudi and Marga knew that her mother had died, and Astrid suspected how her father had spent his days. But no one saw the whole landscape of her life. She made sure of that. She described parts to the people who could picture them best and hoped they would never meet to connect the pieces.

Erik's appearance on Mehringstrasse threatened to do just that. She hated to think of him judging her life. With his mother's sense of culture, he had always laughed at poverty—not at suffering, but at the joy-seeking ways of the poor. Julia had often imagined his apartment in Frankfurt, where he taught music at a *Gymnasium*. Erik would have walls of books, Persian carpets, and a grand piano with gleaming black curves. Johanna, an executive for Diebel Insurance, helped to pay for it all.

Still, when Erik appeared in Julia's courtyard, she felt a flash of joy. Last time she saw him, at his wedding, he had been red-faced with laughter. With champagne frothing his emotions, he had chortled like a boy too happy to take the world seriously. On this warm September morning, he was wearing a blue T-shirt and jeans and dragging a small black suitcase. Erik looked down, frustrated, as the wheels caught on a bush, and he yanked to tear them free. Five stories up, Julia leaned out over her table.

"Hey, Erik! Up here!"

Erik smiled radiantly and waved a pudgy arm. He seemed to have doubled in size.

Breathing heavily, he approached Julia's open door. His fluffy red hair had thinned, but a few bumps still troubled his shiny forehead. Sweat stains darkened the blue under his arms, and his belly pushed his shirt out from his jeans. Whereas Julia carried her weight gracefully, Erik looked as though someone had stuck a hose in his mouth and blown him up with a bicycle pump. Never at ease in his body, he moved bewilderedly, as though he had gained forty pounds overnight. At the sight of Julia, his brown eyes softened with relief, and she sensed that he hadn't relaxed in a long time. His warm, damp hug felt wonderful, his belly resting easily against hers.

Erik glanced into Julia's living room with no apparent objection to what he saw. His eyes moved quickly to her table of plants below the bright open window. Stuck behind the protrusion in the Vorderhaus, Julia's apartment got little light. Plants could thrive only in this favored spot, nourished by a few western rays. The shiny, dark table with its floral border supported a rich tangle of green.

Erik wandered toward the cascade of leaves, then stopped before a black-framed picture. "Hey, there's your Dürer print!" he cried. "I can't believe you still have that! I wonder what happened to mine."

In the ninth grade, he and Julia had taken a school trip to Nuremberg. At the Dürer House, they had been offered free prints by a man demonstrating the artist's press. Julia's showed a bearded saint holding a church and cocking his head quizzically. Maybe he was wondering what all those squiggles were. From the column under his feet to the vines over his head, wormy tendrils engulfed him. Only his halo poked out spiky and straight, clearing some space between the vines. Pleased by the curves, Julia had rolled her print carefully and splurged on a black wooden frame. Other than her clothes, the saint drowning in tendrils was one of the few things she had brought to Berlin.

Erik asked for a glass of water, which he drank thirstily as he studied Dürer's fine lines. Julia showed him her tiny bathroom and dark bedroom, where Erik parked his suitcase. He seemed interested in little but Julia herself and his plans for the next two days.

"You look just the same! You look great!" he exclaimed as he followed each quiver of her blue dress.

"Is he hot?" Marga had asked when Julia had called to trade shifts.

"Nah, it's just Erik." Julia had laughed.

"So what the hell—why don't you wear that blue dress?" Marga had said.

Simply cut, the navy-blue dress tied in back, so that without pulling, it showed Julia's fullest curves. She had found it last week on a ten-euro rack, strategically placed for people enjoying the last weeks of summer.

"Oh, come on," Julia told Erik. "I can't look the same. It's been so long."

"No, you really do," he insisted.

As Erik sat beside her, his eyes glowed fondly but flickered as his troubles broke through.

"I mean, look at me," he said, waving a hand over his belly. "Johanna's after me all the time to lose weight—and Renate …"

Julia smiled, still jarred by the way he called his mother by her first name.

"I wouldn't worry about it," she said. "There are a lot worse things you can do than gain weight."

Erik grinned and shook his head so that she couldn't tell whether he agreed. Awkwardly, he bent and rummaged in his pack until he found a highlighted copy of *Zitty*.

Erik's plans for the weekend made Julia smile. In the museums section, he had marked exhibits on South Sea art in Dahlem, seventeenth-century landscape painting at the Picture Gallery, and Egyptian sculpture at the Altes Museum. He wanted to hear six concerts and had ranked them in order of preference, from Beethoven's Sixth at the Philharmonie to some French Renaissance songs at the Apostel-Paulus-Kirche. Erik blushed as Julia laughed deep in her throat and asked what they could do for extra credit.

"I just want to *do* something," he said. "Frankfurt's not like Berlin. We're always working, or Johanna's away. There's so much going on here! I don't know when I'm going to get back."

For someone so ambitious, Erik didn't move fast. He seemed content just to sit and talk, with occasional glimpses at the bearded saint.

"That was the funniest trip." He chuckled. "You remember Frau Köhler? She had no idea where the Dürer House was, but she pretended she did."

"Yeah, and that kid who took off—he just split—what was his name?" Julia laughed.

"Oh, yeah! Robert! Robert Ruder!" Erik leaned back and laughed, his face bright pink.

"Geez, who would name a kid Robert Ruder?" Julia giggled. "Maybe that's why he ran away."

They laughed with the same jazzy rhythm.

"So did they ever find that kid?" asked Julia.

"Yeah. I remember we went home without him, but I think the police got him."

They quieted, and Erik spread his arms along the back of the couch. He sighed exaggeratedly and laughed at himself. "This is nice," he murmured.

"So who have you heard from?" asked Julia.

It had been a long time since she had thought about Henningsthal, and suddenly she craved the scoured streets, over which people passed at the same times each day. Informed by Renate, Erik knew everything about everyone, and one by one, he told her their stories. Almost all of their classmates had left Henningsthal for big cities, and some had landed in the East. A few were married, but hardly any had children. Laughing at life, Erik described their successes and failures in teaching, medicine, and law. Inge Albrecht, obsessed with fashion and clothes, had ended up teaching gym in Hoyerswerda. A kid who had taken no end of grief for wearing a back brace had joined the police. And Christian Wendt, known for having sex with any girl who would let him, was now a gynecologist in Düsseldorf.

Julia shrieked. "No way! Has anyone sued him yet?"

"No, not yet. He has a very loyal practice."

Julia swatted him, and he tried to tickle her, but she was faster and grabbed his wrist.

"I surrender!" He laughed, but then his features softened. "So did he ever come on to you?" he asked.

"Yeah, like a leech." Julia smiled. "The little creep kept coming by the Imbiss. I told him to get lost, but he wouldn't listen." She chuckled. "Then one night he showed up when my father was there."

"Oh no." Erik's eyes brightened.

"Yeah." Julia laughed. "He told him if he didn't leave me alone, he would do something that would make him remember Julia Martens to the end of his days. It was great—I can still hear him saying it. 'I might go to jail for maybe ten, fifteen years, but what the hell. It'd be worth it.'"

"Wow!" Erik gasped.

"Yeah. The little shit never came back."

Erik rubbed her arm. "Oh, God." He sighed and glanced at his watch. "So should we do something?"

Based on Erik's wish list, they drew up a plan. If they took the yellow U-Bahn to Potsdamer Platz, they could try for Philharmonie tickets when the box office opened. If they got them, they could see the landscape exhibit at the Picture Gallery next door. The paintings of lush meadows and puffy clouds seemed like a good match for the *Pastorale* Symphony.

"It's such a beautiful day, though," said Julia. "I'd love to walk in the park. We could see if the gray heron's by the pond."

Lazily they made their way down four flights of stairs. As they crossed the courtyard, Julia felt eyes and spotted Birgit in the Vorderhaus window. Erik grinned and returned her wave. His good-natured friendliness flowed easily through a wide, parched summer bed.

The stifling U-Bahn made their faces flush, and with his pink skin, Erik reminded Julia of a Dorrie's Donuts box. The Berliners had bared sturdy limbs and pale flesh to celebrate the September day. Erik's eyes settled on some girls in sundresses, one of whom was swinging around a pole. Laughing, she shook out her shiny brown hair and brushed it from her pimply shoulders.

As they walked between red- and yellow-brick buildings, Erik shook his head, reflecting. "Can you believe that ten years ago, none of this was here? Things change here so fast."

Julia couldn't imagine Berlin without Potsdamer Platz, whose pointy towers guarded the East-West boundary like wedges of yellow cheese. Since she had come to Berlin, the shining Potsdamer Arcades had welcomed her, but according to Astrid, twenty years ago the place had been a wasteland. Julia and Erik crossed the double brick lines where the Berlin Wall had once stood. In her mind, she tried to erase the skyscrapers. Just dirt and weeds, Astrid had said, and a whole lot of dust. "And mines! Don't forget the mines!" Astrid had exclaimed.

In the summer of 1990, Astrid had watched as soldiers dug mines from Berlin's best-loved ground. Looking down at her feet, Julia hoped they hadn't forgotten any, but a sweet-smelling breeze dissolved the thought. It hadn't rained in weeks, and from the nearby *Tiergarten* came the smell of dry leaves and the heavier scent of dirt. If only she could follow the park's raked paths to see yellow branches against the glassy black pond.

At the Philharmonie box office, Julia learned that only the most expensive seats were left: block A, third and fourth rows, for thirty euros each.

"I'll invite you." Erik beamed. "You can get lunch."

In the museum, he studied the paintings so closely that two guards told him to stand back. After his hilarity that morning, his silence worried Julia, but she didn't press him. She sensed that whatever needed to come out would have to emerge by itself. Letting Erik set the pace, she stared at ponds, cows, and gray-green leaves and breathed the paint's faint, oily tang. Erik turned to her with an almost guilty look, then blinked and smiled. He shuffled to a new painting with his toes slightly turned in. Funny—in spite of his new weight, he moved just like he used to.

After a hot, packed burrito, Erik lost his desire for culture. It was over eighty degrees, and even with air-conditioning, the Mexican restaurant they had chosen radiated heat. Tourists trying to quench their thirst with margaritas were discovering they were more than half-drunk. Julia leaned back, feeling peaceful despite the din.

Erik cupped his hands to his mouth and tried to make himself heard. Julia shook her head, and they leaned forward to speak into each other's ears.

"It's good to see you," said Erik. "In spite of everything that's happened, you haven't changed. You have this grounded quality. I've missed that. The people I know are so different."

Julia shrugged. "They're probably okay. They just think about different things."

To escape the noise, they moved to a café across the street, and Erik ordered an Irish coffee. Its sweetness invaded his breath, and he seemed sensitive to the stuff. Whether it was the coffee or the whiskey, he began to talk freely. Julia settled in the sound of his warm, flowing voice and gave up on a walk in the park.

"So you've got a degree from the Hans Breithaus Academy? That's wonderful." Erik smiled.

"Yeah," said Julia. "This guy helped me—the conductor of a choir I sang with. I had to get my high school equivalency first—I did that at night. It took a long time. Then I started studying voice.

"I'd love to hear you sing," said Erik. "Where do you sing?"

"Oh, around. In churches, when they need a soloist. The duet in *Christ lag in Todesbanden*—that was great! And the *Christmas Oratorio* in the Johanneskirche."

"Wow!" exclaimed Erik. He turned his glass mug upside down until the last creamy drops rolled into his mouth. The people at the next table stared at him, and he gave them a sunny smile.

"How about you?" asked Julia. "Are you still playing?"

"Yeah," he said sadly and nudged his glass. "I still play at home. And at school when I teach. But not concerts. I'm not that good."

"Yeah you are," said Julia. "I've heard you play."

Erik looked at her, amused. "People will listen to a sixteen-year-old who's pretty good," he said, "but not a thirty-year-old. You've got to be great. I'm not."

Julia sipped her iced coffee and gazed at him, unsure what to say. His round face seemed as ready to laugh as it always had but equally ready to cry. She sensed sad, black water rising in him, concealing angry snags.

Only at the Philharmonie did Erik's eyes brighten. In his stuffed pack, he had been carrying a folded shirt and pants, into which he changed while Julia waited outside the bathroom. When he emerged, he raised his eyes to scan the enormous space. Irregular and vast with unexpected stairways, the Philharmonie looked like an exploded city. Overhead, round lights hung like balls of plankton, and 360 degrees of eyes ringed the stage. The circular space made Julia think of ruins that had come alive to shelter vagabond music.

With a sigh, Erik settled into his third-row seat, spread his legs, and studied the orchestra. The conductor, William Handshaw, strode onstage, and Julia suppressed a fit of giggles as she thought about what Arno called the frizzy-haired Australian maestro. Arno's kindest comparisons likened the edgy director to a dancing vegetable brush. Others targeted his sexuality. Watching Handshaw's slim body shape Beethoven's melody, she could hear Arno's voice, fast and deep.

"He can count," Arno had growled late one night at the Onion. "But the guy's light on his feet. If his string section turned on him, he'd piss himself."

Julia doubted the truth of these slurs since her Breithaus Academy teachers called Handshaw a first-rate artist who treated his musicians well. Tonight, the strings seemed happy with his direction as the music gathered for a joyous burst. But something in Julia couldn't help laughing. "*Schrubber!* Scrub brush!" She could hear Arno grunt, describing Handshaw's style in every sense. Responding to her quiver, Erik stuck a finger in her ribs and caught her hand as she poked back. It had been a long time since anyone had held her hand, and she let him keep it. She shivered as his thumb stroked her palm.

Erik seemed fully absorbed in the music, which rose swirling as the melody emerged. He seemed personally connected to the fragile theme, aroused when it surfaced and subdued when it died. He shuddered at the violent chords of the storm and breathed more softly when its dark waves passed. Every now and then he squeezed Julia's hand, which was sweating. He freed her fingers only to brush off tears that began to flow in the last movement.

Worried, Julia glanced up at him. His red nose looked broader than ever. His eyes were fixed on the musicians, but he wasn't seeing them. Sniffing quietly, he sat helplessly as tears trickled from his eyes. Was it the music? To Julia, Beethoven's symphonies were calls for running and jumping. The swirls of this *Pastorale* made her think of wind rushing through high trees.

"Would you like to go?" she hissed in Erik's ear as the applause began.

Wordlessly, Erik nodded. Holding hands, they rushed to retrieve his daypack, from which he dug a packet of tissues.

"Are you okay? Let's go somewhere we can talk," said Julia. Erik smiled ashamedly. "I'm all right," he insisted. He stopped to blow his nose.

Julia led Erik to Billy Wilder's, which at nine o'clock still had free booths. Strategically placed, the restaurant caught people streaming into the mouth of the Sony Center. Julia liked Billy's for its satanic warmth but also for its Viennese cakes. Besides offering drinks of all kinds, it served creamy concoctions of chocolate, marzipan, and cherries. The glittering bar shone like an altar, illuminating black-cushioned seats and red walls. On the counter, clear glass bottles with silver siphons shot gleams toward the movie stars on the wall. Erik smiled at Audrey Hepburn and ordered a Black Russian. Telling herself that she would make it last, Julia asked for a beer.

"Tell me," she said, the way she used to when they were little. Erik smiled, embarrassed. "Mm!" He sipped his drink, which looked like chocolate milk with ice cubes. "I—I don't—I'm so sorry," he began. He cleared his nose again. "It's … Everything—"

Julia watched him steadily and waited for his voice to settle.

"It's everything," he murmured, shaking his head. "It's all turning—I don't even know where to start."

"Start anywhere." Julia smiled. "We've got all night." She tried a sip of beer.

Erik took her hands and clenched them. His puffy forearms against the black table made her think of Arno's, which were so much broader and tighter. For a conductor, Arno played piano brilliantly, but with wrists so thick, he looked more like someone you would call to move a piano than play it.

"You're so nice," Erik was saying. "You're so nice. You deserve better than what you've had. I'm so glad you're singing. Are you seeing anyone? You haven't told me that."

Julia shook her head. She had been out with men and had enjoyed their caresses, but there hadn't been anyone—

"No one special? *Der Eine?*" asked Erik ironically.

"Well, there's someone I like. I have for a long time." Julia's voice wavered.

"Is it that guy who helped you?" he asked.

"No, no!" Julia laughed, blushing. She freed a hand and swallowed some beer. "No—no, he doesn't like me that way. He just ..."

"Do you wish he did?" asked Erik.

"No—no, it's different." Julia shook her head. "He respects me as a singer. That means more to me."

"Yeah." Erik nodded. "But it can be hard living with just respect. I mean, when you want something more."

"You hear me complaining?" asked Julia wryly.

As long as Erik didn't talk about himself, he seemed steady, so she let him ask her about her life.

"I'm sorry about your dad," he said. "That must really have hurt."

With warm eyes, Erik stared intently. In a fine stream, Julia found herself releasing a breath she hadn't known she'd been holding.

"I dealt with it. It seems like a long time ago," she murmured.

A bottle flashed over the bar.

"I was in America, or I would have come. I'm really sorry about what happened," said Erik.

Julia grimaced and shrugged. "It had to happen. It could only have ended one way."

Her throat tightened, and the bottles blurred.

"I'm sorry," said Erik, taking her hand again.

"He used to call me!" Julia sobbed. "At first he was angry. He called me a thief—and a lot of other things. Sometimes he didn't say anything—sometimes he just breathed. But I knew it was him. Some—" Her voice broke. "Sometimes he was nice. He called me Julchen. He asked me when I was coming back home."

"I'm so sorry." Erik's eyes swelled. "But did you? I thought—"

"No, I never did," whispered Julia. "I never did."

"So what happened?" asked Erik. "Renate told me, but I wasn't sure."

Julia's insides tightened. "He killed himself. He was in a clinic, but somehow he got out. It happened so fast. He was dead before they knew he was gone."

"What did ..." Erik couldn't manage the question.

"He lay down on the tracks. The engineer couldn't stop. I met the guy. I felt sorry for him."

"So you did go back—"

"Yeah, for the funeral ... Just for the funeral, to clean things up."

"Oh ..." Erik clenched her hands.

"These people kept calling me! The police, the detox people." Julia's stomach wrenched. "They asked me to come. They said it would help, but I never did."

"Were you doing a lot—here in Berlin?" Erik frowned.

"No!" Julia sobbed. "I could have gone back. I should have gone. But I didn't."

Erik's eyes burned with steady warmth.

"I was so sick of it!" she blurted. "I was glad I left. What's the point taking care of someone who's throwing his life away? Fuck that!"

"You have nothing to be ashamed of," said Erik. "Nobody's done more for her parents than you have. At some point you have to live your own life."

"I let it happen!" she moaned. "I let it happen!"

"No, you didn't!" Erik raised his voice. "He did it to himself. God knows why. No one could have had a nicer family than he did."

Julia held his hands tight and tried to stop crying. Now that she had found the words, they wouldn't stop coming. They were bringing the sounds of her father, the rich voice that had thickened like a river in a black city. His smoky smell had turned rancid and unclean until it no longer warmed her. She told Erik about parts of Henningsthal he hadn't seen—the hidden ugliness of her family life. His eyes swelled, and he fingered a gouge on the table.

"I didn't know," Erik breathed. "I would have helped. I—I would have done something."

"I don't think anybody could have done anything." Julia shrugged. "Once a guy starts drinking, you have to deal with it, and you can't let it drag you down."

Erik nodded. "You're a wonderful person," he said. "I've always liked you, but now I respect you even more."

Seeing that his chocolaty drink was all gone, he ordered another. To collect herself, Julia told him about the singing she had done, then about Dorrie's Donuts and her shifts with Marga. She didn't mention Marga's songs or Basti's furniture or Dr. Kowalski. She would have hated getting laughs at her friends' expense. Erik loosened his belt and spread his arms. He seemed relieved to step outside his own life, and he listened with easy sympathy.

"I'm glad I came." He sighed. "I've missed you so much. I've missed you ever since—"

He frowned, trying to remember, and laughed when he couldn't. He flipped his glass to catch the last drop. As a brown stream crested on the tumbler's rim, his tongue wriggled with anticipation. The waitress brought him another drink, but Julia waved her away since her beer was half-full.

"It's been a long time," she said. "Can you tell me what's happening?"

"Okay. Okay," he said. "It's actually pretty funny."

It wasn't, though Erik laughed when he told it. Soon after he and Johanna got married, she had abandoned her music. After she failed to enter a professional orchestra, she'd stopped playing her flute and vowed not to touch it again. Instead, she'd decided to do something she did better than anyone, which turned out to be selling insurance. Julia didn't doubt it. In her wedding dress, Johanna had rolled her sleeves up to the elbow, and her legs had seemed eager to kick themselves free. She had a straight back, a hard jaw, and short, swinging hair. At thirty, Johanna showed no interest in having the grandchildren Renate craved and told her mother-in-law to back off. Her passion, evident in late-night emails to New York, was for managing a well-run office. When Johanna was gone—which was often—Renate called, and like migrating birds, her thoughts all flew one way. Erik should divorce Johanna and start over. He was a nice-looking man with an excellent job. Any woman would want him. Except— Except—

Erik dug for his packet of tissues. He picked up his drink and set it down hard.

"You know she must have over fifty scarves?" he murmured, pressing three fingers into his forehead. "Every color of the rainbow. She has one to go with everything."

Julia waited to meet his eyes.

"I drink now," he mumbled. "Not like ... but more than I should. I eat too much. I hate myself. I just wish I knew. I just wish I knew ... if she loved me."

"I bet she does," said Julia. "I bet she does. She seems like a person who does what she wants. If she didn't want to be with you, she would have left by now."

One tear clung to Erik's flushed cheek. "If she left me, I don't know what I'd do."

"You'd be all right," said Julia. "People can stand a lot more than they think. You'd be okay."

"No, you don't understand!" Erik's voice sharpened.

Julia looked up at Audrey Hepburn, whose tiara twinkled over her kitten face.

"She's seeing someone. Not someone. A lot of guys. A lot of guys from work."

"Oh, come on! How do you know?"

Erik's smile showed more pain than cynicism. "She types emails at three in the morning. I wake up, and I hear this tapping. Ugh! It makes me sick! When I touch her, she winces. Then she goes away for a second, like she's switching something in her brain—and when she comes back, she's thinking of someone else."

"But she always comes back to you. You must mean a lot to her."

"Yeah, like an aircraft carrier. She goes out on missions and comes home to refuel."

Julia couldn't help laughing. She could picture Renate's outraged monkey face.

"It is pretty funny." Erik laughed. "When we were ten, who would have thought I'd end up like this?"

"Not me," said Julia. "But this is just one point in your life. You don't have to stay this way. You can make it better."

"You think so?" asked Erik.

"Yeah, sure!"

Sipping his chocolate, Erik talked about Johanna. His stories always evoked vivid pictures, and he told lurid tales in which Johanna played the heroine. He described her high-fashion clothes that shamed New York women and her deft handling of office intrigues. She had beaten out three guys for a recent promotion and foiled another who framed her for stealing his work. More than anything, he wanted Johanna to be happy. That was all he cared about.

"I bet she is," said Julia. "I bet she is. Are you?"

"Right now I am." Erik sighed. He beckoned for Julia to leave her seat and settle down next to him. He draped his arm around her and took her hand.

Moving slowly, the waitress brought them their check. Somehow it had gotten to be three in the morning. Erik laughed at his dizziness when he stood, but his legs carried him along doggedly. Outside, Julia shivered in her loose-fitting dress, and Erik offered her the wadded T-shirt from his pack. They drifted into the Sony Center, empty except for a few hooting teenagers.

"Wow!" Erik breathed.

He plopped down on a bench. Overhead, the limpet-shaped roof changed from turquoise to lavender, then from lavender back to turquoise. The ribbed dome glowed magically, pulsing in the black night. A fresh gust of wind brought the smell of cool leaves.

"Mm." Julia sniffed the air.

Erik nuzzled her hair.

"Let's go for a walk in the park!" she exclaimed.

"What, now? Are you crazy?"

His quick breath said that he wanted other things.

"No, really. It must be wonderful right now."

"But it's dangerous!" he said. "There are junkies—crazy people."

"What, crazier than us?" Julia laughed. "Come on."

Taking one hand in hers, she pulled him to his feet. Erik clung to her as she led him out the back, and he turned his head for one last look at the purple roof. For the first time all day, Erik seemed at home in his body. He let his belly hang loose and matched Julia's pace with even steps.

Empty of cars, the Hauptbahnhof tunnel gaped. Julia spread her arms and whirled, claiming the space as she crossed it. In the park, the Bellevue promenade was lit like a runway, flanked by lights that met at a distant point. Instead of following it, Julia chose a black path, where darkness quickly swallowed them. She breathed the sweet air with animal pleasure.

"What is this? I've never seen you like this," said Erik nervously.

"There, see?" she teased. "I'm not the same as I used to be."

In the warm darkness, they shuffled blindly until Julia pulled out her phone. Erik had an emergency light on his keychain, and their faint beams revealed clumps of black brush. From their padding steps, Julia knew they must be on a trail. Only once did she hear another sign of life, footsteps crashing through the brush. They snapped off their lights, and in absolute blackness, Julia clung to Erik. Listening desperately, she tried to make out where the steps were headed. The crunches grew fainter, and she exhaled slowly, Erik's warm belly expanding against hers. Their embrace softened, and his hand traced circles on her back. Laughing gently, she pulled away, and they ambled onward.

Clang! A burning pain shot through her hip.

"Owa! What was that?" asked Erik.

Julia had walked into the rabbit gate protecting a luxuriant bed of flowers. She fumbled for the latch and angled her phone toward a sign that said, "Please keep the gate closed at all times on account of the rabbit plague."

The flowers' soft scent beckoned, and she led Erik into their midst.

"This is nice," he murmured. "Let's sit down here."

Julia lay facedown at the garden's edge, the cool blades of grass wetting her belly and breasts. Scrunching forward, she stuck her nose into the flowers and tried to identify them by their scents. Charcoal-gray petals quivered with each exhaled breath. Within seconds, Julia had found marigolds, lavender, and red begonias. She knew them by their bitter scent, more enticing than that of the tight pink blossoms.

"This is nice," Erik breathed dreamily. "I like this. Let's stay here."

He pulled her close. Julia turned to face him, and he kissed her. He tasted like chocolate. Rolling in sweetness, she lay on her back and spread her arms and legs.

"Mm," she moaned, rubbing her hair into the wet grass.

With a wry chuckle, Erik settled onto her. His body felt warm and heavy, more insistent than she would have guessed.

In the darkness, his voice came like a far-off message. "You're so nice. You're the nicest girl I ever knew. The nicest girl ..."

Instinctively, she wrapped her arms around him. Erik pushed up her dress. Smiling, she stroked his soft hair. She felt him shaking, but she wasn't sure whether he was laughing or crying.

———————————— ■ ————————————

Julia woke up stiff, wet, and cold. In the gray light, the flowers were coming into focus, intricate and still. Erik moaned as she nudged him, but when she insisted, he staggered to his feet.

"God, it's cold!" He rubbed himself. "Let's get out of here! Do you know the way?"

Disoriented, Julia led them out of the garden and sought the main trail to the pond. Unable to find it, she chose a dark, narrow path between some bushes and a black creek.

Erik pulled out his flashlight. "Do you know the way out of here?"

"Yeah," she murmured, feeling tired and old.

When they reached a straight, diagonal path, she turned to the right. Erik quieted and trudged with quick, even steps. In a few minutes, the path opened into a vast traffic circle, and Julia stopped, gazing up in awe.

Far above her, a brilliant gold angel raised her powerful arm. Around her flew a hundred screaming crows, worshiping her in a mad reel. Erik took Julia's hand, and she leaned into his warmth.

That day Erik didn't cross a single item off his list. They spent the whole day under Julia's blue comforter, laughing and talking, eating and sleeping. Erik felt sick, but Julia was kind to him. He kept saying that. She was so kind. At the end of the day, she went with him to the Hauptbahnhof and waved warmly as his train pulled away. Erik leaned out the window and said he would call, but he never did. She hadn't heard from him since.

7

Then Shall the Eyes of the Blind Be Opened

Julia awakened floating in blackness. She had been sleeping so soundly she had no idea who she was, let alone where. There was only a pleasant feeling of warmth, and she pulled the comforter closer around her. Her mind felt as though it had been erased and she were starting life over again.

The clock radio said it was 18:32. Like a picture coalescing, her world came back to her—fragrant roses, the lullaby aria in her throat, and a scaly spot on the bathtub that needed scrubbing. And that feeling—a warmth, a fullness, the insistence of a living force. The words that had been eluding her coalesced into a melody, and suddenly she felt ready to call Erik.

Julia snapped on the radio, and "Hey There, Delilah" filled the room, D major hope against B minor longing. Behind the music, the house was making Sunday-night sounds. Julia's building had a life of its own that expressed itself in slamming doors, flushing toilets, and gusts of conflict. On summer nights, the open windows offered ten arguments at once and, in the gray hours, the gasps of people having sex. A snorer sometimes woke Julia with his rasps, and once she had been roused at four in the morning by onions sizzling in butter. Tonight, the knocks and swishes formed a gentle percussion that failed to find a beat.

Julia pulled on her bathrobe and turned the knob on the white iron radiator. "Hey There, Delilah" ended with sad optimism, and a harsh voice loudly praised the new shopping mall, Alexandria. Julia made her way to the living room and listened to the steam heat hiss. What would Erik be doing? Probably grading his papers. This seemed as good a time to call him as any.

While Erik's phone rang, Julia studied the ceramics on her shelves. A red bowl caught her eye, one she had bought at a flea market in Reinickendorf. In the dim light, its curve glowed softly, begging to be stroked. The bowl had a chip on the back, but you couldn't see it unless you picked—

"Hello?"

"Erik?"

"Julia! Oh, wow …"

In Erik's voice, delight was swimming in dread. Julia's heart pounded, but she loved his musical tones.

"Hey, Erik. Is this an okay time to talk?"

"Yeah … yeah … Sure. It's okay." Erik's voice dipped nervously.

"Oh—should I try again later?"

"No, no, now's good … Johanna's out with a friend. We're going to a concert later. She could be home anytime."

"Oh—okay." Julia's melody had dissolved.

"So—how have you been?" he asked. "I'm sorry I—"

"Oh, pretty good. That's okay. I've been busy—you know, singing. Last night I sang the *Christmas Oratorio* in the Remembrance Church."

"Oh, wow, that's great! Did anyone record it? I'd love to hear you sing."

"Yeah, yeah, I guess so …"

"Yeah?"

Feeling faint, Julia sank onto the couch and fingered the ripples on her blue-sprigged quilt. Erik must have guessed. He was smart, and he had always been able to read her voice.

"Julia? I—I'm really sorry about … not calling, after … That was such a crazy time. I was drinking. Things are going so much better now—with me and Johanna, I mean. We're going to New York for New Year's. With this exchange rate …"

Erik's voice sounded higher, sharper than usual, without its good-natured rolls. Julia wondered whether one of Johanna's business friends had left her and she had come home to refuel. In the soft light, a blue-and-white pitcher shone on the shelf over the red bowl. Julia felt ashamed of her smile.

"Something's happened, hasn't it?" asked Erik. "Is that why you're calling? What's going on? Is everything okay?"

"Yeah, yeah, I'm all right …"

"But … something …"

Even frightened, Erik sounded sympathetic. He did seem stronger than he'd been three months ago.

"Yeah. Erik … I'm—"

Julia's words had fled, even though she had heard her voice saying them minutes ago. Miserably, she studied the waxy, heart-shaped leaves of a philodendron.

"I'm going to have a baby."

"What? Why, that's great!" Erik breathed. "So you are with someone. That's—"

"No."

"No?"

"No. It's from—"

"Oh, God!" All the warmth left Erik's voice. She had never heard tones like this from him before.

"But—but—you can't be!" he gasped. "Weren't you using something? I mean—your singing. You weren't *trying* to get pregnant, were you?"

"No, no, I didn't want to. I don't know how it happened."

"Well, come on …" Erik's throaty laugh released his voice.

"I can't take the pill," she said. "The doctor told me—when my mother—" She wavered.

"That's okay." Erik's voice hit firm ground. "That's okay. I'm sorry. Of course. I should have known."

"He said the risks were too high."

"Of course," he said again. "That's right. So what do you …?"

"Condoms mostly," said Julia. "I had a diaphragm for a while, but I kept getting infections. So condoms, or I count. I'm very regular. That's what I don't get. I had just had—"

"So you weren't using anything?"

"No. I had just had— It has to be in the middle. I had just had—"

"But that was … Shit! That was almost three months ago! How are you going— Why didn't you tell me sooner?"

Julia had no words left. That was the question she couldn't answer. She stared down at her plants, her shadow dimming their gleam. With her index finger, she stroked the fuzzy, sticky leaf of an African violet.

"Julia!"

"Yeah." She sighed.

"Why didn't you tell me? Look, let me help you. There isn't much time left. Find a clinic, and—"

"It's too late," said Julia.

"What?" Erik's liquid tones congealed. "No! That can't be right!"

Julia's lips twitched, and she swallowed a laugh. Erik was freaking out.

"It's past twelve weeks." She kept her voice steady.

"Look, this isn't right!" Erik's tone grew lower, more forceful. "This isn't fair. Isn't this my decision too? Don't I have anything to say about this? You wait until it's too late, and … Why did you even bother to tell me?"

"I guess—I guess—"

"You guess what?" Erik sounded like the schoolteacher he was.

"I wanted to know how you felt," said Julia.

"Well, I would have felt a lot better if you had called me two months ago."

His acidic words seared her. She sensed how far apart they had moved since their days together in Henningsthal.

"So you don't want any part of this."

"I didn't say that!" cried Erik. "Look, you're my— We've known each other so long. There are things nobody can understand but you. I loved being with you, and I think we both needed it, but …" Erik's voice softened. If he had been there facing her, she was sure he would have touched her. "But … Julia, I—I love Johanna. I can't tell you why. Half the time I think she despises me. But I need her. Haven't you ever … It's just something I know. I want to go through life with her, or—or I don't want to go through life at all. When I see her coming out of a gate at the airport, smiling at me, I can't believe—" His voice broke.

"That's okay," said Julia. "That's okay. I understand how you feel."

"Yeah? So you've—"

"No, not like that. I don't think anyone's ever felt that way about me."

Julia glanced at the couch, whose blue-flecked cover was askew. Yellow light blasted the ripples of cloth, and she peered at their shadowy valleys.

"I care about you," Erik was saying. "I care what happens to you. But we can't have a baby. It isn't right. I love someone else. And—and you will too … A baby needs two people who love each other."

Julia imagined Astrid's reply. Fathers were scarce in their Kiez. Julia smiled at her red bowl and spread her fingers over her belly.

"Look—if it's really too late, what about adoption?" asked Erik. "I know people dying to have a kid. It's so sad. They have to go to all these clinics—"

"No," said Julia. The strength of her voice surprised her.

"No? Think what you're saying. You want to do this without me—just when your music … It's crazy! Why do you want to have this baby?"

On Basti's table, the wooden leaves formed a rich brown ring, over which greenness silently breathed.

"It's hard to say in words," she murmured.

"It's okay," urged Erik. "Try anyway."

"It's a feeling. It's just a feeling," she said.

He exhaled, and she remembered his lips on her skin.

"I—I feel something alive in me," she said, struggling to find the words. "I felt it as soon as the sickness started, but I don't feel sick now. I've never felt this good. I—I feel something—someone. My voice is stronger, as though someone were singing with me. Everyone says so. Everyone hears it."

"That's great," said Erik, "That's the pregnancy—the hormones. But once it's born, how are you going to take care of it?"

"I'll figure it out," she said. "Everyone does. I don't want to go through life without having kids. No one has kids anymore. I see all these old ladies, all alone …"

"That's crazy," said Erik. "You've got ten, fifteen years. You might meet someone. Someone who loves you. That would be the time. Not now!"

"I can feel it!" she burst out. "It's alive! It's here! It's—it's me—and it's someone else—someone who wants to live, and I have to take care of it!"

"Hey, hey, take it easy! No one's asking you to—"

"And I can't give it up. It would be like giving up my heart or my brain. Oh, you don't understand!"

"I'm sick of hearing what I don't understand!" shouted Erik. "That's not an answer! I'm a guy, so I can't understand anything? If I can't understand, you explain it!"

"I'm trying to explain it!" yelled Julia. "It's alive. It's part of me. If I give it up, I'll spend the rest of my life thinking about it."

Erik breathed deeply. "What about the baby?" he asked. "You'll be working—it'll be in day care. A couple might adopt it who could take time off. One person, two people there with it all the time? A great school, lots of culture, travel—"

Erik's burnished tone sounded foreign. Had he changed that much? Or had he always—

"You think I'm not good enough," said Julia. "You think I can't do it. This place isn't good enough for a kid?" Behind her she felt Astrid, Basti, and Birgit. Arno loomed in the shadows.

"I didn't say that!" Erik's melody expressed ongoing pain. He had been bruised and was sick of always being knocked in the same place.

"Just think about it," said Erik. "You don't have to do anything now. You've got six months. Just think about it."

"Yeah." Julia sighed, cupping her breasts. With little pushes, she jounced them up and down. "I'll keep thinking. I'm going to the clinic tomorrow."

"Oh, that's good," said Erik. "That's good. They can tell you your options." Someone else's words seemed to have hijacked his voice. Was this really his child?

"Yeah." Julia glanced at Astrid's kitchen window, which was dark. Her neighbor must have gone out.

"Look, why don't you tell me how it went when you get back from the clinic. Johanna's in Stuttgart this week. You could call tomorrow night."

"Yeah, okay."

"Look, I'm not going to tell her about this. I don't want her to know."

"That's okay." Julia sighed. "I can see that. I won't tell."

"Thank you—" Erik's voice trembled. "Thanks for understanding. I don't think most women would do that."

"Oh, it's okay," said Julia.

She stared at her shelves until the red bowl's shine dissolved. Up above, the blue-and-white pitcher shimmered. How long would it be before Johanna walked? How long before the excitement of her guys overcame the comforts of Erik? Julia dropped the phone into its waiting cradle and settled onto the couch. She leaned against its unyielding arm and squeezed a pillow against her breast.

———————————— ■ ————————————

At the clinic, a thin nurse with straight blond hair scanned Julia with a practiced eye. A faint blue frost gave her eyes a youthful shine that defied the puckers around her mouth.

"You're just over three months, aren't you?" she asked. "Why didn't you come in sooner?"

Julia flushed, hating to be scolded. She was twice as old as the miserable teens in the waiting room. The saddest one, a Turkish girl in a white headscarf, looked as though she wanted to disappear into her swollen raincoat.

Julia gazed steadily into the nurse's blue eyes. "I felt fine," she said.

"Well, that's good," answered the nurse. "But for your baby's sake, you'll need to keep regular appointments."

In the chilly room, she made Julia strip down and smeared ice-cold jelly on her stomach. Round and glistening, her belly lay like a hard-boiled egg waiting to be bitten. The nurse explored its curve with a plastic wand that looked like a detached penis. Thinking of Dr. Kowalski's stethoscope, Julia began to laugh.

"What, am I tickling you?" asked the nurse.

"No, no, it's okay," said Julia, straining to see the nearby screen.

In a gray triangle, a faint white shape was pulsing like a jellyfish in a tank. The nurse typed, frowning critically.

"Is everything okay?" asked Julia.

"Yeah, everything's fine," said the nurse without looking up. Julia studied the dark roots of her hair, which lay like a grasping centipede.

The nurse ordered Julia to return in four weeks and gave her some nutrition pamphlets. She didn't ask whether Julia wanted to keep her baby—apparently the time for that had passed. She didn't ask about adoption either. Maybe Julia didn't look like the type to give up her child. In that neighborhood, few women did. The nurse handed her towelettes to wipe off the jelly, but her belly still stuck to her shirt.

Julia came home to a message from Arno, who had lost no time finding her a gig. On January 19, the Bartholdy Choir would be singing Bach's seventy-second cantata, replacing the Bach Choir, which was performing in Leipzig. Because of their special concert in the Thomaskirche, they couldn't do their regular Berlin service and had asked the Bartholdy Choir to step in. Arno's voice sounded rushed and breathless, and his orders were punctuated by harsh coughs.

"You'll be singing your aria with Udo and Jakob," he said. "Just you and the two violins. I want you to memorize it. There are a whole bunch of places where—" He drew a troubled breath and dispersed it in angry coughs. "Fuck! Fucking cold! I need you all with me, hear? Nobody goes off into la-la land this time. Get yourself a score, and memorize it. Oh—and you have to wear black. I like the red, but you know these church types. Call me! Ca—"

His last order broke up into a burst of coughs, and he hung up without repeating it. Laughing aloud, Julia listened to his message three times. She spread her arms all the way and bent her knees. Through her west windows, the first rays of afternoon sun were greeting the lonely leaves.

Normally Dagmar Schleifer sang the alto solos with the Bartholdy Choir, and Julia wondered what Arno had done to get her out. With her big head and long, skinny neck, Dagmar sang better than she looked and ran through Bach's runs like a laser printer. Unlike Sascha Neumann, Dagmar had little vibrato, but she lacked Sascha's warmth and power. Arno must have chosen Sascha for the *Christmas Oratorio* because Dagmar just didn't sound joyous. The alto aria in the seventy-second had little coloratura, and Julia understood why Arno wanted Dagmar gone. But how had he managed it in thirty-six hours? What had he promised her instead?

Rather than going to a music store, where scores cost seven euros, Julia called Rudi, who downloaded the cantata from the net.

"Wasn't Dagmar going to sing this?" she asked.

"Yeah." Rudi laughed.

"So what did he do? I'm not singing the solo of someone who's been maimed or kidnapped, am I?"

Julia pictured Rudi's eyes glowing at Arno's shenanigans. "No, you're singing the solo of someone going to Leipzig with the Bach Choir." He chuckled. "He got her an upgrade."

"But what about the woman who was singing with the Bach Choir?"

"Oh, she got maimed and kidnapped," said Rudi.

Julia laughed deep in her throat and gently cupped each breast. Each one filled her hand with supple warmth, and she gave them a fond little bounce.

"He told you to wear black, right?" asked Rudi. "No more red. It's January. Time to get serious."

Rudi brought Julia the music that night, and she set right to work. For once, Bach had been kind, and her aria seemed made to be memorized. Its light melody caught her ear like a folk tune, and it moved so cheerfully she could hardly believe it was D minor. Composers used deep, brown D minor when they didn't want to mess around: Beethoven had created his Ninth Symphony from it, and Mozart, his Requiem. In the seventy-second cantata, the poignant melody belied its building blocks, since part of its energy was a reaching sadness. Its main motif, like a whorl in a fingerprint, was a leap of a minor sixth. As always with Bach, the jump surprised you at first, but once you had heard it a few times, you couldn't imagine the tune any other way. That one plaintive interval expressed the longing at the song's heart, a promise by someone with very little that she would give everything she had.

Within days, Julia was singing the tune everywhere, lugging food up the stairs, soaping her hair in the shower.

"Mit allem, was ich hab' und bin," she sang as she wiped her plants' leaves with a wet sponge. "With everything I have and am."

"Will ich mich Jesu lassen!" she sang, dusting her knickknacks on the coffee table and arranging them on different shelves. "I'll give myself to Jesus."

Bobbing up and down before Dürer's tendrils, she sang to the old saint and savored the new arrangement of her body. As Julia swayed to the music's pulse, she filled herself with air and released it as warm, liquid sound: "Kann gleich mein schwacher Geist und Sinn des Höchsten Rat nicht fassen"—"My weak mind and senses can't grasp God's advice." She felt the prickle of eyes and saw Basti in his kitchen window. He started and fumbled with something on his table, then looked back at her and waved.

Julia had more trouble with the thorn-and-rose section, where Bach had turned perverse. Anyone who followed his simple line, "He keeps leading me down thorny and rosy paths," was in for some rough surprises. Never considerate to singers, Bach had turned roses and thorns to sound with long, sweet notes and hellish, chromatic runs. What his coloratura lacked in length it made up in snags. Julia wished that she could move from note to note as easily as Dagmar Schleifer. She could overpower Dagmar on the roses, rich pulses of B-flat, A, and G, but the thorns were a different story. The thorny path started with a major-sixth drop, and finding it was like grabbing a thin branch while falling off a cliff.

With her own special method, Julia mastered the runs by dividing the notes into groups of four. She sang each group slowly until she saw its shape, then gave it a name like "Waterslide" or "Lobster Claw." Its form came not from the notes on the page but from the feeling she got while singing them. After a few repetitions, Julia closed her eyes and saw an image turning in space. The worst thorn, A♭–C–F♯–A, she called "the Stethoscope," because it slid over the major and minor thirds like Kowalski examining Astrid's chest.

After a day of practice, she no longer needed music, but she checked to make sure she wasn't inventing variations. Whether singing or not, she heard the thorns and roses everywhere she went. Putting doughnuts in baskets, buying cookies at Ohlmann's Market, she hummed through Bach's leaps until she performed them like a gymnast. Singing them was like prancing on a balance beam because in fast runs, how you hit each note determined how you landed on the next. If you were off on one, you would flub the next one worse until your arms flailed and you fell with a thud.

In her throat, in her belly, Bach's runs felt just right. Julia smiled as she sang them at her window, admiring the unkempt bushes in the *Hof.* What their branches lacked in fullness, they made up in spunk, seeking light between bicycle spokes and recycling bins. At four o'clock, the sky glimmered stubbornly. The days were growing longer, and Julia had never felt better. She stood up straight and relished the flow of air into her lungs. Gently she pressed her growing belly.

By now few of her clothes would fit, and Astrid helped her to find more. One day she took Julia to Czeplinski's, a lingerie shop on Kantstrasse. Until now, Julia had ignored the place because the bras in the window looked so unappetizing. Their stiff, dull-brown cups hung awaiting mudslides of flesh, which they would shape into aching cones. Even though none of the lacy bras in lingerie stores fit, Julia had forgotten Czeplinski's. Only when Astrid dragged her there did she realize she needed their clothes.

"Oh, yeah!" The owner smiled. With one look, the Polish woman with squashed gray curls guessed Julia's new size: 46F.

"This is where you come when you don't want a bra for decoration," she said. "You'll be needing nursing bras now too, right?"

Julia must have looked shocked, since the old woman laughed. "Oh, we all need 'em sometime. When are you due?"

"June 9." Julia was surprised at how little sound her voice made.

June 9, that was what the nurse had said. Five months from now.

Finding clothes for the cantata proved even harder. Julia couldn't afford new ones, and it seemed like a waste since after June she would be back to her old size. Her black gown threatened to split, so she tried on a black skirt and blouse. In her new bra from Czeplinski's, her chest pulled wide smiles between the waxy buttons, and the skirt's zipper stopped halfway up. The main thing was whether she could breathe. She looked anxiously in the mirror and drew in as much air as she could. The zipper fell back a few teeth, but the buttons held. If she wore the blouse outside the skirt, no one would know the zipper was halfway down. Yeah, that would be the way to go.

When Julia saw Arno at the Friday-night rehearsal, he had lost his harrowing cough. His movements were freer, less hectic than usual, and his energy burned without flaring. He greeted Julia with a lingering hug, then stood back and caressed her sides.

"You've been eating a few *Lebkuchen*." He grinned. He knew Julia's passion for spicy cookies.

"Yeah. I've been eating."

In Arno's eyes, something snapped mischievously. "Well, it's good to see you. You look good," he said. "Now let's hear how you sound."

He told her he had been in New York the past week, having left once the marathon of holiday concerts had passed. He looked more relaxed than she had ever seen him, but when she started singing, his demanding soul emerged. Without breaking rhythm, he called to her to lengthen this note, to shorten that one. About her perfect rendering of the thorns and roses he said nothing. Arno expected flawless intonation and rhythm, and he used rehearsals to play with the remaining variables.

Saturday afternoon, Julia sang the dress rehearsal in her gray sweat suit, covering herself with her coat while the choir sang. For the service, they would be sharing the loft with the orchestra, so jammed in they would need a shoehorn to slip the soloists behind the continuo.

Down below in the church, Julia listened with awe and realized how good the Bartholdy Choir had become. Under Arno's direction, they brought the opening chorus pulsing to life: "*Al*-les, *Al*-les, Alles nur nach Gottes Willen"—"Everything only according to God's will." Against the fast-moving orchestral background, the accented notes shot out like divine fiats. Julia looked fondly from singer to singer, watching Anja lead the sopranos and Rudi strain openmouthed with the tenors. In the alto section, Julia didn't see Carola. What a shame, to lose a rich voice like that. Julia rubbed her back and wondered when Carola was due. How far along had she been at the *Christmas Oratorio*? A flash of Arno's hand drew her eyes, and the thought dissolved. Like a lightning rod, he led all her energy into the music.

Viewed from below, Arno's direction looked even more athletic. When you stood in front of him, all you saw were his hands and eyes. At this last rehearsal, every musician fixed his or her gaze on the conductor. To sing those strokes of divine will against sixteenth-notes required perfect timing, and Arno must have made the singers memorize their parts.

In the practice room, Julia changed into her skirt and blouse while the young soprano soloist from the Singakademie guarded the door. The zipper sat lower than it had a few days ago, so Julia reinforced it with a safety pin. The metal teeth held when she inhaled as deep as she could and blew out her breath fast and hard. Jakob, the second violin, hugged Julia in the hallway and didn't notice his hands met over a divided zipper.

"This is going to be great," he said. "Udo's been running me ragged. We've been practicing this aria for weeks. But with you—it's a whole new experience."

A quick movement pulled Julia's eyes to the orchestra room, where Udo was pantomiming the strokes he wanted. With a bold, energetic style, the first violin played with his whole body, so that in the hardest movements, he combined self-assurance with a child's delight. Usually he and Arno got along well, and confrontations between them were quickly settled. When they disagreed, Arno always prevailed, but Udo found ways to show his disapproval.

The organist began the prelude exactly at six. On the bench next to Julia, Arno tapped his watch and mouthed, "Friggin' Prussians." The singers had to sit through two hymns, two readings, and a sermon before Arno could start the cantata. He could reach the podium only by turning sideways to slide between the bass players and continuo. During rehearsal the loft had seemed cold, but now, lit by spotlights and packed with bodies, it was glowing with heat. Julia fanned herself with her program but forgot how hot she was once the music started.

An A minor chord rose up like a living force and resounded with excruciating beauty. Every eye followed Arno, who cued the strokes of will against the moving texture so perfectly the music came alive by itself. Behind Udo, Jakob concentrated with all his strength, his round face flushed under his blond hair. Udo guided the violins with broad, keen strokes. Immersed in the music, Julia almost forgot she was next and jumped up when the chorus ended. She had more trouble than Arno squeezing between the keyboard and the bass players. Smiling, one of them slid his chair forward. Julia stood exactly where she had been shown, angled sideways so that she could sing to the congregation while maintaining eye contact with Arno and the violins.

Udo and Jakob stood with their bows poised and looked intently at Arno. With the light blasting her, Julia felt her hands starting to sweat. Arno was staring at her in disbelief. What was wrong? Why didn't he start her recitative? Frightened, she glanced at Rudi and saw his mouth hanging open. He was gazing fixedly at her, as were most of the choir and orchestra. Arno's lips contracted once, and his eyelids flicked so that she saw some white above the blue. Then he cued her and the continuo player to start her recitative.

"O, selger Christ," sang Julia. "Oh, blessed Christ." A tremble in her voice drove the thirty-second-note turns. With her eyes on Arno, she moved through the lines without pausing, since her voice formed the ground from which the music grew. White-faced, Arno offered minimal guidance. Only his lips told her when to swell or withdraw. He gave her no cue until the violins joined her and the recitative slid into an aria.

What in the hell was wrong with Arno? Udo's and Jakob's intertwined melodies gave Julia time to think. That light. Standing sideways in its beam, she must suddenly have become visible. Everyone in the loft could see through her blouse, and to even the least observant, her rounded profile was unmistakable. Julia tried to turn, but no matter how she stood, there was no escaping the musicians' gaze. She was on display, and she was going to stay that way until she was done singing.

Arno brought her in, but not with the inviting gesture he had given in the *Christmas Oratorio*. He pointed at her with accusing violence, as though daring her to sing. Nurtured for weeks, the melody burst out, demanding to be heard: "Mit Allem, was ich hab' und bin!" At the sound of those notes, Arno relented, and he shaped her phrases with a few rough gestures.

During the next interval, Julia glanced at the violins. Tense as his strings, Jakob followed Arno like a puppet, but Udo's pointy face signaled protest. Amid curving phrases, he shot Arno an indignant look. This was no way to treat a soloist.

With three pairs of eyes on him, Arno led them into the hardest section. "Er führe mich nur immer hin auf Dorn- und Rosenstrassen," sang Julia. She let Arno's hand guide the opening of her throat. Despite his anger, she felt fully centered, and the notes spun out from her core. At the crucial fermata, she and the violins followed Arno perfectly when he hesitated a tick longer than usual. United, they slid through her final run even though he took it slightly faster. Masking the tension, Udo and Jakob's final duet gave a feeling of deep serenity. The young bass stepped forward, and Julia squeezed back to the bench. She stared down at gouged gold wood, unable to look at Arno another second.

The cantata ended with a powerful chorale: "Was mein Gott will, das g'scheh allzeit"—"What My God Will, May That Be Done." The minister intoned his blessing, and the musicians were free to go. The old continuo player smiled behind his musty breath and complimented Julia warmly. The others pushed their way toward the stairs, unwilling to mention what they had seen. Julia joined the stream and tried to merge with the black-clad bodies. She had almost reached the practice room when someone grabbed her arm.

"Get in here!"

With one wrenching motion, Arno pulled her into his office and slammed the door behind him. As she flew in, Julia caught a glimpse of Heike's shocked face. Arno gripped her shoulders and pushed her back against the wooden door, which rattled as she struck it. His fists were clenched, and his face was white. Violently he kicked a bookcase, so that papers cascaded to the floor. Julia ducked her head.

"Oh, sit down," he said disgustedly. "I'm not going to hit you."

Julia didn't move, so he seized her arm and pulled her to a chair. She looked up at him, defiant.

"What have you done to yourself? What is this?" he demanded, pointing to her belly.

His eyes fired warning shots, as though he were looking for something to smash.

"When were you going to tell me about this?" he shouted. "You said you'd sing the *St. Matthew Passion*! What about *Messiah*?"

"I can still sing," said Julia. "I still want to sing."

She looked up to see worried musicians peering in through the glass. There stood Jakob, openmouthed, and Anja, her dark eyes narrowed. With effort, Arno lowered his voice.

"You want to sing with a *baby*?" he hissed. "You know what that means?"

Through a crack in his anger, Julia thought she saw pain. Arno met her eyes, pleading.

"Look—think this over. How much time have you got? Can you still …?"

"I can't. It's four months," she said softly.

"Shit!" Arno kicked a wastebasket, and its contents scattered: an apple core, a sticky bag, and some balled-up papers. With his fists clenched, he loomed over her. "Why do you want to do this now? Why now?" He took a breath, but his arms tightened. "My God! Just when … You've got a gift! You're just starting—"

"I want this baby," she said. "I can feel it."

Arno's face erupted in ridges. "Anyone can have a baby!" he cried. "Anyone! What you can do, only one person in a million— A *baby*? Who did this to you anyway? I'll fucking kill him!"

Julia pictured Erik trembling before Arno and started to laugh. His right arm twitched, and she turned her head, bracing herself for a blow.

"You think it's funny?" he demanded. "How can you do this?" He brought his hands to his head. "The *St. Matthew Passion*! The RBB Choir! *Messiah!*

"I still want to sing that," said Julia. "I still want to do all that."

Arno looked down at her, surprised. "You think you can? When—when—"

"Beginning of June," she said. "I can still sing the *St. Matthew Passion*. Do you want me?"

"Yeah." Arno flushed. "Yeah. I just don't—"

Three uneven raps sounded at the door.

"Just a minute!" yelled Arno.

The knocking increased.

"What the fuck!" Arno strode furiously to the door and yanked it open. There stood Rudi, his dark eyes determined. He stepped back at the sight of Arno, but in his high voice, he spoke words he must have been rehearsing for the past minute.

"I need to talk to you."

"Not now!" shot Arno in his deepest, most intimidating tone.

Rudi glanced at Julia, gripping her chair.

"I want to talk to you right now," he said, "or I'm quitting this choir. I'll never organize another tour."

With his eyes on Julia, Arno jerked his head and motioned for her to get out. She backed out slowly, worried for Rudi, but he smiled faintly with his rabbit teeth.

Supposedly the glassed-in rooms were soundproof, but Julia heard most of their mismatched duet. Once she had emerged, the musicians melted away. She stood with her back to the door, held in place by the clash of voices. With her eyes squeezed shut, she drew quick, tight breaths.

"I'm sick of this! I'm sick of you!" yelled Rudi. "Always cleaning up messes! How could you do this to her? And then treat her— What about Linda?"

"You fucking—" roared Arno, stopping before he uttered the fatal word. "You think— It wasn't me!"

Rudi replied quietly, and Julia couldn't hear him.

"No, I don't know who the fuck it was! She doesn't have any—"

Their voices grew lower, and she guessed they were speculating about men they knew.

Rudi's tenor emerged, clear and shrill. "Look, I don't care who it was! If you hurt her, I'll never sing with you again!"

Julia couldn't make out the reply, but it sounded conciliating.

"So it wasn't you, huh? You sure?" Rudi's voice penetrated clearly.

"Hey!" Someone jostled Julia's arm, and she winced. A band of pain was burning where Arno had grabbed her. Before her stood Basti, fidgeting in a brown wool jacket.

"Here." He offered her some yellow daisies wrapped in gleaming wet cellophane. From the size of the drops, she guessed it must have been pouring.

"We came to hear you sing. You were great. I'm just waitin' for Birgit to come outa the bathroom."

"Thanks," murmured Julia.

Basti looked uneasily at the passing musicians, who cast worried glances through the glass. Arno had settled on the piano bench and Rudi on an office chair. The tenor leaned forward with his arms extended.

"You were fantastic!" Birgit ran up beaming, her bare arms covered with gooseflesh. "Do you like your flowers? Basti let me pick 'em out. We're going to dinner now. At Mövenpick."

"Yeah. You wanna come?" asked Basti.

Birgit looked at her with anxious eyes.

"Oh—I—I've got to go out with some singers," said Julia.

The bass and tenor notes broke through the glass. Arms tense, Arno leaped up from the bench. Rudi leaned back, bracing himself.

"I *do* treat my—"

"You think that by sleeping with—"

"I did *not* fucking—"

"Quite a pair of mouths on those guys." Basti jerked his chin toward the office. "I hope you're not goin' out with them."

But Julia had stopped listening. With her hand on her belly, she stared down in disbelief. Inside of her, something had moved—something that wasn't her but that spoke through her, saying it didn't like being yanked across the room.

8

For unto Us a Child Is Born

In Charlottenburg, word spread quickly about Julia Martens—that big, brown-haired girl with such a nice shape. Speculation about the father was rampant, and men in bars chided each other and laughed. Knowing of her success in the music world, most people suspected an outsider. One insistent rumor identified him as a fat, red-haired man who walked pigeon-toed and dragged an expensive suitcase. Others protested that Julia would never go for a type like that. No one in the Kiez held it against her. Nowadays, when women got pregnant, men became scarce. It seemed like a shame, though—such a good, hardworking girl—a girl who could earn €200 in just one night!

Of everyone Julia knew, Basti took it the hardest. As Julia's shape changed, he averted his eyes. He offered her gifts and greeted her warmly, but his voice skulked in its lower register. Basti worked long hours on his beat-up wardrobe and stripped and finished it in record time. Selling it took longer, because of a new law that made antique dealers wary of tax-free deals. In the end he sold it to a used furniture dealer in Kreuzberg for half of what he had hoped to make. True to his word, he bought Birgit a gift, an indigo sequin dress that she modeled for Julia and Astrid.

"Two hundred pounds of shit in a hundred-pound bag," muttered Astrid as Birgit jiggled across the yard.

"She looks pretty nice, don't you think?" asked Julia.

In her sparkly blue dress, Birgit's eyes had shone as though Basti were caressing her all over.

"Yeah, like a sow on her way to the opera," said Astrid, blowing smoke out the side of her mouth. "Let's hope you don't give her any ideas."

"Oh, come on." Julia laughed. "He's way too smart for that. He just feels sorry for her. I think it's nice, the way he tries to make her feel good."

"Yeah? Well, if he keeps on tryin', he's gonna get stuck with her. It's the smart ones that always get caught."

Astrid frowned at the budding bushes, which were showing faint touches of green. Her downcast eyes seemed to envision future pain. Astrid shook her head disgustedly. "She's not like you," she said. "She wants a man. But she's not gonna get my Basti."

"What do you mean? I like men," said Julia. She massaged her rounded belly.

"Yeah, but you want one to have fun with, not to feed you."

"Don't worry. He just feels sorry for her," said Julia.

By now she and Astrid had made more trips to Czeplinski's, and Julia could wear only limp clothes from secondhand stores. To feel pretty, she put on colorful scarves, but everywhere she went, people treated her differently. At work, men spoke to her in tired voices, as though she were one with them in weariness, not a beauty to be conquered. Marga kept asking if she wanted to sit down, and in the U-Bahn, people offered her their seats. In the eyes of well-dressed women she saw frightened pity, the kind you would feel for a man with no legs. At times she hated this thing that had taken over her body and turned her into a swollen cripple.

For weeks now, she had heard nothing from Arno or Rudi, and she worried about how they would react to her new size. She was glad when she came back from Ohlmann's Market one morning and found her message light flashing.

"Uh ... Julia ..." Arno's voice was so deep it was almost a growl. Either he was sick again or just emerging from a rough night. Julia eased her canvas bags to the floor, where they settled with glassy clunks.

"Uh ... Julia ... Listen. I'm sorry. I shouldn't have ... uh ... I'm really sorry. We can work with this if we have to." Arno cleared his throat. "Uh ... Linda says she won't sing unless you do. I need my Mädels. I need you to sing. Start practicing the *St. Matthew Passion*, all right? Call me. Oh—and Linda wants you to do 'Erbarme dich.' She's right. Only an idiot would give that to a soprano." Arno coughed loudly. "Jesus, what time is it? Just call me, okay?"

Julia reached for a box of chocolate-topped cookies, whose yellow corner peeped from a floppy bag. She bit into a glossy square the color of Basti's cabinet. Exhaling slowly, she let the chocolate melt on her tongue. Down in the Hof, a freezing rain had coated the bushes, so that their knobby branches bowed to the bins. Watching flickers of rain trouble the puddles, she finished her cookie. Then she called Arno and said she would be ready anytime he wanted.

When Arno met Julia for her piano rehearsal, he couldn't hide his alarm. In the two months since the seventy-second cantata, she had grown much wider, and in some places she was deeper than she was wide. Driven by inner calls for food, she had been eating whenever she was hungry. Arno wrapped his arms around her, but he didn't squeeze, as though fearing she might break.

"Good to see you!" he said breathlessly. "You look … different. Now let's hear how you sound. Let's hear you sing."

He settled at the piano and frowned at her as though she had inflicted crippling wounds. His abrupt movements told her he was still angry and anything could set him off.

Arno started her on the aria that opened the second part: "Ach, nun ist mein Jesus hin"—"Oh, Now My Jesus Is Gone." With most of the orchestra behind her, Julia had to hold an F-sharp for four measures, and after the third one, her note wavered and died.

Arno stopped playing. "What the fuck was that?" he demanded.

Julia laughed, relieved to hear him back. She hated being treated as fragile.

"I'm not getting as much air in a breath as I used to," she said. "Let me do it again."

Arno looked at her sharply, then withdrew to calculate. With two days to go, he must have been thinking of Sascha, Dagmar, and some young altos from the Breithaus Academy.

"Try it again," he said tightly. This time Julia's F-sharp held its richness, even though he slowed the accompaniment.

"Don't even think of doing that in church," he snapped. "Jesus! Breathe through your ass if you have to, but get the air in there! What do you think this is?"

Julia smiled, her teeth digging into her lower lip.

When Linda saw Julia's swollen shape, she concealed her shock more gracefully. In a black velvet gown, Linda stood more beautifully than ever. Her fluffy blond hair now reached softly to her straight shoulders. With her perfect posture and slender waist, she looked readier to dance than sing. Julia wondered how many Lindas would fit into her shapeless black dress, bought at a secondhand store called Round Two.

Gray and tired, Rudi didn't look as fresh as Linda, but he dared to squeeze Julia and whispered, "*Geil!* More of you to love!" In his thin arms she relaxed as she hadn't in weeks, and she felt a strange urge to cry.

In the hallway before the performance, Julia felt the pull of watching eyes. She turned her head and discovered Arno staring uneasily through the glass. He smiled and waved, mouthing encouragement, but inside she shivered. He didn't trust her and was probably wishing he had called Dagmar Schleifer.

In the three-hour epic of mourning and shame, Bach had given the alto a lot to do. If she was the mother's voice at Christmas, now she was leading the dirge. Almost all her arias were about crying, but if she broke down, the piece would dissolve around her.

At least no one else seemed to doubt Julia. Jakob smiled radiantly, and Udo said how much he was looking forward to their "Erbarme dich" aria. In the soprano section, Anja and Heike grinned and waved. Anja, the mother of two, puffed out her cheeks and made a broad curving gesture over her belly. Rudi blinked and smiled supportively, but an inner vortex seemed to trouble his smile. Julia worried about him all through the heaving opening chorus.

Since Manfred had been shunned, an earnest blond tenor played the Evangelist, a creamy-faced boy of less than twenty. As always, Arno had chosen well. The young tenor looked directly into people's eyes and sang the words so that each person in the audience felt their force. The notes flowed so naturally from his lips that his recitatives sounded more like talking than singing. Jörg made an impressive Jesus but yielded the bass arias to Michael, a rich-voiced African American singer whom Linda had recommended. Again, Julia wondered about the American invasion, this need to sing in Berlin as a rite of passage. Would German singers be as welcome in New York? For a moment she dreamed of singing at Lincoln Center, applauded by people whose language she barely spoke. Jörg gave Julia a friendly nudge as he stood to reprimand his disciples for chiding a woman with perfume. Then it was her turn. Julia pushed herself to her feet.

Drawing in as much air as she could, she sang that she would anoint Christ with her tears. Arno nodded slightly and led her into her first aria. Against a duet of flutes, a Vietnamese girl and the pretty dancer from Christmas, Julia followed Arno's hands through chromatic turns. "Buss und Reu knirscht das Sündenherz entzwei," she sang. "Repentance and regret crush the sinful heart in two." The aria defied all orientation, as though she were seeking firm ground in a kaleidoscope. In runs full of surprises, she and the flutes cut in and out, none of them showing the others what to do. With her line memorized, Julia kept her eyes on Arno and watched his hands and the shape of his lips. Their soft roundness said that he liked her intonation, but his long fingers asked for more sound. By the time she sat down, the church looked dimmer, and she didn't know what more she could give.

Arno looked happier when she and Linda rose after Jesus reproached his followers for sleeping. Before cuing the orchestra, he wiped his brow and grinned, his eyes shining with anticipation. In the slow, writhing movement, Julia's voice intertwined with the soprano's, glowing in the warmest part of her range. With easy movements, Arno led them in and out, as though they were dancing under water. "So ist mein Jesus nun gefangen," they mourned. "So now my Jesus is captured." Against them, the second chorus sang in short, sharp cries, "Lasst ihn! Haltet! Bindet nicht!"—"Release him! Stop! Don't bind him!" Seeing only blackness behind Arno's white hands, Julia couldn't judge the audience's response. She sensed that she was doing something extraordinary. Playing, caressing, she tried to match Linda's light tones, and Linda opened her throat to mimic Julia's. With a look of wonder, Arno guided their blending, his mouth half-open with delight. Julia stole a look at Udo, who was smiling softly. As she quivered to the end, a third below Linda, she knew that Arno was satisfied.

During the break, the musicians congratulated her.

"That's the best I've heard that done," said Udo.

Julia asked Rudi where Carola was—the second-chorus altos sounded thin.

"Oh, she had her baby," he said. "In January, I think. I don't know when she's coming back."

"Are you okay?" asked Julia.

"Yeah, sure!" Rudi gave her a bright smile in which his eyes didn't participate.

"Yeah?" asked Julia and felt her face scrunch up like Marga's.

Rudi's smile was just starting to fade when Arno walked up. He draped a heavy arm around each of them.

"Pretty good, huh?" He grinned. With a quick caress, he lifted Julia's hair. "*Breathe!*" he whispered. "Just breathe!"

Before cuing the orchestra for the second part, Arno smiled reassuringly. The singing would start with Julia's long F-sharp, and he led the orchestra faster than usual. Udo looked worried as he shot through the opening turns, hoping the others could follow. Ashamed, Julia filled herself with air and spun her F-sharp so perfectly the note had a hypnotic quality. Alternating with the chorus, she maintained a rich flow of melody. Lips parted, eyebrows raised, Arno looked relieved if not thrilled. In his sleepless night, he must have been most worried about this movement.

"Ach, mein Lamm in Tigerklauen!" sang Julia, enjoying Arno's smile. "Oh, my lamb in tiger's claws." At the movement's end he nodded, and she met his eyes. For the first time since Christmas, she felt joined to him.

Julia's most vital moment came when Peter realized that he had denied Christ three times. Udo stood, and Arno paused before cuing him, then started the slow, exquisite aria. Arno's gesture to Julia was more an acknowledgment than an invitation. "Erbarme dich, mein Gott, um meiner Zähren willen," she sang, reaching out to embrace Udo's melody. "Have mercy, my Lord, when you see my tears." Her voice and the violin's moved like separate beings as they rose, lightly touching and turning. Arno held them back so that the tension mounted and their dance moved with soft tranquility.

There were moments, though, when Arno asked her for more sound, with a twitch of his outstretched hand. Julia tried to breathe deeper, but she had hit the bottom of her well. Looking at Arno, she sadly refused. For an instant, the conductor's eyes softened, but his pulse of feeling quickened to rage. His thick fingers trembled as he glared, unwilling to believe she had no more air. To match her tone quality, Arno pulled Udo back, and as they approached the climax, the violinist raised his brows. Udo took every suggestion and finished the piece just as Arno wanted it. The conductor nodded to each of them with compressed lips.

With Michael, the American bass, Arno took a different tack. Rather than guiding Michael's powerful voice, Arno simply unleashed it. Radiating energy, the passionate man shook the audience with his cry: "Gebt mir meinen Jesum wieder!"—"Give me my Jesus back!" The listeners started and sat up straight, feeling the force of his outrage. Awed by the story of Christ, Michael seemed honored to be telling it. Udo accompanied him with gliding strokes, smiling admiringly. When they had finished, the audience murmured and stirred. They checked their programs to see when Michael would sing next.

Arno took Julia's last solo aria at top speed, demanding everything his strings could give. The piece had only one sustained note, but she needed every ounce of air to spit out the words so fast. Feeling as though she were being dragged, Julia struggled to shape Bach's phrases. Arno's eyes pierced her, insisting, demanding, and she lost touch with her center. Amid the strange words and fast-changing notes, Julia began to panic. She forgot where to breathe in the twisting lines, and against the darkness, Arno's hands dissolved. By her third entrance, she felt her voice growing fainter. Arno stretched out his hand, fingers shaking, and while Udo and Jakob played, she gathered strength. When the aria began again at the da capo, she wasn't sure she could sing, but she heard her voice blend with the violins. She made it through to the end without pleasure, ashamed of the pale sounds she was making.

Julia sat back down, and Linda took her hand. "Bend over," she murmured in English. "Put your head down. You're white."

Julia bent double and felt her chest expand and shrink. In the black minutes, she listened to Michael's voice, vital and sincere in its richness. "Mach dich, mein Herze, rein," he sang. "My heart, make yourself pure." In the last movement, which the four soloists sang with the chorus, Julia recovered some of her warmth.

Hot and exhausted, the choir sang their last chord in a barely audible sigh. Arno lowered his hands a millimeter at a time, so that for half a minute no one dared applaud. Then the church exploded. Three times, four times, Arno led the soloists off and on. This time, too, the audience had favorites—not the Mädels, but the two new men, the serious young tenor and the radiant American. They stepped forward together, and Arno placed himself between the two, squeezing their upraised hands. A soprano handed Julia some orange-and-yellow daisies, which she clutched gratefully.

In the throng of patrons and well-wishers, almost no one addressed Julia. Several people shook their heads, impressed by her courage but convinced that a three-hour oratorio was no place for a pregnant woman. A tall, gray-haired man talking to Arno jerked his head her way, apparently asking why Arno had let her sing. Seeing that she had become a liability, Julia slipped downstairs. She wasn't the kind of soloist you could put on display.

In the basement, Rudi hugged her and said he would call. He was going home with Norbert, who didn't like to eat with the choir. Arno went out with Michael and Linda. He said they would come by Löwenstein's later, but they never did. Eating bratwurst and fries, Julia spent the night talking with Anja and Heike. "Sleep while you can," they told her. "Get lots of sleep. You have no idea what's coming."

———— ■ ————

Julia sang just one more time before June, at a small wedding in the nearby Johanneskirche. She had always liked weddings, and the minister recommended her often. Her rich voice, he said, set just the right tone for affirming a loving bond. In May, a thin blonde girl with bad teeth hired Julia to sing "Gracias a la Vida," a Joan Baez song from the 1970s. She was marrying a thick-necked Peruvian half a head shorter than she was. Julia liked them instantly and tried to memorize the strange words, matching syllables to notes in the tune. She wished she were better at foreign languages. Erik picked up words as if they were tools and then just started using them. Julia sang with a round-faced friend of the groom's whose guitar chords floated like passing moods. He sought the best key for Julia and grinned admiringly, his dark eyes snapping with fun.

As Julia's voice danced in the bright space he shaped, she felt the force of people's eyes. They weren't looking at the guitarist or even the bride and groom. They were staring at her in her enormous black dress, which broadcast her pregnancy rather than hid it. The baby inside her liked the music, and as it kicked spiritedly, Julia tried to keep still. An older blonde woman, probably the bride's mother, ogled Julia as though she were stark naked.

The Peruvian guitarist spoke to her in Spanish. He smiled broadly and pointed at her belly. Laughing, Julia shook her head and raised her hands to show that she didn't understand. Seeing it was hopeless, he grinned and hugged her with the fondest embrace she had felt in months. The minister didn't call her again. Apparently, a wedding was no place for a pregnant woman either.

Nowadays, when Julia left her apartment, people everywhere looked shocked. She had never imagined she could get this big, and the glances of pity and fear made her feel deformed. Some greedy, malevolent force seemed to have hijacked her body. When she went to the Wilmersdorfer Arcades after work, teenage girls stared horrified, then whispered to each other and giggled. Groups of young, brown-haired guys looked startled, maybe picturing their girlfriends in a similar state. The older men seemed to view her as a walking time bomb that they hoped wouldn't go off on their watch. No man gave her that sideways glance like a ray of sun from a clearing sky.

At the clinic, almost every woman was big, though Julia never saw one as huge as she was. Since September, she had grown from 160 to 195 pounds.

The blue-eyed nurse squinted at the scale indicator. "You know, you don't have to eat every time you're hungry."

But seeing Julia appear punctually every two weeks, the nurse had begun to treat her better. She pointed out features on the ultrasound and fought to get Julia a reservation at the Wasserstrasse clinic. Since Julia had come in for prenatal care so late, the reputable West Side clinic was booked, but Wasserstrasse was willing to take her. When the nurse learned that Julia was a singer, she turned almost friendly and asked her where she performed. The receptionist's call—"Frau Martens?"—sounded like a phrase from a different tune. The nurse's scolding took on a more human quality, and in the eyes frosted with blue, Julia saw reluctant sympathy.

Julia was starting her forty-first week—not a problem, the nurse said, but time to think of inducing labor. Staring down at the Hof, Julia laid her palms on her belly. She spread her fingers and circled her hands. It sounded so awful—taking drugs to make your muscles contract. Weren't they supposed to do that by themselves?

Twice last week and then again last night she had been awakened by a tightening across her belly. Each time she got up and sat holding the phone, thinking of Marilyn Monroe. Astrid said they had found her with her hand on the phone. She'd been calling for help but couldn't get through. Alone in the dark, Julia started pressing buttons, but some instinct told her to stop. Her belly was right, as always. Each time the cramps had eased by themselves, and she'd ended up falling asleep.

Now in the golden stillness, the stores would soon be closing, and she had a hankering for rice pudding. She was low on milk, but more importantly, she was running out of water. In her building, lead joints in the basement made the tap water unsafe to drink. Rubbing her back, Julia wondered whether it was worth walking down four flights of stairs and then back up again. Once the metal gates on the shops rattled down, the only place to go until Monday would be a gas station that charged twice as much.

In the last few months, the stairs that left Julia panting had changed from an annoyance to an obstacle. She had found herself willing to go without things rather than drag herself up and down. In the Vorderhaus, where rents were higher, Birgit and her mother rode up and down on an elevator. It creaked and clanked, but it hoisted them up to their high perch. Without having to schlep juice up four flights, the two of them drank it by the crateful. Thinking of the gas station prices, Julia decided to go out.

On the warm June evening, her Hof was unusually quiet. The house sighed in the late-day sun, glad to be rid of its noisy inhabitants. As Julia crossed the courtyard, she heard only a pan lid clanging and a woman scolding her son. Astrid's windows were closed since she had gone with the Kiez management crowd to celebrate someone's birthday. Basti had ridden down to Lichterfelde to see some BSR friends with tips about dump sites. Rudi and Norbert had driven to the Baltic coast to enjoy some rare time alone. As Julia's due date had approached, her friends had called her each day, but once it passed, they had grown more lax.

"Just do whatever you were gonna do—it'll come when it comes," she told everyone.

She had orders to call if she felt a contraction, but after two weeks, her friends seemed almost to have forgotten.

Instead of going to Ohlmann's Market, Julia walked slowly to the discount chain, which was only six blocks away. The air seared her throat, and her shirt grew damp. Great. More laundry. That was all she needed. She wondered about Rudi, who seemed depressed, and about Marga, who was singing at a club out in Friedrichshagen. Marga said it was the best place Ultraviolet had ever played, and they were going to try a new song she had written.

At the discounter's, Julia bought six bottles of water and two of apple juice, plus some cookies and half a dozen rice puddings. She admired the shiny circles of foil that sealed the plastic containers.

"You sure you can carry all that?" asked the skinny boy at the register. His voice echoed down an empty aisle, and his long, ruddy face drooped.

"Oh, yeah, I got it," Julia answered softly.

She divided the weight between her canvas bags, the way she had heard they did in elevators. After two blocks, the bags' pull seemed to have doubled. Without trees, the heavy facades radiated heat like oven walls, and she set down her bags and tried to breathe. On a balcony above her, geraniums glowed like silent fireworks. Crisp socks hung from a line, stiffened by Berlin's hard water. If Basti were there, he would have helped. Lately he had done a lot of her shopping. Julia looked up and down, but the street was empty. She picked up her bags and trudged on.

In her gateway, she set the bags down again to check the graffiti for new shapes. She had always been pleased by the smoky black scrawls, like the tracks of mysterious animals. In broken curves, words lined the entryway like writing on an Egyptian tomb. Most were illegible, and some were in Turkish, but she noticed a new looping green line. "In memory of hers," it said, with rounded *e*'s. Probably some girl had sprayed it out, recreating a line from her favorite song.

Julia had missed the start of the eight o'clock movies, and as she dragged herself upward, she wondered which one to watch. The one with Harrison Ford and that skinny blonde woman seemed best. Julia hoped she hadn't missed the part where he said that her breasts were too small. She bent slowly to gather the cloth handles, which had flopped while she paused to breathe.

Pop!

Oh, no, the stairs were all wet. One of the bottles must have broken. Feeling warm wetness along her leg, Julia looked down at her pants. The bags weren't wet, but her pants were. She froze.

From between her legs, warm water was trickling down the steps in a fine stream. Gripping her bags, she watched it darken the green linoleum that Janek and Katrin, the Polish house cleaners, had scrubbed that morning. Was this river really coming from her? When it dried, would it stink like piss? How was she ever going to get those stairs clean again?

At the clinic, they had told her to call an ambulance as soon as her water broke. There could be an infection; it could hurt the baby. Just at that moment, the lights went out. The stairway lamps were on a timer, and she had used up her five minutes. Without any windows, the stairway was a black shaft. Julia gripped her bags and kicked each successive step to find where to place her foot. Up above, the light switch glowed orange. When her right foot struck matting, she shuffled toward the shining square and punched the timer. A dim light revealed chipped brown walls and hemp floor covering. Julia leaned her bags against a wall, lay down as the nurse had told her, and dug for her phone. Before she had finished telling the dispatcher where she was, the lights went out again.

In the blackness, Julia counted her breaths. She propped her feet against the wall and pushed. Her belly tightened in a way it never had before, and she gasped as hot pain seared her back. She clawed the prickly bumps of the matting and breathed its musty smell. You could scrub stray fluids off of naked stairs, but carpets held on to their memories.

"Hey!" called Julia. "Hey!"

Her voice careened through the empty stairway.

"Hey!" she yelled.

Miserably, she thought of Marga on stage and Rudi kicking up sand. The folks from her house would all be out drinking, shouting to their friends and laughing loudly. And Arno—what would Arno be doing? Maybe composing as he often did at night, his thick fingers testing crystalline chords.

"*Hey!*" screamed Julia. Her voice broke.

Far away, a siren practiced its fourth, the pitch twisting upward as it approached. Footsteps sounded in the Hof, and Julia cried out with all her strength. The steps moved toward the stairs, and the landing filled with light. With syncopated taps, two sets of steps rose toward her.

"Well, what do we have here?" A red-faced man grinned. With his sharp nose and fun-loving dark eyes, he looked more like a cabaret host than a paramedic. "Oof, Mädel." He grunted. "Have you made a mess!"

To Julia's embarrassment, her voice collapsed. "Ple-ease could you help me?" She wavered. "Please could you put away my food? Could you get my suitcase? Here are my keys!"

"*Na, na,* take it easy," he growled. "What do I look like, a butler? Take it easy, Mädel. Don't have a baby."

Still on her back, Julia laughed, and a fresh squirt of fluid wet the matting. That would be just her luck, to get the biggest smart-ass on the *Feuerwehr*.

"So where's your guy tonight, Tenerife?" he asked.

"Geez, Oli, give her a break," pleaded his partner, a pale, blond boy with an anxious look.

Julia was in no mood to be offended. "Frankfurt." She grimaced.

"Oh, that ain't far enough. We'll catch him there." The jokester grinned.

His partner took Julia's keys and the bags of food and in a few minutes returned with her suitcase. From the length of time he was gone, she guessed that he had put the puddings in the refrigerator.

Once the funny man got down to business, he proved to be quite kind. He pulled down her pants and touched her belly more tenderly than most men she had known. Julia shuddered at the feel of her wet pants, which were beginning to turn cold.

"It's okay," he said, patting her stomach. "He ain't in no hurry. Or is it a she? Do you know?"

"No, I don't want to know," said Julia. "I like surprises."

"My kind of girl," he muttered. "Let's hope someone in Frankfurt does too."

On the way to Wasserstrasse, Julia was tossed by every bump in the road. Ordinarily, she would have walked to the nearby clinic herself. Nestled between the palace gardens and the autobahn, Wasserstrasse lay in a hodgepodge area of rest homes, research institutes, and warehouses. Wincing from the jolts, Julia wondered how much this ride would cost her and whether her insurance would cover it. Despite all her planning, she had slipped into a whirlpool and could survive only with other people's help.

When the paramedics opened the doors, the swish of traffic revived her. A tree formed dark lace against the glowing sky. The paramedics wheeled her to the emergency room, where a lithe blonde doctor began to probe her. As she leaned over Julia, her mouth hung open slightly. Deep circles underlined her red-rimmed eyes.

"Who's your midwife? Does she know you're here?" asked the doctor.

She squeezed Julia's belly like a cantaloupe.

"Oh—I don't have one," said Julia. "I've been going to the clinic. They told me to use someone here."

"Okay." The doctor smiled. "Well, you've passed the point of no return. You're having a baby tonight. You're dilated one centimeter."

As the doctor bent downward, a strand of soft hair tickled Julia's cheek. Except for her weariness, the wiry doctor didn't look much older than Julia herself.

"It's going to take a while," she said. "I'll look in when I can. We're having a busy night."

Another pain hit, and Julia gripped the metal table. All by itself, her belly tightened and hardened, and she shrieked as a white-hot flash stabbed her back.

"Don't worry—we've got you," said a big, red-headed woman, who introduced herself as Frau Tannen. She was going to serve as Julia's midwife.

Following the midwife's directions, an orderly wheeled Julia to a contraction room, which looked nothing like she had imagined. Instead of a hospital cot, it offered a double bed with a brown-and-purple quilt. Stiff drapes guarded the window, and a TV sat poised on a metal arm. With the broad bed and twin nightstands, the room seemed made for couples riding out contractions together. The midwife looked at Julia with deep-set brown eyes.

"Is there someone you can call?" she asked. "Someone who can be with you? You're not supposed to use a cell phone in here, but if you do when I'm not around, I can't help it."

Julia's throat hardened. "They're all out doing things," she said. "They don't know—"

A scream broke through the wall, a tearing, animal shriek. Julia drew in her breath.

"Don't worry." Frau Tannen's dark eyes penetrated her. "This is going to hurt, but there are ways to deal with it. Some women do it by screaming. They've taught you how to breathe, right? You can scream right back at her if you want, but there are better ways. Have you ever swum in the ocean?"

Julia pictured Rudi whooping in the surf and Norbert rolling his eyes. She had been to the Baltic but not the Atlantic. For that you had to go to France or Spain.

"Hey, are you paying attention?" asked the midwife.

Surviving contractions, she said, was like riding waves. You had to breathe in as they gathered and breathe out as they broke. If you misjudged a wave, it would grind you up.

"Like surfers—wipeout." She chuckled, and Julia glimpsed Rudi again, the froth closing over his narrow head.

The surfer strategy sounded good, except that you couldn't know when the waves would come. Julia hated feeling her body out of control after so many years of practiced movements. Once Frau Tannen had guided her through a few contractions, the midwife apologized and left. There were five other women on the ward that night, and she had been assigned to one of them.

Awaiting her next pain, Julia stared at a painting of fruit, which settled when she blinked her eyes. In a grooved ceramic bowl, apples and grapes lay bunched on one side, and she wished she could rearrange them so that they filled the space. She rode out one contraction fairly well but got smashed by the next because a scream from next door distracted her. The high-pitched sound pierced the wall like the yelp of a dog whose tail has been crushed by a heavy foot. Julia thought she heard Spanish and wondered where the suffering woman might be from. Was she alone too? She wished that she could talk to her.

Between pains, Julia kept calling her friends. Rudi had turned off his phone, as Norbert insisted when they went out together. Had Rudi said they would be back on Sunday or Monday night? She couldn't remember.

"It's here—it's happening—I'm at Wasserstrasse," she said, her voice muted by the room's stiff fabrics.

For Marga she left the same message. It surprised her that Basti had shut off his *Handy*, which for him was a living organ. Maybe he had met a girl, and Julia wondered what she might look like. Miserably, she realized she had forgotten her charger, so that her phone had a limited life. Hungry for another voice, she left the fading thing on. She tried Erik and murmured a vague message for him to call her. She even whispered a few words to Arno.

Frau Tannen returned to Julia when she could, laughing and shaking her head. She confided that her other woman was much younger, a frightened girl with an angry boyfriend.

"It's not fair, but that's the way it is." She sighed. "You're strong, you're healthy, and everything's happening the way it should. Pretty fast, actually. Six centimeters now. You look like you can handle this. If you want something for the pain, now's the time. How are you doing?"

"Oh, I'm okay," said Julia. At the clinic they had told her you couldn't push well after an epidural, and she wanted to force the baby out herself.

"It's tough being on your own," said Frau Tannen. "Really, honey, isn't there anyone you can call?"

"I've tried everyone," said Julia softly. "I've called everyone I know."

Frau Tannen left the door open, and another scream filled the room. This time there were words: "*¡Ai, Dios!*"

"Cuban." The midwife grimaced. "She's doing fine—but they're screamers."

Frau Tannen rarely stayed more than a few minutes, her face drawn with worry over the younger girl. Distractedly, she asked Julia what she did, and her dark eyes warmed when she heard she was a singer. She began to treat Julia like a doctor or professor, but she didn't come by any more often.

In the muted room, time passed differently than in the world outside. It stuck at some points, then slipped away in landslides. It was 11:42, then 11:43, then suddenly 2:13. Once Julia turned on the TV, but she didn't feel like watching. It was more comforting to follow her own thoughts.

Between pains, Julia remembered her mother, who appeared as a gray shimmer around tired eyes. Had her mother gone through all of this? Had it hurt this much to bring her into the world? Julia thought of her mother cleaning the sidewalk by electric light. More clearly than her mother's face, she saw the striated slabs of cement and heard the moist scratches of the *Schrubber*. There were still mornings when Julia awoke at four, fearing she wouldn't get to the Imbiss on time.

The pains were growing worse, and they tore into her bones and flesh. As her belly pulled back, she felt like a wishbone being yanked apart. When a pain hit its peak, she hated the vicious thing torturing her in its relentless drive to come out. No wonder so many women died in childbirth. Breathing didn't help, and neither did plan B, making moaning sounds like "ooooh" and "aaaah." When she tried it, her voice turned into an animal cry like the Cuban woman's.

"Oh, great," quipped Frau Tannen. "Now we've got 'em in stereo."

She checked between Julia's legs, and her features hardened.

"Ten centimeters," she said. "Let's get you to delivery."

To Julia's relief, the room to which she was wheeled looked as though it belonged in a hospital. She lay down on a high bed covered only with blue sheets. In a corner stood a bath with U-shaped grips and a stool that looked like an alternative to the bed. Soon after she settled, the slim doctor appeared, her blond hair stuck to her face like Arno's. She pushed on Julia's belly and listened for a heartbeat.

"Oh, yeah." She smiled. "You're our best woman tonight. Everything sounds the way it should."

The slim doctor watched Julia handle a pain and nodded as she exhaled slowly. When Julia cried out, the doctor frowned sympathetically, as though remembering a thousand women's sufferings. The waves came so quickly now that Julia couldn't talk or think. She pictured the angry red thing inside her, fighting its way out no matter how much it hurt. Gritting her teeth, she tried to focus on breathing, but she felt dizzy and sick. Frau Tannen stayed to talk her through the contractions, but the pain ground up her words.

"Come—good!" she heard. "That—one more—"

After a nod from the doctor, the midwife told Julia to push. A freckle-faced nurse appeared, and metal instruments clicked on a corner table.

"We're close," said Frau Tannen. "We're getting real close."

Another pain struck, and Julia gasped. Her body pushed by itself, and she felt herself float out of it and hover in an unknown space. As though watching from above, she saw the midwife climb onto the table and use her weight to help her push. Julia could barely breathe, but the pressure of that great big body was wonderful. For the first time all night, she didn't feel lonely.

"Okay! Okay!" called the doctor. "Try again! Try it again."

Frau Tannen gripped Julia's shoulders, and the nurse stood ready with a blue cloth. Back in her body, Julia bore down with all her strength. She heard a dull, wet sound and felt something give.

"Okay, there's the head! You've got the head out!" called the young nurse, who had dark smears under her eyes.

"One more. One more," murmured Frau Tannen. Julia didn't have much strength left, but she pushed and felt something slide. The little nurse blinked shining eyes.

"You've got a baby girl," said the doctor. Impulsively, she touched Julia's cheek.

Julia raised herself to see the bloody, squirming thing they had placed on her belly. It didn't look anything like what she had pictured inside her—a round, pink baby with soft curves. With fierce eyes, it was staring straight at her. It didn't cry, but with an animal instinct it wriggled its way upward. There was something frightening in the blind force of it, but Julia reached down to help it find her breast. Frau Tannen watched critically as its tiny mouth closed on her nipple. The sucking tickled pleasantly, like the lips of a nice man in bed.

"Yeah." The midwife sighed. "I wish it always worked this well."

Julia smiled dreamily and stroked the baby's sticky head. It was an odd sensation, this eager mouth sucking at her, but she already knew that she liked it. A quick rush of steps slapped the hallway.

"Where is she? How's she doing? Is she in there?" asked a hoarse voice.

The freckled nurse answered like someone who had never shed a tear in her life. "Look, you can go in there if you clean yourself up. But the guys stay outside. Is that clear?"

The burst of protest sounded like the snarls of three mishandled dogs. Minutes later, Marga rushed in wearing an aqua gown, her arms wet up to the elbow.

"How ya doin'?" she cried. Several pieces of her voice were missing. "Lemme see it. Are you okay?"

In the doorway, the bass player from Ultraviolet blinked like an owl. Coming straight from her gig, Marga must have brought the whole band with her.

Julia should have been exhausted, but with the baby at her breast, she felt only joyous excitement. She called out to Kevin, the bass player, and laughed as Marga described the Friedrichshagen audience.

"Tell her about that fat guy!" said Kevin, gripping the door frame with long fingers.

"Oh, yeah—this one guy stayed up front and played air guitar all night, and then around three—"

"No, no, it was after that. It was after 'Moving Pictures,'" called Kevin.

"Oh, yeah, so anyway, around four his wife comes in, this great big woman even fatter than he is, and she drags him out—"

"Ooh … Hey, I think—" Julia called for Frau Tannen.

She and her midwife shooed the musicians out as the afterbirth emerged. Frau Tannen raised a green plastic dish to show it, a twisted, bloody mess. Marga wanted to stay, but Julia urged her to come back again the next night. Vibrating from her success, Marga ran off with Kevin and Tony, the drummer, who were driving her to Dorrie's Donuts.

At eight o'clock Frau Tannen's shift ended, and she gave Julia a card with a tiny black footprint. "Willkommen im Leben," it said. "Welcome to life."

That animal track stirred Julia, the sign of an independent being. Its five round spots formed a major chord that resounded with sunny harmony.

"You did a beautiful job," said the midwife. "I'll be back again tomorrow night. You'd better rest now. If everyone you called is this happy, tomorrow's going to be a busy day."

Julia knew that Frau Tannen was right, but she couldn't sleep. Her body wanted to dance. She lay staring out the door, watching people pass, trying to make sense of the sounds they made. At the same time, she ached from the steady pull of the baby's mouth. Her breasts were red, hot, and swollen, but the little thing couldn't get enough of them. At times Julia feared it would tear them apart, but it pleased her to know that they were doing what they had always been meant to do.

A fresh shift of nurses moved her to a new room, where they said she would spend the next three days. In the other bed, a Turkish woman smiled in solidarity, although she couldn't speak German. Her round face lit up when her family came in—her husband, an old woman in a black headscarf, and a bright-eyed boy with a mischievous smile. Gesturing at Julia, the old woman offered her a sweet. Then, narrowing her eyes, she jerked her head Julia's way and emitted a long stream of *ö* and *ü*. The boy, who had been staring at Julia, looked away with troubled eyes. She guessed that the speech had contained some judgment. The old woman frowned as her daughter-in-law nursed, then scolded and repositioned the baby. Julia sucked her sesame candy, and the boy's eyes returned to her, registering each move of her lips. Rich and buttery, the sweet melted on her tongue, and she smiled into his questioning eyes.

"All right! All right, let's see it!" Astrid rushed in with Basti, looking sheepish and tired. Her rough voice scraped the bottom of her range, and her breath smelled rancid. She was carrying some pink and white carnations, but with her bumpy hair and sticky eyes, she couldn't have washed. When she saw the baby, she sprang forward with a delighted cry. Basti glowed, smiling shyly.

"Oh, how beautiful!" She gasped. "Just look at all that hair!"

After the baby's first bath, the brown fuzz on her head had stood up like a sun-drenched thicket after a long rain. Her features were pink folds, but those frizzy brown curls showed who her mother was.

"It's a girl, right?" asked Basti, peering down inquisitively.

When his dark eyes caught Julia's bare breast, they turned and settled on the Turkish family. The mother-in-law had not stopped talking, and her harangue was punctuated by sharp looks at Astrid. Basti, who understood some Turkish, shot her a glance that stopped her in midstream. The old woman bent over her grandchild, and Basti turned back to Julia. He focused carefully on her face.

"What are you gonna call her?" he asked softly.

Julia had been asking herself this for months, and she heard her voice speak the answer.

"Bettina."

"Bettina ..." echoed Astrid. She nodded thoughtfully. "Where did you get that? You name her after somebody, your mom, your grandma maybe?"

"No." Julia smiled. "I want a name that never belonged to anyone I knew—nobody in my family."

"Bettina Martens." Astrid frowned so seriously that Julia wanted to laugh.

Astrid's face was lined more deeply than usual. The soft blue sweater slipping off her shoulder revealed a black strap like a pencil stroke under a painting.

"Bettina Martens, I like that," said Basti. "That sounds natural."

He stepped outside, and murmurs circled in the hall.

"So ..." Astrid lowered her voice. "You hear from her dad yet? Is he gonna come by?"

"He knows I'm here," said Julia quietly. She eyed the baby's brown head. When the overhead light caught the delicate curls, they shone with a ruddy glow. "I called him last night," she murmured.

"So is he comin'?" asked Astrid.

"I don't know," said Julia. "He hasn't called."

Basti reappeared with a chair in each hand. When he saw his mother's face, his jaw set.

Astrid took a chair but held tight to her subject. "So if he doesn't call, are you gonna go down there?" she asked. "He's gotta help."

Basti looked at his hands, then down at the baby.

"What is he? A conductor? A musician?" pushed Astrid.

"No, no, a teacher." Julia's face burned.

Astrid fumbled for her mirror and muttered angrily. "A teacher, huh? Must be a pretty cultured guy."

"Mom—" Basti glared but kept his voice low. "I'm sorry we didn't get here till now. I was out all night with these sanitation guys. I've been havin' trouble sellin' furniture, and they think they can get me a job."

Against Julia's breast, the baby sputtered and squirmed. She tried switching sides. So far, the little thing seemed to prefer the left.

"Oh, don't worry about it." Julia smiled. "You're practically the first ones here. So you might be able to get a BSR job? Don't you have to go through the job center?"

"Yeah, but these guys can make a few calls ..."

"It'd be steady work." Astrid frowned at the baby's fuzzy head.

"It's lousy work, but I could do furniture on weekends," said Basti. "If I got an apprenticeship, I ..."

The Turkish boy crept toward him and stared with big, soft eyes. Basti smiled, searched his pockets, and pulled out a red Swiss Army knife. With a few words and gestures, he asked the father's permission and took the boy aside.

"I got an appointment tomorrow," whispered Astrid in a puff of fermented breath.

"Yeah?" Julia smiled.

"Yeah. I think this is gonna be it. I can feel it. The way he touched me last time—so slow ..." She traced a wavering path across her breast.

"Are you sure?" asked Julia. "You've gotta be careful, you know. If he—"

"He has magic hands." Astrid's eyes burned, and she leaned in closer. "I was thinking about it all last night—I think I should go for it."

"Gee, I'd be careful," murmured Julia, glancing at Basti and the Turkish boy.

Fascinated, the boy was fingering the corkscrew. With quick twists of his wrist, Basti showed him how to use it.

"Why don't you let him make the first move?" asked Julia. "What if he freaks out or something?"

"Oh, he won't freak out." Astrid chuckled. "I know how bad he wants it. Sometimes they just need a little nudge."

She met Julia's eyes and laughed naughtily, her teeth nicking her lower lip.

Tired as they were, Astrid and Basti stayed on, except for a few cigarette breaks. They brought Julia pudding from the cafeteria and Mars bars from the gift shop. Basti offered to set up her baby bed as soon as she got home. He had built a small platform, so that Julia could lie next to the baby and feed her at night without worrying she would roll over and hurt her.

"And I can bring you stuff till you can get around again," said Basti. "Diapers, milk, that kind of thing."

He gazed down with calm, dark eyes as though he had been through a hundred births. Only a crust at their corners betrayed his sleepless night—that, and an edgy restlessness.

On Julia's breast, the baby whimpered and stirred. Julia tried shifting her, but she only got louder. Finally, Bettina reared her head, gathered strength, and let out a piercing scream. The violent sound cut into Julia's head, and frantically, she tried to still her. Like a blade run amok, her cries were stabbing everyone in the room, and Julia felt it must be her fault.

"Oh, Jesus!" Astrid covered her ears.

"Why don't you guys get some sleep and come back when she's better?" Julia called over the storm.

"Hey-hey!"

In the doorway stood Rudi, quivering with delight. Behind him was Norbert, round-faced and solid. They had gained some color from their days at the shore, and Rudi's red-brown skin set off his soft gray hair. A bouquet of red roses tickled his chin, and Norbert was clutching a soft polar bear. Julia introduced them to her neighbors, who were rising to leave, and against her breast, Bettina quieted. Basti stared frankly as he pushed past the men, and they studied his broad, straight shoulders. With a look of amusement, Norbert settled into one of the chairs, but Rudi was too excited.

"We got here as soon as we could," he said. "I had my phone turned off. When we heard your message, we threw everything in the car and started driving."

The smoky circles under Rudi's eyes made them look darker than usual. He seemed thinner and, if possible, even more high-strung than he was at rehearsals.

"How are you feeling?" asked Norbert. "You must be exhausted."

Like Rudi, he had a combed moustache, and his graying hair was beautifully cut. Rudi's agitation made Norbert look stiller and rounder. Under his clean-shaven face hung the soft curve of a double chin. He looked fondly from Rudi to the baby.

"Oh, I'm okay," said Julia. "They said it went about as well as it could have."

Already she felt twinges of pain between her legs where the local anesthetic was wearing off. They had said that the tearing was minimal, but she didn't like the sound of that word *tearing*.

"So you were all alone? You didn't have any help?" asked Rudi.

"Oh, the people here were great," said Julia, but Rudi looked down and shook his head.

"I should have been here," he said. "I should have been here."

"Well, we're here now, aren't we?" Norbert glanced at him. "It's great to see you both doing so well."

Rudi smiled and waved at the Turkish family, who were returning from their midday meal. The husband and mother stared suspiciously, studying the two men's familiar gestures and expensive shirts. Only the boy grinned and waved back, but his father held him close.

Norbert laid his hand on Rudi's shoulder. "I've got to go," he said. "I've got to get ready for school tomorrow. Are you okay if I take the car?"

"Sure," said Rudi without moving his eyes from Julia.

Norbert rose, and Rudi patted his arm awkwardly. He kissed Rudi's bald spot and lingered, savoring the smell of his hair.

"Good to see you, Julia," he said. He offered her a warm, meaty hand. "I'm glad to see you doing so well."

As Norbert's footsteps receded, Rudi relaxed on his chair as though all his cells had loosened. Exhaling, he reached for Julia's free hand. The baby stirred, and Rudi grinned guiltily. With a movement of his head, he offered the teddy bear to the Turkish boy, whose parents seemed more tolerant of Rudi alone than of the two men together.

"Are you okay? You don't look so hot," said Julia.

"Huh! You're one to talk!" Rudi snorted.

Their eyes met in a mischievous glance, but the spark in Rudi's faded.

"What am I saying?" he said. "You look beautiful. You look like a Raphael Madonna."

Julia wondered if Raphael Madonnas had burning breasts and crotches that stung like they were full of soap. But she smiled, appreciating the compliment, and tried to focus on Rudi.

"No, seriously, what's wrong?" she asked. "I've been worried about you. What's going on with you? What's happening?"

"Oh, I'm okay," he said. "Come on, I didn't come here to talk about me."

"Well, you might as well. You've got a captive audience." Julia laughed.

Rudi looked at her, ashamed. "We were fighting all night," he said. "That's why I turned off my phone. I thought it would clear the air, but it was awful."

His thin face barely concealed his anguish. Julia felt a sudden hate for Norbert's round chin.

"I'm sorry," she said. She squeezed Rudi's hand and waited for him to go on.

"It's just—sometimes it's so good, but sometimes I feel as though I've been kidnapped. He gets mad when I work late. He doesn't understand—he teaches school. A physics lab runs twenty-four hours a day, and night's when they need me most. I have to ask his permission to do things, as though I were some little kid. He says I'm not committed, but his idea of committed …"

"Yeah," murmured Julia.

Rudi's hand trembled as he fought for control. "I—I don't want to break up with him. I want to stay with him and be who I am. I want to live with him and still have a life."

The little boy stared sadly and rubbed his chin against the bear's fuzzy white head. In Rudi's mind, a safety loop snapped.

"Who am I kidding?" he said. "We were fighting about Arno. We've been fighting about Arno since the day I met him."

Julia gave the tiniest nod. The baby stirred, probably aroused by her thumping heart.

"But he knows Arno's not gay, right?"

"Does he?" Rudi raised his eyebrows slightly.

"Shit! Arno's … You haven't …?"

"No," said Rudi. "Have you?"

"No." Julia's voice was nothing but air.

The boy and bear stared like a two-headed totem pole.

"You say he's not gay. How do you know that? How much do you know about him?" Rudi's voice tightened.

"As much as you do, I guess." Julia squirmed. She had to go to the bathroom, but her crotch stung so badly she wasn't sure she could stand it. In the chair next to her bed, Rudi leaned forward until she saw green flecks in his eyes.

"Do you know where he's from?" asked Rudi.

"Yeah, from Bonn. We were ragging on him that time at Löwenstein's, when the whole place started yelling, 'Go back to Bonn!'"

"Yeah, even the ones who didn't know what it was about." Rudi laughed.

Many Berliners viewed the government's arrival as an invasion and wished that the noisy Rhinelanders would go home.

"That's not what I mean," said Rudi. "You know what his father does?"

"No, what?" Julia bristled.

Rudi lowered his voice as though revealing something dirty. "He's a construction worker. So's his brother. No one in his family has ever studied."

"So what?" said Julia. "He's smart as hell. He might be the best choral conductor in Germany."

"I know that! That's not what I mean!" Rudi's voice sharpened, and the Turkish parents turned to look.

"So what do you mean, then?" asked Julia.

"I mean—how he *is*, how people treat him, how he ... Look!" Rudi dropped her hand to make a broad gesture. "You know where he was that time he disappeared?"

"Yeah, for six weeks. That guy from the Singakademie had to take over. They said he was sick."

"Oh, he was sick all right." Rudi snorted.

"You don't mean ... He doesn't ..." The room dimmed to gray snow.

"No, no ..." Rudi took her hand again and pressed it. "He doesn't drink—at least not that much. He doesn't do drugs. Hey!" He reached up to touch her cheek. "We shouldn't be— I didn't mean to upset you."

Julia's throat tightened. "What happened? Please tell me."

"His father broke his jaw," said Rudi. "They were fighting. He was home for some holiday. His brother grabbed him from behind and pinned him, and his father hit him as hard as he could. He had to drink through a straw for six weeks. I helped him. He hasn't seen them since."

"Jesus!" Julia breathed. "What were—"

"It was about his music," said Rudi. "They're all jealous of him. They baited him, called him a pussy. Said that what he does isn't real work. His father called him—" Rudi stopped and smiled at the little boy. "Well, you can guess. His family thinks he's gay."

Despite the burning, Julia began to laugh. "They think he's gay?"

"Yeah, a lot of people do."

"Yeah? Does Linda?"

Rudi's eyes pulsed. "He wants that woman for her voice. Anything else he gets is a fringe benefit."

Julia suspected otherwise, but she let Rudi keep his illusions. Sitting there next to her, he looked happier than he had been in months. A few tufts of gray hair were sticking up, and his smile revealed his large front teeth.

"You know we used to work out together?" he said. "Until Norbert— Half the guys at the gym made passes at him. I never knew."

"So does Norbert want you to quit the choir?" asked Julia, her energy returning. "Does he want to ban you from seeing Arno?"

"Yeah, something like that." Rudi sighed. "It's almost an ultimatum. Either I quit Arno, or Norbert quits me. I don't know what to do."

"You almost did quit Arno," said Julia.

"What? Did he tell you?" Rudi drew back.

"No—no—" She faltered. "I heard it. I—I shouldn't have— but I did. Thanks—thank you for doing that."

"Heike said he was going to hit you. I was scared to death. We all were." Rudi frowned into the memory.

"But they sent you."

"Yeah—I guess they thought he'd never kill a tenor." Rudi's front teeth dug into his lower lip.

"Guess they were right." Julia chuckled.

"Hey, did he ever apologize?" asked Rudi.

Julia frowned. That must have been one of Rudi's conditions. "Yeah." She nodded.

"He's a real bastard, isn't he?"

"Yeah, a real asshole." Julia's eyes filled with tears, but she felt an odd pang of relief.

Rudi reached up to stroke her hair. "You know, for someone who doesn't care, he seemed awfully interested in who the father was."

Julia nodded, unable to speak.

"Did you call him?" he asked quietly.

"Yeah." She gulped. "Yeah. He knows I'm here."

"You bet he does." Rudi smiled. "I left him three messages. I'd threaten to quit again, but he doesn't believe me. He knows—" Rudi's voice broke, and he waited to speak. "I know he's in town. He's holed up in his apartment in Mitte. He's composing some music. He gets crazy when he writes—doesn't see anyone for days."

"Yeah." Julia sighed. "Yeah, I can imagine. Listen, I'm gonna call for the nurse. I need to go to the bathroom."

"Okay." Rudi smiled. He pulled out a technical journal with silver pipes on the black cover.

———————————————— ◾ ————————————————

During the next three days, Julia's friends came by in shifts, almost as if they had planned it. Astrid appeared in the morning before her appointment, Marga stopped by when her shift ended, and Rudi visited at night on his way home from the lab. Marga wanted to know when Julia was coming back to work, since her replacement talked about nothing but clothes.

"When my six weeks are up, I guess, if I can find a *Krippe*," answered Julia. She had heard that single mothers had priority for day care but hadn't tried to find a spot.

With Frau Tannen and the nurses hounding her, Julia barely had time to think. Every few hours they weighed Bettina, and if she lost a few grams, they watched Julia nurse and squeezed her breasts. They taught her about burping, diaper changing, and "reading" the baby to see why she was crying. Bettina wailed at all hours, and Julia soon recognized her powerful screams the way she knew her own face in the mirror. Not even Frau Tannen could say why Bettina howled at times when she couldn't be hungry or wet.

"She's just getting used to things," she said. "Sometimes they're like that. She'll settle down soon."

But Bettina quickly became known as the strongest voice on the ward. She seemed happy only with Julia's breast in her mouth. When her tiny lips closed on it, she radiated triumph, as though enjoying a well-earned reward.

Her last afternoon in the hospital, Julia closed her eyes as the baby sucked away. Basti and Astrid had offered to take her home the next morning, but she wondered what she would do after that. Home lay up four long flights of stairs, and the pain between her legs was so bad she could barely walk. If she couldn't leave the baby alone, how was she going to take a shower? How was she going to do anything?

As her thoughts spiraled, she must have dozed off, since her name sounded twice before she opened her eyes. In the doorway stood a woman with wide-spaced dark eyes, a snub nose, and brown hair streaked with gray. She was clutching some yellow flowers, and she smiled hungrily at the baby. Julia held Bettina close, fearing the woman might be crazy.

"Julia!" she exclaimed. "I'm so glad to see you!"

It was no madwoman. It was Renate Kiepert.

9

The People That Walked in Darkness

For a moment Julia could only stare. Since Erik's wedding, Renate's skin had loosened to form drooping pouches under her coffee-brown eyes. Yet for a woman over sixty, Renate looked fresh. Her big upper lip curved youthfully, as though just compressed by a baker's finger. Her white slacks hung loosely over her narrow hips, and a silk scarf with a buckle pattern brightened her navy-blue shirt.

"May I see?" she intoned, as though asking to see a six-year-old's drawing.

Julia clutched Bettina, who was nursing contentedly, as Renate tiptoed in closer. With the baby's face hidden, Renate eyed the pink blanket.

"A little girl?" she asked. "Have you picked out a name?"

"Yeah. Bettina." Julia smiled for the first time.

"Bettina ..." Renate frowned. "Have you thought— Oh, well. Bettina." She sighed.

Julia gazed at the baby and enjoyed the pull of her tiny lips.

"Erik told me you called," said Renate. "He was so excited. He's going be here as soon as he can. He said he knew it was time. He could tell by your voice."

"But how did you know to come here?" asked Julia.

She could barely be civil to Erik's mother after Renate had snubbed her at his wedding. In her coral dress, Renate had flitted past Julia several times before stopping to ask about Berlin. While Julia spoke, Renate's eyes had drifted to Johanna's bright-haired family group. As soon as she could, Erik's mother had slipped away and for the rest of the night had offered only lukewarm smiles.

Renate's eyes cut deep. "Well, Erik told me where you lived, and a nice young girl in your building told me how to get here. I just don't understand why you kept this to yourself for so long."

"Oh, there were reasons," said Julia flatly.

"Well, of course … I can understand that, but you'll be needing help now. Erik and I will be happy to help." Renate's lips quivered with anticipation.

"That's good," answered Julia, keeping her voice low.

Renate asked the nurses to bring a vase for her flowers. Her eyes settled on the two bouquets by Julia's bed.

"I see you've had visitors," she murmured.

Julia raised her chin. "Oh, yeah. I've got lots of help. Bettina already has quite a fan club."

"Well, you may not realize—" Renate aborted her sentence. "I'm glad you have such nice friends. But Erik and I want to help you too. With school in session, I'm just here for today, but in a few weeks, I'll be able to spend more time."

"Oh, yeah?" said Julia.

Bettina stirred. Julia was beginning to understand her signals, and her daughter was saying she had had enough milk. Relaxing her lips against the nipple, the tiny creature turned her head and sniffed the room's stale air.

Renate gasped. "Oh, isn't she beautiful! Just look at that face! She looks just like Erik!"

Julia glanced dubiously at Bettina, whose squirrel-ear features hardly looked human. Yet emanating from this little body were invisible loops that bound her to Erik and his mother. Since her father's death, Julia had moved quite freely, and she found herself in an unfamiliar harness.

"Is Erik coming?" she asked.

"Of course. As soon as he can. He's teaching, and this is the hardest time. But he'll be here soon. May I hold her? Do you mind if I burp her?"

Reluctantly, Julia handed Renate the baby and suppressed a smile as Bettina wailed. Despite Renate's sympathetic noises, the baby screamed like a cement cutter until a nurse came to see what was wrong.

"I think you'd better give her back to her mama," the nurse said.

Renate lowered the baby, and a flush rose against her blue-and-gold scarf.

Back on Julia's breast, Bettina quieted, but Renate stayed until the last train back to Henningsthal. If she changed in Dortmund, she wouldn't get home until eleven, but she said it was worth it to spend time with her grandchild.

The next morning, Julia left the hospital with three bouquets of stiff flowers and Norbert's white bear, which the Turkish boy had relinquished. Astrid and Basti escorted Julia and Bettina to a taxi. The nurses waved goodbye, looking relieved to lose that shattering voice. As glass doors sliced the air, Julia felt the baby stir and shift her head so that she could drink the June breeze.

Julia had practiced walking each day, but nothing could have prepared her for the stairs. Each time she lifted a leg, searing pain tore at her crotch. "We've got to get a fucking elevator," muttered Astrid, shaking her head. She picked up Bettina, who rode surprisingly well against her breast. Basti wrapped his arm around Julia's back until he was supporting most of her weight.

"You can do it," he murmured and gave her a barely perceptible push.

"She's gotta." Astrid snorted. "Come on, honey. Once you're up there, everything'll be okay."

One step at a time, Julia crept upward. She clenched her teeth and felt wetness between her legs. She took comfort in Basti's smoky smell and his unyielding body.

When Julia's door swung open, her apartment looked strange. The empty rooms offered no relief, and she had an odd feeling of having landed in someone else's space. She recognized the baby clothes, carriage, and diapers she had bought, but Bettina had risen in her mind like a mountain range, dividing her memory into lands of before and after. To check the alignment of her baby bed, Basti made Julia lie as she normally slept, but she couldn't remember how. For six months she had been lying on her back or her side, and sleeping facedown didn't feel right. Only her drooping plants spoke of continuous time. Despite her pain, Julia left the baby on the bed and shuffled to the sink for water.

As soon as Bettina left Julia's body, the little one shrieked with rage. She hadn't minded Astrid's breast, but the flat, empty bed appalled her. Julia turned back, pitcher in her hand, and the truth struck her like a resounding chord. For the next few years, everything she did, she was going to have to do with this little thing attached to her. Astrid, who had opened the windows for air, quickly closed them again.

"Here, lemme get that," Astrid said and reached for the dripping pitcher. While Julia comforted the baby, Astrid watered the plants. Basti stalked from room to room to check the doors, outlets, and faucets.

"Mom, watch that table!" he cried, seeing spots quiver on the dark wood.

"Aw, don't be so fussy!" Astrid spluttered. "Geez! Like we have nothin' else to worry about!"

Frowning, Basti wiped the table with a towel. "I'm gonna be on the lookout for a nice entertainment center for you," he said. "And some new shelves. You're gonna be in here a lot, so you might as well have somethin' nice to look at. You've got my number, right? You can call me anytime." He glanced at Julia and ducked his head.

"Thanks," she said.

Basti hesitated in the doorway, his tired eyes full of concern. In his wrinkled blue T-shirt, he looked like a boy longing for bed. His voice and manner belonged to an older man, determined but reluctant to trust. As he shifted his weight from foot to foot, the shadows moved under his angular jaw. He grinned with a self-conscious, boyish smile.

"I'll come by and check on you. I'll be right downstairs. Anytime you need me, you just call."

"Okay." Julia smiled.

Astrid shooed him out. "Such a fussbudget." She sighed. "So I haven't had a chance to tell you!" She brightened.

With the baby squirming against her breast, Julia tried to remember what she hadn't been told.

"My appointment, Monday afternoon!" said Astrid. "There's been so much goin' on, so many people ..."

"Oh, yeah," murmured Julia.

"So anyway, I thought you'd wanna hear about somethin' other than baby puke."

Julia nodded. Envisioning her plants sucking up water, she listened to Astrid's tale.

For her appointment, Astrid had worn a red push-up bra and a gauzy red shirt. When Dr. Kowalski came in, he had been in a lousy mood. Astrid could tell from the way he said her name, "Frau Kunz," like she had herpes instead of a heart condition. Maybe he had had a fight with his wife, who didn't look so thrilled with life either. Kowalski smiled at Astrid as he brushed a red thread on her chest. She told him to blow on it, and he did. He listened to her heart and frowned a bit and then, for the first time, asked her to take off her bra.

"I can't hear you." He smiled. "You're a well-nurtured woman, and I just can't hear you like this."

"So I thought of askin' him how he's been filin' reports on my aortic valve for a year and a half when he can't hear me, but I take off my bra, real sexy-like, and his eyes—he's got the most gorgeous blue eyes—they light up like a little kid's at Christmas."

"No!" Julia laughed deep in her throat.

"Yeah." Astrid grinned. "So with this big smile on his face, he says, 'All right, now, Frau Kunz, let's try this again.' And when that cold metal stethoscope hits me, I freeze up like two raspberries."

"Oh, no!" Julia laughed. Bettina had quieted against her warm, quivering chest.

"And he blushes—have you ever seen a doctor blush?"

Julia thought about it. "No. Never."

"He turns bright pink. He has such blond hair, y'know, such fair skin—he's almost purple. So then he gets all professional and makes this big show of listenin' to my heart. But while he's doin' it, I brush my hand against his, y'know, like you can pretend it's an accident if he doesn't like it, but if he does, he can take it any way he wants."

"So what did he do?" asked Julia, her breath quickening.

"He just looked me in the eye for a minute. That one look said it all. He liked what he saw, but he was scared."

"Well, yeah," said Julia. "If he goes for it and she finds out, it's his practice *and* his marriage. If she gets mad enough—"

"Oh, she'll never find out." Astrid waved her hand disgustedly. "He's way too smart for that. He didn't tell her anything. I know, 'cause she said, 'So we'll see you in two weeks, Frau Kunz?' with that same fake, cheerful voice, just like the ladies whose houses I used to clean."

"Yeah, I know that," muttered Julia. Playfully, she formed the sounds that her mind was hearing. "So we'll see you in two weeks, Frau Kunz? And next time be sure to check under the beds—and the stove—and the refrigerator—and no blow jobs, okay?"

The women erupted in laughter, and the shaking proved too much for Bettina. As she cried out in protest, Astrid pushed herself up.

"I think she needs some peace and quiet," she said.

The door clicked shut, and Astrid's footsteps faded. With the baby crying angrily, Julia was alone.

In the house, people soon learned that Julia had a *Schreikind*, a colicky child with piercing cries. The June heat was searing, and in a world without air-conditioning, Berliners lived with their windows open. Day and night, the house became a multicelled creature in which each cell knew what the others were doing. Flushing toilets and the clinks of dishes made it clear when everyone got up. If anyone watched television, the whole house listened with her. People who fought had twenty witnesses, and even quiet conversations were closely followed. Hearing the moans of lovers, people smiled in their beds and rolled over, thinking of the bodies they longed to hold. Saddest of all were the sharp cries of Frau Riemann, who pleasured herself in the early-morning hours with no idea that she was being heard.

When Bettina screamed, her voice shot off the Vorderhaus walls and gained strength as it ricocheted around the building. Like torture, it lacked a definite pattern and could erupt at any time of day or night. At three in the morning, windows slammed and then reopened as people gasped for air. The whole house cursed Julia for bringing this monster into the world. What was wrong with her? A talent like that, and all she did was get herself knocked up like the dumbest girl in the Kiez.

Alone with Bettina, Julia struggled to do as she had been taught. When the baby cried, she tried to feed her, and if she didn't want milk, she checked her diaper. Thinking Bettina must be too hot, she tried to sponge her down, as she did for herself many times each night. Swollen from the heat, Julia shivered as she ran a sopping-wet washcloth over her body. She walked back and forth and flapped her arms, enjoying the prickly feel as her hairs rose and trickles of water ran down her back. But Bettina hated wetness. Julia tried to fan her, and she didn't like that either. After each nursing, Julia carefully burped her. She tried singing to her, but Bettina screamed louder. She seemed to take Julia's voice as a challenge, an invitation to a noise-making contest. At night, she shrieked with shattering cries that must have evoked violent thoughts in the best-natured tenants.

At the clinic, Julia didn't need to say a word. Nurses heard Bettina's voice for themselves. Used to teenage mothers, they scolded Julia at first, but seeing the baby well fed and dry, they frowned at her chart. Bettina was colicky. With time, her hunger would settle to a pattern, but as summer wore on, none emerged. She slept much of the time but woke up hungry every few hours, sometimes every twenty minutes.

At night, the sun retreated grudgingly at ten and showed its impatient face again at four. Day and night merged into a glowing haze, and Julia resigned herself to her captivity. Bettina fell asleep around six in the evening, then awoke crying at ten, twelve, three, and five. In a dream state, Julia offered her breast, and if this didn't work, she walked Bettina from room to room, jouncing and patting her until she quieted. Julia's eyes had always been good, but at night the blue digits on her stereo turned to fuzz. In Iraq, the Americans had used sleep deprivation as torture in that place where a woman led men on a leash. Now Julia was the prisoner, enslaved by this relentless, screaming invader. She had sunk below the surface of life, and to most people, she was no longer visible.

One night she dreamed she was facedown on a sled, pushing herself through wet grass. Ahead of her, the ground turned soft and wet until she was paddling in warm, black water. Something rough and scaly bumped her from behind. An alligator! She spread her arms and groped for firm ground, but the mud dissolved in her fingers. All around her was inky water, and alligators kept nudging her from behind. Any second now, jaws would close on her legs. She plunged straight ahead into the black water and awoke in drenched sheets with the baby fussing. She had fallen asleep with her breast in Bettina's mouth, and milk leaking from the other one had soaked the bed.

Too tired to think, Julia dozed through the day and spent much of her time looking out the window. She breathed lovingly on her plants and treasured every living leaf of them. In a soft green pool, they underlay her view of the world and became inseparable from her notion of it. Down in the Hof, she watched each movement with fascination. Trash thudding in the bins pulled her to the window, and she quickly learned who dumped garbage when. From the squeaks and plops, she guessed what had fallen, Styrofoam packing or oozing potato peels. She studied the shapes of the bushes holding the bins in a scratchy embrace. Before long she knew which bicycles belonged to whom and which ones had been abandoned. The forgotten bikes filled her with sadness, their wheels warping, their tires fused with the hard ground. She learned when people left and came home, and she knew how some tenants looked naked. At the window with the baby at her breast, she imagined she was a captive princess. Who would have guessed the demon holding her was the tiny thing in the blanket? Staring down at the melting bicycles, she tried to remember her life before Bettina.

Nursing day and night, she paced in the heat and drank a gallon a day. With loyalty that shamed her, Basti kept the crates of water coming. Julia never left her rank apartment, but outside, the world ground on. Dorrie's Donuts and the government wired money to her account, and with her bank card, Basti bought bread and *Wurst*. On the statements he brought, the numbers drew steady breaths: *Kindergeld* in, phone and electricity out. When Basti left, he took out the garbage.

"You can't keep doing this," said Julia one night when he arrived streaming with sweat.

Some obstreperous object had left a gray streak across his white T-shirt.

"That's okay. It's only for a while." Basti smiled, the skin wrinkling around his eyes. "Pretty soon you'll be takin' her out for walks. Then you can bring me things. You'll see."

In those days only Basti's voice reached Julia with all its human fullness. The others were flattened by her phone. The mechanized voices sounded like airy ghosts of pulsing, breathing forms. Still, Julia welcomed the calls, and she ran to interrupt the phone's melody. Unable to face sixteen flights round-trip, Astrid called daily or shouted out her kitchen window. Rudi checked in faithfully but had little to report since the Bartholdy Choir was on summer break. Marga begged Julia to come back to work and urged her to look for a day care center. Renate asked about Bettina's crying, recommended specialists, and reproached Julia when she didn't see them.

Sapped by exhaustion, Julia just sat. Her cells seemed to have lost their uniting bonds. She had given up her voice students, and the thought of selling doughnuts overwhelmed her. When she tried singing now, her voice was breathy and rough, so bad that wedding guests would want a refund. Once, Erik called to say he was coming, and he seemed glad to hear she was doing well. He was thinking of her and had more to say, but he didn't want to say it on the phone.

The phone rang at eleven one night, after a long, torturous Friday. Bettina had refused Julia's breasts and then screamed for hours. Astrid told her of a twenty-two-year-old couple arrested for shaking their baby, and Julia feared she would be next. Eager for any voice, she grabbed the phone but heard only a seashell rush. Then came a hiss of exhaled breath.

"Dad?" she whispered.

Someone choked, then coughed roughly. "No—God, no," said a deep voice. "It's Arno."

Julia's throat stuck. She couldn't make the feeblest sound.

"Julia?"

"Yeah," she said finally.

"I'm sorry. I—" Arno's voice turned to mud, and she hoped he wasn't drunk. "I hear you have a baby girl."

"Yeah," she murmured.

"That's great. I'm sorry I haven't— I've been composing." Arno's voice regained strength. It stuck in places, as though he had been in his apartment all day and hadn't stretched it out. "I—I'm sorry I haven't got anything for you right now. All the choirs are on summer break."

"Oh, that's okay," said Julia. "I'm in no shape to sing anyway."

Arno revived with an angry cough. "What? What do you mean, no shape to sing? You get in shape, you hear? No shape to sing! Fuck that! The only time you're in no shape to sing is when you're dead!"

Julia laughed for the first time in weeks.

"Yeah? That's more like it." Arno chuckled in his lowest register. "Have you got a *Messiah* score?"

Julia squinted at her lower shelves. "Uh … no."

"Well, you tell that tenor friend of yours to get off his ass and buy you one. St. John's, Smith Square, December 11. You're my alto. You can bring your kid if you want, just not in the church, okay?"

"Yeah." Julia smiled.

That night the air turned wet and cool. Bettina slept gently, but Julia lay awake as rain pecked at her window. Like an orchestra, the drops offered a feast of sound, kissing leaves, slapping bins, christening mud. The soft taps aroused her, and as she listened, she wished for a strong, hungry body. She had grown to love Bettina's clinging arms, but she longed for an embrace that would swallow her.

Next morning, Julia called Basti to ask if he would go for a walk. The pain between her legs had faded, but she had only been out twice, each time to go to the clinic. In her mind, the long green stairway outside her door had turned to a mossy cascade. One misstep would send her and Bettina sliding helplessly downward.

At first Basti didn't answer, and she suspected he was busier than he let on. Ever since Herr Stahl, the building's owner, had fired the *Hausmeister* Herr Beck, Basti had become the unofficial superintendent. To save money, the landlord had replaced the hard-drinking old man with a house-management firm that did little but send out letters. In the old days, when your toilet got plugged, you bought Herr Beck a bottle of schnapps, and he blew out the clog in a jiffy. Nowadays, the house-management firm told you to contact the landlord, and Herr Stahl told you to call house management. Instead, most people turned to Basti, who for years had been unclogging drains, oiling hinges, and hanging curtains. People paid him in cash when they had it, and when they didn't, in food, liquor, or cigarettes. Rumor had it, some female tenants offered other compensation, but Julia didn't believe it. Probably people were saying the same thing about her.

Urged on by Astrid, Julia had regained favor in the house. In ninety-degree weather, the tenants' annoyance at having to lug drinks upstairs had turned to rage. Since most people in the neighborhood were schlepping water, the Kiez management association used Julia as a test case. In a formal letter they drew up, she threatened to sue Herr Stahl for forcing an infant to drink leaded water. Unless he replaced the pipes and installed filters in thirty days, she would withhold her rent. The ploy worked so well that within a week, Herr Stahl offered filters for all fifteen apartments. For the tenants, this meant not just ten euros a week saved on water but also relief for their tortured backs. Despite Bettina's wails, Julia became popular. Basti, who installed the filters, had always been a favorite.

When Julia reached him that morning, he promised to come instantly.

"But if she's goin' out, you better put somethin' warm on her," he warned. "It got a lot colder last night."

Bettina smiled as Julia slid her legs into a pair of pink baby pants. Only when Julia heard Basti's steps did she realize she was wearing a saggy gray sweat suit. Blushing, she asked if he could watch Bettina while she changed her clothes.

"Sure." He beamed.

The baby gurgled cheerfully as he counted her fingers and toes.

With the bedroom door closed, Julia undressed as fast as she could. It had been so long since she had cared what she looked like! Her well-rounded body had softened and spread, and she felt flabbier than she had a year ago. Since she had no scale, only her clothes revealed her new size. The dress she had worn with Erik pulled at the waist, and she couldn't zip any of her pants. Finally, she put on some loose-flowing black clothes with a red Guatemalan scarf for color.

"You look great," said Basti, coloring.

It took Julia fifteen more minutes to get ready since she needed diapers, a pacifier, a bottle of breast milk, and a cover in case of rain. Basti took the baby carriage downstairs but ordered Julia not to bring Bettina until he was there to steady her.

When she reached the courtyard, Julia paused to breathe. Sun was boring through the overcast sky, and she turned her face toward the light. Eager for cool, fresh air, people had opened their windows, and a curtain flickered high in the Vorderhaus. A puff of wind carried the smell of burned toast and wet leaves. Tears welled up in Julia's eyes.

"Feels good to get out, huh?" said Basti. He patted her shoulder gently. "Hey, you all right? Pretty soon you'll be doin' this every day. Goin' back to work … You'll see. Hey, come on." Awkwardly, he wrapped his arms around her.

The warm, solid feel of Basti's body made her tears flow faster, and for a moment she clung to him and sobbed. She hadn't realized how lonely she'd felt, chained to a tiny person who couldn't commiserate and who separated her from those who could. Julia raised her head to see Birgit hurrying from the Vorderhaus, a little out of breath.

"Hey, you guys goin' out? Is that Bettina? Can I see?"

Dressed in white capri pants and an indigo blouse, Birgit bent to admire the baby. Basti stepped back with a self-conscious smile, and Julia motioned for Birgit to pick Bettina up. Drunk on the sweet, heavy air, her daughter didn't protest. She stared fascinated at Birgit's brown curls, which had blossomed in the damp.

As they moved toward the gate, Birgit chattered in sweet soprano notes. Julia let the high voice ripple into the background. In the entryway, she tried to read the new graffiti, her eyes drinking a flood of pink scrawls. She lowered her gaze just in time to avoid a glistening pile of dog dung. On Mehringstrasse, she stopped reverently before each window, even though the businesses were truck-rental firms and appliance repair shops. She read the menu of every restaurant on Hildemannstrasse.

"I'll take you here if you want," said Basti. "Both of you—and Bettina too." He scowled at a description of liver, apples, and onions and flexed his fingers in his back pockets.

Birgit paid close attention to Bettina, whose bright eyes followed her brown hair. "She's so beautiful!" she exclaimed. "You must be so happy!"

"Yeah." Julia nodded.

She watched two people slicing sausages at a nearby table. They had the same pinched noses and thick blond hair, and she guessed they were brother and sister. When they looked up, their gray eyes settled on the baby and ignored Julia, Basti, and Birgit.

Basti's phone erupted in tinny arpeggios.

"Yeah," he answered in a deadpan voice. "No kiddin'!" He brightened. "It's oak? You sure? Yeah … yeah … Well, look. Just don't let him know you're interested, see? Don't look at it. Don't go back there no more. Don't let him— Yeah, yeah. I could do that." Basti frowned at his watch. "Look, I'm doin' somethin' pretty important right now. You're sure it's oak? 'Cause if I get down there and— Yeah. Yeah, okay."

"Basti, what's happening?" asked Birgit eagerly.

"That was Sergei at the Treptower Market. Some idiot's sellin' sewin' machines on an oak table."

"You better get down there," said Julia. "Birgit can help me back upstairs."

"Oh, I couldn't do that," said Basti.

"I can help her," said Birgit. "Lemme do it. I'd love to."

Basti looked questioningly at Julia. She could almost hear his heart pound.

"Go get that table," she said. "We'll be all right."

"Okay," he said finally. "If it works out, I'll take you out someplace nice."

"Thanks, Basti." Birgit sighed.

He set off at a dead run. As he disappeared around the corner, Julia smiled to herself. She hadn't seen him so happy in months.

———————————■———————————

A few hours later, the growl of voices drew Julia to her living room window. Down below, Basti and a bald, stocky man were carrying a table across the courtyard. From four stories up, it didn't look like much. It had been painted white, and with large bare patches, it resembled a crazy world map. Through the biggest bald spot ran an inlaid border of dark wood. Basti's tense arms told her the table had value.

Julia stayed at the window and rocked Bettina, who had fallen asleep. During new experiences, she frothed with energy, then quickly crashed from exhaustion. Today the wash of new sensations had apparently done her in. When the two men emerged from the shop, Basti handed his *Kumpel* some money. The bald man thumped Basti's shoulder, then plodded toward the gate.

The old carpenter Herr Seidemann passed him on his way across the yard. In the daytime Basti's friend was often sober, and the urgency in his step said he had had little to drink. It pained Julia to see how thin he looked, with his pinched face and stringy red hair. Since she had last seen him, he seemed to have aged ten years, as though some monster were sapping his life force. Striding toward his unofficial apprentice's workshop, he looked almost like a craftsman again. With one hand on the railing, he swung around the corner, ran down the basement steps, and disappeared.

Climbing the stairs with Birgit had boosted Julia's confidence, and with Bettina sleeping, she yielded to curiosity. Balancing the baby on her hip, she clutched the railing. She eased her way downward step by step until she was inhaling the sharp scent of Basti's workshop. The carpenters' faces brightened when she came in. Basti was squatting beside the table, stroking it with his palm and squinting along its surface. Herr Seidemann came over to admire Bettina, and Julia smelled urine, alcohol, and dirty clothes.

"Now here's somethin' even prettier than this table." He grinned. "Hey, little one!" Seeing Bettina asleep, he damped his voice to a whisper. Basti just smiled, but his easy movements told Julia how pleased he was to see the baby in his shop. In low tones, he went back to the story she had interrupted.

"So Sergei says, 'Yeah, my girlfriend's been askin' for a sewin' machine,' only he doesn't know any more about sewin' machines than he does about opera. So the Bulgarian guy starts showin' him this big one, an' I can see it's a piece of shit—oh, excuse me—"

"That's okay." Julia laughed low and deep.

"So Sergei keeps lookin' at the table, an' I try askin' the guy some things about sewin' machines. But this Bulgarian, he's smart, an' he catches Sergei lookin' at the wood where the paint's scraped off. Meanwhile, I'm tryin' every way I can to get a look at the end grain. I try accidentally droppin' one of those things—whaddaya call those things, you know, with the thread on 'em?"

"Bobbins," said Julia.

"Yeah, wish you were there." Basti sighed. "All I had was Sergei, the genius. So like I was sayin', I try droppin' a bobbin, but it goes bouncin' way the hell off somewhere, an' when I bend down to get it, all I see on the way back up is dirt and paint. It could have been oak, or it could have been some cheap piece of shit—oh, excuse me, I'm sorry. Sergei was right—from those patches on top, it looked like good oak, but you never know."

"Yeah, you gotta see the rings," muttered Herr Seidemann.

"So finally, the Bulgarian looks up at Sergei an' says, 'Maybe you like table, eh? Eez good, *dobro*? You want table? For you, two hundred euros.' So I start laughin', an' we walk away, an' I tell Sergei to stop lookin' at the goddamn table. After a while we come back, an' I make the guy an offer on a sewin' machine—somethin' I know he'll never take. But by now it's gettin' time for the market to close, an' he's startin' to take his stuff off the table. So I give him a hand, an' I drop somethin' on the other side. When I bend down to pick it up, there's a big patch of paint missing, an' I finally get a good look."

"Solid oak," murmured Herr Seidemann, fingering a bald spot. "Standing years, not too far from the center. These boards are over an inch thick."

"Yeah." Basti sighed. "It's a beautiful piece. And an ebony border! That guy was smart, though. I had to carry all his stuff back to the truck. I've gotta bring him a new table next week, an' he still wanted a hundred and fifty euros."

"A hundred and fifty euros!" Julia gasped.

"It's worth ten times that," said Herr Seidemann. "Look at the width of these boards. It's probably all from one tree."

With her free hand, Julia reached out to stroke the table. The wood felt cool and smooth under her fingers, but it was badly gouged. Although the top was straight, it was pitted and soiled, with white paint surrounding bare patches like spilled milk. Enduring mutely, it bore its wounds with dignity, making Julia wonder what it had been through.

"What kind of table is it?" she asked.

Herr Seidemann rubbed behind his ear. "Well, it's too small for a dining table," he said. "I mean, one of those big tables for dinner parties. I don't think it belonged to anyone rich."

"A smaller dining table, right? For a family," suggested Basti.

"Yeah, that sounds right," muttered the old man. He fell silent, his gaze dissolving in the battered surface. He ran his index finger around a bare spot and shook his head. "You're gonna have a hell of a time with the top," he said. "Even if you can get the paint off, if it hasn't sunk in too deep, the ebony runs a quarter inch, max. Some of these dents are deeper than that."

Basti frowned and forced his finger into a wedge-shaped gouge. "Yeah, I'm gonna have to patch it," he muttered. "Geez! Sewin' machines! Who the hell would put sewin' machines on a piece like this?"

Herr Seidemann shrugged. "Table's made to be used. Good, strong, solid oak? Probably he knew it could take the weight."

"How old do you think it is?" asked Julia.

Herr Seidemann squatted and probed the carvings on one leg. "Oh ... I'd say about a hundred and fifty years."

"Wow!" she breathed.

Basti ran his palm over the mottled surface. "It's well made," he said. "Somethin' like this, it'll last a long time. I like things that're well made."

Julia met Basti's eyes and smiled. The electric light had harshened his angular face, distorting it with brilliance and shadows. Against her breast, Bettina sputtered and squirmed. She wanted to nurse, but Julia hesitated to bare her breast in front of the men.

"You guys, I've gotta go," she said.

"I'll come up and check on you," promised Basti.

She left them talking excitedly about which paint remover to use. In their eagerness, they sounded as anxious to see the wood as a pair of teenagers to see a naked girl.

With the baby fussing, Julia struggled to pull herself upstairs. Unaccustomed to her right side, Bettina thrashed and screamed while Julia clung to the railing with her left. In the living room her message light blinked insistently. While she had been talking to Basti, Erik had called.

In a voice that was half laugh, half apology, he said that his school year had ended. His students had finished their *Abitur*, and he would like to come up. She suspected that more than school had delayed him four weeks. Renate hadn't come either, and Julia guessed they had made some kind of deal. The thought of them discussing her made her fume, and she didn't look forward to seeing him.

———— ■ ————

When Erik appeared in the Hof, Julia couldn't help smiling. He had lost some weight, but as he stood talking to Birgit, he still had quite a belly on him. Erik grinned and leaned one arm against his suitcase's long yoke while Birgit laughed and tossed her head. The July sun ate into her brown curls and brightened Erik's soft red hair. Astrid rested her elbows on her windowsill and shook her head disgustedly. She jerked her head toward Erik, and Julia nodded slowly. Great. Now the whole neighborhood would know that Bettina's father was in town. Julia opened the door and listened to him trudge slowly up the stairs.

Erik stared amazed at Bettina, as though every thought had been erased. His eyes widened, and they turned moist and red. With one finger, he reached down to touch her, like a god scared of his creation.

"Wow," he murmured. "Just look at her. She's beautiful." He hugged Julia appreciatively. "She's so little!"

"Oh, she's gonna get bigger." Julia laughed.

At first, she found it impossible to talk to Erik. Her thoughts glided through murky depths, refusing to seek the surface. His bulk squashed her couch, and if she hadn't been in her own apartment, she would have looked for an excuse to leave. Erik's eyes seemed to register the changes since September—dandelions of dust, the cluttered changing table, the garbage bag waiting beside the door. He caught her eye and smiled, then shook his head.

"I'm sorry," he said. "I want to help. God, this is such a mess."

Fascinated, he watched Bettina's mouth pull at her nipple. He admired the baby with warm, dark eyes.

"Gosh," he murmured. "That is so amazing. Reminds you we're really all animals."

"Yeah," said Julia. The sucking aroused her, and it pleased her to feel waves of pleasure without him knowing it.

Erik sighed. "So how are you doing? What can I do to help? Are you— How are you fixed for money?"

"Oh, I'm doing okay," answered Julia. "I've got *Kindergeld*, plus some money for maternity leave from my job—that'll last six weeks."

"Your job?" asked Erik. "You mean singing?"

"No. Dorrie's Donuts." She smiled.

"You're kidding!" He laughed. "Why do you work there?"

Resentment flashed, but she tried to laugh with him. Between those who worked because they had to and those who worked because they wanted to lay a gulf so wide that most attempts to span it failed.

"Oh, I don't know," she said. "The fringe benefits, the great career prospects ..."

Behind Erik's eyes, thoughts drew together as though someone had pulled a string. "So you can't live from singing," he murmured.

"Nobody can—except Shakira and Pavarotti."

"He's dead." Erik laughed.

"Well, there you go," she growled in Basti's low tones.

"So would it help if I gave you some money? I mean, I really should. Renate's been asking me to." Erik twisted his back and resettled each broad thigh.

Julia shrugged. "Sure, if you want. But I'm doing okay. You don't have to unless you want to."

"I'm sure you need help," he said. "I don't know—cooking, cleaning. That sort of thing. You ought to hire somebody."

Julia looked at him blankly. Other than Erik, she had never known anyone who hired people to clean.

"Do you want me to help take care of her—babysit?" he asked. "I don't know how, but I could learn."

Julia exhaled. "Sure, if you feel like it."

"I just—you've got to tell me what to do! I'm trying to do the right thing here!" Erik's eyes burned with frustration. "What do you want? You want me to divorce Johanna? Marry you? Raise the baby together?"

"No!" she cried.

"Look," he said quietly. "I want to declare paternity. If it's okay with you, we could go to a notary. It was Renate's idea, but I want to do it. It would be good for Bettina. If something happened to you ..."

Julia glanced at him sharply. She liked the idea of Bettina having a father on paper, but she resisted her having one in fact. It struck her as a ploy on Renate's part, and she wondered what Renate stood to gain by it.

Erik was looking at Julia anxiously. In his hunger to participate, he seemed to have more than Bettina in mind.

"It's just an idea," he said. "We don't have to do it unless you want to."

"I'll think about it," muttered Julia, wondering what Astrid would say.

Bettina spat out her nipple and began to cry. Julia tried burping her, but she seemed troubled by more than air. Her screams pierced Julia's ears. Erik rose up, frightened.

"My God, what's wrong with her? Should we do something? Should we get a doctor?"

"Oh, she's just colicky," Julia called over Bettina's cries.

In the Vorderhaus, a window banged. Erik pressed his palms to his ears.

"My God, this is horrible!" he cried. "It cuts into your head! Aren't you worried?"

Julia jounced Bettina and grimaced. "Well, I guess we could try changing her."

Erik followed Julia to the changing table. She bared her daughter's fine skin while Bettina screamed, red-faced. Sure enough, her diaper had wrinkled and darkened like a napkin too close to a tea bag.

"Ugh!" Erik gasped.

Julia showed him how to wipe the baby down, and he rubbed her sticky bottom with trembling hands. When he fastened her diaper, he got it too loose, so he pushed it aside and took another. With the wetness gone, Bettina looked up and gurgled with pleasure. Miraculously, her red face cleared and radiated amused delight.

"Wow!" said Erik. "I never saw anything like that. She goes from screaming to smiling just like that! When she's wet, she screams; when she's dry, she's happy—I guess we're all like that, only we're not allowed to show it. I wish I could scream like that."

Julia raised her eyebrows. "Well, just don't try it, okay? I've got enough to deal with here."

"Okay, I'll try." Erik grinned. He glanced at the rejected diaper, and his smile faded.

"Look, I should tell you," he said. "Renate's given me an ultimatum. We've talked a lot about this. She wants me to raise the baby—and to tell Johanna ... I still haven't."

Erik met her eyes, and his voice dipped strangely. "That's why I didn't come until now. If I'd gone away at *Abitur* time, she would have suspected something. Johanna knows I would never do that. But Renate—"

"She didn't tell Johanna, did she?" asked Julia.

"No." He sighed. "But she's going to. I told her I should be the one to do it, and Renate said she would wait until I came to see you. But once I'm back ... if I don't tell Johanna, Renate's going to."

Julia bristled. "What the hell kind of deal is that? Why can't she mind her own business?"

"It is her business," said Erik. "At least she thinks it is."

"How is it her business?" demanded Julia.

Erik held out his hands, fingers spread. "Well, she made me. I helped make Bettina ..."

Julia stifled a stinging reply, but Erik seemed to read it in her face. "Look, I realize I haven't done much until now, but she's dedicated her life to me, and she wants grandchildren."

Julia looked into his anguished eyes, golden brown under a triangle of pimples. "What do you want?" she asked.

Erik gazed back, struggling. "I want everyone to be happy," he said. "For you to sing ... for Johanna to work ... for Bettina to have a good life ... for Renate ..."

"But what if that can't all happen?" asked Julia. "What if you have to choose?"

Erik turned his eyes toward her dusty shelves. "I want to be with Johanna," he said.

Julia swayed silently, rocking the baby. She envisioned her mother's quiet smile. Her own mother would have loved Bettina. She could almost hear her soft voice saying, "A baby? A baby girl?" She would hope that Julia would bring her to Henningsthal, so she could breathe the sweet scent of her curls. Her own mother would never get to know Bettina. Her mother, who had never demanded a thing in her life. Julia's eyes overflowed, and she nuzzled Bettina's sticky head. Erik touched her shoulder.

"I'm sorry. I've hurt you."

"No, no, it's okay," she said. "I was just thinking. You've got to tell Johanna. But you do it, okay? Don't leave it to Renate."

"Okay, I promise," he murmured.

Erik had wanted to go for a walk, but Julia let inertia take hold. On the street, the whole neighborhood would see Erik, and she feared what people might say to him. The summer light burned to a blaze as they talked about what to do. Sensing how badly Julia wanted to work, Erik scanned the yellow pages and made a list of all the nearby day care centers.

"You'll have to visit them all, though," he said. "Ask people."

"Yeah, sure." Julia rocked the sleeping baby.

Around five, Bettina woke up crying, and Julia nursed her and burped her.

"Are you still singing?" Erik asked as Julia walked back and forth, jouncing the baby.

"Well, I'm doing *Messiah* in December. My friend just brought me the score."

"Hey, that's great!" he exclaimed. "But what about now? Are you practicing? Are you singing somewhere?"

"No," she said quietly. "I've tried, but any time I sing, she screams."

The late-afternoon sun had turned Erik's eyes to amber. "You've got to find someplace to practice," he said. "Once she's in day care …"

Bettina cried out, and Erik followed Julia to the changing table. Bettina's diaper was wet again.

"Jesus, it's like Sisyphus," he muttered.

Erik had suggested they go out to dinner, but he had long since abandoned the plan. When Bettina fell asleep, he was glad to eat bread and cheese and watch a reality show about remodeling people's houses. Julia brought out a box of chocolate-covered marshmallows, and one by one the brown puffs disappeared. Julia smiled as she cracked the dark chocolate and sank her teeth into the sticky filling. When the light faded, Julia invited Erik to bed. After everything that had happened, there was no need for him to sleep on the couch.

He nestled comfortably behind her, and his urge filled the crack in her bottom. She sensed he was only responding to her warmth. With each breath, she felt him thinking of Johanna—of how he wanted to touch her long, taut body. Erik's arms were comforting, but Julia knew she didn't want to spend her nights with him. As she spun into sleep, her mother appeared in a rippling gray image. Julia was slapping *Bouletten* when the screams cut her ears. With her eyes closed, she offered the baby her breast.

Erik propped himself up on his elbows. "What time is it?" he asked. "What's wrong? Is she all right?"

Bettina sputtered angrily.

"Yeah," whispered Julia. "She's fine. She's just hungry."

Wearily, she carried Bettina back and forth. Some dark region of her mind knew her apartment so well she could walk in the loose embrace of sleep. Just before she reached her table of plants, Julia opened her eyes. The stereo's blue digits coalesced. 00:38. Outside, stillness had conquered the day. Astrid's window was dark, but a shadow flickered, as though someone had stepped back suddenly. Against Julia's breast, Bettina quieted.

"Is she okay?" whispered Erik as Julia settled.

"Oh, yeah," she murmured.

Under her ear, the mattress creaked with each inhaled breath, a fleeting, dissonant chord.

A scream shattered the darkness.

"Jesus!" Erik bolted up. "What's wrong with her?"

Julia reached for Bettina. "God, I don't know. Hungry. Wet. Sometimes I think she's just lonely."

She picked up the baby less gently this time. In the living room, the stereo said 02:02. Bettina twisted her neck and refused Julia's breast, and her diaper shone pristine in the electric light. Outraged by some unknown offense, Bettina drew in air and forced it through tiny vocal cords with all her might. Julia wished that she could throw the screaming thing out the window. If only it would hurtle off into the black, so that her life could belong to her again. Instead she clutched Bettina tighter and hoped the pressure would silence her cries. Erik appeared in the doorway, puffy and miserable in blue pajamas. From the Vorderhaus, a curse resounded. Julia bounced the furious baby and wished she could grow two more hands to cover her ears.

When Bettina woke again a little past three, Erik tried to comfort her. She would tolerate only Julia's soft body, however, and in suspended time Julia paced the living room. Soon after Bettina quieted, the morning light turned the curtains to sad, glowing squares. Julia ignored them, determined to keep her eyes shut as long as Bettina would let her. The bed rocked, and she guessed that Erik had gotten up. When she wandered groggily into the living room, she found him on the couch reading her *Messiah* score. Next to him lay a yellow cloth wadded with gray fuzz. Erik looked up as though he had come back from far away.

"This is beautiful!" he said. "I'm so glad you're singing this."

He followed her eyes to the dust cloth and smiled. "I dusted your shelves for you," he said. "They really needed it. I—I started to make breakfast, but I didn't know what you like."

Erik's red hair looked as though two small animals had had a fight in it.

"Thanks," said Julia. She kissed the top of his head. Under her lips, his hair was soft and sweet.

Erik slipped back into *Messiah*, but he stopped and looked up at her. "That light," he said. "It was like Zarathustra. I had to get up. Julia …" His broad lips quivered. "As soon as we eat, I'm going back home. I'm going to tell her today."

For breakfast they finished the bread and a jar of Nutella. Erik ran his finger under the rim and sucked it thoughtfully. By seven, the wheels of his suitcase were grinding across the Hof, waking anyone who was still asleep. When he disappeared, Julia glanced at the filthy yellow rag on the couch, and her eyes filled with tears.

■

On a murky July morning a few weeks later, Julia stepped out into the courtyard. The air was heavy and cool, but the gray sky revealed nothing of what the day might bring. Overhead she recognized the kind of clouds that could sit for a week, permitting neither sunlight nor rain.

Hearing a scrape from the cellar, she wheeled Bettina toward the back stairs, though she was due at day care at 7:30 a.m. In a burst of energy, she had called all the centers Erik had found, and one of them, Kinderfreude, had an opening for an infant. As a single mother she had priority, and suddenly she found herself in the world again. For eighty euros a month, negotiated after a careful scrutiny of her earnings, Kinderfreude would take Bettina weekdays from 7:30 a.m. to 1:30 p.m. Julia had to pump milk anytime she could duck into a bathroom, but as she walked through the Charlottenburg streets, the rhythmic movement revived her. Last week she had gone back to Dorrie's Donuts, and she was headed there again this morning.

In the semidarkness of his shop, Basti stood planing his table. Between strokes he checked it with his level, then shook his head and muttered to himself. Hearing Julia's steps, he looked up, startled. Clutching his planer, he smiled warmly at Bettina.

"Wow, you've done a lot," said Julia.

In the past few weeks, the table had changed, though not yet for the better. Basti was taking his time, and with his *Hausmeister* tasks, he couldn't work too often. With painstaking care, he had removed the legs and clamped the top into a rock-solid frame. Stripped of its paint, the bared wood had the rough look of a wet dog. Basti glanced at the level and breathed out hard. He ruffled his hair with his hand.

"This is nice wood, but it's full of dents. Looks like somebody went at it with a hammer. With the ebony, I can't go much deeper, and if I patch it, it's gonna show."

Julia reached down to touch the wood. Under the dust, it felt hard and dense. She could see the boards now, about six inches wide, each with its pattern of tiny brown lines. When she rapped the surface, it answered with a low, muted sound.

"It's beautiful wood, beautiful!" exclaimed Basti. "I have no idea how I'm gonna match it. Hell!" He fingered a gouge that must have haunted his dreams. "Looks like the damn thing had chicken pox!"

Julia laughed and relished the sweet, burnt smell of sawdust. "Where's Herr Seidemann?" she asked. "I haven't seen him in a while. Is he still helping you?"

Basti shook his head disgustedly. "Nah. He was all excited at first, in here every morning. He was givin' me orders like I really *was* his apprentice, an' then one day he just stopped comin'. It's always like that with him. What a waste."

"Yeah." Julia sighed and shifted the baby.

Basti squinted at the table and gave the middle another scrape. His smooth arms flexed over the rough wood.

"But you're still gonna do it, right?" asked Julia. "You're still gonna fix it up?"

"Oh, yeah." He sighed. "Gonna patch it—give it some natural finish—lots of coats. I—I turned down that sanitation job. Everybody thinks I'm crazy. My mom's still mad at me."

Julia waited in silence and watched his shadowed eyes. His throat tightened as he sought for words.

"I just—I go out drinkin' with these BSR guys, an' they're good guys, you know? They tell me, yeah, it stinks, but the pay's good, an' somebody's gotta do it. They tell me when I'm not dumpin' garbage, my time's my own, an' I can do furniture at night an' on weekends."

"That's true," said Julia softly.

"Except that out of all these guys, not one of 'em's doin' anything. Not one of 'em. Nights, weekends, they just all go an' get wasted. Sometime they must have wanted to do somethin'. I mean, nobody *wants* to collect garbage."

"Yeah," said Julia. "But maybe …"

"Nah." Basti shook his head. "Only difference between them an' me is thirty years liftin' cans. I bet once every one of 'em thought he was different."

"Yeah." Julia nodded. "You're right about that."

"So I'll take my two hundred and eighty-one euros a month," said Basti, gripping the tabletop and testing its hold in the frame. "This ain't so bad. I'd rather be a carpenter gettin' called a bum than a bum collectin' a salary."

"Who's calling you a bum?" Julia frowned.

Bettina gurgled and stirred.

"Oh, my mom, for one," he grunted. "Birgit's mom. Not Birgit."

Basti grimaced, his eyes warm with amusement. Frau Schicke's habits were none too regular. What Basti felt for Birgit he didn't say, and so far, Julia had seen no signs of interest. To a guy his age, Birgit's looks must have been tempting, no matter what went on in her head.

"Well, I think you did the right thing," said Julia. "You're the furthest thing from a bum I know."

"Thanks." Basti smiled with flushed cheeks. "Just tell that to my mom, okay?"

"Yeah."

Wide awake, Bettina clutched at her breast.

"I've gotta go," said Julia. "Can I get you anything?"

Basti's smile broadened until she saw his eyeteeth, stained yellow brown from smoking.

"Nah." He shook his head. "I'm good. See you tonight. Maybe then this thing'll look less like swiss cheese."

Julia settled the baby under her blue-checked cover, and the rasping continuo resumed. Bettina raised her chin and inhaled deeply as clean air replaced that of the dusty shop. After a stormy night, she enjoyed the morning, especially if she could go outdoors. The light in her eyes and the crinkles around her nose revealed what interested her and what she liked and disliked. Even wrapped in a blanket, she relished fresh air, and above all, she loved sunlight.

The sky offered little of it today, but as the carriage jolted, Bettina opened her eyes and smiled. The flash of delight warmed Julia, and she beamed back down at her girl. Bettina looked up at her, and for the first time, Julia was sure of what she had sensed. Behind the bright eyes lay a thinking person with a robust will. She wanted to get to know Bettina, to watch her change as she grew. Remembering her nighttime urge to throw her away, she felt a sickening wave of shame. She gripped the rubber handle and eased the carriage over a stony bump in the Hof.

At Kinderfreude, a burly woman greeted her cheerfully. Her good-natured voice surprised Julia, since Bettina had been tagged as a screamer. By law, no facility could reject her for crying, only for having an illness that could infect other children. In a center for thirty kids, crying was the most infectious disease, and many *Krippen* scared off mothers of colicky babies through sheer meanness. Frau Marlies, who was in charge today, seemed instinctively to like Julia. Maybe it was her singing, which the cropped-haired woman revered. Julia suspected the real reason was their bigness, a solidarity among women who couldn't wear the clothes in shop windows. That, and the fact that Bettina's father was nowhere to be seen.

"Oh, she's happy today! Look at that!" Frau Marlies bent over Bettina and grinned. The baby's eyes shone, and her lip wrinkled as she sniffed the strange woman's smell. She stared fascinated at her earrings, which dangled like popcorn kernels from her fleshy ears.

"Yeah, it's the walk," said Julia. "She likes to go out."

"Don't we all." Frau Marlies chuckled.

Julia handed over four bottles of breast milk and parked her carriage in the "lot," a shaded room used for storage. The place seemed well run, and Julia admired its blithe murals. She stepped back to smile at a family of bears carrying grape bunches of bright balloons. With a devilish look, a baby bear was extending a pin toward the blue balloon of his older brother. Even now, in the chaos of arrivals, Frau Marlies and her colleagues had matters well in hand.

With Bettina in her arms, the matron called to Julia, "When're you singing next? I'd like to hear you."

"Oh, not for a while," she said. "December definitely. But I don't know about before then."

Outside, Julia found herself walking with only her purse, a sensation so odd that, at first, she was sure she had forgotten something. The morning air fondled the front of her body, and the people she passed didn't know she had a baby. As she walked, her green top fluttered in the breeze, and her breasts contracted in the morning coolness. Yet as she had noticed last week, no one was looking at her. Her body clung fiercely to the weight it had gained while the forces holding it together had loosened. She felt big in a disorderly way, and it must have shown in her face. Men who passed her on their way to work took no more notice of her than of a parked car. Even the Turkish fruit seller, who watched women as he enjoyed a good meal, glanced her over and went back to his mangoes. By the time she reached Dorrie's Donuts, she was glad to be off the street.

"Oh, thank God!" exclaimed Marga, vibrating from the morning rush.

In the years Julia had worked at Dorrie's, the flow of customers had increased. People grumbled that the American chain had spread like a pink weed, but everyone drank their coffee. Although the neighborhood bakeries offered firmer rolls, Dorrie's sold creamy coffee drinks. With the doors open wide, the sweet-smelling shop lay in wait for anyone headed to work on the Charlottenburg S-Bahn. At a bakery, you drank your coffee and ate your *Brötchen* standing up, and for commuters, eating on the *Bahn* meant a few more minutes of sleep. Julia had tried all the drinks, and they were delicious. Among the regular customers, she was known for her free hand with the whipped cream.

Unhappy about Julia's maternity leave, the manager had eased her return. On weekdays, the store was open from 6:00 a.m. until 8:00 p.m., with two workers handling each seven-hour shift. Since Bettina's day care ran from 7:30 a.m. to 1:30 p.m., swing shift wouldn't work, and 6:00 a.m. was too early. At Marga's suggestion, Julia came in at eight, so that Marga opened alone. Between six and eight she rushed between the coffee machine and toaster, but she would have done anything to get Julia back. Eighteen-year-old Silke, Julia's replacement, spent all her free time tracking new clothes in the chain stores and agonizing over which ones to buy.

Seeing the crowd at the counter, Julia ran to her locker. She had no time to pump milk, and as she pulled on her purple jersey—while she was gone, the color had changed—she checked her milk pads. They clung reassuringly to her distended nipples, which could squirt liquid like protesting squid. Julia smiled as she remembered her maroon velvet dress. The best she could offer customers today was a wet T-shirt.

For two hours she and Marga worked steadily, too busy to think. The red-haired jokester came in with his crew, but he stared at Julia without recognition. His face was pale and swollen, and he looked as though he hadn't laughed in a week. Once he had paid for his coffee, he left, and she watched his blue overalls recede.

By ten, those going to work had long since been there, and those out shopping weren't ready for a break. With the store empty, Julia closed her eyes and leaned back, breathing out in a slow, controlled stream. Marga's voice broke the flow.

"Are you okay? How've you been doing? You get any sleep last night?"

In her purple jersey, Marga looked more waiflike than ever, her skinny arms half the width of the sleeves. She had removed a stud from her nose, leaving a red, wounded spot, and her skin was oily and bumpy. Her black hair had grown so that it started to curl, but it hadn't chosen a direction. Her look of concern had a troubling energy, as though she were ready to fight.

Julia's smile emerged from within. "Oh, a little." She shrugged. "She goes to sleep around six, then wakes up at eleven, twelve, two, three, five ... whenever. Last night was pretty good, nothing between eleven and three. They say she'll settle into a pattern, but she hasn't yet. She can wake up anytime and start screaming."

Marga shook her head. "Yeah, my sister's first one was like that. She just kept crying for no reason."

"There's gotta be a reason," said Julia, reaching for a rag. After the morning rush, she liked to wipe down the tables. "I just wish I knew what it was. I wish she could tell me. I nurse her, burp her, change her, walk her around ... Maybe she doesn't like the dark."

"Sometimes I think they just cry because they can." Marga rubbed a tabletop energetically. The artificial wood resisted coffee well, but several tables wobbled, creating brown puddles.

"No, I think she's trying to tell me something," said Julia. "I feel connected to her. Even here I think about her all the time, as though she were sending me signals."

"Did you give birth to an alien or something?" Marga giggled and glanced back over her shoulder. Her impish face revived Julia's laughter, crushed flat by her ravaged nights.

"Could be," chuckled Julia. "But I can't see an alien entering Erik's body. If I wanted to impregnate a human woman ..."

"Yeah, I'd go for that Bollywood guy, that one with the big nose," said Marga. "What's his name?"

"Something Khan," answered Julia.

"Yeah, or that blond guy, your conductor friend," laughed Marga. "Have you seen him? What's he been doing lately?"

Julia gripped her damp rag and studied the squiggly lines that were supposed to make the plastic look like wood.

"I haven't seen him since the *St. Matthew Passion*," she said. "That was ... gosh, maybe four months ago. He called me once. He didn't sound good. I heard he's composing some music."

"You better call him," said Marga. "Just to let him know you're alive. Tell him you wanna sing again."

Her cadence of words sounded strange. Julia didn't think of singing as something she wanted to do, only as something she did.

"I've got to start practicing," she murmured. "My voice is awful right now."

"So do it," said Marga. "What do you do afternoons after work?"

A flicker of movement pulled Julia's eyes to the street. A Turkish woman was fumbling in the back pocket of her stroller. Her mound of hair swelled her shimmering gray scarf, and green stalks sprouted from her orange grocery bags. With hooting cries, she was calling to her little boy, who had clambered out, demanding a doughnut.

Julia frowned. "Well, I pick up Bettina on the way home," she said. "And once we're there, I can't sing. There's something in the sound that drives her nuts—at least, when I sing full force. She always starts crying."

"Could you get more hours at day care?" asked Marga.

"Well, I'd have to find the money." Julia reflected. "I could do it if I got one of my students back—but they've all found new teachers. And I've got Renate after me …"

"What? Is that bitch still giving you a hard time?" cried Marga. "Shit! I can't believe that!" She squeezed her rag, and her knuckles rose like white mountains across her skinny hand.

During the slow hours last week, Julia had told Marga about Renate, who vehemently opposed day care. Since Julia had entrusted Bettina to Kinderfreude, Erik's mother had been calling to warn about sex abuse, sensory deprivation, and stunted learning. What was the point of giving your child to strangers during the most critical period of her growth so that you could sell doughnuts? Julia protested that this was just a start and that her real goal was singing. But Renate was relentless. To develop creatively, babies needed constant stimulation, and strapped in bed like a Romanian orphan, Bettina was getting no attention. Renate wanted to come up, and only an all-out crisis had kept her away.

As soon as he'd gotten home, Erik had told Johanna about Bettina. He had called Julia right afterward, and his wounded voice haunted her ears.

"She hit me!" He'd marveled. "I mean, I knew it would be bad. She has a right, but … She was screaming at me, and her face got all red, and then she started hitting me—with her fists, punching me—screaming that she was going to kill me, that she was going to kill you—"

Erik had called as soon as Johanna left because he wanted Julia to phone the police. He feared Johanna was going to kill her, and he repeated exactly what Johanna had said so that Julia could tell them at the precinct: "I always knew you'd find some whore since you haven't got the guts to be with a real woman. Well, she'll regret the day she spread her legs for you."

Julia hadn't gone to the police, since she had interpreted Johanna's words quite differently. So far, she'd been right. Rather than hiring a hit man, Johanna had enlisted a lawyer. She had left Erik that night and moved in with a colleague, and for the next decade, Erik probably wouldn't see much of his salary.

In the weeks since Johanna had left, Erik's will had dissolved. He couldn't eat or sleep, and Renate was trying to decide whether to move him to a clinic. When Julia spoke to him, his voice sounded flat. Nothing she said stirred its musicality. Somehow, between calls to lawyers and psychiatrists, Renate had found time to demand that Bettina be removed from day care.

"The bitch backed the wrong horse." Marga cleared a table of crumbs with one swipe.

"Yeah, no kidding," muttered Julia.

Marga shook her head. "My sister has to deal with this kind of shit. You know, when you have a kid, it rips a big hole in your life, and every bitch in the world comes through it. I think that as part of the wedding ceremony, the bride should slit the groom's mother's throat. It would save so much trouble."

"Yeah, but you get it whether you're married or not." Julia reflected.

Marga paused, clutching her rag. "Women her age, they haven't had lives," she said. "They've lived through their kids, and now they want to live through their grandkids. They're all fucking parasites. She doesn't want a daughter-in-law. She wants raw material to make a new little Erik."

"Well, she ended up with a girl." Julia laughed.

"Same difference." Marga shrugged. "She wants you to do the shit work and pass on as little of yourself as possible. When it's time for the cultural polish, she'll move in and take over."

"No, she won't." Julia mopped a pond of coffee that looked like a small brown bear.

"Now you're talkin'," said Marga. "You know what my sister's mother-in-law said? 'I know it's hard to manage, but with a little more willpower ...' Shit, if my sister had a little more willpower, she'd rip that woman's fucking face off. But she never fights back, 'cause she's scared to hurt Jens. Least that's what she says. I think she just doesn't have the balls."

"God, how horrible—to be *trapped* like that!" murmured Julia.

An old woman hesitated in the doorway, then walked slowly to the counter. She studied the loaded baskets with confused hunger. Her wispy hair, beige slacks, and padded shoes were of the same pale shade, and with her limp green hat, she looked like a sun-starved crocus. Julia served her a Black Forest muffin and hot chocolate, to which she gave an extra puff of whipped cream.

"So what about you?" she asked Marga when the woman had left. "You had any good gigs lately?"

"Oh, a few." Marga frowned. "It's hard, though. There're so many bands in Berlin. The clubs will let you play, but most of 'em won't pay you. It's depressing to have to play for nothing."

"Yeah, I know what you mean," muttered Julia.

"We need some new material. Hey, you can help me. I've got this new idea for a song."

"Yeah?" Julia brightened.

"Yeah, yeah. Remember when I told you about Nils?"

Nils. Who was Nils? Julia studied the doughnuts pushing forward in their baskets. In their eagerness to be sold, each pressed its round belly into its neighbor's back until she could almost hear them sigh. Again, she sensed the changing landscape of her mind, where Bettina had risen in a molten burst.

"You know. The guy who threw me out at two in the morning."

"Oh, yeah." Julia nodded.

"Well, I want to do a song called 'Across the Floor.'"

Marga sang the guitar line, playing chords on the table like Arno. Against Julia's memory of his hands, Marga's fingers moved like spiders' threads in front of thick brown sailors' ropes. Julia wondered what Arno was working on this morning.

"Hey! Hey!" called Marga.

Julia realized she had fallen into a dream, as she so often did after nights of sleepwalking.

"C'mon! What rhymes with floor?"

"Door," said Julia.

"And out the door!"

Marga leaped up and shimmied, shaking her tiny breasts to an electric guitar solo only she could hear. With her spare body, she didn't have much to shake. In her oversized shirt, she moved with the energy of an ocelot trapped in a tent.

"Okay, so what else?" She panted.

"Whore!" Julia chortled.

"God, that's good!" Marga stopped in midmove. "You no-'count whore!"

"Suppose—suppose you do it from the guy's point of view," said Julia. "You know. He wants her out. He wants to make a clean sweep—"

"Oh, it was a clean sweep all right!" Marga laughed in her lowest tones. "That's what gave me the idea. His floor was a mess. I don't think he ever cleaned it, and when he dragged me across it, all this dirt collected under my butt—grit, dust balls, all these hard, sharp little things—"

"God, that's great!" Julia's laugh penetrated to her core. "Suppose you call it 'Gonna Mop My Floor.' The guy wants to clean up his life, and he starts by mopping the floor with his girlfriend's ass."

"Oh, man, I love it!" cried Marga. She reached for a stiff brown napkin. She seized a pen and began to write, tossing her hips from side to side. With her left hand, she pressed chords into the counter, then stopped to record them over the phrases. Julia bit into an apple-cinnamon doughnut and felt a rush of delight as cool filling dripped between her fingers.

Hours later, she heard Marga's melody as she walked down Wilmersdorferstrasse. She smiled at a window of indigo dresses and felt the song emerge with each exhaled breath.

"Gonna mop my floor!"

Her throat hadn't felt this open since Christmas. For the first time in as long as she could remember, Julia wanted to sing.

10

He Was Despised

The school year, not the clinic, brought Erik around. In mid-August the new term began, and color bloomed in his voice. As he talked about his sixteen-year-olds learning counterpoint, the singsong quality returned. Like a crushed thing, his voice sat up and shook itself, trying to recover its lost fullness.

With Erik coping, Renate announced that she would come up, this time with her husband, Horst. They wanted to visit their grandchild, and next weekend seemed like the best time.

When Astrid heard of the visit, she offered to help Julia clean.

"Gee, I hate to go through all that just for her," said Julia.

"You gotta." Astrid blew smoke at the ceiling. "You can't let her get you on that."

Next morning, she stood panting at Julia's door with a blue bucket of cleansers and sprays. The gray streaks under her eyes looked like tire tracks, but her teeth caught her lip in a broad smile. Working systematically, she and Julia scrubbed through the rooms. The vacuum cleaner frightened Bettina, so they took turns holding her.

"This place ain't so bad," said Astrid as she wiped the bolts on the toilet. "When you got men around, they shed hairs all over. Plus they piss on the floor. Once I had to work for this Italian guy, and it was hell on earth. He had practic'ly no hair on his head, but from the neck down, he was a gorilla. Every week I went through a pack of dust cloths, and I still had my hands full of hair."

Julia laughed and fondled Bettina, who was sucking away energetically. In turquoise gloves, Astrid's hands rubbed the toilet's white curves with masterful efficiency. She gripped the porcelain in a determined embrace, looking happier than she had in weeks. In her last two visits, Kowalski had treated her with sober, professional distance.

"As though I was just anyone!" she moaned.

Julia thought he was scared and had been urging Astrid to give him more space.

"So when's your next appointment?" she asked.

"Oh, a week from Monday."

With one strong arm on the toilet seat, Astrid pushed herself up. "Whew!" She reached for the wall with outstretched fingers. With her eyes shut tight, she rested her forehead against the tiles.

"Hey, are you okay?" asked Julia.

"Oh, yeah." Astrid shook her head. "Circulation."

She looked sharply at the shower curtain rod and pushed the stiff white curtain to one side. She ran a cotton pad along the top and held it out to Julia. A gray smear defiled the fluffy white round.

"See that?" she asked triumphantly. "That's the first place they look. Things up high, things you wouldn't think about. That, and down low. Under the beds."

Astrid moved on to the bedroom, where Julia helped her dust. From the open windows, fine black powder had settled onto every surface. Perched on a chair, Astrid called for a fresh cloth to wipe the wardrobe top.

"Oh, come on! She'll never look up there!" Julia laughed.

"Oh, you'd be surprised," said Astrid, squinching the corner of her mouth. "I worked for a few that were too frail to clean, but when it came to checking up on me, they were athletes."

Astrid finished by washing the windows.

"They really notice those," she said. "One streak, and they're on you."

While Bettina slept, Astrid and Julia rubbed the encrusted panels and dropped blackened paper towels on the floor. To clean the living room window, they shifted the table of plants, and Astrid paused as she gripped its carved edges.

"Boy, he sure did a nice job on this," she murmured, pressing her thumb into the floral border. Glowing like chestnuts, the rounded petals looked alive under her tobacco-stained fingers.

"Yeah, he's really good." Julia sighed. "I can't believe he can't find an apprenticeship."

"Oh, it's got nothin' to do with bein' good." Astrid snorted. "It's all luck. Just timing. He shoulda taken that sanitation job."

"He thought it was a dead end," said Julia. "It would have used up all his energy."

Astrid breathed out hard. "I don't think the electric company could use up all his energy. He gets up at five. Runs around all over the city. Just so long as he doesn't have any left for that little slut in the Vorderhaus."

Julia smiled. With school out, Birgit visited the workshop each day, displaying gauzy tops and snug jeans she had bought with her friends. When she ran into Julia, she begged to hold Bettina and asked when Erik was coming back. Sometimes Julia admired her clothes, and excitedly, Birgit told their stories. A blue-green blouse had started at the Potsdamer Platz Bella for €32.90 in March, then had dropped to €19.90 by July and €14.90 by August, except that by then all they had was extra small.

"Figures," said Julia.

"But then, but *then*," exclaimed Birgit, her blue eyes brightening, "I found a large at the Alexandria Bella hanging in *totally the wrong place*—for only €9.90!"

"Wow," said Julia.

Birgit filled her top admirably, and with two loops of green bangles against her chest, she must have inspired fantasies. What Basti felt for Birgit remained a mystery. As he varnished his table, he listened patiently to her tales of the hunt and banished her only when he needed to concentrate.

"Oh, I wouldn't worry. She's back in school now," Julia told Astrid.

"Learnin' what, how to give a guy a hard-on?" Her neighbor grunted.

Julia's laugh turned to a cough as she inhaled ammonia.

"Hey, you're usin' too much!" cried Astrid. "It'll streak!"

Stretching, she wiped the window from top to bottom with expert strokes.

"Hey, who's that?" asked Julia.

A familiar, stocky man was crossing the Hof, followed by a short, round couple she hadn't seen before. Though it was eighty degrees, the little man was wearing a fine gray suit, and the woman, tight jeans and a long-sleeved white blouse.

"Oh, those must be the people comin' to see the table," said Astrid.

"What people?" asked Julia.

"Russians," mumbled Astrid. "Somebody who knows somebody from the Treptower Market."

"Let's go see!" exclaimed Julia.

With passion that exceeded Birgit's, she had been following the restoration of the oak table. She couldn't bear the thought of it being sold without a chance to say goodbye. Gently she picked up Bettina, and she and Astrid slipped down to the shop.

After hours of cleaning, Julia relished the cool air and the scent of varnish, burnt sawdust, and sweat. Basti was negotiating intently with his visitors. Under the electric light, Julia recognized the heavyset man who had brought the table six weeks ago. He must be Sergei, since he was trying to translate, but Basti, who knew some Russian, was preempting him. Fingering the table, the woman kept her eyes on Basti and spoke in a hard, shrill voice. She struck the wood, and her frothy sleeve slid down over her long red nails. Impatiently, she pushed the gauzy white back up again. She sized up Astrid and Julia with one quick smirk and turned back to the men.

"*Dub?*" she asked, rapping the table. She squinted at the side to check the end grain. Standing behind her, her husband followed her movements with shadowed eyes.

"*Da. Dub. Dobro,*" said Basti.

With a wave of his arm, he invited her to inspect it, and she squatted so suddenly Julia wondered whether her jeans would hold. She twisted herself sideways to examine the underside, and her gold sandals ground the sawdust. When she stood, her curls were askew, and she squinted fiercely at Basti. She held one palm flat in the air and jabbed it with a poppy-red nail. Basti shrugged as a stream of Russian splattered him.

"Sure, it was dented!" he cried. "Sure, I had to patch it! You shoulda seen it before! It's a hundred-and-fifty-year-old table! You want a new one, go to Ikea!"

Shining in the darkness, the table stood solidly on rounded legs. In six weeks, Basti had worked a near miracle. Honey colored with reddish-brown lines, the table's surface looked good enough to lick. The inlaid ebony beckoned like dark chocolate. Under the new varnish, the wood glowed so beautifully Julia wished she could wear a piece of it around her neck.

The Russian woman whispered to her husband, who grunted and shrugged.

"Five hundred," said Sergei.

Basti laughed. "*Dub? Pyatsot?* Are you kiddin' me? I don't need to sell this. I'll eat off it myself!"

The Russian man stepped forward until the table bit his paunch, and he ran his fingertips along the grain. He said something to Sergei, but Basti shook his head.

"Two thousand. That's my price."

The husband blew out his breath, and the woman laughed loudly, jabbing her hand and glaring at Basti. The Russian man spoke again.

"A thousand," said Sergei.

"Two thousand. *Dve tysyachi!*" Basti held up two scarred brown fingers.

The woman shook her head, but her curls didn't move. With a disgusted look, her husband threw up his hands, and they turned to leave. Sergei looked desperately at Basti, who stood impassively with folded arms.

"Geez!" said Astrid when they had disappeared. "What's wrong with you? A thousand euros!"

"It's worth two thousand," said Basti. "I worked on it six weeks."

"Who were they anyway?" asked his mother.

The stairs creaked. On the top step, the well-dressed husband sang out a rounded phrase.

"Fifteen hundred," said Sergei.

Basti ran his fingers gently over the table. He raised his eyes to the Russian and nodded. "*Da.*"

The man called to his wife, who smiled her way down the steps. Basti shook her hand, and a change in her curves showed how much she enjoyed his grip. Amazingly, the flood of Russian didn't wake Bettina. Julia had always loved the sound of that language, nasal and melodic with sudden halts in unexpected spots. With one last sideways glance at Astrid and Julia, the woman walked out while her husband peeled off three five-hundred-euro bills. Basti folded them and put them in his shirt pocket. He and Sergei carried the table up the steps, and its tilted surface shot off a few last gleams of light.

"Geez!" Astrid gasped.

Julia stared at the place where the table had stood.

Basti tramped down the stairs, shaking his head. "Sergei's takin' them and the table to the Hotel Adler. Y'know, I bet they're payin' more for one night in that place than—"

"C'mon! Fifteen hundred euros!" exclaimed Astrid. "You never made that much! Not even for a wardrobe!"

"Aw, she'll probably just use it to put her makeup on," said Basti.

Astrid fondled his shoulder. "It ain't big enough for her makeup."

The following Saturday, Horst and Renate Kiepert walked through the green gate into the Hof. Under Julia's window, they leaned together, and Renate pointed toward the dumpsters. Her short gray-brown hair curled against her blue blouse, and her white capri pants sheathed her slender thighs. Horst was heavier, in light pants and a beige vest full of pockets. After a look around, they disappeared into the entryway.

Julia waited in the doorway, baby on her hip, and listened to their unmatched rhythms as they climbed. At the sight of Bettina, Horst smiled with delight and blew kisses over Renate's shoulder.

"Hi!" said Julia. "Come on in."

She offered them water, then gave them a quick tour. Horst glanced through the rooms to be polite, but Renate's eyes mapped the space like security cameras. Julia was glad that she and Astrid had put in all those hours cleaning.

"Those stairs must keep you in shape." Renate smiled. She sipped water from a six-sided glass.

Julia offered Bettina to Horst, who took her awkwardly and grinned with pleasure.

"I guess you have quite a view, though," said Renate, watching her husband mistrustfully.

Bettina twisted and whimpered.

"Here, let me take her," said Renate.

On her lean blue shoulder, Bettina quieted, then spat up a sticky puddle. Julia swallowed a laugh as Renate twisted her head to check the damage. If the blouse was silk, it could be considerable.

"Here, let me get you a rag for that," said Julia.

Balancing Bettina on her hip, she sponged Renate's shoulder. The wet material had turned purple against her skin, and a few strands of hair clung together in damp spikes. Uneasily, Renate settled back onto the couch. Julia cradled the baby against her breast.

"Erik tells me you're singing," said Renate. *"Messiah?* In London?"

"Yes, that's very nice," murmured Horst.

"Yeah," said Julia. "That'll be in December. I'd like to find something before that, though."

"What about the opera?" asked Renate. "Do you sing there much?"

"Not yet." Julia smiled. "I'd like to, but it's complicated. My friend who helps me—"

"But why don't you go down there?" Renate broke in. "Ask them to set up an audition? It's so close by." She and Horst had walked from their hotel near the Deutsche Oper, where they had tickets for *Tosca* that night.

"Sure, it wouldn't hurt." Horst watched Bettina search for Julia's breast.

"Well, it isn't easy," said Julia. "There are so many good singers. You have to approach them the right way. You can't just walk in there—"

"But why don't you try?" asked Renate. "It would be so much better than that doughnut place. You could spend more time with Bettina. You could come down and see Erik."

"Sure, if that's what he wants," said Julia. Bettina's mouth tickled her pleasantly.

"He always has such a good time with you." Renate smiled. "He used to come home so happy—back in the days when you both took music. These past few years, it's just been awful for him."

"Yeah, he's had a rough time," muttered Horst. He studied the crease of his clean beige pants, then raised his eyes to the west window.

"What a nice table of plants you have there!" exclaimed Renate. She rubbed a fuzzy leaf between her thumb and finger as though it were the ear of some small animal. Her eyes shifted to the thriving bushes in the Hof.

"Would you like to go out?" she continued. "Horst and I thought we could go see the Berggruen Collection. They have a new Cezanne, and it's just down the street."

In rippling murmurs, she and Horst conversed while Julia gathered diapers, pacifiers, and disposable wipes. Horst waved a digital camera.

"You haven't sent us any pictures," said Renate, "so we thought we'd take a few. We could go to the Charlottenburg Gardens. You're so lucky to live near such a beautiful place."

Bettina stretched as she breathed fresh air, and Julia watched her register the new voices. Day by day, her curly-headed daughter was gaining awareness. She still screamed at all hours, but she was beginning to enjoy life. On their walks through the neighborhood, she exercised her young senses, and she fell asleep blissfully when she had drunk her fill. In her likes and dislikes, she was becoming a unique person.

The gray woman at the museum admissions desk glanced dubiously at Bettina. Sure enough, the unfamiliar sounds and smells proved too much for her. Before Renate could locate the Cezanne, Bettina was howling red-faced, and Julia had to take her out. While Horst and Renate studied the paintings, Julia paced the sidewalk, gazing at the yellow palace across the street. Even at this distance, its lemon dome seemed remote, threatening to dissolve into a puff of moths.

For lunch Julia suggested the Café Mehring, close and comforting with its panels of dark wood. She ordered half a chicken with crispy fries, but before her food came, she had to carry Bettina outside. Twice the baby quieted, and Julia tried to eat, but Bettina screamed so piercingly that Julia leaped up with her mouth full. Studying the palace's long, still wings, she wished that she could park her daughter the way you parked a car. If she could just eat one meal, just have one conversation, even with Renate and Horst! Confidently, Bettina nuzzled her breast, sure of her right to Julia's body. Julia pushed through the café door with a rough shove, and Bettina cried out angrily.

In the Charlottenburg Gardens, the heat shimmered in waves. The half-chewed food lay heavy in Julia's stomach. She followed Horst and Renate past an unmoving parade of red, yellow, and purple flowers. The still bursts of color hypnotized her, holding her eyes like an unfulfilled promise. Renate turned to admire the yellow palace, which hung behind them like a mirage.

Horst focused his silver camera carefully on Bettina and took a picture. He pressed a button and squinted at the image. "Oh, yeah, that's nice," he murmured.

In the afternoon sunlight, the brilliant yellows seemed to pulse. Daggers of red stabbed clusters of blue. A delicate, bitter scent aroused Julia, and she started as she recalled the last time she had smelled it.

"Is something wrong?" asked Renate.

"Oh, I was thinking about singing," said Julia. "There's someone I need to call."

———————————— ■ ————————————

As soon as the Kieperts left Sunday afternoon, Julia telephoned Rudi. While Renate had droned about Erik as a boy, Julia had been starting to plan. Like Erik, Norbert had to be back for the new school year, and he and Rudi had returned from the Greek Isles. Late August meant the end of *Chorpausen*, and next week the Bartholdy Choir would start rehearsing *Messiah*. Julia planned to ask Rudi if she could sing at his place since she no longer had access to a practice room. The keyboard she had bought her first year at the Breithaus Academy clunked like a little child's xylophone.

A curved black piano formed the centerpiece of Rudi and Norbert's apartment in Friedenau. If Julia left work at one, she could reach their apartment by two and sing for an hour before she picked up Bettina. How to pay for those three extra hours of day care would be a more complicated matter. If she got a gig or if Erik lent her some money … Before Julia called Rudi, she left a message for the minister at the Johanneskirche, saying her maternity leave had ended and she could sing weddings again.

Rudi sounded overjoyed to hear Julia's voice and told her to come by next Saturday. She found him tan, a little balder, and antsier than ever. While Bettina slept, he showed her pictures of him and Norbert posing next to white stone ruins and brilliant sprays of pink flowers.

Lined with books from floor to ceiling, Rudi's living room looked like a library, except for the black piano dominating the space. With glossy confidence, it stood on the blue Persian rug as though the room existed solely for its sake. The tall windows looked out on a wooded square, where playing children laughed and shrieked. From Norbert's study came the sound of books and papers shuffling, but he didn't come out to greet Julia. When Bettina whimpered, he closed the door.

Rudi offered to play for Julia, and he took her up and down some midrange scales. Her rough, breathy voice frightened her at first, but Rudi offered her water and made her continue. Slowly her throat recognized the shapes of the notes, as though hugging lovers she hadn't felt in years. The low C was broad, sweet, and open; the A, bright, shiny, and clear. When Bettina protested, Julia bounced her gently and sang over her rising whine.

"Let's try your arias!" cried Rudi. He ran to a bookcase for his *Messiah* score.

Rudi began with his favorite piece, "He Was Despised." He played with soft grace, offering a carpet of notes against which Julia sang. She was still trying to quiet Bettina. When Julia struggled with the words, Rudi joined in and guided her through the strange English sounds. The rich alto aria was an unexpected gift for his finely spun tenor voice. Together, he and Julia slid from G down to B-flat: "A man of sorrows …"

The long, slow movement hovered in the heart of her range, offering phrases like chocolates in a box. When she sang of people's contempt for Jesus, her voice would throb naked in the dark, answered only by faint breaths from the strings. Rudi had said the aria was a favorite of Arno's, and she tried to understand why. Arno loved intensity, and he took things at kick-ass speed. In this song about suffering, the phrases were oddly separated, and without continuity, they didn't build momentum as they might have. To please Rudi, she kept the phrases coming. He was having so much fun with the whiplash chords.

"He gave his back to the smiters, and his cheeks to them that plucked off the hair," she sang.

Her voice dissolved into giggles. "What? Did they shave him?"

"Oh, come on!" Rudi glared and smashed out a G-major chord.

To humor him, Julia swallowed her laughter and sang, "He hid not his face from shame and spitting." Rudi pulled her through the entire aria, even the da capo repeat. He played the last E-flat chord with a haunted touch. He had to cough before he could speak.

"This is going to be beautiful," he said softly. "Arno was right. He always is. You've got a lot of work to do, but your voice was made for this."

Against Julia's breast, Bettina had quieted. "How's he doing?" she asked.

Rudi glanced nervously toward the study door.

"Better, I think," he murmured. "He's been composing all summer. Some big, powerful thing for full orchestra. He gets so isolated when he's writing. Sometimes I call him just to keep him sane. And then I see him sometimes. But you don't know that, okay? The deal is, I have no contact with him except for rehearsals. This London thing—I don't know how we're going to work that."

"Oh, it'll work out," said Julia.

She leaned into him and stroked his shoulder. Rudi closed his eyes and stretched his neck, rubbing the back of his head against her breast.

■

For Julia, the three extra hours each day made the difference between existing and living. With Norbert's approval, Rudi gave her a key, and in the empty, sunlit room, she closed the windows and sang full strength. At first, she had the eerie, guilty feel of haunting someone else's space. Rudi's apartment had an odd, spicy smell, and Julia tiptoed from room to room, sniffed the cakes of sandalwood soap, and stroked the brown plaid comforter. The Persian carpets shuddered under her steps, and she paused to study their designs. On the living room floor, bursts of flowers pushed against six soft frames and winced at the piano's sharp feet. Three walls were filled entirely with books, and she dizzied herself trying to read the highest titles. Except for her textbooks from the Hans Breithaus Academy, Julia hardly owned any. When she wasn't working, she played with Bettina, talked to friends, or listened to music.

Alone at the piano, Julia plunged into her arias, singing for two or three measures and checking to see where she had landed. If the piano contradicted her voice, she repeated the phrase determinedly. She pondered every odd interval until its strangeness dissolved. "He Was Despised" came easily enough, though she wished it would move along faster. Cheerful and melodious, "O Thou That Tellest Good Tidings to Zion" swung along like a cow on her way to pasture. In her throat, "Behold, a Virgin Shall Conceive" resonated like the words of a canny midwife. She had no doubt that her duet with Linda, "He Shall Feed His Flock," would be liquid joy. She could hear her voice flow toward Linda's light, clear F like a current warming a cool stream.

Julia and Rudi worked together on the fast-paced duet "O, Death, Where Is Thy Sting?" Built on contrasts, it raced along like a lovers' quarrel, with both singers crying out at once. They gestured and grimaced as they cut in and out, but they couldn't wreck the duet even when they hammed it up. Rudi reminded her how much fun it was to create a world with her voice. Julia also sensed that the music was helping him escape the sadness holding him in its grip. Adamantly, he refused to talk about his troubles and insisted they spend each minute singing.

Of all the arias, only one daunted her, and that was "Refiner's Fire." Its bursts of notes defied every sense, and she had an idea how fast Arno would take it. The solo opened easily enough, with a strong, sad melody. "But who may abide the day of his coming?" asked the alto. Unlike Bach, Handel had used no Evangelist. He let the soloists tell the story of Christ, and he had a gift for turning sensations to sound. After the first slow section, fire flared out in a roar as the strings shot tongues of flame. The transition always shocked the audience, and her voice had to guide them through it. At a pace so fast the notes barely sounded, she would have to slide down four crazy scales. She could hardly catch her breath before some broken arpeggios, D minor and A7 in alternating blows. Without pausing, she had to rush down another slope insane in its choice of intervals. For relief, "Who may abide?" returned, but then came more fire, and the second time, it was worse. In the last section, she had to run through six measures of arpeggios, leaping from A7 to D minor. For a singer, Handel had created the fire of God's judgment. He had entrusted life and death to an alto.

At the Hans Breithaus Academy, they had joked about Bach, who gave altos the leftover notes in his harmonies after he had written melodic lines for the others. One female teacher had been sure Bach's mother-in-law was an alto and he had written descending major sevenths to torture her. Usually altos sang about motherhood, weeping, and mourning. "Behold, a Virgin Shall Conceive" was standard fare. Arias about the wrath of God went to tenors and basses. It was their job to scare the shit out of everyone. But after writing a simpler version of "Refiner's Fire" for a bass, Handel had transformed it for a virtuoso male alto. Arno thought Julia could sing it just as well, and he was taking the choir to London to show her off.

Since Arno knew she could create the flames, Julia had no doubt. She began by imagining Handel's runs as individual, living bodies. Each phrase formed part of a musical whole yet maintained its own personality. The slamming arpeggios became Muhammad Ali and Mike Tyson, striking with A7 and D minor fists. The four descending scales turned into John, Paul, George, and Ringo, since each moved with a different flair. The toughest scale, the one after the first four arpeggios, Julia named "Motherfucker." In its fearful intervals she heard the cry of a person falling into hell.

At first Julia left *Messiah* in Rudi's apartment, but by mid-September, she took it out with her. Under her breath, she hummed its melodies while Bettina slept, and she ran through the Beatles scales on the U-Bahn. When there were no customers, she performed for Marga and balconies of doughnuts listening in their baskets. Late at night, she sang with her daughter in her arms when every window in the house was dark.

In three months, Bettina had found no sleeping pattern. Julia felt encouraged when her daughter slept three hours, but the next night she was up every forty-five minutes. Julia's nights became a Tantalus torture in which sleep was snatched away just as she touched its velvet surface. When Bettina's cries stabbed her, she wished she could awaken from this mother nightmare to the tranquility of her old life. Instead, relentless yells ripped her dreams, and the nightmare became reality. How wonderful it had been, just to work and sing! Why hadn't she appreciated it? Swimming through days between sleeping and waking, Julia stopped caring what she looked like. All that mattered was keeping the baby fed and changed, getting to work on time, and learning her music.

It did please Julia to watch Bettina grow. Almost every day brought a surprise. Her features settled, and her eyes darkened until at moments Julia saw her own face looking back at her. Bettina's eyes mirrored Erik's, but her nose was Julia's—and that of Julia's father. Her piercing cries cut Julia's ears, but she and Bettina were learning each other's signals. A certain shadow in her daughter's eyes meant that she wanted her diaper changed, and a focused glance meant she was trying to interpret something. Bettina loved nursing, fresh air, and sunlight, and she resisted unfamiliar sounds and smells. When Julia burped her, she dribbled sticky white liquid onto her shoulder, so that some of her hair was always crusted.

Bettina spent much of her life in day care, but she never got sick. Every few days Renate called to talk about Erik's illnesses and warned Julia to check whether Bettina pulled her ears when she cried, which could mean an infection. Renate found Bettina's health astonishing since she spent her days in a germy sea. The curly-haired baby exuded health and demanded milk, bouncing, and fondling.

In October, Julia's spirits rose when the minister asked her to sing a wedding. A round, good-natured couple wanted her to perform the love theme from *Titanic*. Rudi hooted when she practiced, but she told him that for €200, she would sing the love theme from *Shrek*. After the ceremony, the brown-haired bride thanked Julia tearfully. The girl's father compared Julia to Celine Dion.

"You should be on the radio," he rumbled. "You're way better than her. The way you do it, it's got more oomph to it."

After the wedding, Julia began meeting with Arno. At first, he fumed when she said she couldn't come at night, but after long harangues with Rudi, he agreed to work from two to three in the afternoon. The first time she saw him, he grasped her in a violent hug and clasped her back with open fingers. Arno had lost weight, and his face felt like a dried cactus against her cheek. He stepped back, breathing fast, and his ardent blue eyes narrowed.

"Have you been okay?" he asked. "You look tired."

"Sure, I'm okay," said Julia. "Can we sing? Let's sing."

Arno sat at the piano, and against the white keys, his wrists were twice the width of Rudi's. He frowned at Julia's first notes, but as her throat opened, he relaxed.

"More!" he called. "Give me more! Put your gut into it! More sound!"

It took several sessions before Julia tapped the power he wanted, in a state where the volume increased as she relaxed. When the notes came from her center, she had to dampen the sound, or she would have blown him off the bench.

"Yeah!" cried Arno without breaking rhythm. "*Jawohl!* Wide open! I want you wide open!"

By the end of November, even Arno was satisfied. Singing day and night, Julia had resurrected her voice, so that it sounded richer than it had a year ago. Rudi, who had booked seventy-five people's flights, bought her a ticket for 9:00 a.m. Friday morning, December 11. The downbeat would be at 8:00 p.m. that night. Rudi, Arno, and the others had flown the day before, but they were letting her arrive late. For the past few days, she had been pumping milk and giving it to Astrid, who would watch Bettina until Saturday afternoon.

At day care, Frau Marlies greeted Julia with a frown.

"I'd keep an eye on her if I were you," she said. "She's been spitting up a bit. And she's been quiet. They all slept. We didn't know what to do with ourselves."

Julia studied Bettina under the white pool of each streetlight. She lay still, unmoved by the rattles of trucks and the whiff of burnt crust from a pizzeria. At home she nursed eagerly, and as her little mouth pulled, Julia mentally reviewed her packed suitcase. Her marked score lay under her maroon velvet dress, which Arno had requested and a Serbian seamstress had let out with a genius comparable to Handel's.

Bettina released Julia's nipple, and she eased the baby onto her shoulder and patted her warm back. Julia reached for a cloth to soak up the dribble, but before she could catch it, a geyser of milk burst from Bettina's mouth. Lukewarm streams ran down Julia's back. Fearing Bettina might choke, Julia laid her on the couch and braced herself for a shriek. But even when Bettina lay on the blanket, she didn't cry. Her brown eyes looked up, bewildered. Julia cleaned her carefully and checked her diaper, which was dry. Reluctant to put her to bed, she walked up and down slowly. She thought of calling her pediatrician, wiry Frau Kielmeyer, but by now her office would be closed.

Julia had ordered a taxi for 6:00 a.m., and she planned to give Bettina to Astrid just before that. At ten, Bettina grimaced with a familiar, irritated look and cried out in angry whimpers. Relieved, Julia put her to bed and lay down beside her, but with Handel's scales in her head, she couldn't sleep. Note by note, she hummed through Motherfucker, which she still hadn't mastered and was going to have to fake.

At four Julia awoke with a cry, bursting out of a dream that she forgot instantly. Beside her, Bettina was sleeping peacefully. She had never slept for six hours. Julia gathered her up and snapped on the light. She smiled with relief when Bettina's face screwed up and she screamed with rage. Her voice didn't have its usual piercing quality, and somehow, her body felt limp. When Julia opened her diaper, it was dry.

Julia offered her nipple, and Bettina seemed more than happy to drink. When she finished, Julia watched her and held her breath. Bettina raised her chin, swallowed once, and gurgled. Julia followed each ripple of her daughter's lips and throat. Bettina sighed, twisted her head, and spat out a river that drenched Julia's nightgown. Terrified, she telephoned Astrid.

"Jesus!" Astrid growled. "Is it time already? Did I oversleep?"

"No, no, it's early." Julia's voice broke. "Listen, I think she's sick. I don't know what to do. I don't think I can go."

"Oh, yeah?" Astrid's voice focused quickly. "What's she doin'? Throwin' up? I've seen that before. I can deal with that. You should go."

"Yeah?" asked Julia miserably. She mopped Bettina's face with her sleeve.

"Yeah, sure. If anything happens, I'll just take her to a doctor. I can do that. You get ready."

Julia threw her nightgown into the hamper and wiped herself down, unwilling to leave Bettina long enough to shower. She put on the clothes she had laid out for the trip, her nicest pair of black pants and a red sweater. On her bed, Bettina was resting quietly. Julia looked into the bag she had prepared for Astrid with diapers, toys, and wipes. It was ten to six. Even though Bettina was still, Julia laid her out one more time to check her diaper. It was still dry. Bettina opened her eyes and looked up, frightened.

With the baby on one arm and both bags in the other, Julia ran down the stairs. The taxi was waiting outside the gate. Seeing the tears on her face, the driver took her bags hurriedly.

"Where to, miss?" he asked.

"The West Side clinic," said Julia. "The emergency room."

———————————◼———————————

From the hospital lobby, Julia called Arno at seven. The gray-haired nurse glanced at her disgustedly as she slipped out. In a steel crib, an electric octopus was feeding Bettina fluids, its limp arms holding her without love. Under Bettina's flattened curls, her eyes were closed, and Julia longed for them to open. She would have welcomed even a reproachful look, any sign of the bond that now ruled her life.

Julia's *Handy* cropped voices as a zookeeper clips wings, but Arno's uneven rhythm expressed his confusion. He sounded disoriented, as though he hadn't slept, and he seemed not to know who was calling. The alarm in Julia's voice helped him recognize its tones.

"What is it? Where are you?" he snapped.

"I—I'm at the West Side clinic," she said. "Arno—Bettina's sick. I can't come."

She had expected an explosion, but there was only silence. "Arno?" she whispered.

"Yeah." He sighed. "Yeah. You're—you're at the clinic? She's in the hospital?"

"Yeah—" She faltered. "She—she's very sick. I'm scared."

"Sorry." Arno's voice deepened. "Julia, I'm sorry."

There was some static, then a long exhaled breath. Probably he had lit a cigarette. As the silence lengthened, Julia's stomach wrenched. Finally she spoke.

"I can't leave her." Her voice wavered. "I just can't leave her. I'm telling you, so—so you can find someone else. Can you? Can you get— Because I just can't leave her!"

"Right," murmured Arno. "Find someone else. Fuck!"

She heard a clunk and guessed he had kicked something over.

"I'm sorry," she whispered. "I don't know what else to do."

Arno seemed not to hear. "Find someone else. To sing *Messiah*."

His sarcasm sickened her, but it was useless to fire back. Arno's mind had disengaged. Scanning his memory, he was seeking another voice, one as close as possible to hers.

"Someone in the choir?" she suggested, and the explosion came.

"Of course I can find someone!" he roared. "Of course I can! But it won't be you! It won't be you!"

Arno's rage roused a voice she had forgotten she had. "Look— my daughter may be dying! Fuck *Messiah*! I'm tired of saying I'm fucking sorry!"

As fast as it had emerged, her Henningsthal voice drowned in tears. From London came dead silence, not even a breath.

"Take care of your daughter," said Arno tightly. "I'll find another singer."

He hung up with a curse.

Astrid came in a taxi as soon as Julia called, and all day long, they sat by the steel crib. Astrid urged Julia to eat, but she couldn't. At nine, eight London time, she pulled out her score and heard the music as she flipped through the pages. She imagined Rudi straining in the front row and Udo smiling as he rushed through the flames. And Arno's hands, white against the darkness. She saw Arno's hands. In each measure she pictured his broad, blunt fingers showing her the sounds he wanted to hear. At her entrances they beckoned, begging her to sing. Glancing from her score to Bettina, Julia breathed out slowly. At ten, a doctor told her Bettina was out of danger. The choir would just be starting the slow minor dance "Behold the Lamb of God."

Longing to breathe, Julia stepped out the next gray afternoon and found five messages from Rudi. To learn about Bettina, he had called three times Friday night and then again that morning. The last call had come twenty minutes ago. In his morning message, he had said his flight home was at two and that he would check in again that night. Why wasn't he up in the air? Julia bit her lip and jabbed the tiny keys, canceling twice when she hit the wrong numbers.

Rudi's tenor came in with perfect clarity. "Julia—has Arno called you?" he asked.

"No," she said. "I haven't heard from him since I told him. How mad is he?"

"Oh, he's mad," answered Rudi. Stripped of its gentleness, his voice moved briskly.

"So what happened? What's going on?" asked Julia, her stomach tightening.

"He's disappeared," said Rudi.

"Oh, come on," she scoffed. "He's just off somewhere. He'll be back when he's ready."

"No, this is different!" Rudi's voice rose. "He—I'd better tell you what happened."

"Okay." She kicked the concrete walk with her toes.

"Well—it was bad," said Rudi. "Not terrible, no major fuckups—God, I'm starting to sound like him—but ... just ordinary. It's the first thing I've sung with him that felt that way."

"Oh no," murmured Julia, her heart accelerating. "Who did he—"

"He gave 'Refiner's Fire' to Michael, and Linda did 'Feed His Flock' alone. For the other arias, he got a girl from the choir. I don't think you know her—Sabine, a first-year student from the Hans Breithaus Academy."

"Jesus," Julia breathed.

"Well, who was he going to get?" demanded Rudi. "She did a damned good job too, no major mistakes, just … faint. She sang every note, but she was scared to death. And he didn't help her. He treated her like—"

"That doesn't sound so bad," said Julia. "I mean, considering—"

"That wasn't it," he broke in. "There were lots of things. Michael was all over the road on 'Refiner's Fire.' You can't blame him. He's done it before, but he— Linda was the problem. She's fed up. Arno didn't say anything, but I think she's dumped him. She sang fine. Everybody sang fine—but there was no passion to it. There was no point. Afterward we all went out drinking—he drank a lot. Then he didn't show up at breakfast this morning. We had to go, and I couldn't find him anywhere. I—I couldn't get on the plane. He's not answering his phone. They let me into his room, and his stuff's still there."

Julia reached for a concrete pillar, cold and dusty against her palm. "Where—where—" she gasped.

"It's awful," said Rudi. "I called Norbert, and he says this is it. He was already mad about my staying overnight with him. He says if I stay here now instead of flying back when I said I would, there's no point in coming back at all. But I—I—oh, God!"

Seven hundred miles away, Rudi broke into sobs.

"Find him!" whispered Julia fiercely. "Find him! Stay there as long as you have to, but find him!"

11

A Great Light

Arno turned up around six the next night, sober, stubbly, and hungry. After talking to Julia, Rudi had gone to the police, but they couldn't file a missing person's report until Arno had been gone forty-eight hours. Rudi said a bristly old bobby had listened sympathetically, but he'd guessed the disappointed conductor was out on a bender.

"Don't worry, sir. He'll be back soon," he'd reassured Rudi, who had spent a sleepless night clutching Arno's *Messiah* score.

Turned away by the bobbies, Rudi had carefully packed Arno's things, then moved to a cheaper hotel. Late Sunday, Arno found Rudi's message at the Meridian and an hour later was crushing him in a smoky hug. Arno wouldn't talk about where he had been for two days, and Rudi wouldn't say what passed between them that night. By Monday evening, they were back in Berlin rehearsing the Christmas song, "Über's Gebirg Maria geht."

The next week, Rudi called Julia often and asked about Bettina in tense tones. She heard that he cared, but he was calling from hell. Norbert was evicting him, and they were living the hideous, slow-motion crash in which a well-run machine crumpled to scrap. Despite Julia's pleas, Rudi wouldn't let her see him until he had found a furnished studio in Steglitz. Probably he wanted to protect her from the pain, which she guessed was acute. Not given to displays of emotion, Norbert had concealed the cutting edge of his anger, and once unsheathed, it must have inflicted deadly wounds.

At least she could tell Rudi that Bettina was fine. The gastrointestinal virus had sapped her, and the doctors scolded Julia for not bringing her in sooner. After a day of fluids, she was sucking as though wanting to make up for lost time and terrorizing the nurses with her screams.

"Geez! I liked her better when she was sick!" called Astrid through her kitchen window.

"Yeah, it'll take more than a virus to do her in!" Julia yelled back.

She nuzzled Bettina's fuzzy head and wondered what life would be like without her. From her daughter's brown curls rose a warm, honey smell that spiraled into her consciousness. Bettina could have died—that was what the doctor kept saying: "We might have lost her." In the hospital, his words had echoed through the halls as Julia fled outside to phone Rudi. "What if I just keep walking?" she had wondered—back to the days when she could go where she wanted, back to the days when she could sing. She longed for the time when she was just herself, not the mother of this hungry, noisy thing. In London, no one would have said her arias sounded faint. The trouble was, she couldn't get there. Feeling her daughter's weight, she wondered where else she couldn't go, what else she wouldn't be able to do. How long would it be before Arno stopped calling? Little Sabine Buchholz didn't have the guts for "Refiner's Fire," but someday someone would. In the murky morning, Julia dared to think it: What if Bettina just weren't there?

Still, her daughter's recovery moved Julia in a way that nothing had before. Inhaling her scent, Julia sensed Bettina's toughness, and her eyes filled with tears. She was proud of her girl's powerful voice and her voracious appetite. Slowly, she pressed her lips into Bettina's hair and savored its warm sweetness.

The Saturday before Christmas, Bettina had recovered enough to go out, so Julia took her to visit Rudi. As she settled the pillow on her daughter's breast, Bettina looked up, questioning. From the glassy new shopping center on Walther-Schreiber-Platz, Julia pushed her carriage west into gray residential streets. Rudi's new building lay on a diagonal intersection, where cars waited impatiently on their way to the shops.

Five stories high, Rudi's apartment house varied from soft pink to light brown. A coating of grime made it hard to determine the original color. Up top, the expensive flats had arched windows and curved balconies fenced by white wrought iron webs. Down in the Hof, some birch trees rose from a hollow waiting to be filled by spring daffodils. Rudi's apartment faced the busy street to the west, so that the swish of traffic penetrated the hall window.

When Rudi opened his door, Julia tried not to look shocked. The skin of his face had loosened, and with smoky circles under his eyes, he looked years older. He had dropped weight he couldn't afford to lose, and his oatmeal sweater hung on him. His broad smile, cleft by two large teeth, seemed not to belong on his face. His real feelings came through in a passionate hug that lasted until Bettina began to whimper.

With his usual energy, Rudi showed Julia his apartment, designed for foreign businessmen on short stays. The room had white walls, gray carpet, and stiff blue drapes that looked as though they had been disinfected recently. One corner with a sink and some cabinets served as a kitchen, and in the gleaming white bathroom, Julia could touch both walls. In a nook fenced by shelves lay a bed so narrow she doubted she could fit into it. Rudi did, but its taut gray blanket made her think he didn't spend much time there. Across from the bed was a desk with a built-in shelf, on which stood a picture of Rudi and Arno.

Against a background of haze, the two were grinning, cheek to cheek. Someone must have taken the photo on the Vienna tour, since the yellow honeycomb of Schönbrunn Palace was visible beside Arno's ear. The narrow, dark-eyed face and the round, blue-eyed one couldn't have been more different, except that both were beaming with happiness.

"Great picture, huh?" said Rudi. "Heike took it. We were all kidding around that day. I'm glad I can finally put it up."

"You got a nice frame for it," said Julia. She fingered the Greek key pattern that circled Arno and Rudi like a golden chain.

"Yeah." Rudi sighed. Too quickly, his smile returned. "Would you like some tea? I got you some *Lebkuchen*."

Julia settled into a chair and parked Bettina's carriage close beside her. As long as her daughter stayed in her familiar cocoon, the new surroundings were less likely to bother her. Bettina's eyes opened, and her nose twitched a few times, but Julia doubted the space would offend her. Rudi's apartment smelled like nothing. She had never seen any place so clean.

"Is peppermint okay?" he called over his shoulder.

"Yeah, sure, that's my favorite," she said.

Against the legato of running water came staccato cracks of cellophane. The sight of six Lebkuchen on a white plate—a complete set, two chocolate, two glazed, and two plain—made Julia's eyes well up with tears. Rudi must have bought them especially for her since he hadn't even opened the package. At her place, a pack of Lebkuchen never lasted a day, usually not more than a few hours. As Rudi filled her plain white cup, she reached for a chocolate cookie.

"So you're doing okay?" she asked. "How have you been?"

Rudi's bright smile shone again. "Oh, pretty well," he said. "This place is great. I'm closer to work now, and I can stay as late as I want. Nobody—" His voice faltered.

Julia reached for his hand. "You did the right thing," she said. "Things couldn't go on like they were. Something had to happen."

Rudi looked into his cup and closed his eyes. He massaged his forehead with thin fingers. Julia bit her Lebkuchen and savored the bitter chocolate against the soft, spicy inside. She longed to ask what Norbert had said, since Rudi's pain might lose force if he could describe it. Uncertain whether he could stand to tell her, she chewed as quietly as she could.

"I miss Norbert." He sighed. "In spite of everything, I miss him. He was so—so *civilized*." Rudi smiled, enjoying a memory.

Julia nodded. "You guys were together a long time."

"Yeah, fifteen years," he murmured. "We can't separate our things. Except for our clothes ... The books, the CDs, the kitchen stuff ... neither one of us knows who owns what."

Julia wondered how Rudi was doing financially. The spacious apartment with the grand piano belonged to Norbert, who came from a family with money. Without fighting, Norbert would probably see to it that his household remained intact. Julia suspected that Rudi would never see more than his clothes and the computer he had carried out with him.

"Is he giving you a hard time?" she asked.

Rudi rubbed his forehead. "Oh, he could if he wanted to. He's the injured party. But that's Norbert. He never fights over material things. He's not vindictive. He just told me he couldn't stand being someone's second choice anymore. He's right. Things only got bad when he tried to make me admit it."

"Admit what?" asked Julia. She didn't like the sound of this.

Rudi smiled ruefully. "Oh, that for the past six years, every time he touched me, I was wishing it was a big blond guy with the manners of a tyrannosaurus."

"Oh, God." Julia imagined the soft, insistent accusations. "So what did you tell him?"

"The truth!" Rudi's voice rose. Julia glanced at Bettina, whose eyes had caught him. "I love them in different ways. I love them both. But I don't think I've ever thought about Arno when—" Rudi's voice broke, and he swallowed a mouthful of pain. "At any rate, he didn't believe me. He said he won't play second fiddle to someone's adolescent crush. He's worth more than that."

"It's not an adolescent crush!" exclaimed Julia. "You guys work together. You've never— Norbert's the one acting like an adolescent!"

Faint and timid, Rudi's smile looked real for the first time. "You want to call him up and tell him that?"

"Ba!" said Bettina.

Under her moon snail canopy, she stared, bright-eyed.

"Wow, is she talking?" asked Rudi. He reached for a plain Lebkuchen.

"Nah, it's too early," said Julia. "But she will be before long. She's making all kinds of sounds."

Rudi sniffed his cookie dubiously and bit it. His delicate smile shone again.

"So how's the object of your adolescent crush?" she asked. "Has he told you anything more about London?"

Rudi shook his head vigorously. "No, not since that night. He told me he felt like walking, so he followed the river. All this red brick, so dark, so cold—then some really bad neighborhoods. He said something about some Jamaicans ..." Rudi glanced toward the window as a bus shuddered by. "When he came back, he was starving, so we went out, and he ate this huge steak. Then he wanted to sleep ..." Rudi met her eyes and shrugged. "That's it. In the morning we went to Stansted and got a flight home."

The quick shifts of his eyes made Julia sure he was concealing something, but she didn't want to grill him. Rudi took another bite of cookie and looked up, ashamed.

"You know, when Norbert asked me to leave, that night after the rehearsal, I called Arno." Rudi's gaze settled on her face. "I called him, and I asked him if I could stay with him for a while. He told me to come over, and I did. We talked all night. I asked him if I could live with him."

"What did he say?" Julia breathed. Her voice had dissolved.

"He said no." Rudi smiled and tried to imitate the voice an octave deeper. "C'mon. You know that wouldn't work."

Imagining Arno's reaction, Julia smiled back. "Could you live with that smoke?" she asked.

Rudi laughed. "You know, I never even thought of that?"

Julia squeezed his hand. He tried another bite of his cookie.

"We spent most of the night talking about music," he said. "He played me some of what he's been composing. It's beautiful. D minor, really haunting, a lot of work in the strings ... He wants the Philharmonie to play it, but he doesn't want Handshaw to conduct."

"Oh, that's good. How's that gonna work?" quipped Julia.

In the melody of Rudi's laughter, she thought she heard his old self.

"Ba!" cried Bettina insistently.

Lately, her curiosity about the world had grown into a determination to join it. Sounds caught her interest, and when voices reached a certain pitch, she gleefully added her own. Seeing that she felt left out, Julia scooped her up and rocked her against her breast. Bettina smiled, and Julia grinned back at her. While she played with the baby, Rudi opened his desk drawer.

"I can't believe I forgot to show you this," he said.

It was a short article in English dated the Monday after the concert. "Middling *Messiah* at St. John's, Smith Square," ran the title. Reading English was easier than speaking it, but Julia struggled. She sounded out the words as Bettina squirmed on her lap:

On Friday evening the Berlin Bartholdy Choir and Orchestra delivered a passable performance of Handel's *Messiah*, a disappointment after the recent achievements of this ensemble directed by Arno Weber. Known for his fast tempi and impulsive style, Weber is emerging as one of Germany's most exciting young choral conductors. While this performance affirmed his artistry, it also confirmed some doubts that have been raised about his artistic choices. The fast pace at which he took the early arias proved too much for Michael Tiller, whose powerful voice lacked its usual control. From Linda Larson, whose ethereal soprano has awed New York audiences, he drew an uninspired performance. The weakest link in the chain was the young alto, Sabine Buchholz, who replaced Julia Martens and, despite a laudable effort, was unprepared for a performance of this caliber. One can find no fault with the choir or orchestra, who performed admirably under Weber's direction.

Given his recent virtuoso performances of Bach and Mendelssohn, one wonders why Weber chose Handel's *Messiah* and why he wished to perform it in London. For the talents of this group, Bach's *Christmas Oratorio* would have been a wiser choice. Except for the Americans, Weber's singers seemed uncomfortable with the English text, and their pronunciation—

"Oh, shit." Julia looked up at Rudi, who had stopped smiling. "This is terrible. Has he seen this?"

"Yeah." Rudi sighed. He picked up the last bit of his cookie, looked at it, and put it back down again.

"Why did he pick Sabine?" asked Julia. "Why not Carola? She has a beautiful voice."

"Carola hasn't come back yet," said Rudi. "I'm not sure she will. Sabine's a crack reader, and—well, she sounds a little like you. She doesn't have your guts, though. He must have known that, but he took a chance. He would have done anything to get that sound."

Julia nodded sadly. "And that guy thought the English was bad?"

Rudi shrugged. "Well, you know what his English is like."

"Yeah," she said softly.

With lyrics in German, Arno made his singers repeat each phrase until every consonant clicked. Julia remembered him excoriating the basses for singing, "Brich dem Hungrigen dein Boot"—"Break your boat for the hungry."

"*Nicht dein Boot!* Jesus! *Brot! Brot!* What do you, have—"

As always in rehearsals, Arno cut himself off before a four-letter word passed his lips. Sloppy German provoked him to rage, but with English, unsure how it was supposed to sound, he might have been more lax.

"He made me take him through that review word by word," said Rudi. "He made me go online and check the dictionary. We googled the guy who wrote it. He's not one of the main *London Times* music critics. Some up-and-coming guy, I think. Then after—"

"Is Arno going to do something?" she cut in.

Seeing that Bettina wanted to nurse, she raised her sweater with trembling hands.

"No, no, I thought he was going to blow up, but he got very quiet. God, it's so wonderful to talk about him like this, to think about him!" Rudi beamed with energy. "I feel so clean now—not having to hide it. I can remember him saying things, I can picture him, and I don't have to feel ashamed." He gazed fondly around the small gray room. "It's been awful—but at least I have that. I can think of him whenever I want."

Julia wondered how often Arno thought about her and Rudi. She said nothing, but he followed her mind.

"He's been asking about you," he said. "I know he's thinking of you."

"So he doesn't blame me?" asked Julia. "You know, this was really all—"

"No, it wasn't!" Rudi looked at her fiercely. "Did you make her sick? Was it your idea? Things like this happen all the time. He should have been ready."

That was what had been puzzling Julia: why Arno, who attended to every detail, had had no plan B. She looked questioningly at Rudi, but his mind had returned to London and the night he had only half described.

"As I was saying, when he finally understood the review, he got very quiet," said Rudi. "'You know,' he said, 'every word that guy wrote is true.'"

Bettina paused, then went back to her sucking.

"That doesn't sound like him," said Julia. "What's going on?"

"I don't know," said Rudi. "He's changing so fast."

"So he's not going to kill the guy?" She smiled.

"No." Rudi shook his head. "He wants us to sing it again."

Unlike Norbert, Johanna spent all her rage in one burst. It wasn't that she forgave Erik—it was more as though he wasn't worth fighting. Why he could laugh, he still couldn't say. But by spring he was giggling in his calls to Julia as he described his students' efforts to write a three-part fugue.

Erik didn't visit Julia often, since he was setting himself up in a new place. As she expected, the breakup had left him broke. Johanna had proved less vindictive than Julia had thought, but the woman was no fool. Since Erik could prove no infidelity on her part, she had emerged as the victim, with rights to their car, their condo, and most of their assets. To avoid a long fight, Erik gave her whatever she wanted, but what she wanted was to eject him from her life. Instead of demanding high alimony, she had taken what she could and kept communications minimal. In a way, said Erik, it was almost a relief. He had sensed her contempt as an underground river, and when the ground finally collapsed, he knew what had been happening under his feet.

There was something beautiful about starting over—finding your own place, filling it with furniture you chose yourself. To save money, Erik had wanted a small apartment, but Renate had insisted he rent a three-bedroom flat with a sunny guest room for Bettina. Usually Renate occupied this room herself, since she spent most of her weekends in Frankfurt. For the time being, she was paying most of the rent. You learned a lot about life, said Erik, when the worst occurred and you had to let people take care of you. It wasn't nearly as bad as you'd think.

In June, when Bettina took her first steps, Erik was still with Renate in Frankfurt. Bettina had been crawling since March, and one afternoon, she used the couch to pull herself up. Julia called

Basti, who rushed up to cheer her on. Even more than Astrid, he loved Bettina's reddish-brown curls and her determined squint. That day she clung to the blue-sprigged blanket and frowned from her new upright perspective. Within a week, she was lurching across the room to Julia, who knelt and called her with open arms.

As Bettina grew, her face changed from minute to minute, resembling everyone who had gone into her making. Her wide-set brown eyes looked a lot like Erik's or maybe more like Renate's. When she concentrated as hard as she could, Bettina frowned just like Horst. While staring, intrigued, at some new object, she got Erik's schoolteacher look. When she screwed up her face and screamed full strength, Julia recognized her own nose and mouth. She rarely saw signs of her mother's pinched face, since Bettina almost never looked fearful. Instead, some perverse sculptor had molded her father's fleshy features on her daughter's fine face. Bettina's playful laugh reincarnated his love of fun.

With her penetrating voice and relentless curiosity, Bettina was a child you couldn't ignore. She learned to talk early by watching people's responses to her broadening repertoire of sounds. Seeing that "Mama!" brought Julia running, she sang the phrase whenever she wanted help. Astrid beamed with pleasure when Bettina piped "Assi!" And "Bassi!" made the young carpenter blush. Astrid said it must have been the schoolteacher genes that made Bettina so fond of her own voice. Seeing Bettina's sparks of pleasure at their responses, Julia thought her daughter was a scientist, experimenting on everyone around her.

With her *Kindergeld* and twenty-five hours a week at Dorrie's, Julia could barely get by. She asked the minister at the Johanneskirche to spread the word she was available for weddings, but she was competing with hundreds of other singers. Through Rudi, she heard about Arno's doings. He was seeking an orchestra to perform his piece, which he kept remolding obsessively. In

October he was taking the Bartholdy Choir to Prague, but he had asked Dagmar Schleifer to sing since the alto solos vibrated with coloratura. Rudi insisted that Arno wasn't mad at her—Julia's voice just wasn't right for the pieces he had chosen. When she tried to reach Arno, he wouldn't call her back, and she guessed his anger ran deeper than Rudi knew.

At Julia's urging, Rudi rented a bigger apartment in Steglitz, where he could unpack the books Norbert had sent. Within days Rudi's shelves filled with stripes of color and brightened his life with rainbow smiles. He bought a keyboard that could mimic twenty-seven instruments, but he complained the keys sank under his fingers. On a respectable piano, the keys fought back, each demanding a special touch to release its tone. From the workout Rudi gave that silver keyboard, Julia knew he loved playing it—when he could find the time. Each morning at seven thirty, he left for the lab, and unless he had a rehearsal, he stayed until midnight. At work, he spent much of his time planning the Prague tour: changing hotel reservations, haggling with the railroad, trying to communicate with Czech technical crews. Physically he looked better, but Julia worried. Rudi wasn't someone who could live alone, and many men might take advantage.

She spent most afternoons in Rudi's book-lined space, where she experimented with his keyboard and sang. Sometimes she wasn't sure what to practice, since she didn't have even one gig. At Renate's urging, she had written to all three Berlin opera companies and asked for an audition as a choral singer. What made the once divided city so good for musicians, Arno joked, was that there were at least two of everything: two orchestras, three operas, and several hundred choirs. But the three operas quickly replied that they had no openings; they would contact her when they did. She advertised for pupils and got a few responses, but most people wanted voice lessons at night. The two she eventually took answered signs that

Basti and Birgit had hung in local markets. On Thursdays she taught Bärbel, a lusty, tone-deaf woman who reserved 80 of her 347 euros a month for her dream of learning to sing.

Besides the keyboard, Rudi had an extraordinary collection of music, and he taught Julia how to download what he didn't own. Scores bloomed from his color printer, and she worked her way systematically through Bach's arias. Some days she pulled out *Messiah* and slid through its treacherous runs. Just the sight of the score made her heart beat faster, and sometimes she clapped it shut in midphrase. Although she maintained her range, her voice had a thick, pudding-like quality. From her womb to her lips, she felt like an engine forced to run on congested streets when it was longing for the autobahn.

That Christmas, for the first time since she had come to Berlin, Julia had no singing engagements. For the *Christmas Oratorio*, the Bach Choir had booked Sasha Neumann, and for the Bartholdy Choir's *Magnificat*, Arno had chosen a younger singer. The *Magnificat*'s alto solos demanded mastery, but they were short, and two of the three were duets. Always on the lookout for new talent, Arno had given the part to a Korean student with a sweet, rich, liquid voice. It would be a while before he offered anything to Sabine Buchholz again. Arno said he would do it the day she grew balls.

For Christmas, Erik invited Julia down to Frankfurt as a special housewarming for his new place. It was Bettina's first train ride, and she stared fascinated at the rain-drenched fields whose furrows converged in elusive points. When she grew used to the brown lines whipping past, she started kicking the seat. She squirmed and whined through most of the four-hour ride despite Julia's efforts to keep her busy.

Erik's apartment smelled of fresh, clean wood. The guest room offered a bright forest of toys. Bettina dropped her white bear, Knuti, and banged enthusiastically on a keyboard whose keys lit up when she struck them. Each note had a color: blue for C, green for E, bright pink for F-sharp. As Julia watched the colors flash, she wondered what synesthete had chosen them and how many synesthetic players would be repulsed when the notes and colors failed to match.

Renate was thrilled to hear Bettina talk and wanted to help her learn. In a slow, serious voice, she maintained a running narrative about everything around her. She explained why there was a spruce tree in the corner, why its branches held glowing candles, and why it wasn't good to eat all the Lebkuchen on the red plate. Renate had prepared a potato salad and *Bockwurst*, which they tried hard to eat, although they had been swallowing cookies since four.

Erik had no room for a grand piano, but he had found a used upright. After dinner, he announced that it was time to sing. Julia's voice emerged rough and sticky with food, but after a few carols, her throat cleared. It had been so long since she had really sung! Erik hadn't lost his fine touch on the keys, and with Renate holding Bettina, Julia let loose. When they ran out of carols, Erik pulled out Schubert's *Lieder*, of which he was fond. Julia felt her body open, effortlessly doing what she feared it had forgotten. Breathing from her belly, she sang for the sheer love of it and let her impulses guide her gestures.

"What a voice!" murmured Horst.

On Renate's lap, Bettina stared, mesmerized, her face changing as Julia moved from note to note. One instant she laughed, and the next, she seemed to be in pain. When she inserted her own voice, Renate didn't shush her. Some of her sounds fit the harmony.

"*Ja!*" Renate beamed after "Erlkönig." She bounced Bettina, who continued to squeal. "Your mama has a beautiful voice! Would you like to sing like that too?"

Erik said it was time to open the presents. "What kind of place is this, where the grown-ups want their toys and the kids want to keep singing?" He laughed.

Sprawled out on the rug beside Bettina, Erik helped her liberate her gifts. Except for the stuffed monkey Julia had bought, every package Bettina tore contained something educational. There were books with bright pictures of children from other lands, and games where you fit colored shapes into waiting holes. Bettina seized a red triangle and slid the apex into her mouth. As Erik tried to reason with her, Julia laughed harder than she had in months.

"Does it really taste good? Why don't you try it in that spot over there? Don't you see how nicely it'll fit? We have so many better things to eat—"

"Taste good!" cried Bettina. She clutched one point of the triangle in each fist and stared greedily at the apex.

"That'll never work." Julia laughed. "She'll never do anything she knows you want her to."

Erik looked into Julia's eyes and smiled. He picked up a blue square and pretended to spread it with Nutella. "Mmm!" he said with a greedy smile.

Bettina frowned indignantly and grabbed for the square.

It was late when Julia tucked her into bed with her matted bear and floppy new monkey. Once Bettina had settled down, Julia helped Renate clean while Erik and Horst sat sleepily near the tree.

"It's wonderful to have you here!" said Renate. "It's doing us all so much good. To hear you sing—what a voice you've got! You're better than most altos in the opera here. Have you heard anything back about your applications?"

Julia groped for words. "Thanks. I'm on a waiting list for the operas, but I'm not expecting much."

"Why not?" asked Renate. "You should keep calling them. With a voice like that!"

"Well, you have to have a connection," said Julia.

"But you went to a good school!" exclaimed Renate. "You've sung with the Bartholdy Choir. You've sung in London!"

Julia flushed. She hadn't told Renate about Bettina's illness, and she wasn't going to if she could help it. Some powerful instinct told her not to, and she didn't like the penetrating look in Renate's dark eyes.

"You really don't have the connections?" she asked softly. "After all these years in Berlin?"

On a white plate, a lonely chunk of pickle sat marooned in yellow paste.

Julia didn't know how to explain. At auditions, people admired her warmth and power, and every conductor she'd worked with had praised her voice. No fear had ever dampened its strength, but she had noticed something that happened when she spoke. She didn't swear, and her grammar passed merit, but after a few phrases, people got a certain look. Not *a* look, but many looks that slid past like the notes in Handel's runs. Somewhere in those runs were surprise, disgust, and pity, the startled frowns evoked by a pretty girl with bad breath. When Julia spoke, people heard her father swearing. They heard the Henningsthal truck drivers delivering drinks. Once she saw those looks, she had a hard time talking, since she found she had no more to say. Arno suffered from the same problem. He could charm the most cultured people in the world, but eventually they learned that they turned his stomach.

Renate was gazing so fixedly that for a moment Julia was sure she had read her thoughts.

"Well, you certainly have talent," said Renate. "I think it's a crime! I would pay to hear you." She rinsed the plates Julia had scraped into the compost. "You know," said Renate without turning, "if you can't find anything in Berlin, why not try here in Frankfurt? Maybe there's too much competition there."

"I like Berlin," said Julia quickly. "I know it's the best place for me. There are so many opportunities."

"But if you're not getting any chances—with a voice like that ..." Renate reflected.

Despite Julia's sleepiness, her belly tightened, and her heart picked up its pace. "I have a lot of friends there."

Renate turned to her and sighed. "You know, Horst and I aren't getting any younger. We'll be retiring soon, and we want to stay close to Erik. If you were here, we could watch Bettina, and you could work on your music full time. You could teach, practice, apply for more jobs. You wouldn't have to work at that doughnut place, and Bettina wouldn't have to be in day care."

Julia's heart beat blood into her head. "I want to stay in Berlin." She gripped a red plate strewn with crumbs.

Renate blew out some extra air. "Well, if you don't want to ..." She dampened her voice so that the phrase spiraled through space.

On the way home, Julia watched the brown fields whip past, hypnotized by the crop rows' rolling lines. She tracked beads of water jerking their way across the window and tried to guess when they would fuse. The warm, tired girl with her head on Julia's lap had loved her weekend in Frankfurt. At home Bettina played in a corner of the bedroom, but nothing in her heap of toys compared to the games at Erik's house. Someday when Bettina applied for jobs, Julia didn't want her getting disdainful looks. Infuriating as Renate was, she did have something to offer. The question was what attitudes infested her learning, lurking in it like black spores of mold. Worse than the thought of Bettina getting those looks was that of her giving them to someone else. Julia felt wetness against her leg and dug in her pack for a tissue. Fast asleep with her breath warming her mother's thigh, the future job applicant was drooling.

———————————■———————————

That year in Berlin, winter never came. Januaries had been growing milder, and on the blackest evenings, the temperature suggested a ghostly April. On the skating rinks, boys scoured along in white T-shirts, and on the Kudamm, women fidgeted in their fur coats. The New Year's fireworks exploded in balmy air, and the sidewalks filled with mushy red paper, broken bottles, and dried trees. Overburdened, the BSR couldn't keep up with the dog dung, which Basti swore desecrated their Kiez more than anyplace else. Since they rarely saw dogs, Astrid joked that they trucked it in from Wilmersdorf, where every widow had her yapping little pooch.

"Nah," said Basti. "Prob'ly they pay somebody to walk their dogs here." He kicked a crusted green bottle. "Geez, I don't envy the guys who have to clean this up."

Lately his sarcasm had acquired a harder edge, and Astrid confessed she was worried. Basti had lost weight, and he moved more abruptly, with an impatience Julia hadn't seen before. He smoked more than was good for him, and it was pretty clear what was wrong. Without pay, he was doing the work of a *Hausmeister* and a master carpenter, while his scouts demanded more for their tips. Sergei had a good eye and knew plenty of customers, but he wanted 50 percent of the take. Gradually, Basti's stream of applications had dwindled. What was the point? Who wanted a twenty-two-year-old apprentice? If anything, his teachers would be learning from him. Over Christmas, he had gotten blind drunk with his friends out in Lichterfelde.

"Doesn't seem to have hurt him any," said Astrid. "Prob'ly did him good. What he needs is a girl. Not the clingy kind, one who can handle herself. Geez! At his age! Sometimes I wonder."

"Oh, he knows what he's doing," said Julia. "He just doesn't want to waste time."

"Yeah?" Astrid sniffed. "Well, he'll waste a whole lot of it if he keeps it all bottled up and then loses it with some tramp."

Astrid, too, had been feeling depressed. Convinced of her ailment, the job center wanted only monthly reports, and her visits to Kowalski lasted just minutes. With maddening courtesy, he called her "Frau Kunz." And in the *B.Z.*, there was bad news from France. After renewed investigations, the case of Princess Di's driver had been closed. No one could prove it was more than an accident.

"Yeah, right. And who's payin' those guys?" scoffed Astrid. She continued to believe that the queen had had her daughter-in-law killed.

On these warm, murky days, Julia hated the dark. When dawn came at eight and dusk at four, icy air had a quickening effect, but darkness in fifty-degree weather was deadly. One morning before work, she ran her theory by Basti, who looked up pointedly from a chair he was stripping.

"Yeah, warm and dark. We ain't made for that. What're you doin' after work? You wanna go somewhere with me? If you want, I can take you someplace nice."

A new directness in his stare made Julia flush. Until now, she had always liked it when Basti looked her straight in the eye.

"It's okay," he said. "I think you're gonna like it. It'll be great for Bettina too."

When Julia pushed the stroller into the dim Hof that night, she found Basti waiting. Scowling at the bushes, he stood perfectly straight and brought his cigarette to his lips in broad stitches. For the expedition, he had removed his work clothes and was wearing corduroy pants and a maroon sweater. As Julia approached, he took one last drag on his cigarette, then crushed it with the ball of his foot. Spears of pungent cologne penetrated his smoky smell.

"You look nice!" said Julia. "Let me go change. Can you watch Bettina for a minute?"

"Yeah, sure." He took the girl's tiny hand and led her down to the shop.

As fast as she could, Julia tried on clothes, tossing twisted rejects over her shoulder. In the past year, the jaded cells of her body had been pulling themselves back together. Last week a man had glanced over his shoulder when he passed to see whether the front looked as good as the back. For six months, Bettina had been on solid foods, and Julia's breasts were remembering their former shape. She smiled when she saw the mounds her push-up bra created under her fuzzy red sweater. Since it was nearly fifty degrees, she left her jacket open.

When she entered the shop, Bettina was frowning with concentration as she rubbed a chair leg with both hands.

"That's it," said Basti. "Now you're gettin' it. Pretty soon I'll let you strip the paint. I could use some help around here."

Smiling at his secret, Basti wouldn't tell Julia where he was taking her. On the U-Bahn, he joked in her ear about his mafioso customers, and cinnamon gum enlivened his spicy scent. He nudged her to exit at Wittenbergplatz and led her and Bettina into Westhof, the poshest department store in Berlin. Julia had always viewed the Western showplace as a kind of museum, where you admired things before you bought them at Woolworth's. On a Tuesday night, the tiered foyer was a marvel of light, and Bettina ogled the shiny labyrinth of makeup counters. The escalator bred conversations in English, Spanish, and Russian.

"They come here first before they come to me." Basti grinned.

She followed him through tents of brocade curtains toward a brilliant display of lights. Laughing, Julia pulled off her jacket. Basti had brought her and Bettina to the biggest lamp department in Berlin.

As far as she could see, lights were glowing, shimmering, twinkling. She pulled Bettina into their midst until she was surrounded by radiance and warmth. On one side, enormous globes shone softly, some perfectly round, others oblong. One sat like a translucent egg aglow on a silver post. Overhead, crystal chandeliers turned slowly, their gemlike drops projecting rays. Mesmerized, Bettina tilted her face upward and tried to follow the shooting sparks. Some of the lamps were built like trees, with silver leaves among their shiny tips. The most fascinating ones looked like tiny sea creatures. From central globes, squiggly branches protruded, supporting tiny lights or crystal balls. Cut like gemstones, the crystals multiplied the glints. Julia found herself floating in an ocean of twinkling diatoms.

"Ah!" Bettina reached toward a lamp. Under its light, her red curls shone brilliantly, and her brown eyes sparkled.

"Ain't this somethin'?" asked Basti. "Better than Christmas, huh?"

Impulsively Julia hugged him, and he clutched her in a way he hadn't done before. As though he owned the place, he strode through the display, describing the light of each lamp and judging its value.

"Now, you take somethin' like this." He pointed to a lamp with a red porcelain base. "Two hundred forty-nine euros. You could get somethin' like this out in Spandau for less than twenty."

"May I help you?"

A tall blonde woman stood behind them. Her hair shimmered in the dazzling light.

"May I help you find something?" Her eyes shifted to Basti.

"Oh, that's okay. We're just looking," said Julia.

The woman's eyes flickered over Julia's chest, then settled on her face. Their gazes met, and Julia saw that descending scale from pity to distaste. It wasn't Julia's looks that had set it off but some inflection of her voice. Maybe it was Bettina's squeals, which in that sea of crystal must have signaled danger. Basti glanced at Julia and faced the woman.

"We're lookin' for a lamp," he said. "Somethin' feminine. Somethin' nice for a lady's bedroom."

In a niche below the glowing red lamp stood a larger one with a soft pink peony. It was on sale for €169.

"You like that one?" he asked, reaching down.

Against the white porcelain, his brown fingers lay like handprints on a finger painting. Crusty red cuts on his thumb and forefinger contrasted with the lamp's perfect smoothness. Whimsically painted, the peony had a Japanese look. The tapered shade crowned the base exquisitely.

"It's lovely," said Julia.

Bettina stared hypnotized at the diatom lamps, which cost €899.

"Good, we'll take it," said Basti. "Can you wrap it up for us?"

Without a word, the blonde woman unplugged the lamp. Her hair swung as she carried it to the register. While Basti watched, she unscrewed the shade and wrapped the elegant base in three staggered sheets of white paper. After she angled the shade into a black Westhof bag, Basti peeled off two hundred-euro bills. Her eyes flickered, but his face remained motionless.

"Thanks," he said. "You have a nice evening."

Only on the escalator did he begin to smile. "Wonder how many of her customers pay cash?"

"Only the Russians," answered Julia.

In the Hof, she took the package from Bettina's stroller, where it had been riding in her daughter's place. Holding the sleeping girl, Basti looked down warmly, and Julia reached up to kiss his cheek.

"Thanks," she said. "It's a beautiful lamp."

"Oh. Oh, gosh." In the dim light, Basti faltered. "I—I can go back." He blushed. "I can go back and get you one just like it. But I was gonna give it to my mom. She's been so down lately."

Julia laughed at herself. "No, no. That's a great idea. Let's go up and give it to her right now."

Astrid was reading the *B.Z.* at her kitchen table, a crumpled pack of cigarettes at her elbow.

"What's up?" she asked. "What've you got in there? Somethin' fall off a truck I should know about?"

Basti laid the bag on the table, and Julia pulled out the shade. Laughing, Astrid tried it on as a Chinese hat.

"No, no, Mom, check this out!" cried Basti.

He ripped open the paper, and when she saw the pink peony, Astrid stopped. In a few quick moves, Basti assembled the lamp and plugged it in. With her lips parted, Astrid fingered the porcelain flower. She raised her hand to her face as she began to cry.

"That's the most beautiful thing I ever saw." She threw her arms around Basti and clung to him, shaking. "I don't deserve you," she moaned. "I don't deserve you."

"Aw, c'mon, Mom," he muttered.

Bettina added her voice with a mezzo wail, weary from their evening adventure. Astrid's sobs turned to laughs, and she pushed Basti back.

"This is nuts," she said. "It's a beautiful lamp. And you know what—I'm gonna need it. As soon as I can, I'm goin' back to work. Dr. Kowalski says I can if I want. He says I'm a borderline case."

———————— ■ ————————

After a winter when crocuses bloomed in January, the icy spring came as a rough surprise. By mid-February the buds were swelling, and daffodils were poking their noses between hardy green shoots. Down in the Hof, Basti stared uneasily at tiny green nubs along wiry branches. Then ten days into March, the temperature dropped, and the wind whipped up. When it snowed, Julia took Bettina walking down the green strip in the middle of Schlossstrasse. Purple violets peeped out from under the white crust. Thrilled by the snowflakes, Bettina raised her arms, tilted up her face, and tried to catch them in her mouth.

"*Lecker!*" she squealed. "Yummy ice!"

Astrid was less enthusiastic about the snow, which could dissolve into rain or harden into pellets. Most days now she was up at five, sliding to the U-Bahn at Sophie-Charlotte-Platz. All it had taken was one trip to the job center. Hearing that Kowalski was letting her work, the *Beamtin* had voided Astrid's paperwork with a resounding stamp.

"Practic'ly gave me a heart attack right there in the office," she said. "Geez! You're sick, and then you're well again, just like that."

As Astrid had predicted, she found work in a week. The city was in debt and the economy staggering, but cleaning ladies were in demand. Astrid went to work for Putzarama, a temp agency that dispatched women all over Berlin. The job suited her since she loved exploring the city, and she saw no end of wealthy homes. With a regular gig, you went to the same place each week, and the woman got on your nerves. This temp work could be disgusting as hell, but you never fell into a rut. In the late afternoons over doughnuts and coffee, Astrid spent hours describing the places she cleaned, scandalized by other people's messes.

"These guys out in Pankow—you wouldn't believe! Some kinda rock stars, I think. They had a flat-screen TV, four electric guitars, a stereo that musta been worth a couple thousand euros— and dust all over everything. I didn't know whether to dust the stuff or shave it. And socks—jeans and socks—all over the floor. I can't organize their stuff for 'em—they oughta know that!"

"Wow, so what did you do?" asked Julia.

"Aw, I picked it all up in a laundry basket. I wasn't gonna, but finally I washed it. Whoever they are, I kinda felt sorry for 'em. Two overgrown kids with a lotta money."

If a woman was involved, Astrid rendered a harsher verdict, and between bites of strawberry-frosted doughnut, Bettina echoed her gleefully: "*Sauerei! Schlamperei! Schweinerei!*" At twenty-one months, she was repeating words like an Amazon parrot. Seeing a pile of wood shavings on the basement floor, she squealed "*Schwein'rei!*" until Basti doubled over with laughter. In a neighborhood restaurant, she caused a different reaction when she frowned at a wobbly table and cried, "Cheap pieceashit!"

On a regular basis, Basti took Julia and Bettina out, since he loved watching the little girl discover the city. When the snow stuck, he brought home three strips of plastic, and they slid screaming down the slopes of Viktoriapark. He treated mother and daughter to huge, gooey slices of cake and took them walking in the Charlottenburg Gardens. Bettina adored Basti, and when he was busy, she sulked. Julia didn't sulk, but she missed his low voice and attentive eyes.

"Does he talk to you?" said Astrid one afternoon when rain was pecking at the window. "I can tell he's not doin' so good, but he won't say anything."

"Not really," answered Julia. "He talks about what we're doing, about what he's working on. But not ... I know what you mean."

"Somethin's eatin' him," said Astrid. "It's this job stuff—givin' up on the apprenticeship, workin' for nothin' ... But there's somethin' else. He's always had a shit deal, but before, he could live with it. You know if he's seein' anyone?"

Julia shook her head. "If he were, he wouldn't tell me."

"He gets so mad when I ask him." Astrid sighed.

"So don't," said Julia. "I know what you're saying, but I don't think he can talk about this kind of stuff."

"He doesn't have a problem talkin' about furniture," Astrid grumbled. "Ask him about a cabinet, and he'll go on for an hour."

Julia smiled and shrugged.

"What do you guys talk about, on those long walks you go on?" Astrid pressed.

Julia tried to think. "Stuff we're passing," she said. "Buildings. Cars. Furniture ..." She laughed low and deep.

Julia thought about Basti as she led Bettina downstairs, then coaxed her up four flights to their own apartment. Most of the time Basti seemed angry and tense, but the noisy toddler always drew a smile from him. He never mentioned a girl, and he stayed close to Birgit, who was due to graduate in June. Sometimes Julia wondered whether he preferred male company, but she saw no sign of that either.

In her apartment, Julia found the message light flashing, but instead of Rudi's tenor, a low female voice emerged. It was Inge Caro, the assistant manager of the RBB Choir, who wanted to audition her in two weeks. With a gasp, Julia sank down on the couch and welcomed Bettina's wiggly embrace. She had been waiting for this call since she had graduated from the Hans Breithaus Academy.

Founded back when cultural events were broadcast by radio, the RBB Choir was a world-class professional group. Its sixty singers sang fifty concerts a year and earned over €2,000 a month. In the hands of Nigel Hunt, its British conductor, the opera-quality voices blended into a powerful wave of sound. Besides the sixty regulars, the choir employed several freelancers who sang in large productions or replaced people who got sick. Julia would be trying for one of these freelance positions, which paid €200 per concert and €160 per rehearsal. From her Breithaus Academy friends, she knew they didn't call freelancers often enough to make them rich, but they called often enough to make them singers. If she got the job, it would mean that for the first time ever, she would be able to support herself through music.

The RBB Choir channeled an endless stream of applications, and Arno had advised her to wait until the time was right. On paper, her Hans Breithaus degree looked good, but she needed experience, and he wanted her voice in top form. Freelancers had first crack at permanent positions, and through unknown sources, Arno was tracking the age and health of the fifteen altos. When he didn't return Julia's calls in January, she'd applied to the choir on her own, along with the three city operas. Over time, she had begun to doubt Arno's judgment. His talent stood like a deeply rooted oak, but his influence was a net of loose vines.

When Julia called back, Frau Caro told her what to expect. She had to prepare two pieces that all the applicants would sing, "Buss und Reu" from the *St. Matthew Passion* and Brahms's "Sapphische Ode." To complement these, she had to learn a piece of her own choosing, something that showed her strengths as a singer. She would need to do sight-reading, and she would be asked to sing the alto line in pieces the choir often performed. To check her range, they would run her through some scales and arpeggios. The whole audition would take half an hour, and they wanted her to come at 4:00 p.m. on March 20.

Relentlessly, Julia called Arno, trying his cell and landline in quick succession. Having forged ahead without him, she suddenly craved his deep, angry voice.

"Julia!" he growled a little uneasily at eleven thirty that night.

Picturing Bettina in bed, Julia tried to keep her voice low, but excitement boiled up in her throat.

"Arno! I'm auditioning for the RBB Choir!"

"What?" He sounded befuddled. "What? You applied?"

His voice had a thickness she didn't like, but with him, there was no knowing what caused it. He might have downed several beers, or he might be hearing her through a rocking forest of chords. He might not have spoken to anyone all day.

"Yeah," she answered in her lowest tones. "In January. I applied to them when I wrote to the operas."

"Oh," said Arno.

There was a long pause. Some bumps suggested he was lighting a cigarette.

"Okay," he said finally. "Okay." His voice gained strength. "All right. So this is it. This is your shot. What do they want you to sing?"

"'Buss und Reu,'" said Julia.

He grunted his approval.

"And Brahms's 'Sapphische Ode.'"

"Oh, shit. That thing's a real cesspool."

Julia giggled. Arno had no fondness for romantic music, and she hoped his reaction wouldn't tickle her when she sang it.

"So what should I sing as my elective piece?" she asked.

"'Schlafe, mein Liebster,'" answered Arno without hesitating.

"Yeah, that's what I was thinking. It's lower than 'Buss und Reu,' and it's got more sustained notes—"

"No," said Arno. His voice slipped into gear. "No. You should sing it because you sing it better than anyone else. You've got—" His voice wavered, then came back fast and deep. "Bach wrote it for you. That's your aria."

"And 'Refiner's Fire'?" she asked. "I thought about that one."

"Boy, you are a piece of work!" He laughed. "Don't worry— you're going to sing that. And I'm going to conduct it. But not now. You're not ready."

"How do you know?" demanded Julia. She gripped the phone.

"When was the last time you sang? I mean for someone who knows what music is supposed to sound like?"

"Last weekend at Rudi's." She laughed.

"Oh, that—"

"Don't call him that!" she cried. "Don't you call him that!"

"I didn't call him anything," grumbled Arno. "Look. Just don't sing 'Refiner's Fire.' If you want to get into that choir, don't sing it."

Arno fired off a bullet-point list of tips. Nigel Hunt, the conductor, was a real musician. He had gotten the job because some bureaucrat thought only Brits could wave a baton, but there was no denying the man could count.

"With him, just figure you're naked," said Arno. "He'll see everything. He'll hear your thoughts. He'll hear things that don't even come out of your mouth."

Besides Hunt, she could expect the manager and assistant manager, the choir's elected representatives, and most of the altos.

"Don't dress sexy." He chuckled. "Keep 'em outa sight. Women hate good-looking women. The one you've gotta watch out for is that assistant manager."

"Frau Caro?" asked Julia.

"Yeah. Everyone trying out will be good. There'll probably be four or five of you. She has to plan it all, and she hates disorganized people. You don't want to piss her off. Julia—don't fuck this one up. You're—you're …" His voice faded. "You're the best alto I ever heard. You should be singing. I— You should be singing. Get this job. Don't fuck this up."

"Okay," said Julia. "Okay."

The next week she borrowed Rudi's keyboard, and he left the lab early to play until Bettina went to bed. As though she were doing spring cleaning, Julia peered into every corner of her voice, testing and retesting each note. In slow motion, she wound through each measure of Bach's coloratura, and when she had mastered it, she tried it backward.

For the sight-reading, Arno had told her to practice modern music.

"They know you know Bach." Julia mimicked his voice, recreating his resonant, low growl. "They're gonna hand you some piece so weird it's gonna sound like aliens wrote it."

On his computer at work, Rudi generated series of random notes, and Julia turned them to music each night. Although they seemed to have no inherent connections, once she sang the tones, they formed a pattern to her ear. The more she sang, the quicker she was to hear melodies in constellations of notes. It had been a long time since she had worked herself so hard, and instead of rebelling, her voice thanked her.

Julia's singing reached into her neighbors' kitchen, attracting Astrid and Basti. Astrid tried to quiet Bettina, who squealed along with her mother. Basti nodded admiringly and shot occasional looks at the skinny man at the keyboard. Astrid promised to watch Bettina on the twentieth, since she had only a morning cleaning job. Basti wouldn't be able to serve as backup, because he had to meet some men out in Treptow. After his week of short days, Rudi couldn't leave the lab early, but Birgit was willing to step in.

"Don't worry. You won't have to leave her in charge," said Astrid. "She'll prob'ly leave her with one of those bathroom ladies at the mall."

The night before the audition, Bettina sensed something was up. She often slept through the night, but she wouldn't settle down even when Julia read her favorite book about the Laplander girl who saved her reindeer. Around eleven she finally fell asleep, but at two she was clamoring for a drink. Since she had stopped nursing, Bettina slept in a crib near Julia's bed, and even asleep, Julia followed her dreams, her whimpers, her tiny breaths.

Probably Julia wouldn't have been able to sleep anyway. In the gloom, notes perched on staves hanging like broken gates. She followed the tones, uncertain where they led, but a thin, angry man interrupted her voice. At six the radio popped on with the breathy, little-girl sound of "Almost Lover," and Julia felt more relieved than anxious.

As on any other day, she showed Bettina how to eat her raisin roll while she wolfed down a *Kaiserbrötchen* with salami and cheese. When it came to feeding, Bettina needed little help. After just a few weeks, she lost interest in using food as makeup and became a serious eater. She was eager to put everything into her mouth, especially anything pink or red. That night, Astrid had promised to give Bettina her favorite dinner, strawberry Müllermilch with macaroni and tomato sauce.

At work, Marga wished Julia well. "Knock 'em dead," she said, but her voice lacked force.

Lately her frenetic movements had slowed. Despite all the raw songs she was writing, Ultraviolet couldn't find paying gigs. When the weather improved, she wanted to give an open-air concert, but getting permission was a hassle.

Right after work, Julia picked up Bettina, who was lively despite the gray day. The cold, damp air felt as though it could produce snow any minute, and Julia pushed the stroller hurriedly across Schlossstrasse. The red flash of her answering machine stopped her heart. Was it Frau Caro? Was she going to cancel? Instead, Astrid's low growl emerged, saying she was way the hell out in Wannsee, and the woman who was supposed to drive her to the S-Bahn hadn't returned. Julia fingered her plants and looked down at the Hof, where round drops were pattering the blue and yellow bins. The glistening bushes had drawn in their arms, embracing themselves to keep warm. Julia sang up and down and smiled when Bettina joined in. She checked all the music in her black folder. At a quarter past two Astrid called again.

"Listen," she said. "This ain't lookin' good. This woman picks me up this morning at nine, and I tell her I have to be back at the S-Bahn by two, 'cause I gotta be home by three. 'Oh, I'll be back long before that,' she says. 'I just have to pick up a few things.'"

"Where are you?" asked Julia, breathing faster. "Could you just take off? Could you walk to the S-Bahn?"

"I don't know where I am," said Astrid. "Somewhere out in the woods. It took us a while just to drive here. Look, I'm sorry, honey. She said she'd be back. 'Just pick up a few things.' I hope the bitch picks up herpes."

"So you're really stuck, huh?" asked Julia.

"Yeah." Astrid sighed. "Looks like you're gonna need the Princess after all."

"Okay," said Julia. "Thanks for letting me know."

She jabbed buttons to summon Birgit. No voice broke the string of high tones, and the Vorderhaus windows were lifeless. With her stomach clenched, Julia tried Birgit's cell phone. It was off. On the stereo, the blue digits changed from 2:36 to 2:37. Birgit had seemed so eager to watch Bettina. She couldn't possibly have gone far. Julia scanned the house windows and saw glimmers only down at Frau Riemann's.

Although the RBB building wasn't far off, Julia had ordered a taxi for 3:15. No matter what happened, she mustn't be late. Breathing swiftly, she pushed Bettina into her outdoor clothes and led her down the stairs. After two flights, she grabbed her and ran the rest of the way, then across the wet courtyard to the ground floor apartment.

No sounds answered Frau Riemann's shrill bell. Maybe the stringy woman was hunkering down in her dim kitchen. Frau Riemann read the police report daily and apprised Astrid of the criminal trends. There were so many stories of men who rang women's bells, pretended to check their meters, and then raped, robbed, and killed them.

"Frau Riemann!" she called. "Frau Riemann, it's Julia!"

"Fwau Wiemann! Fwau Wiemann!" cried Bettina.

Julia pounded on the door and pressed her ear against it. She squinted through the peephole. She saw only a distorted coatrack bearing a dingy rainbow of wool. Miserably, she led Bettina back through the rain and up four flights of stairs.

It was ten to three, and by this time, neither Marga nor Rudi could have made it. Julia tried Birgit again and left a message asking her to come to the RBB building. She hesitated a moment, then left the same words for Marga. In a panic, she thought of calling to change the time, but what would they think of a singer who canceled an hour before her audition? Remembering Arno's warning, Julia decided to go ahead. At 3:05 she pulled on her coat. Against the Vorderhaus, sodden flakes of snow were forming among the drops.

"Where we go?" asked Bettina crossly.

"We're going to an audition."

"Awdisha." Bettina frowned.

In one of those flashes she had had since *Messiah*, Julia wished she could plunk Bettina on the couch and lock the door. How simple all this would be without Bettina! As though reading her thoughts, Bettina looked up questioningly, her frown of concentration darkening. Sweating, Julia led her back downstairs, and they waited in the gateway. White mush was accumulating on parked cars. After a few minutes the taxi came, and Julia helped Bettina inside. As she fumbled with the seat belt, icy kisses burned her exposed skin.

"You sure you want to go out in this?" asked the driver. He angled the stroller into the trunk. "Y'know, we could all just snuggle up and watch a movie."

"Oh, I'm sure," said Julia. "Nice idea. Maybe some other time."

Clusters of white splattered the windshield as though thrown by mischievous hands. Excited by any moving vehicle, Bettina was shouting with enthusiasm by the time they reached the RBB building. Among the pelting drops, she twisted and whined, unwilling to go in and miss the snow. Julia had to drag her up the steps since she refused to sit in the stroller.

At the reception desk, an older man frowned uncertainly when Julia asked where she could park the stroller. He told her to go up to the second floor, and when she opened the heavy stairwell door, she spotted a group of women halfway down the hall. At twenty to four, they looked dry and ready, while Julia had snow in her hair, and her wool coat smelled like a wet dog. A tall, slim woman with short brown hair was taking information from the other three. In profile, she looked like a sapling in winter, and Julia guessed she must be Frau Caro. Clutching Bettina's hand, Julia walked toward them as fast as the little girl would let her. As Julia got closer, she recognized two of them. One was a young Breithaus Academy alto with a solid, substantial voice. The other was Dagmar Schleifer.

"Hi!" called Bettina.

Frau Caro started, and her mouth opened slightly. Energetic and thin, she was wearing a gray sweater and fine wool pants. Her restless feet shifted in boots of smoky-gray leather with a raised scroll pattern. Rather than hiding her eyes, her gold-rimmed glasses intensified them.

"Julia Martens?" she asked.

"Yeah." Julia nodded.

"Okay, great," said Frau Caro. "So we're all here. Listen, Julia—you're not going to be able to take your little girl in there. Do you want to come back another time?"

"No!" said Julia. "No. I—I'm sorry—"

"Oh, we'll watch her," said the third applicant, a tiny woman with curly hair and warm, dark eyes.

Frau Caro's black eyes darted back and forth, marking the movements of her quick thoughts. "Is that all right with you, Julia?" she asked. "I think we should reschedule."

Julia sized up the short, doe-eyed woman. "Oh, it's okay," she said. "I'm ready, really. It's just—someone I was counting on—"

Frau Caro's eyes penetrated her, but they seemed sympathetic. "Okay, then," she said. "I'm going to take you to some practice rooms where you can warm up. Then we'll take you in alphabetical order: Arens, Martens, Schleifer, Schulze."

In a soundproof cell with a black piano, Julia took off her coat and Bettina's and hung them on hooks near the door. To catch their drips, she laid a bed of tissues on the brown carpet. Shakily she began some descending scales. First, she would clear out her lower register, then work her way up. It was useless to shush Bettina, who added her shrill voice to Julia's full one. In spite of everything, Julia felt her throat opening, and Bettina smiled as though she were making the rich sound herself. Whatever happened, Julia knew that her voice wouldn't fail her.

The short, dark-eyed woman appeared in the doorway. With her cropped hair and tiny nose, she looked like a squirrel.

"Hi, I'm Didi Schulze," she said. "Who's this?"

"Bettina!" crowed the little girl, bouncing on the bench.

"This is so nice of you," said Julia. "I really can't—"

"Oh, it's okay." Didi's hand swept the air. "I'm last, and I'm scared to death. This'll give me something to do."

Watching the second hand circle, they talked in low tones. They tried the short chromatic runs of "Buss und Reu," but it only made them more nervous. At four, Dagmar came in, looking pale.

"They've started," she said tightly. "Kathrin's in there now. Frau Caro's coming for you next."

Dagmar smiled at Bettina, who was obsessively playing a C-sharp. "That's a nice note," she said. "Do you like that one?"

Bettina scowled. Like her singing voice, Dagmar's speech held your attention, but not for its pleasant qualities. She spaced out her syllables like beads on a string, and her words wound along like a jeweled snake.

"Hey, how was Prague?" asked Julia.

"Oh, it was great." Dagmar smiled. Behind her round glasses, her gray eyes warmed. "You know Arno. All business. He worked us so hard we didn't even know where we were."

"How did the concerts go?" asked Julia. She traced slow circles on Bettina's back. Bettina was pounding the middle C now, bouncing each time that the earnest note sounded.

"They were wonderful," said Dagmar. She glanced amusedly at Bettina. "About as close to perfect as you can get. I love working with him. He makes you do things you never knew you could."

"Who?" asked Didi, looking up from her Brahms.

"Oh, Arno Weber," said Dagmar. "If you want a workout, try singing with him."

The door opened.

"Julia?" said Frau Caro, smiling at the three women. "Bonding, huh? Don't worry—we're not a bad bunch."

Julia hugged Bettina and followed Frau Caro into the hall.

"Mama! Ma—"

The cry ended as though someone had pulled a plug. Julia winced. Didi and Dagmar must have shut the door, sealing themselves into a screaming hell.

Frau Caro led Julia to a large, bright room where a dozen singers sat self-consciously on metal chairs. As the assistant manager introduced them, Julia tried to register their names, but she kept hearing that stifled wail. Their faces made a stronger impression, half allowing empathetic smiles. Nigel Hunt, the conductor, stood tall and straight in tight jeans and a red sweatshirt. His long face radiated warmth, and he moved with broad, easy gestures. His brown eyes glowed with dangerous energy, but his voice flowed like moonlight.

"Okay, Julia. Thanks for coming today. Why don't we start with the Bach?"

The pale young boy at the piano played so deftly that Julia could imagine a small orchestra. With him as her ally, she drew a bottomless breath and began the sad, chromatic aria about sin and regret. In the damp air, Julia's voice had a rich, liquid quality, and she met each listener's eyes. She lingered longest on the conductor's. As though meditating, he seemed fixated but remote, registering each quiver but impossible to read.

As the melody emerged, Julia pictured each note as a pulsing, floating shape. Smiling inwardly, she raised her eyes to follow the forms, but instead she left her body and ran down the hall. Bettina must have thrown a fit as soon as she left, and Didi and Dagmar weren't equipped to handle her. Her daughter had never bitten anyone yet, but Dagmar seemed like a good candidate. Julia tried to focus on the mournful lines and squinted to see the dissolving shapes. Flashes of the embattled practice room cut their sides. As Julia formed the notes, she strained to hear the imprisoned voice. Concentrating as hard as she could, she forced herself to feel each word in Bach's descending phrases. When she finished, Hunt deflected his searching beam, then thanked her and told her to try the Brahms.

Determined to give them her warmest sound, Julia spun the sweet, heavy notes. This time she sang to the altos, the women Frau Caro hadn't introduced. They sat impassively like moss by a brook, absorbing each drop of her tune. Hovering on a C, Julia saw Arno's hand cup the note and fondle it like a fragrant orange. Remembering everything he had said about Brahms, Julia smiled as she floated his tune. "No matter what he writes, the guy puts you to sleep. He should have stuck to lullabies."

Images loomed from the shrill opera down the hall, and Julia forced herself to focus. Hunt seemed pleased she had chosen "Schlafe, mein Liebster" as her elective piece, and she swelled and throbbed on the low notes. Somehow the melody felt wrong in that brilliant room. In a dark church full of people, it could work its magic, but in this tense place, no one could imagine sleep. During one rest, Julia thought that she heard a distant cry, and her air ran short as though someone had kicked her belly. Without the slightest tremor, she glided to the conclusion, and Hunt smiled. His straight shoulders relaxed.

Julia enjoyed the melodic alto lines he gave her, the opening dirge from the *St. Matthew Passion* and a clear, cutting section of Britten's *St. Cecilia*. Arno had been right about the sight-reading, a contemporary piece so weird she suspected not aliens but drugs. Realizing she would fail if she tried to make sense of it, she read like a short-order cook. She took orders with her eyes, then filled them with her belly and throat. Hunt took over the piano for her scales and arpeggios to test aspects of her sound the melodies hadn't revealed. She emerged from the music to find herself the crux in a burning array of gazes.

"That was nice, Julia," said the conductor. "You have a very rich sound. I'd like to ask you something, though."

Her stomach clenched, and she looked at him wordlessly. His dark eyes pulsed with curiosity.

"Where do you go?" he asked.

Julia blushed. "Where do I go?"

"Yes. Where do you go? When you sing. You left us there a few times, and I was wondering where you were."

"Oh, I—I was thinking about the music," she breathed.

"Oh, well, I can understand that." He smiled. He glanced at a sheet on the piano. "Okay, Julia, you'll hear from us soon. We'll be making our decision later this week, and we'll let you know right away if you can join us."

Julia looked around the bright room one last time, but the faces had merged to a blur. So that was it. Her throat hardened and swelled, and she hoped her eyes weren't red. As the singers complimented her, she did her best to thank them without exposing her failing voice. In the hallway, she studied the backs of Frau Caro's boots, which were scratched and worn compared to the decorative fronts. In that echoey space, their footsteps fell out of sync, Julia's longer stride breaking Frau Caro's quick beat.

Julia pushed open the practice room door and heard high-pitched singing.

"Okay, try this one," said Dagmar. She played a high F, and Bettina squealed out something close to it.

"Hey, your kid can sing!" Didi laughed.

From Bettina's red face, Julia knew she had been howling, but on the bench next to Didi, she looked happy. Dagmar slipped out behind Frau Caro, and when the door had closed, Julia murmured, "How was she?" She rubbed the curly little head.

"Well, for a while we were glad the place was soundproof."
Didi smiled. "I don't think I've ever heard anything make that
much noise. But then Dagmar started playing, and she got really
interested. We said it was a game. We would play something, and
she had to sing it back. She can do it. She's pretty good. What is
she, two?"

"Play that! I want that!" cried Bettina, pointing to a slim,
black F-sharp.

Julia wheeled Bettina to Theodor-Heuss-Platz since she couldn't
afford eight euros for another taxi. The cool air had shaken off the
wet snow, leaving patches of mush on the grass. Feeling trapped in
her heavy, ill-smelling coat, Julia opened a button but shivered as
the wind touched her breast. In her stroller, Bettina was squirming,
so Julia reached down to adjust her blanket. Bettina cried out
angrily, and Julia yielded to a thought she usually resisted.

Most hospitals had *Babyklappen* where mothers could leave
unwanted infants. Why didn't they have one for kids of two?
Probably they would be overrun, she thought, stifling a laugh.
In the misty twilight, Julia didn't see a soul. What if, right now,
she just walked away? She stopped and lifted her hands from the
stroller's bar. She had enough saved for a cheap plane ticket. She
could fly to London, Paris, New York. With her fingers curled
over the battered bar, she stood transfixed, imagining the joy of
walking unencumbered. The steady pace of an approaching man
reminded her of Basti, and she pictured his ironic grin. When the
grit crunched under her feet, she realized she was moving forward,
her fingers clasping the bar.

As Julia approached the U-Bahn, she remembered her cell
phone and found messages from Birgit and Marga. Wildly
apologetic, Birgit said she had thought the audition was tomorrow.

She was down on the Ku'damm with some friends, and she would come as fast as she could. Marga, who had called just minutes ago, asked if Julia still wanted her since it was after five. From the U-Bahn station, Julia called them both and told them not to bother.

As she cooked dinner, she stared into the pot of macaroni, inhaling the steam and watching the foam rise. The curled noodles danced in a heaving ring, jounced by a million tiny bubbles. From Astrid's dark windows, Julia guessed she wasn't home and wondered if she was still trapped out in Wannsee. She hoped that Astrid wouldn't set out alone on those black, icy roads. Bettina sensed Julia's dejection and ate her food quietly, studying her mother with troubled eyes. She frowned while Julia read to her and looked up anxiously when her voice faded. In her crib she lay still and drew quick, silent breaths until sleep finally took her.

Julia picked up the black folder she had tossed on the couch and pulled out the music to put away. She hesitated with the pages on her lap, staring at them until the notes dissolved. From the stairwell came the steady beat of determined legs. That must be Basti. She snuffed up her tears, wiped her eyes, and looked toward the door. The bell's shrill note jabbed her even though she expected it. She lost a slipper getting up and fumbled to put it back on. By the time she reached the door, she was almost breathless. Standing before her she found Arno Weber.

12

The Voice

All Julia could do was stare. Panting from the climb, Arno stood with his mouth open, his frown melting as he looked down at her. Rain had darkened his hair, and snowflakes crusted the shoulders of his gray jacket. Each time he breathed out, Julia smelled smoke, and she found herself smiling before she had recovered enough to move.

"Hi," he said finally. "I had to see you. I heard how it went, and I had to see you."

"You heard—"

Frozen in the doorway, Julia gazed up at him. Arno was so much bigger than she remembered. In the faint light he loomed over her, breathing hard. In all the years she had known him, he had never come to her apartment, and she had no idea how he had found her tonight. From the look of him, he must have set out at a run as soon as he hung up the phone.

"How—" she tried again but felt herself caught in a hug. A big hand passed roughly over her hair. Arno pushed her back and gripped her shoulders. Looking down ironically, he shook his head. "Julia," he murmured.

She fell back a few steps, and Arno walked into her living room. His eyes took possession of her space. In one sweep, they scanned the shelves, the plants, and the couch and settled on the fallen music. The cold air tightened her back, and Julia closed the door.

"What's this?" asked Arno. He picked up the fallen pages. Smiling faintly, he conducted with quick jerks of his hand. With his eyes on the page, he followed the notes with his lips. The sheer craziness of the moment made Julia laugh.

"Arno." She cut into his music. "Can I take your coat? Can I get you something to drink?"

"Huh?" He grunted. "Oh, yeah, yeah." He put down the sheets and handed her his heavy gray jacket. His jeans were damp from the knees down, but his gray flannel shirt was dry.

"You got any coffee?" he asked. "I could use some coffee."

"Yeah." She smiled.

She brought out two Nescafés in warm red mugs and found Arno settled on the couch. He was conducting with one hand and humming a line that jumped from one voice to the next. Smelling the coffee, he stopped and smiled up at her.

"Thanks," he murmured. He slid to one side.

"We've gotta be quiet," said Julia. "Bettina's sleeping."

"Be—" Arno squinted, confused. "Oh," he muttered. "Oh. Oh, yeah."

With the bedroom door closed, Bettina slept through most conversations, but she might be jarred by an unknown male voice. Julia took a sip of coffee and looked at Arno's thigh, which was warming her even though he had just come in from the cold. Arno sighed and put down his mug.

"Julia," he said, "you didn't get into the RBB Choir."

"I know," she breathed. The denim over his leg was so taut she could feel the force in the drawn white threads.

"You do?" he asked, hesitating. "Did they call you?"

"No." Her heart thumped. "But I guess they called you, huh?"

"Oh, I know somebody." Arno leaned back and sighed. He scowled at the wrinkled blanket between his legs. "I called them. I wanted to know. They said that you brought your daughter. They said you sang well, but you seemed distracted. Hunt liked your voice best, but he didn't trust you."

"How do you know all that?" demanded Julia. "What are you, a Stasi? Do you sleep with people to find out what's going on?"

Arno leaned forward with clenched fists. "I know Nigel Hunt," he said in his lowest tone.

"You called him?" she asked. "He told you that? Does he know you're sitting here right now telling me this—before they've even called me?"

"I don't give a shit what he knows," growled Arno. "I wanted to hear how you did. Is that so awful?"

"Yeah!" She glared.

A bush of capillaries flared on his cheek.

"I'm a person! A thinking, feeling person!" she choked out. "I'm not something—something you make—" Julia broke off, unable to find words.

Arno turned on her, his eyes blazing. "I want to know why you fucked up!" he hissed. "I want to know why you've fucked up everything! The *St. Matthew Passion* you die on me, *Messiah* you don't show! And now this! You could be the best alto in Germany—in—in the world, maybe! And Didi Schulze beats you out for a freelance job in the RBB Choir!"

"What?" Julia gasped. "They didn't take Dagmar?"

Arno shook his head, refusing to be distracted. "Do you *want* to fuck up?" he demanded. "Do you not want to sing? Do you have any idea how hard I've worked—the kinds of deals I've had to cut? And you fuck things up every time! Is it built into you or something?"

"Fuck you!" she spat.

She raised her arm to hit him, but he seized her wrist. With her free hand, she slapped him as hard as she could and caught the side of his head. Arno grabbed her other arm. Julia fought viciously and dug with her knees, but in an instant he had her pinned. Pressing down on her, Arno's body was a terrible thing, yet she sensed that he didn't want to hurt her.

"Julia!" he gasped. "Julia! Stop!"

On her arms, the crushing grip relaxed. Julia sat up and smoothed her hair.

"We've got to talk about this," he said. "Before I take another chance, I want an answer from you."

He took hold of her chin and forced her to look at him. On his flushed face, she saw signs of age. There were fewer tufts of gold in his hair, and his eyes were red-rimmed. The intensity of that gaze was relentless, and Julia felt herself dissolving.

"I know it's your kid," he said. "It's always been your kid. But other people have kids, and they sing. I want to know why—when you're almost there. After the *Christmas Oratorio*, you could have sung anything! You come out of this shithole, you work for so long—and then you have a kid with a guy you won't even live with? Who is this guy anyway?"

Julia's tears flowed onto the fingers gripping her chin. The anger was fading from Arno's eyes, but there was fury in his grasp.

"Who is this guy?" he demanded. He wasn't going to let her go until she answered.

"His name is Erik," she said. Sick as she was, she left out his last name, uncertain what Arno might do to him.

"Okay, so Erik," he growled. He gave Julia back her face and nodded for her to go on.

"He's from Henningsthal." She sighed. "I knew him growing up. He knows about everything. He knows about my father—"

She lost her voice in a surge of tears. This time Arno's crushing hug felt comforting.

"It's okay," he said. "You don't have to talk about that." He kissed the top of her head.

The rest of her story was muffled by Arno's shirt, and he shifted her to make sure it reached his ears.

"He came up," she said. "He was having problems with his wife—she's left him now—and I was so glad to see him. After it happened, I felt something alive in me. I couldn't kill it—I couldn't give it up. Not because of him—because of how it felt!"

She looked up and met the full force of his eyes.

"What does he do?" he asked.

"He's a music teacher."

Arno grunted and nodded as though something finally made sense.

"And he's free—his wife's left him? But you don't want to live with him?"

Julia shook her head violently, and Arno grinned.

"A real pussy, huh?"

Julia smiled and reached for a tissue.

"Yeah," chuckled Arno. "There's nothing worse than a faggot who fucks women."

Too exhausted to protest, Julia shook her head, laughing, and Arno stroked her hair playfully.

"So is he helping you out at least? Where is he, Henningsthal?"

"No, Frankfurt." She sighed.

Arno nodded and frowned. "So he can't help you watch her?"

"Well, he wants to," said Julia slowly. "His mother does. She's after me all the time. She wants me to move to Frankfurt."

"Oh, shit!" Arno straightened. "You wouldn't do that, would you?"

"No, no," she said hurriedly.

Julia stared at the red mugs of coffee, which had somehow remained upright.

"So why don't you let them take her sometimes?" asked Arno. "I mean, if she wants to—just let her take her off your hands for a while."

"I don't trust her," said Julia. "I don't like her. I don't want Bettina to be around her."

"Well, what's wrong with her?" asked Arno. "Even if she's a bitch on wheels, it's not contagious at your kid's age."

"She looks down on people," said Julia. "Anyone who doesn't know the plot of *Turandot*, she basically wants to shove 'em in the ovens."

"Oh, yeah." Arno sighed. "I know the type."

Julia wondered how many poisonous looks he had endured from people who thought him unfit to make music.

"Y'know," said Arno, "music—" He paused and drew a deep breath. "To be a good musician, you don't have to read the arts page of the *Frankfurter Allgemeine*. You don't have to memorize the program notes. It's something you *do*. Talking about it, writing about it—that's something else."

"You're not kidding," muttered Julia.

"You can do it—better than just about anyone. How, why—who cares? With the voice you've got, you should be singing. Give her the kid! Shit, today you left her with Dagmar Schleifer!"

Through the closed door, Julia heard a faint cry, and she jumped up guiltily. Arno followed her to the bedroom. In her crib, Bettina was dreaming, openmouthed. She grimaced as though someone were pinching her and clutched the blanket with one tiny hand. Arno stared, fascinated, at the expressions passing over her face as her pain gave way to anger, then to something that looked like awe.

Julia touched Bettina's damp red-brown curls, and she smiled in her sleep. Arno drew in his breath. Julia pointed toward the door, and they crept back to the couch.

"She looks like you," murmured Arno. "I never saw anything like that—her face—like changing keys every two measures."

"Yeah," said Julia quietly. "She's like a mirror. Everything I do, she reflects back to me."

"Listen." Arno gripped her hands. "I want to know if you still want to sing. I mean if you really want to. You know what I mean. Because if you do—"

"I want to sing," said Julia.

Arno nodded and squeezed her fingers. "That's what I thought. You don't act like it half the time, but when I said you didn't, you just about knocked my ear off."

Julia stared back, unapologetic.

"Okay." He exhaled hard. "The *St. John Passion*. In four weeks. I've asked Hyun-A, but I'll find her something else. I want your word that you'll show up and that you'll sound like yourself. No matter what. Even if your kid's puking pea soup and her head's spinning."

"I'll do it." Julia laughed.

Arno's grip tightened. "I'm going to make this happen. You're going to sing—really sing, like you were meant to. Even if I have to kill someone."

"I'll do it." Julia's joy surged.

Arno cupped her face in his hands.

"That's not all," he said softly. He let his hands drop. "I've been talking to Linda." With a sudden frown, he fumbled in his shirt pocket. "She's pissed off at me, but we're still talking. She thinks she can get us a gig in New York."

"What—for the *St. John Passion*?"

"No, no, *Messiah!*" he exclaimed. "You, Linda, Michael, Markus—same team as the *St. Matthew Passion*. At Christmas. Not this year, but next year, or maybe the year after. Could you do that?"

"Yes," said Julia.

"Don't say yes unless you mean it," he warned. "Don't say yes and make me pick some kid from the choir."

"I'll do it," said Julia. "I'll go with you. I'll figure something out. I'll do it."

Arno leaned forward and kissed her, and she opened to his firm lips and smoky taste.

"Hey, easy." He grinned, pushing her back. "There'll be time for that. But tonight—there's just too much—"

Julia nodded, blushing. Arno pulled out his cigarettes and matches.

"Hey, not here," she said. "Not with Bettina. Out in the hallway, okay?"

"Okay, yeah." He grimaced. "But bring me my coat, will ya? It's fucking freezing out there."

In the dingy hall light, Arno drew on his cigarette. Gray-brown stubble broke the line of his cheek.

"You been okay?" she asked quietly.

"Yeah, yeah." He sighed. "I'm almost done with my orchestral piece. It's not right yet. I hear it, but when I write it down, it's not what I'm hearing. It's just one beat off somewhere—one instrument, one note. It's driving me crazy—like chasing something that disappears just as you're about to catch it."

Julia nodded, feeling his frustration. Arno kicked the wall and watched his round black shoe bounce off it.

"And imagining who'll play—that's part of the problem. I want the Philharmonie, but only if I conduct."

"Would they let you do that?"

Arno smiled cynically. "I'll have to cut some kind of deal. You wanna give *Schrubber* a good time for me? Or should I send Rudi?"

Julia choked on her laugh. "Y'know, that's not funny. Do you realize how much he does for you? How much you mean to him? You know what he had to give up?"

Arno stopped smiling. "Yeah, some uptight prick who fucked him up the ass and kept him on a short leash. The time you spend with him, you know that better than I do."

Arno's deep voice echoed through the stairwell, and Julia shushed him. She had to swallow her laugh.

"So you could be nice to him sometime," she said. "You ever thought of that? Be nice to Handshaw, and he'll give you his orchestra."

"*Schrubber?*" Arno ground out his cigarette. "Every time I see him, I want to shave his fucking—"

"Sh!" Julia laughed. "Shut up!"

"Boy, has this neighborhood gone to shit!" growled Arno in a voice so much like Astrid's Julia thought she was hallucinating.

"C'mere, Mädel." Arno enfolded Julia in a hug and held her until her breathing matched his. Under her ear, his coat rose in pulses. They expanded into each other in waves.

Arno stepped back and kissed her gently.

"Okay." He smiled.

Before she knew it, she was hearing his quick steps fade down the stairs while she bent to retrieve his cigarette butt.

———— ■ ————

At work the next day, Julia had trouble following Marga. She was saying something about the street construction office. Unable to find gigs, Ultraviolet had decided on an outdoor concert, and they would be singing next Saturday at Alexanderplatz. They had to set up their gig as a publicity event, and for weeks they had been visiting offices and filling out forms. Their sponsor was Manny's Ice Cream, which would power their amps as long as they advertised aggressively. Next weekend, Marga and her band would be singing in the biggest square in Berlin for anyone who cared to hear.

"There must be a couple thousand bands in Berlin," muttered Marga, shaking her head. "Our demo CD's good, but it's hopeless. You can't get bookings without an agent, and you can't get an agent unless you're singing clubs. At least this way someone will hear us."

Marga frowned at a chocolate muffin whose mound had lost a dark avalanche. She culled it from the basket and headed for the trash.

"Hey, wait a minute! I was gonna eat that!" cried Julia.

Marga smiled. "First time all day you've sounded like yourself. What were you doing last night, drowning your sorrows? I thought Bettina was sleeping better."

"No," said Julia. "I still can't believe it. Arno came over."

Marga brushed aside a few strands of black hair. "Holy shit! That conductor guy?"

"Yeah. He came over to yell at me for blowing the audition."

"Oh, that was nice of him." Marga's blue-green eyes sparkled. "You sure that's all he came for?"

"Pretty much." Julia laughed. "He wants me to sing again— the *St. John Passion*. Maybe another *Messiah*."

"Hey, that's great!" Marga handed her the chocolate muffin. Still bright, her eyes dug into Julia's. "So nothing happened, huh?"

"Nope." Julia took a bite, and Marga watched her chew, her smile deepening as the silence pulsed.

Unlike Marga, Birgit felt responsible for Julia's failure, and Basti let her know she had fucked up royally. Gleefully, Astrid recounted Frau Schicke's tirade about her son's mistreatment of her daughter. Basti's harsh upbraiding had produced a meltdown, and for days Birgit had refused to leave her bed. "Irresponsible," he had called her, "irresponsible," her Birgit, who was about to graduate from *Realschule*! That was more than could be said for that wannabe carpenter, who had yet to land a full-time job. Astrid replied that maybe he should call the Socialist Party since that was how Frau Schicke had found most of her work. Either that, or maybe the local husbands. The beautician had stalked down the stairs, and the two women hadn't spoken since.

Basti saw Birgit as a problem to be solved and the feud between their mothers as intolerable. When Frau Schicke wouldn't let him in, he offered—through the closed door—to take Birgit out on a job hunt. In June, Birgit was about to become one of the few in the house with a high school diploma. Although she had registered with the job center, her search hadn't come to much yet. Clicking listlessly through online files, she had never been sure what to write down, and jaunts to stores with her friends had turned to shopping trips. Next Saturday, Basti was taking her to Alexandria, the most luxurious mall in Berlin. Usually his excursions with Birgit worried Astrid, but this time she grudgingly approved. Since Astrid had gone back to work, she had been ill-tempered and tired, and under the kitchen light, her face was gray. She had outlined her eyes with dark-blue pencil, but under them, a perverse hand had etched deeper crescents.

"He's not as dumb as he looks." She sighed. "It's like he's makin' an investment. If he spends time gettin' her a job now, it'll pay off later. She'll have somethin' to do, an' she'll meet lots of new people. If she meets a guy, he's rid of her for good."

Julia shrugged, sharing Astrid's wish that Birgit would drop off the face of the earth. She was furious at Birgit for wrecking what might have been her only chance to sing professionally.

Birgit didn't deserve a job shoveling shit, but Astrid was right. If the Princess found her dream job selling clothes at a mall, it would be the best for all concerned.

Saturday morning, when Julia saw Birgit in her new gray pants suit, she found it hard not to smile. Hearing that Julia was taking Bettina to see Marga, Basti had combined their missions. He and Julia would spend the day helping Birgit find work, then listen to Marga that afternoon.

Birgit looked down and drew a deep breath. "I'm so sorry," she said. Her round blue eyes showed genuine shame. "It won't ever happen again. I swear to God. Anytime you need me to watch Bettina, I'm there."

Birgit looked sideways at Basti, who was nodding energetically.

"That's okay," muttered Julia.

Bettina eyed Birgit's uneasy, shifting curves.

"Do I look okay?" asked Birgit, glancing at Basti. From her tone, Julia was sure she had been consulting him all week.

There was no denying how good Birgit looked. Fine vertical lines on her gray pants suit made her seem taller and slimmer. Although the jacket's button pulled, she appeared full-bodied rather than fat. Her shiny turquoise blouse revealed dangerous cleavage, and she had clipped back her hair, giving her round face an earnest look. With a minimum of makeup, her blue eyes and full lips had a winning freshness.

"You look nice," said Basti. "But you're gonna have to close up that blouse. That don't look professional."

"Okay." Birgit giggled.

She buttoned it all the way up to the neck, stuck out her chest, and made a prissy face. Basti undid the top two buttons.

"But that's all, you hear?" he warned. "No more. Not until you get a job and we go out to celebrate."

The stroller jolted Julia's shin. Anxious to move, Bettina was kicking with a quick beat. In just a few days, a warm wind had chased off the cold, and the mush underfoot seemed to belong to another era. The urge to bare one's flesh was irresistible, and Julia had put on a purplish sweater with a deep V-neck. On the U-Bahn, Basti sat between her and Birgit, so that his breath warmed Julia's cheek when she leaned over to give advice.

"It's gonna be hard," she shouted over the U-Bahn's rattle. "Some people are gonna treat you like crap. You've gotta be ready."

Birgit nodded anxiously and clutched the black folder she had brought to hold her application forms.

"You just gotta keep goin'," said Basti. "You gotta keep tellin' yourself, 'This is what I know.' Clothes, shopping, how much stuff costs, where to find stuff—who knows that better than you?"

Bettina hated the din of the U-Bahn, so Julia covered her daughter's ears playfully. Each time Julia lifted her hands, Bettina let out a shriek that pierced the U-Bahn's roar. It was a relief to escape into an aqua tunnel, which led to a pond of sunlight in front of Alexandria.

The mall built by foreign investors had been an instant success, drawing people who had once shopped on windy Karl-Marx-Allee. All over the city, signs proclaimed that Alexandria was open six days a week from ten until nine. From fluttering banners, the Alexandria woman smiled, a red-haired, long-necked beauty. The night Alexandria opened, the police had called in ambulances to save people nearly crushed at the media store. Since that first rush, the flow of customers had been steady, a never-ending line of ants from Alexanderplatz.

Against the morning sun, Alexandria loomed before them. Its supporting ribs curled out as they rose, making the mammoth mall look top-heavy. Surrounded by panels of rosy stone, its cubist murals glittered.

"That red stone sure is nice," said Julia. "It must have cost a fortune."

Basti smiled cynically. "Same stuff they use on the bike paths. Looks good, but it can't cost that much."

In her mind, Julia compared Alexandria's walls to the bike lane they had just crossed. Sure enough, it was made of the same pink squares—they just looked so much better beside the Picasso murals.

Once inside, Julia forgot the red walls and enjoyed the vast, open space. Between inner and outer horseshoes of stores, a central corridor hummed with voices. Sun shone through the third-floor skylights, brightening the red, blue, and green marble under her feet. On a flag two stories high, the Alexandria woman rippled. Brilliant shop windows pulled Julia's eyes a dozen ways.

"We've gotta do this systematically," said Basti, glancing around uneasily. "Otherwise ..." His voice trailed off. Confidently, he smiled at Birgit. "Okay. We do one floor at a time, first the outside stores, then the inside. Every store, no matter what they sell."

Birgit giggled nervously, suddenly realizing what the day was going to be like.

"We're gonna keep a checklist," continued Basti. "Every store. When you come out, we write down what they told you. 'Cause some'll tell you to get lost, an' some'll tell you to come back, an' you'll look like an idiot if ..."

Birgit's round face drew together with anxiety.

"Don't worry," said Julia. "What are they gonna do to you? What are they gonna do?"

As soon as the words left her lips, she knew they were her father's. She had spoken them just as he did, with the same defiant bluster.

"Yeah." Basti grunted. "No matter what they say, nobody can hurt you unless you let 'em."

"What should I say?" asked Birgit, breathing quickly.

"You say, 'Hi. You need any extra help? Are you hirin'? Are you lookin' for any new salespeople?'"

Birgit liked the sound of the last one best. "Hi," she breathed. "Are you looking for any new salespeople?"

"No, not like that," said Julia. "That sounds like Britney Spears. You've gotta breathe deeper. Get the right kind of support. Get a big belly full of air, and say it in a real strong voice."

"Hi. Are you looking for any new salespeople?" Birgit laughed at the sound of her new tone.

"That's it," said Basti. "You've just gotta do it. Here. Start with this place. Go in here."

"But that's a jewelry store!" Birgit gasped.

"What—so you can't sell jewelry?" he said. "There's nothin' to it. Get in there!"

Slowly Birgit walked into the shop, and the man behind the counter approached her dubiously.

Julia worried the day would be hard on Bettina, who loved new sensations but had a saturation point. She had brought along a good supply of juice and raisin buns, but she feared what would happen when the tunes and flashes wore her out.

"You really think she's gonna get something?" she asked Basti, who was watching the tall, bald man lean toward Birgit.

Basti shrugged. "She won't if she don't try." He sighed. "She's got as good a chance as anyone. She looks great. She loves new clothes. Most of these places are gonna throw her out. We've just gotta keep her goin' till she finds one that's right for her."

Birgit returned to them with lowered eyes. "He said I had no experience."

Basti grimaced. "Aw, they all say that. C'mon, let's go try the next place. Gimme that pad I gave you."

On the pad, he drew a thick, straight number one, noted the name of the store, and wrote "No experience." He slid the pad into the back pocket of Bettina's stroller. Birgit had drifted over to the jewelry store window, where a garden of wonders was sparkling. Julia and Basti joined her, and he followed her eyes to a flower of light-blue stones on a silver chain.

"You like that?" he asked softly.

Birgit nodded and shifted her body so they were almost touching.

"When you get a job, I'm gonna buy you that," he promised. "Come on. Next store. Bettina's gonna get tired. We can't stay here all day."

Birgit entered the shops one by one. In some of them, the saleswomen sniggered, but in others, they handed her applications. As Birgit's sheaf of papers grew, the drama became routine, and she stopped rushing back elated or near tears. After she was rejected by a lingerie store, Julia and Basti followed at a greater distance. Seeing the stroller, the manager had quickly dismissed Birgit, wary of any girl associated with a baby.

As a luxury mall, Alexandria offered shadowy nooks with soft black armchairs. Seeing two of them free, Julia and Basti settled and took turns reaching into the stroller to play with Bettina. Basti boxed with her, and the little girl squealed, protesting when he withdrew his brown fists.

"Looks like Bettina's doin' great." He smiled. "What about you, though? I'm sorry about that choir."

"Oh, it's okay." Julia sighed. "I'm not sure it would have made any difference. Even if Birgit had been watching her ... I'll never know. Anyway, it's no excuse."

"I've heard you sing," said Basti. "Your voice is beautiful. You could sing opera—or one of those big shows maybe …"

"Thanks," she murmured, kneading the yielding chair.

She raised her head to find Basti gazing at her steadily. His small, dark eyes registered something she didn't know she had revealed.

"Is … that guy … helpin' you out?" he asked. "What's goin' on with him?"

"He's in Frankfurt," said Julia. "He teaches there. He and his mother want me to move down there."

She glanced at Bettina, on whose face her features and Renate's were inextricably blended.

"So are you gonna do that?" asked Basti. His eyes flicked downward.

"No," said Julia. "I want to stay here."

Basti breathed out slowly. "So you don't love him?"

"No." She sighed. "He's just an old friend. He means a lot to me. Talking to him makes me feel good sometimes, but I don't love him like—"

Basti ducked his head. "I saw you together," he murmured. "I didn't think you loved him either. He's not right for you."

Julia studied the taut threads of her jeans, then forced herself to look up. "I know," she whispered. "I know you watch me at night."

"I want to take care of you," said Basti.

He took her hand and squeezed it. He breathed in and out before he trusted his voice. Julia clutched his rough fingers, and encouraged, he found his words.

"That guy can't take care of you. It's written all over him. He can't even take care of himself. It's great you've got Bettina, but I can see why you don't want him. I'm younger than you, and your music—I could never do anything like that. But if you want someone who's there for you—for you and Bettina—I— You're the most wonderful woman I ever knew!"

"Basti!" Julia gasped. She covered her face with her hands, hiding sobs she couldn't hold back. When she looked up, she found him in torment, unable to embrace her in public.

"You've gotta tell me what you want," he said. "If you want me to be with you, you've gotta tell me." He searched her face and struggled to go on. "I've been thinkin' about goin' to Norway—or Canada. Or America even. They need carpenters there. They pay good money. I've been talkin' to some guys. Over there, they don't have this apprenticeship stuff. You just do it. You do it, and if you're any good, you make it."

Julia nodded. "That sounds good for you."

Basti drew in his breath. "You want me to go?"

"I don't know," she murmured. "I don't want to hold you back."

Basti's face darkened. "My life is a crock of shit," he muttered. "Workin' for nothin', fixin' up good furniture for trashy people. You're what keeps me goin'—you and Bettina."

He peered through a tree of purses into a handbag shop, where Birgit was pleading her case. Basti shook his head and smiled cynically.

"You know I'm just—" He broke off, searching for words. "You know I don't want to be with her. I'm just tryin' to help her. I know she—"

He glanced at Birgit a little more fondly. "She looks real good, and she's tryin' so hard, but compared to you ..."

Julia followed his eyes to Birgit, who was drinking the lean manager's words. The brown-haired girl nodded in a slow, even rhythm.

"Basti," whispered Julia, ashamed.

His dark eyes probed her. "There's someone else, isn't there?" he asked, sensing an answer in her quick shudder.

"No!" she exclaimed, but Basti nodded slowly.

"Yeah." He sighed. "Not her father." He looked down at Bettina, who was falling asleep, lulled by the soft, familiar voices. "It's somebody in music, right? Somebody you sing with?"

Feeling herself overpowered, Julia gave a tiny nod.

"And you want to be with him?" Basti began to look older, his mouth tense, his jaw hard.

"No ... I don't know," she murmured. "This is crazy. He doesn't feel anything for me."

Basti's smile returned for an instant. "That's what you think," he whispered.

"Hey, you guys!" Birgit rushed up and frowned at Julia's swollen eyes. "What's goin' on?" she asked, bewildered. "Are you okay?"

"Yeah, she's good," said Basti. "We were talkin' about some heavy stuff. Tell me where you been. We gotta keep up with that list."

Birgit glanced uneasily at Julia.

"I'm doin' real good," she said. "A lot of these places, they got stores all over Berlin. You apply to one of 'em, you apply to all of 'em."

"That's great," said Basti. He took his left hand in his right and reached for the skylights to stretch his back. "We gotta write that down before we hit the other malls. Tell me everywhere you been."

"Are you gonna go to the other malls with me?" Birgit's round face brightened.

"Sure." Basti smiled. "Until you're gainfully employed, we're goin' everywhere."

He pulled out the list and noted the stores Birgit had visited, asking her exactly what the managers had said.

"Let's get goin'," he muttered. "When you get done with the second floor, I'm gonna buy you lunch."

Basti and Birgit set off together, leaving Julia and Bettina in a teddy bear store. For half an hour, Bettina squeezed plushy bears and pulled pink tulle skirts, examining them without mercy. At last the job hunters returned, looking weary.

"You like those bears? Lemme get you one," said Basti.

Bettina chose an open-armed white bear with jeans and a purple top like Julia's. Once it was in her hands, she clutched it fiercely. She wouldn't release it even to eat. Julia was famished, and in Bettina's tight grip, she also saw signs of hunger. She had been chewing on raisin buns since morning, but she needed some solid food.

Julia sized up the food court restaurants and wondered which one might let her use a microwave. She led the others through the full circuit of eateries, staring hungrily at pizza, foil-wrapped potatoes, and enchiladas. Julia shook her head at the hamburger place, hungry for something more substantial. She hurried past a health food store that displayed plastic cups crammed with fruit. Basti pointed toward the Turkish restaurant, where a man in white was shaving a shaggy, rotating joint of meat. Basti asked for three pungent, heaping *Döner* platters, and with a questioning look, Julia held out her plastic containers of macaroni and carrots. A girl with thick black hair smiled broadly and popped them into the microwave. She raised her brows over friendly dark eyes and gestured for them to come inside.

The food disappeared quickly from Basti's and Birgit's plates, but Julia emptied hers more slowly. She fed Bettina spoonfuls of macaroni and tried to keep the sticky noodles away from the bear's fur. Bettina smiled with pleasure as she ate, loving the feel of a full mouth. She polished off most of what Julia had brought and then fell fast asleep. By the time Julia's thick, speckled plate was clean, she wished that she could do the same.

"Ooh, I ate too much," moaned Birgit, rubbing her stomach.

Her third and fourth buttons had come undone. Basti stared dreamily into the shady cleft.

"What're you lookin' at?" Birgit giggled, massaging her belly.

"Oh, I'm thinkin' how nice that necklace is gonna look … just where it's gonna hang." Basti smiled lazily. "You better get yourself a job soon, 'cause that sure is gonna look good on you."

He shifted his legs and brushed his foot against Julia's. Full of warm food, she stirred with pleasure, suspecting what he must be thinking. Except for Rudi, she had never known a guy who didn't want two women at once. As if he had read her thoughts, Basti fondled her side.

"Boy, you girls sure can eat, huh? The way you put it away, I dunno if I can afford any jewelry."

Julia and Birgit laughed delightedly while he ordered three strong coffees. The black elixir made Julia's heart race, and she scoffed at the skimpy clothes in the windows they passed. Bettina slept with her mouth open against the bear's head, afloat in warm, soothing dreams.

Energized by the food, Birgit attacked the third floor with her blouse open. Sick of being professional, whatever that meant, she spoke to the salesgirls in her own voice.

"Hey—how ya doin'? You guys need any extra help?"

Most of the women sent her packing, but at Pinkie she made some new friends. Forgetting all about her job search, she exclaimed over a shimmery blue top, knowing how well she would fill it out. Studying themselves in the mirror, she and the salesgirls compared the blues that best matched their eyes. Birgit left with an application for all ten Pinkies in Berlin and a promise to put in a good word with central management.

Even though she seemed to have found a sure thing, Basti made her finish the third floor.

"You never know," he said. "You gotta keep your options open."

Birgit probed every cell of the highest tier, and as a reward, Basti treated her and Julia to sundaes at the *gelateria*. Julia ordered a Black Forest cherry cup brimming with chocolate, cherries, and cream. Birgit swallowed a Jamoca Almond Dream with so much Kahlúa it made her giggly. Basti didn't like sweets, but he watched Julia and Birgit enjoy their creamy goo and kidded them about their appetites. Julia could have sat there laughing for hours, but Bettina woke up angry. Julia offered her a dripping spoonful of chocolate, but she screwed up her face and cried, "No, Mama, cold!" People at nearby tables shot disgusted glances, and Julia decided it was time to hear Marga.

Basti kept Birgit in a never-ending fit of giggles, playfully pinching her sides. He swore that she and Julia together couldn't put away as much ice cream as the last Russian lady who had bought a dressing table. She had nearly split the bench in spite of two oak crosspieces.

Julia tried to comfort Bettina, who was fussing from the change in the air and light. Usually she loved the outdoors, but the sudden drop in temperature had jarred her temper. The morning's warmth had faded, and in spite of the sunlight, the breeze was cutting. Bettina thrashed as Julia forced her arms into a sweater. As she had suspected, the little girl had reached her limit and would reject any new sights and sounds that day.

In the afternoon sun, Alexanderplatz pulsed with a lolling rhythm. Smiling wearily, Julia relished the open space. Its vastness enveloped her, reducing her to a dark speck. On the far side,

Kaufhof stood like a cathedral, its green banners fluttering against its white walls. Square gray windows watched red-and-yellow trains slide through the nearby station. Water surged from a fountain resembling a cluster of toadstools, around which tourists, punks, and drinkers had gathered. The crowd looked rougher down near the Weltzeituhr, a rotating clock that showed the time worldwide. Periodically, yellow trams sliced the square, but people walked fearlessly across the tracks.

Next to the indigo arch of the U-Bahn, Marga was struggling with a broad banner. Between gusts of wind, she and Kevin, the bass player, were trying to secure the sign. As it bulged outward, Julia read, "Manny's Ice Cream Presents Ultraviolet: Rockin' All the Colors of the Rainbow."

"Ultraviolet ain't a color. Ain't even visible," growled Basti. "How'd they come up with that?"

He hurried to help Marga fasten the sign while the guitarist played with the sound system.

Marga's movements had quickened until Julia could scarcely follow her trembling hands. For the performance, Marga had outlined her eyes in black, and she was wearing bleached, beat-up jeans and a fluttery dark top. Despite the chilling wind, her wiry body seemed to radiate heat.

"We've gotta be at least fifty feet from the U-Bahn," she said, "or they can close us down, but the cable from Manny's won't reach."

Her painted eyes looked so wild that Julia wondered whether she had taken something. Probably she was just excited about singing.

"Hey, Bettina!" cried Marga. She bent over the stroller so that her scruffy head was inches from the little girl's.

Bettina screamed with outrage, and Marga backed off, laughing. With a groan, Julia swung her daughter onto her hip, but Bettina thrashed and cried for her bear. With her free arm, Julia bobbled the animal. Each test of the sound system set off a fresh burst of shrieks. On the bench near the fountain, people scowled at the noisy thing stabbing the afternoon calm.

The band was closer to being ready than it sounded, and Marga ran to take her place. The bass player tried a few quick notes and nodded to the guitarist, who played twanging riffs. The drummer started a fast, steady beat that ricocheted off the gray buildings. Marga's hoarse voice turned the band to a living whole.

"Hey, you all!" she yelled into the mike. "We're Ultraviolet, and we're gonna rock this place, compliments of Manny's Ice Cream. All right, everybody! Let's go!"

The drumbeat increased in volume, and with three quick strokes, the guitarist played the opening chords of "Smoke on the Water." A whoop went up from the bench near the fountain. A girl in a pink dress and red-and-white tights leaped to her feet. Down near the Weltzeituhr, some drunks left their bottles. The drum was so demanding Julia felt her heart adjust to its rhythm, unwilling to pump off the beat.

Over the instruments, Marga kept on shouting. "Come on, you all! Let's see you move!"

She clapped her hands over her head. Her skinny hips rocked, and her black top fluttered crazily.

"All right!" she yelled to the girl in the pink dress, who was shimmying in front of the amp.

By the time Marga began to sing, a good-sized crowd had formed. Two British teenagers played air guitar, and a grizzled drunk danced with the girl in the pink dress. Toward the back, two red-faced men in khaki vests stood listening, openmouthed. Their cropped-headed wives jounced good-naturedly beside them. Birgit took off her jacket and begged Basti to dance, but he glanced at Julia and shook his head.

On Julia's hip, Bettina was wailing angrily. Julia put down the bear and set her on her feet, covering her little ears with both hands. Bettina had decided that she'd had enough. She kicked and punched Julia's legs. Julia worked her way over to Basti.

"You guys," she said, "I'm going to have to take her home. She's had a really long day."

"Oh, I'll go with you," said Basti, smiling warmly.

"No, no, that's okay. I'll take her," said Julia. "You guys stay and listen. Let me know how it goes."

"Okay." Birgit grinned. "Thanks so much for helping. It's been a really great day. Hey, do you think you could take this stuff home for me?"

She pawed aside the crumpled bag of raisin rolls and stuffed her folder of applications into Bettina's stroller. The little girl screamed through Kevin's introduction to the next song, but Julia caught some of his words: "A song by our vocalist, Marga Vogel ... about those times you want to end a relationship with a clean sweep."

The drumbeat resounded off of Kaufhof, and the guitarist played eight quick seventh chords. Marga stepped forward, microphone in hand. Bettina wailed furiously in her stroller.

"Gonna mop my floor!"

Low and hoarse, Marga's voice raked Alexanderplatz. Heeding its call, everyone in the square turned to see.

"Gonna mop my floor!"

By the second phrase, Marga had blown off the static. Eyes closed, arm extended, she shouted into the microphone and wagged her hips provocatively.

"Want you out the door!"

The girl in pink whooped at the IV^7 transition and shook out her shiny brown hair.

"What you cryin' for?"

Julia glanced at Basti, who was clutching Birgit's shoulders. Together, they were moving their hips to the beat. Turning his head, he shot Julia a sad, ironic look. Julia waved, then pushed Bettina toward the blue arch of the U-Bahn. From the dank tunnel she heard enthusiastic applause.

■

Within days of the trip to Alexandria, Basti and Birgit were an acknowledged couple. Frau Riemann told Astrid she had heard them in the shop at four in the morning, but no one in the house needed to be told. Although Basti spoke as cynically as ever, his motions had a fluid quality. Fifteen minutes after school ended, Birgit could be seen running across the Hof, her lips parted and her blue eyes shining. Each day Basti helped her fill out applications. On Saturday, they would take them back to the stores.

"Why'd you have to leave 'em alone like that?" moaned Astrid.

She dug her fingers into her hair until the dark roots twisted like a charcoal centipede. Disgusted by cleaning, she was growing ever more depressed. She had more money than she did on disability, but she was too tired to spend it and passed most of each weekend in bed.

"Couldn't you see what was goin' on?" she demanded.

Julia shifted her weight and sighed. "Bettina was throwing a fit," she said. "You should've heard her. I had to get her out of there—she was making more noise than the band."

Astrid nodded slowly, her eyes fixed on the Vorderhaus windows.

"Listen, I wouldn't worry," said Julia. "I don't think this is gonna last. I think—mainly he likes helping her. They have a lot of fun together."

"Yeah, that's one word for it," muttered Astrid.

Julia did her best to comfort her, but in the next weeks, she had little time. Taking no chances, Arno was working her hard, and when she wasn't with Arno, she was with Rudi. The two *St. John Passion* arias were treacherous, and Arno wanted her voice in top form. Busy as he was, he ran her through strange arpeggios and studied the ways her notes changed when she approached them at different speeds.

In the evenings Rudi brought over his keyboard, and like a caged animal, Julia's voice shook the house walls. Once when she opened the window, she saw Basti on the cellar steps, smoking and leaning against the railing. Feeling the pull of her eyes, he smiled and waved. By now he had gotten used to Rudi's visits and nodded jerkily when the technician murmured, "Hi."

Rudi asked so often about Bettina that Julia suspected Arno was making him spy. If the tenor was looking for illnesses, she had none to report. In the wet spring air, Bettina was thriving. Having mastered walking, she was starting to run, and the beat of her steps pounded the floor. As her reddish curls grew, she looked like Julia and Erik in alternating moments. She sniffed the air with her little snub nose. Her voice was shrill, but she was learning to manage it and saved her most piercing tones for crucial moments.

When Julia practiced, Bettina now stayed quiet, squealing only when her mother slowed in the final phrase. Rudi taught her to applaud, and soon she was a champion clapper.

"Say 'Brava, Mama'!" He grinned, gazing down with bright eyes.

"Bwa, Mama!"

Julia spluttered with laughter.

"Bwaa, Mamaa!" Bettina scowled, hating to be mocked.

"Okay, that's good," said Rudi. "You keep working on that."

With Rudi playing, Julia sang through each phrase of her arias. She learned their contours until she could form them effortlessly.

"Von den Strikken meiner Sünden"—"From the Tangles of My Sins"—took all of her concentration. With its bright quality, the D minor aria didn't sound mournful that Christ's death had set people free. Julia recognized the tangles the first time she heard them. In almost every quick run, Bach had embedded two notes twice as fast, creating an odd catch in the rhythm. Listening to the coloratura, you always felt that you had missed a beat, and singing it, you were sure you had miscounted. Although the piece had little coloratura, the short runs were traps. As Julia sang about how Christ's bondage had freed her, she didn't feel liberated.

Although she knew the first aria would be rough, the second seemed to occupy Arno. Agonizingly slow, accompanied only by cello and continuo, the piece demanded an unwavering tone few altos could offer. In the moment of Christ's death, she had to sing, "Es ist vollbracht"—"It is done"—and ask God to comfort grieving souls. The slow pace didn't make the descending lines easier, since Bach had used unexpected notes to convey Christ's agony. The real shock came in the vivace section, when the pace doubled and the full orchestra jumped in. Then, just as the new tempo had conquered the ear, Bach brought back the moment of sorrow. The aria ended with a cello solo and Julia's slow, descending line, "Es ist vollbracht." With no break in the rhythm, the Evangelist would then sing, "Und neiget das Haupt und verschied"—"And he bowed his head and died." To pull it off, they would need unbroken concentration and perfect timing.

Arno ordered Julia not to lose eye contact as he took her through the shifts. With her and Markus, who would be singing the Evangelist, he spent an hour on the transition alone, like an Olympic relay coach perfecting the handoff. Since the *St. Matthew Passion*, Markus's precise tenor had gained strength. With him as the Evangelist, Julia felt secure, and Arno seemed pleased with her voice as well. From her innermost source came a river of sound that ebbed and flowed as he willed it. Gazing up at her, Arno's eyes had a look of wonder that reminded her of that first night in the Friedrichskirche.

"This is gonna be great," he muttered after the first rehearsal with Markus. "This is the best I've heard you. You sing like this Good Friday, you can write your ticket."

Arno gathered her in a hug that outlasted the first squeeze. Savoring her warmth, he pressed her to him and stroked the body that had made those rich sounds.

When Erik, Renate, and Horst learned she would be singing, they insisted on coming up for Easter. None of them had ever seen Julia perform, and they relished the chance to hear Bach in the Remembrance Church. Because of the short notice, most hotel rooms were booked, but Renate found a double room near the Charlottenburg S-Bahn.

To Bettina's delight, Erik stayed with her and Julia. His bulk in bed made Julia restless, but except for some affectionate kisses, he kept to his own side. Since Christmas he had lost weight but also more hair, and he was getting a saggy, middle-aged look. Romping on the floor with Bettina, he seemed years younger than he did when standing upright. Sometimes he sat cross-legged, looked his daughter in the eye, and talked to her like Socrates discoursing with a pupil. Thrilled to be taken seriously, Bettina prattled with her own unique logic and told him about everything in her world.

"Hey, this kid's got quite a vocabulary." Erik was laughing when Julia emerged from a long shower. "*Schweinerei? Sauerei?* Where's she getting this?"

"Oh, just around," said Julia. "She's got a great ear."

"Well, she's got to be getting it somewhere." Erik frowned.

"Probably from my neighbor." Julia smiled. "She spends a lot of time with her."

Julia rubbed her hair, and Erik followed the bobbing of her breasts. He hadn't approached her since Bettina was a baby, but she recognized the look of animal interest. His stare didn't have the sharp edge of a man who had never known her—it was more like a homesickness, an ache. It had been some time since Erik had heard from Johanna, and he hadn't mentioned seeing anyone. Leaning back against the couch with his legs sprawled out, he gazed admiringly at Julia.

Julia found herself with Erik a lot, since Renate and Horst were watching Bettina. She felt strange at first walking without diaper packs and a stroller, but she began to savor the intelligent voice talking back.

The afternoon before the concert, the rain let up, and the sun scorched the edges of gray clouds. Renate and Horst took Bettina to children's day at the opera, and Julia decided to go out as well. Erik wanted to see a Southeast Asian exhibit at the Martin-Gropius-Bau, but he yielded to Julia's wish for a walk in the park. In the spring, her craving for dirt and wet leaves became a desire that surged with each pulse.

Along the pathway near Bahnhof Zoo, the Berliners were out in force. The reprieve from the rain had brought a welcome chance to move. With determined strides, Nordic walkers overstepped brown puddles, and bundled couples scowled at dripping trees. Julia breathed the musty scent of the zoo and peered through the fence to see which animals were out. Through the bushes, she spied two silent deerlike creatures, and she and Erik moved on, unimpressed.

Usually Erik wasn't a big walker, but today he moved in soft, easy strides. Since the gate into the *Tiergarten* was open, she suggested they follow the path along the canal. From the mud under Julia's feet came the rich scent of earth, stronger where bicycles had ground ruts between black puddles. She gave up trying to keep her sneakers clean and laughed at the dirt-encrusted rims. Across the canal lay a brilliant oval of yellow-and-purple pansies, their petals fluttering in the breeze. In an arched pattern, the flowers shone in the sunlight, all the brighter against the black soil. Erik took Julia's hand, and she squeezed it fondly, appreciating his presence on the lively day.

"You seem as though you're doing well." Erik smiled. "Are you ready for tomorrow?"

"Oh, yeah, sure." Julia sighed. "Arno's been working me so hard I could sing this stuff in my sleep."

"'This stuff'?" Erik laughed. "You think that's how Bach thought of it?"

"Oh, you should hear what Arno says." She giggled.

"Crazy guy, huh?" he asked.

"Yeah, wacko." She smiled broadly.

Erik squinted at the path ahead of them, which was about to end under a bridge. They climbed some mossy steps to a quiet street that emptied onto a vast, roaring road.

"Oh, I know where we are," said Julia.

Erik smiled fondly, but noise and exhaust broke the mood. It was minutes before the stream of cars ebbed so that they could run across the street. Erik sidestepped a puddle on the Grosser Weg and scowled at a nearby couple. They had reached the busiest zone of the *Tiergarten*, and he spoke uneasily, aware of the lack of privacy. Julia nudged him to the left.

"What's this?" He bumped her back jokingly.

Playfully, she pushed him a little harder. They had reached a glassy, dark pond, and gripping his hand, she pulled him to the edge. On a log extending out into the water, a gray heron perched. His neck formed an exquisite curve against the dark, wet wood.

Erik drew in his breath. "Wow! How did you know he'd be here?"

"He's always here," whispered Julia.

She held her breath as the bird turned his head, then looked back at the water and arched his neck. Erik stepped behind Julia and wrapped his arms around her. He pressed his face into her hair.

"I love how you find things like this," he murmured. "I like being with you."

Julia relaxed into him, and they breathed together, watching the elegant gray bird. Perfectly still, the wild thing stared into the water, cutting a clean profile against the black pond. Behind them came a rattle and a shout of laughter. Despite the mud, bicyclists were underway. With a jerk of its head, the heron glared, then spread his wings and glided off, his legs hanging limply.

"Wow!" Erik frowned over his shoulder at the cyclists.

He and Julia joined hands and continued, this time leaving the main path. Dripping branches scraped Julia's face and caught in her hair.

"This looks quieter," murmured Erik.

"Yeah," said Julia. "I love the stillness."

Only the high-pitched call of a finch broke the brush of leaves against her jacket. Erik stopped, blocking her way. He laid his hands on her shoulders and kissed her gently. In the sweet, wet air, his warm lips were delicious, and she opened to him eagerly. Sighing, he pulled her tightly against him.

"I feel so good with you," he whispered. "I'm so glad we have Bettina. With you, I have this feeling of peace. I never had that with Johanna."

Julia caressed his back in slow circles. Under her eyelids, she felt tears forming.

"I think—maybe this was supposed to happen," he murmured. "In spite of everything—Renate—Johanna—it's biology." He grinned down at her proudly. "Mm?" He shook her playfully.

Enjoying the feel of his arousal, Julia burrowed into his jacket. "Hm?" He laughed. "Hey, come on! Come out of there!"

When Julia looked up, Erik had lost his playfulness. "I want to live with you," he said. "I want to spend more time with Bettina. I don't want to be just a visitor."

Julia nodded slowly.

"There are lots of ways to do it," he said. "I mean—we don't have to be married. You could live with me in Frankfurt, or you could get your own place. I think it's good for Bettina to have us both around, don't you?"

"Yeah." Julia sighed. "But what about you? Couldn't you come up here?"

"I have my job down there," he said. "It's a great school—such bright kids. I don't think I could find a better place anywhere."

"But I need to be here," she insisted. "For singing—there's no comparison. All my friends are up here."

Julia pulled Erik aside to make way for an old couple, who thanked them and wished them a good day. They were tiny people, starved as children in the war, and the man leaned heavily on his wife. In their green wool coats and old-fashioned hats, they smiled patiently at the knobby branches, as though imagining them rich with leaves. Julia waited for the couple to move out of earshot. Erik gazed down at the muddy path.

"It's not just the singing, is it?" he asked.

"Yeah, it is. It's the music."

Erik frowned slightly. "I think it's more. I think it's that guy who helps you."

Julia shook her head angrily. "Why do guys always have to think that?" she demanded. Her voice focused. "Like—like I have to belong to someone! If it's not you, then it's got to be someone else!"

"Do you just not realize?" asked Erik, half-amused. "If you could see your face when you talk about him—"

Nothing made Julia madder than not being listened to. "It's the music!" she cried. "It's not him—it's the singing! I believed you when you said you loved your job. Why can't you believe me? Why does somebody have to own me?"

"I don't want to own you!" protested Erik. "Come on! I'm just saying I like being with you, and I want to be with Bettina! You should think about her!"

"You want me to move down there!" she accused. "Whose idea is that?"

"Mine!" he exclaimed. "I know what you're saying. I'm my own person! You're the one I wonder about. Do you just not realize—"

"Realize what?" Julia drew herself up. Her throat opened, and her full voice emerged, passionate and tough.

Erik shuddered. "Hey. I'm on your side. I want you to be happy. I can't make you—"

"You're damn right you can't!"

Erik recoiled as the common tones struck him a second time. "Do what you want then—whatever it is! Do you even know?"

Julia looked at Erik and counted her breaths. He was trying to read her eyes.

"Okay." He nodded. "Okay."

Julia wrapped her arms around him and listened to the finches in the nearby trees.

By suppertime, she and Erik were tramping upstairs, laughing and talking good-naturedly. Under their disagreement lay an ocean of understanding, and they had affirmed their friendship with ice creams at Potsdamer Platz. On the couch, Bettina was fingering her shapes and forcing them into their slots.

"Mama!" she cried, pushing the game aside.

Julia gathered her up, and Renate told them about the opera. "Bettina did beautifully," she said. "It was so much fun. Papageno invited the children up on stage. Bettina was one of the youngest, but she was singing. She's going to be quite a musician! You were singing, weren't you, Bettina?"

"Yeah!" she cried. "Pa—pa—"

Renate nodded, smiling radiantly.

"What—what did you …?"

Julia's voice cut into Bettina's song. Her table of plants had been moved to the side, as though its chocolate legs had crept toward the shadows. On its shiny surface, her philodendrons looked as though they had been dusted and groomed. Every faded leaf had been plucked, and the others gleamed as though they had been oiled.

"Oh, I just gave them some love," said Renate.

"But the table!" exploded Julia. "They have to have light! They can't live over there!"

"I found her leaning on the table," said Renate. "She had both hands on it, and she was looking up at the window."

Bettina frowned. She didn't like being talked about.

"But she'd never climb up there!" exclaimed Julia. "She knows better!"

She didn't tell Renate that for pulling off leaves, Bettina had gotten her first and only slap. From the time that she could walk, she had been fascinated by the plants and often blew on them as Julia had shown her. But having seen her mother's wrath when she offered her a fistful of leaves, she had grown more cautious.

"She was probably just breathing on them," said Julia. "She likes to do that. We do that together all the time."

"No," said Renate. "I came out of the bathroom, and she was leaning on the table, looking up. You can't leave it there."

"This is not your place!" Julia's voice came fast and deep. "You should have asked me first!"

Renate smiled patiently. "I understand," she said. "It's hard—adjustments like this. It was hard on me too. But when you've got a little one around, you have to make changes."

Horst and Erik exchanged anxious glances, and Julia lowered her voice.

"Well, at least let me make them."

She took a deep breath, swallowed, and exhaled hard. She wondered how her plants would fare until Monday, when she could move the table back.

———————◼———————

As the first notes of the *St. John Passion* sounded, Julia exhaled in a slow, controlled stream. The soft blue glow of the Remembrance Church seemed void of any soothing presence. Circling anxiously, the music was seeking shelter, and its G minor restlessness worried her like the light from the mosaic floor. With her eyes downcast, she recognized a turquoise chip and realized she was back in the same seat she had chosen at the *Christmas Oratorio* over two years ago. The strings' dark swirls made her feel as though she were lost in the woods at night. No matter which way she turned, she could find no way to orient herself. Spinning, intensifying, Bach's whirls produced no melody, only a feeling of dread. Julia forced herself to inhale slowly and wondered why she was so frightened. She had never been so nervous before a concert.

Certainly Julia had the strings rooting for her. At the dress rehearsal, Jakob had brightened when he saw her, and Udo had said what an honor it was to work with her again. Now, as the violins spun the tremulous phrases, they drove the cycling current under the darkness. Swaying with the pulse, the young flutist from the *Christmas Oratorio* held a high F over their troubling storm. Her brown hair was cut so short Julia hadn't recognized her at first, but in front of the tenors, her rhythmic dance was unmistakable. Just behind her stood Rudi, staring intently into the black church.

Since Julia had last seen the Bartholdy Choir, the group had changed considerably. She spotted Anja's catlike face among the sopranos, but many of the older singers had been replaced by younger ones whom Arno was auditioning ever more rigorously. A flash of light from Heike's glasses reminded Julia who ruled the sopranos, but Carola hadn't returned to the alto section. According to Anja, she had left the choir so she could spend more time with her son. In her place stood several slender, tense singers watching Arno lead the orchestra.

An hour ago, Arno had seemed as nervous as Julia and had spoken shortly to the eager musicians. In the quick hug he'd given her, she could feel his tautness, and his intent face had looked haggard. When he'd released her, he'd given her a pleading look. He'd also whispered, "You're the hottest alto I ever saw."

By now the ladies at Round Two knew that Julia needed concert gowns, and they called when a dress appeared in her size. Tonight, she was wearing a black velvet dress with a deep décolletage, a relic from the 1950s. Between her breasts hovered a small dewdrop diamond, a special present from Basti.

A week ago, after a final interview, Birgit had been offered a job at the Gesundbrunnen Pinkie. The store lay in Wedding, a working-class district of Turkish, Polish, and African immigrants. Ecstatic, Birgit had gone out with Basti in her blue flower necklace and had been half carried home, drunk on strawberry daiquiris.

"I'm proud of her," Basti had told Julia. "I wasn't sure she had it in her after that stunt she pulled with you. But that took guts, goin' into all those stores like that. I think she's gonna be okay—with this job, with her *Realschule* degree."

"Yeah, it's great you're so nice to her." Julia smiled.

"Oh, she's pretty nice to me too." He blushed. "I just like to see her havin' a good time. Who knows how she's gonna end up. I want her to be happy." He fell silent and searched Julia's eyes. "Listen," he said, "I got somethin' for you too. For bein' so nice to her after she messed up like that. I got you somethin' nice for your concerts."

Julia opened the gray velvet box, and he smiled with pleasure at her gasp. She'd hugged him tightly and kissed any part of him her lips could reach.

"So I guess you like it, huh?" He'd smiled. "I want you to wear it. I want you to wear it a lot."

The fine-spun chain felt cold under Julia's finger as she traced its downward course. The church was full, but eight hundred bodies hadn't warmed the blue space. Outside, her breath had emerged in smoky puffs, and flakes of snow lurked among the raindrops. Wet and angry, people had settled into their seats, cursing the clinging winter and wondering why they had left their warm apartments. Somewhere in the audience were Basti and Birgit, probably holding hands as the music rose. Erik and Horst would be sitting straighter, listening for any surprise they could report to Renate. Despite her love of music, she had insisted on staying home with Bettina since she doubted a babysitter could handle her.

As the music gained strength, its swirls scattered Julia's thoughts. Arno extended his arms. His eyes raked the choir.

"*Herr!*" they screamed in one voice, crowned by the sopranos' high G. "Lord! Lord!"

Bright and clean, their chords cut through the church. Guided by Arno, sixty voices joined the strings' spirals, but the sound seemed to come from one instrument. Beside Julia, Jörg and Markus straightened and watched the choir admiringly. The scared young soprano seemed less aware as she attempted soothing meditation. Blonde and fragile, she made Julia think of a butterfly, and she squeezed the girl's cold hand. Except for Jörg, Julia was now the senior singer. Shivering, she watched Rudi sing a high A-flat, his eyes black and his mouth open wide.

As the choir performed, Julia forgot her nervousness. Their pristine sound was inspiring. In their short bits, they sang out sharp and clean, crying "Jesum von Nazareth" with breathtaking precision. Their chorale, "O grosse Lieb"—"Oh Great Love"— was a collective sigh like the breath of some great animal. As they wound through the coloratura in the complex movements, they barely looked at their scores. Julia watched their eyes focused on Arno and wished that she could see his face. From the motion of his back, she could imagine his gaze, the nexus of all that passion.

In the pauses, the dark church was perfectly still. Awed by the music, no one in the audience dared move. With his maturing voice, Markus made an extraordinary Evangelist. Even in the most contorted lines, Julia could understand each word since he seemed to be speaking rather than singing. As Jesus, Jörg offered his lines with unearthly calm. In the play of sound and stillness, Julia heard Bach's understanding of life, the motion that forms its own purpose.

By the time Markus told that Christ had been seized, Julia was longing to sing. Fully absorbed, Arno met her eyes without smiling and demanded her attention with one quick glance. He cued the oboes, who had risen for her aria, and the bright introduction sounded. In D minor, the song about sin wound along with an alluringly cheerful ring. Just before Julia's entrance, Arno looked at her with absolute trust, expecting nothing less than perfection.

Julia entered in the heart of her range, the notes spinning out from her core. Although her sound was full, she had the tranquil sense that she was part of something, that she had merged with pure, dark, liquid force. Arno moved with deft confidence. Glancing from Julia to the oboes, he shaped each phrase. With his hands, he showed the inner life of the music, its feints and postures and sighs. "Von den Strikken meiner Sünden mich zu entbinden, wird mein Heil gebunden," she sang. "To free me from the tangles of my sins, my savior is bound."

Effortlessly, Julia formed the notes, taking her cues from Arno's lips and eyes. Instead of frightening her, his gaze bound her to him. In the middle section, when he asked for more power, she delivered it instantly. "Mich von allen Lasterbeulen völlig zu heilen," she sang, gliding joyfully down from her top C. "To heal me fully from all boils of vice." Exhilarated, Julia released the high notes at full strength. "Völlig, völlig." The Remembrance Church throbbed with her voice.

When the tangles returned, even the high E-flat was easy. The catches in the phrases felt natural, so that she couldn't imagine them any other way. Before Julia knew it, she was holding her last D, releasing it sadly at Arno's command. As the oboes twisted through their final phrases, Arno's eyes had a tranquility she had seldom seen. The young soprano sat stiff and white, but she smiled at Julia as she stood for her aria.

When the soprano sang, the music gained beauty and power. Possessed by its energy, the fine-boned girl sang in a voice stronger than Linda's: "Ich folge dir gleichfalls mit freudigen Schritten"—"I'll follow you, too, with joyful steps." Julia smiled at the bronze Jesus behind the choir and savored the clean, clear notes resounding like a divine tread.

The church had grown warmer, and Julia relished the flow of air into her lungs. A few soft sounds told her the audience was stirring, and although it was unprofessional, she turned to look. Her quick glance caught only a sea of dark heads illuminated by a soft blue glow. They seemed to be a respectful crowd, damping their twitches and suppressing their coughs until the breaks between movements.

Only in the confusion of Peter's denial did a child cry out, "Ma!" She was quickly stilled, but a spasm pierced Julia since she sounded so much like Bettina. For once she was glad to know that her daughter was home with Renate. Bettina could never resist joining a dialogue, and the stormy *St. John Passion* was full of them.

Arno was doing the piece without intermission since a break would have shattered the mood. After a lukewarm silence broken by coughs, the opening chorale of part 2 hit hard. Bright and powerful, the choir sang that Christ had been taken like a thief in the night. As the Crucifixion neared, the momentum increased, the crowd hurtling toward purposeless violence. "Nicht, nicht, nicht, nicht!" hissed the choir in a crazy chromatic climb. The dissonant cries of "Kreuzige, kreuzige!"—"Crucify, crucify!"— were terrifying in their fury. For almost an hour, Julia listened, since Bach was saving her voice for a crucial moment. She stood up to sing only when Christ was dying on the cross and had been offered a sponge full of vinegar.

For two hours Arno had been guiding the music, and his fierce eyes betrayed his exhaustion. Their intensity showed he was fully possessed, but his face was streaming with sweat. He gazed at Julia less with command than relief. She smiled at him, and he cued the cello soloist, who began a sad descending line. As Arno brought Julia in, he looked at her with calm expectancy.

"Es ist vollbracht." She sank through a B minor triad.

Rustles pricked the cello's smooth line as people squirmed to see the singer.

"Es ist vollbracht."

Julia relaxed into her high D, and her voice gained power. This slow movement was harder to sing than the tangles, and she knew how badly Arno needed her. In this agonizing tempo, listeners could hear every nuance of her voice. Each phrase had to form a perfect curve hanging in space. The astute old cellist followed Arno's breaths since the conductor gave Julia most of his attention. As she held a low C-sharp, she watched the light in his eyes and let the note fade when he thought it should. Caressing the tone, Julia felt she could hold it forever if he asked. In all their time together, she had never felt so close to him.

As the vivace section approached, Julia's belly tensed. No matter how many times she had rehearsed the transition, it came as a shock. While the cello concluded his hypnotic solo, she sensed the audience's eyelids droop. Arno's glance was terrifying in its intensity. His arm shot out. Alone, she cried out in the darkness, turning B minor to D major.

"Der Held aus Juda siegt mit Macht!"—"The hero of Judah conquers powerfully!"

Behind her, the orchestra exploded. With the dramatic change in tempo, Bach conveyed Christ's triumph. Arno stretched out his arm and signaled Julia to unleash her voice.

"Der Held aus Juda siegt mit Macht!"

Brilliant and powerful, her voice soared up, shaking the indigo panels in the church walls.

"Und schliesst den Kampf!"—"And finishes the fight!"

Arno's eyes flashed. He demanded full volume with absolute precision, but even in the coloratura section, Julia's voice held. She delivered Bach's second surprise as she had his first, humanizing the vivace's sudden end. With glowing notes, she kept the aria from slamming to a halt, so that the shift back to adagio felt natural: "Es ist vollbracht."

For three excruciating measures, the cello's moan filled the darkness. Julia waited, picturing the shape of her last phrase. Next to her, Markus stood ready. Quietly, sorrowfully, she sank to her last B and released it exactly with Arno. Without breaking the rhythm, he cued the continuo.

"Und neiget das Haupt und verschied," came Markus's precise tenor. "And he bowed his head and died."

There was a moment of dead silence.

"Maaaa! Bwa, Mama! Bwa, Ma—" Unmistakable, Bettina's voice cut through the church.

Terrified, Julia looked up at Arno, whose streaming face had turned white. She expected fury but saw only intense pain. He cued Udo and Jakob, who stood shock-faced, ready to begin the next aria.

13

The Crooked Straight

None of the musicians believed that Bettina had come without Julia's knowledge. When the concert ended, Renate led her up front, and the smiling, curly-haired little girl wrapped her arms around Julia's leg. Erik and Horst joined them, and together they formed their own little group while the singers joked and greeted their patrons. Arno embraced the soprano, who had received enthusiastic applause, and he thumped Markus fondly on the shoulder. He sized up Erik with one sharp glance, but he avoided the family group. Even Rudi gave Julia a reproachful look.

Holding hands, Basti and Birgit emerged from the audience. In his wool jacket, Basti had the edgy look that came over him in crowds, and he eyed the Kieperts cautiously. In a light-blue dress that set off her new necklace, Birgit was smiling radiantly.

"Boy, she's got a pair of lungs on her!" she called. "Hey, little one!"

"Birgi!" Bettina ran to her delightedly.

"You were awesome," said Basti, smiling at Julia. "Even better than last time. That was beautiful, that part about 'Es ist vollbracht.'"

"Hey, Erik, how ya doin'? Nice to see ya!" Birgit squatted beside Bettina and looked up brightly.

"Mom, Dad, these are Julia's neighbors," said Erik.

"Oh—we've met," said Renate, smiling at Birgit.

"Sebastian Kunz." Basti shook Horst's hand and then Renate's. He glanced back quickly toward Julia. "Listen, I wouldn't worry about what happened." He looked fondly at Bettina, who was fingering Birgit's necklace. "You know, about makin' that noise. It was a beautiful concert."

"Thanks," murmured Julia.

When Basti and Birgit had left, Bettina returned to Julia. "Mama," she droned and stroked her velvet gown. Julia was in no mood for affection. As Bettina's breath warmed her leg in strange, hot little puffs, she wished that she could push her away.

"Why did you bring her?" she asked Renate tightly. "You told me you were going to stay home."

Renate sighed and met Julia's eyes calmly. "I changed my mind. I thought she should hear you. She's so gifted—"

"She's two!" cried Julia. "Not even that! You must have known what she would do!"

Bettina frowned, looking ready to cry. Erik laid his hand on Julia's arm. "Look. It happened. We can't change that. It was pretty funny, you have to admit."

"That's easy for you to say!" The inside of her nose felt hot, and she longed to hit him.

"She's been so good lately," said Renate quietly. "And she's got such an ear for music. I wanted her to hear you sing."

Despite Julia's best efforts, her voice broke out. "How could you do that? You said you were going to keep her home! That was deceitful, what you did!"

A few gray-haired people turned their heads, but by now most of the audience had dispersed. Arno draped his arm around

Rudi and whispered something in his ear that made him smile. Screwdriver in hand, Rudi led the demolition of the risers. Julia helped Renate to dress Bettina, who had begun to whimper.

———————■———————

The next morning Julia's anger was undiminished, and Horst, Erik, and Renate left early. Sensing that she had been bad, Bettina turned soft and affectionate, but Julia found it hard to caress her. This time, Arno would not forgive her. Failing to appear was one thing, but wrecking a performance was another. From the *St. John Passion*, the only voice people would remember was the one cutting the silence like a jagged knife. Without Bettina, Julia would probably be a sought-after singer by now. People loved her voice—it was her daughter they didn't want. Absently, she stroked Bettina's red curls, and the little girl squirmed, disliking her touch.

With the shift from winter to summer, Julia's mood changed as fast as Bach's tempi. Within days, the temperature shot from the midthirties to the midseventies, and the buildings cut sharp lines against the sky. Impatient after the mild winter, the trees sprouted leaves in a week, and the air smelled of lilacs, cherry blossoms, and mud. In the parks, fat dandelions appeared in the grass where jaunty crows stalked. When Julia walked by, they cocked their heads and shot provocative looks. Maybe Astrid was right: ever since the wall had come down, these Russian crows had flown in and taken over.

After six months of darkness, the bright spring was maddening. With the cloud cover gone, Berlin glowed from five until nine, making its inhabitants eager and restless. It was the smell that affected Julia's nerves most—the wild sweetness of a hundred blossoms. When she took Bettina for walks in the evenings, Turkish boys roared up and down Kaiserdamm in red sports cars, their sinuous music spinning out into the night. Despite the stroller, Julia felt men's eyes on her, and she savored the delicious air.

Although Julia knew what Bettina had done, she couldn't give up hope. Arno didn't return her calls, and she sensed that for him, that cry was the last straw. With or without him, she knew she would keep singing, the same way that she kept on breathing. Gazing out over her plants on a Saturday morning, she sensed the life around her—a cough, the moan of Amy Winehouse, the high-pitched crash of bottles in the bin. If Arno rejected her, she would sing in Frankfurt. Maybe Renate was right. Still, she couldn't forget the joy of singing notes shaped by his hands. Arno had meant it when he said that she was the only one who could sing Handel's arias. Maybe he would get over it, as Rudi swore that he would.

Unlike Arno, Rudi stayed in touch with Julia, and she let him know what Renate had done. For the time being, he was forbidden to mention Julia to Arno, but before the ban took effect, Rudi had declared it was all his fault for teaching a two-year-old to yell "Bravo." Arno didn't believe him, since Rudi so often took the blame. The tenor couldn't say when Arno would relent, if ever. When Rudi stopped by to sing and play with Bettina, he said only that Arno was immersed in his orchestral piece, holed up despite the good weather.

Hearing steps in the Hof, Julia glanced toward the gate and saw Basti balancing something on his shoulder. Since he had been with Birgit, Basti had filled out a bit, but his movements were as purposeful as ever. With one easy motion, he lowered his burden and stood by the dumpsters, staring down at it. He had brought home a curved, old-fashioned sled adorned with some kind of red emblem. In the warm weather, someone must have thrown it away, doubting whether Berlin would see snow again. Basti pierced the ground with its runners, held it upright, and circled it skeptically. As he raised one arm to his head, his T-shirt tautened.

"Hi."

The soft voice made Julia jump. Somehow, she had missed the steps approaching Basti. With a slender hand, Rudi reached out to touch the sled. He was almost as tall as the carpenter, but next to Basti, he looked frail and old. Side by side, the brown head and the gray one gazed down at the battered wood. The men spoke quietly, but with the Hof's acoustics, Julia could hear every word.

"This is nice," murmured Rudi. "What is it, oak?"

"Yeah." Basti picked up the sled and rotated it so that they could see the end grain. Rudi's eyes flitted down Basti's arm.

"Yeah." Basti nodded. "Pretty nice wood too."

"Where'd you find it?" asked Rudi.

Basti turned and searched Rudi's eyes suspiciously. "Trash heap. Friedrichshain. Somebody was cleanin' out an old house. Guy called me to check it out."

"Oh." Rudi's eyes returned to the sled. He poked the dark, rusty runners. "Looks like the runners are bent."

"Yeah, they're in bad shape." Basti sighed.

With one quick move, he inverted the sled so that they could sight along the runners. He shook his head.

"Yeah, they're bent pretty badly," murmured Rudi.

Basti chuckled. "*Bent* ain't the word for it. Looks like somebody went at 'em with a tire iron."

"Oh, I could fix that," said Rudi.

"What?" Basti put down the sled. "You think so? What do you do anyway?"

Julia stepped back, sensing they were about to look up at her window.

"I'm a lab tech," said Rudi, "in the physics department at the FU. I build equipment for people—and fix it when they need it. Mostly I fix it."

Julia imagined Basti's grin. "So you think you could straighten these out?"

Rudi bent down to pick up the sled, but Basti caught it first.

"Yeah, I think so." Rudi sighed. "But that's not all that's wrong, is it?"

"Nah," said Basti disgustedly. "This thing's a mess. Gotta replace the steering bar …"

The dry wood rattled as he shook it.

"But I guess you like a challenge, hey?"

"Yeah, you could say that," answered Basti, his low voice perfectly level.

"So what are you going to do with it?" Rudi looked up at Basti, whose shoulders tightened.

"I dunno. Sell it, I guess. I know some people who like antiques …"

"Why don't you sell it on eBay?" asked Rudi.

Basti looked at him steadily. "Yeah. Yeah, I guess I could do that. I heard about that."

"Have you ever done it?"

"No." Basti's back remained tense.

"Well, if you'd like to try, I'd be glad to help you."

"Okay." Basti nodded. "So you really think you could do somethin' with these runners?"

They squatted and tried to see how to detach them.

"C'mon," said Basti. "I've gotta get the right tools …"

He took the sled under his arm and started down the cellar stairs with Rudi close behind him.

In the next weeks, Rudi became a regular visitor to Basti's workshop, and Basti, to the metal shop at the FU. Although Astrid and Birgit kidded him mercilessly, Basti stuck close to his new *Kumpel.*

"He's a friend of Julia's," he insisted, jerking his chin toward her window. "The guy knows stuff. He's interested in carpentry."

"You gotta think like a girl," said Astrid. "That's what you are for him. To get into your pants, a guy'll tell you he's interested in anything."

Basti shook his head. "He's a nice guy. Real educated, but practical. He likes to work with his hands."

"Yeah, most of 'em do." Astrid smirked.

Basti gave up protesting and joined in her naughty laughter.

Rudi told Julia how the night before, he and Basti had written the eBay ad. To use Rudi's computer, Basti had entered the tenor's book-lined flat for the first time. The rescued sled now lived up to its Red Baron emblem. With straightened runners, fresh varnish, and a new steering bar, it looked ready to fly. Proud of their work, the two men stared at the screen.

"Let me try," said Rudi, his brown eyes glowing.

"Rosebud," he typed.

"Oh, yeah! That's great!" exclaimed Basti. "Like that movie!"

"Have your dreams eluded you?" typed Rudi. "Fly through the snow on a fully restored Red Baron sled."

"Geez, that sounds great, like a personal ad." Basti laughed. "But we gotta say somethin' about the wood. Somethin' practical, so they know we know what we're doin'."

"Okay." Rudi frowned, then typed, "Solid oak, lovingly refinished. Reworked steel runners. Guaranteed craftsmanship. Contact Sebastian Kunz."

"Do you have an email address?" asked Rudi.

"No—no." Basti blushed.

"Let's get you a Yahoo account," said Rudi. "Then you can check in at any internet café."

Rudi posted the ad, and as the bids came in, Astrid stopped teasing Basti. The results amazed Julia, a hail of desire whose forceful patter promised wealth. Someone named Bugsy offered €1,000, but Ahmed topped it with €1,500.

"Ahmed? Is he gonna carry it around on his camel?" Astrid snorted.

But before long, she was even more excited than Basti. Han Li, Wolfgang23, Morrissey X, Ahmed again! A week later, the sled went to Han Li for €2,700. Basti had to report the income to the *Finanzamt*, but even after taxes, he would clear over €2,000.

"It was garbage!" he cried, his eyes alight. "Somebody threw it away! And now I'm gettin' two thousand euros for it!"

He insisted on giving half to Rudi, who refused at first but finally took the money.

"I think he needs it," Basti told Julia. "I don't think he's in such good shape. He did a great thing for me. From now on I'm sellin' everything on eBay. And he's startin' to work on a website ..."

Julia welcomed the friendship between Basti and Rudi, which seemed to do them both good. She worried that Rudi might get hurt—perhaps physically—but for the time being, she trusted his judgment. Astrid, too, grudgingly approved of the match. "At least he can't get pregnant," she muttered. As Julia expected, the strongest objections came from Birgit, who said that when the skinny old man ogled Basti, he looked exactly like Frau Riemann.

When Birgit and Julia met in the Hof, Birgit complained of her problems at work. As one of the few who didn't speak Turkish, she felt like a second-class citizen, and her blue eyes and full curves didn't help. When the scarf-heads gobbled in their strange language, they looked at her, and they laughed. She couldn't talk to most customers, so they made her pick up the fallen clothes. All day long, four or five days a week, she rescued blouses slipping from hangers and shoved them back into jammed racks. To make things look nice, she had to put the small sizes in front, even though no one could wear them. When the big, dark-eyed women trampled through, they grabbed their clothes from the middle and knocked others aside as they pushed back the rejects. Birgit's job at the mall was nothing like she'd imagined, helping rich, pretty women choose flattering styles.

All Basti would say when she told him her problems was "That's life. That's work. You gotta deal with that. Everyone gives the apprentice a hard time. You gotta put up with it, and watch 'em, and learn. You gotta work your way up. If they get to you, you don't let 'em know it, you hear?"

Lately, according to Birgit, he had seemed more interested in that gay guy than he was in her. No matter what she said, he knew everything already. No scarf-head had ever called *him* stupid for hanging the pants in front of the tops. How could he be so sure he was right?

Since Basti had started this eBay thing, he hadn't been half as nice as Herr Skrzypecki, the regional manager. Spotting half-unpacked cartons of jeans near the entrance, he had bawled out her boss, Frau Jingez, but he'd spoken kindly to Birgit as she straightened dresses in back of the shop. Smiling warmly, he'd asked how long she had been working there and said she was doing a fine job. He'd asked her to leave the dresses and unpack the jeans, but he'd slipped her a ten-euro bonus. She must have been doing something right.

As Rudi's interest in Basti grew, so did Julia's concern. Ever since he had started work on the sled, a new sense of purpose had enlivened him. Warm color in his face absorbed the gray rings, and he began to put on weight. As he talked of Basti's website, his brown eyes glowed. Rudi hadn't been this lively since his breakup with Norbert, and although she hated to do it, Julia knew that she had to warn him.

"It's really nice what you're doing for Basti," she said one golden evening. "He thought he was going to have to go to Norway. Now he can practically run his own business."

"Oh, I was glad to help him," said Rudi. He leaned back on the couch with a blissful look.

"You know ..." The hovering words eluded Julia.

"What?" Rudi smiled. "He's not gay? He's got a girlfriend? But you're not sure how to break it to me?"

"Oh, come on." Julia laughed. She drew up her feet and wrapped her arms around her shins.

"Look, I'm not trying to seduce him," said Rudi. "I just like being with him. I like what he does." Indignation throbbed beneath his irony.

"Sure, so do I! Everyone does! Just don't get any ideas, okay? If there's anyone less—"

"Oh, you don't have to protect me." Rudi smiled archly. "I can take care of myself. You reach a point when— When the worst happens, you're not afraid anymore."

"That's not what I'm saying." Julia looked into his eyes, so closely set in his narrow face. "He's not like the guys you know— the guys we sing with. If you try something—"

Rudi started to laugh. "What are you saying—he might punch me out? He might kill me? Don't worry. I won't insult his honor."

"No!" Julia checked her rising voice. She mustn't wake Bettina.

"There are lots of ways—lots of ways—" began Rudi.

Julia blew out her breath in a slow, fine stream. When the air ran out, her urge to shout ended with it.

"It's not what you think," said Rudi. "No one's just gay or not gay. You can have a girlfriend and like someone else. You can love someone without ever touching him."

Pain sharpened his features, and Julia relented. She studied Rudi as he lowered his eyes. He sat with his knees pressed close together and stared down at his sandals and socks. His yellow plaid shirt hung limply from the fine, tight curves of his shoulders.

"Hey." Julia reached out to rub the back of his head. "I'm sorry. I'm sorry."

Rudi stretched his neck and lowered his lids. "Oh, it's okay. I know you're trying to help. You're trying to tell me I've found the one man less available—"

"Yeah." Julia sighed. "You can pick 'em."

With his eyes closed, Rudi smiled dreamily. He stretched out his arm and pulled her to him. "Mm," he murmured, stroking her hair. "Aren't you going to ask me how he is?"

"How is he?" Julia breathed. She liked Rudi's salty scent.

"Confused." Rudi laughed. "He's in real trouble now. He's changed a lot, but not enough for what's coming."

"What's going on?" asked Julia. She pushed herself up.

Rudi smiled mischievously, as though relishing the news he was about to impart.

"He got a message from William Handshaw. Handshaw called him about his orchestral piece, and Arno faxed it over."

"His music!" Heat rose through Julia's breast. "He finished it? Handshaw called him?"

"I don't know what he said, but Handshaw wants to meet him." Rudi smiled. "I think he wants to do the piece."

"No way!" exclaimed Julia, her face aglow.

"Yeah." Rudi grinned. "All those years of 'Aussies' and 'Schrubber,' and Handshaw leaves the friendliest, most respectful message in the world. I heard it. He's a nice guy—bright, articulate, and a damned good musician. Arno can't stand that. Now he's got to talk to Handshaw for an hour next Tuesday."

"Oh, shit." Their eyes met, and Julia laughed delightedly.

"I asked him to take me with him—you know, to make sure he doesn't act like himself—but he won't let me." Rudi lowered his chin and glared, trying to imitate Arno. "It's a one-on-one thing."

Julia muffled her laughter. "So you really think he can pull it off?"

Rudi shrugged. "I doubt he can hide his sparkling personality, but my guess is Handshaw won't care. The music's good. The question is who's going to conduct."

Under the west window, the setting sun was turning the philodendron leaves to glowing hearts.

"What if Handshaw won't let him conduct?" she asked. "You think Arno will let them do the piece?"

Rudi took her hand. "I don't know," he murmured.

Julia leaned back, mildly aroused by the thumb stroking her palm. "So he still won't talk about me?" She sighed.

"No," answered Rudi. "Believe me, I've tried." He pulled her hand gently until she turned to face him. "It's more than the music. I don't think he even knows it. You're more than a voice to him. He felt … betrayed."

Julia nodded slowly. Rudi's eyes pulsed with an unspoken truth.

"It's everything," he murmured. "The pregnancy—the baby. You ruined his music. But it's more than that."

Her eyes locked on Rudi's, and Julia kept nodding until the motion was barely perceptible. With a sigh he gathered her in a hug, and Julia rested her head against his chest. In a nearby apartment, a sharp clang pierced the sad voice of Dido as someone washed up her dinner dishes.

———————————◼———————————

Despite Rudi's comforting, Julia couldn't forget Bettina's voice stabbing the darkness. When she practiced, she shuddered at each rest, even when her daughter was safe at day care. Behind her full tones, Bettina's cries lurked as a tormenting, insistent ghost. Until she exorcized this specter, Arno wouldn't let her sing again, and she couldn't escape its force anywhere. Julia wondered what he was doing this morning as she breathed the sweet air on her way to work. Picturing him scowling at Handshaw, she smiled at a pyramid of oranges.

"One kilo, two euros!" serenaded the fruit seller, raising his brows invitingly. As Julia passed Round Two, she realized she was humming and stopped to follow the tune. Somehow, she had recalled John, Paul, George, and Ringo, and the rest of the way to work, she sang Handel's arpeggios. She even tried a run at Motherfucker, and wincing, she waited for Bettina after each phrase the way she braced herself for firecrackers at New Year's.

In the doughnut shop, a throng of workers blocked her view of Marga behind the counter. The singer's rough, low voice spun out through gaps in a shifting wall of blue overalls.

"So if I go to Mallorca with you, do I have to buy my own ticket?"

"Hell no, Mädel, I'll take care of everything as long as you bring the coffee."

Laughing, Julia ran to her locker. By the time she had pulled on her purple jersey, she was singing again. It was going to be one of those days when a tune carried her like a pulse, nourishing every movement.

Julia was glad to see Marga so lively, because since the gig at Alexanderplatz, her moods had reeled. One day she would be full of excitement, talking nonstop about new clubs, and the next she would be vowing to quit the band, sure they would never find a label. For the next gig, Ultraviolet was trying a club called Inter Alia where bands handled their own sound systems, publicity, and tickets. With so much to manage, Marga was bickering with Kevin and Tilman, the guitarist. They had long since learned not to delegate anything to the drummer.

The warm weather had created a hunger for doughnuts, drawing people who rarely left their apartments before noon. When the lull came, it was nearly eleven. Marga leaned back against the counter, puffed out her lower lip, and blew out hard. The fluorescent lights blasted her pale, oily skin, but her eyes sparkled wickedly.

"So Kevin still wants to put rainbows on the tickets," she said, "but that friend of yours says no. What's his name? That big guy—that one who's really built. He and his girlfriend went out with us after Alexanderplatz. I didn't like her much, but he's cool."

"Basti." Julia nodded. "Yeah, he's a good guy."

"Man!" Marga laughed. "Those two sure can put it away. I think we all got brain damaged that night." She stared out the window, her smile following her memory's dim shapes. She shook her head to clear it.

"So how've you been doin'?" she asked. "You're lookin' good. You send out those new applications?"

The previous week, Julia had applied to four opera companies in the Frankfurt area. Erik had sent her their addresses.

"Yeah." Julia sighed. "I've gotta sing somewhere."

She pulled her eyes from the empty street. Marga was watching her closely.

"So you still haven't heard from him?" she asked.

Julia shook her head.

Marga scrunched up her mouth. "So fuck him," she said. "It's not your fault the kid screamed. Shit, if he can't see that ... How could you know?"

"Yeah." Julia nodded. "She said she was gonna stay home with her. And then she just ... I still can't believe it."

"Hey, wait a minute." Marga looked at Julia fiercely. "Where'd she get the ticket?"

Julia shrugged. "I don't know. At the door, I guess."

"No!" Marga's thoughts moved too fast for her thin features. "The concert was sold out! Kevin and I came by at five thirty, but there were no tickets left."

"Then she must already have had one," said Julia. "Probably Erik got them all tickets before she decided to stay home."

"No!" Marga's eyes bored into her. "Don't you see? She already had the ti—"

The shop phone pierced Marga's thought. Instinctively, Julia grabbed it. Her voice crossed Marga's in low, smooth waves, creating a choppy dissonance.

"Good morning, Dorrie's Donuts, Martens."

"She fucking planned it!" hissed Marga.

From the phone came a young, desperate male voice. Its fine grain was familiar, but fear had raised its pitch.

"She's at the West Side clinic!"

The man's agony made Julia forget her training. "Who is this?" she demanded.

"Julia! She's at the West Side clinic!" cried the voice. "My mom! She had a heart attack at work. She's at West Side, in the ICU!"

Marga must have heard because she froze, white-faced. "Go!" she ordered. "I'll handle things here."

Julia ran to her locker.

"When do you have to get Bettina?" called Marga. "You want me to pick her up?"

Julia grabbed her purse and ran, without even changing her shirt. Behind the counter, Marga waved with angry solidarity.

Before Julia cleared the door, she heard Marga mutter, "Too bad it wasn't that other bitch."

In the clinic, Julia found Astrid half-asleep, her flesh turned grayish white. A tube formed a plastic moustache under her nose, and wires grew from her gown like loose vines. From two bags, fluids were dripping into her arm. Basti glanced from Astrid's exhausted face to the monitors, a rack of machines following each breath and pulse. Behind the gray curtains shielding her on each side, sharp, anxious voices chopped. Like the monitors, the ward was throbbing with energy, playing ten different melodies at once.

"Julia," mumbled Astrid. She struggled to raise herself. Although groggy, Astrid seemed overjoyed to see her. "Where's your little one?" she murmured. "What time is it?"

"It's okay, Mom." Basti stood up. "She keeps askin' me what time—" His rough voice died in midphrase, and he threw his arms around Julia. For an instant she clung to him, savoring his hardness and warmth.

"Hey," she whispered. "Hey, come on." Gently she pushed him back. Basti inhaled sharply.

"What happened?" she murmured.

Basti's cynical look returned, and Julia released her breath.

"She was cleanin' some guy's house," he muttered. "Some big place out in Westend. She shouldn't have been doin' that. She should never have gone back to work. If only—if only I'd—"

"Hey, c'mon," said Julia. "She wanted to work. It was her idea. That doctor said she could."

Basti's eyes turned ferocious. "I'm gonna kill him," he said. "As soon as she gets outa here, I'm gonna fuckin' kill him."

"Basti, what time is it?" asked Astrid wistfully.

"It's ten of twelve, Mom," he said. "Why do you keep askin' me that? You have a hot date or somethin'?"

With her eyes closed, Astrid smiled faintly. "He said he'd be back around noon," she murmured.

"They found her out on the porch," muttered Basti. "She was havin' these awful pains. She called the *Feuerwehr*, and she got the door open before she collapsed. Otherwise ..."

His eyes narrowed and darkened.

"Julia, where's Bettina?" Astrid breathed. "You got somebody watchin' her?"

"It's okay. She's in day care," said Julia.

"Oh, yeah?" she whispered. "What time is it?"

Outside, a voice resounded with authority. "So no changes? You say she's resting quietly?" Its soft consonants had a pleasing, foreign sound.

"Hey, Basti," said Julia, "who else knows about this? You want to go call Birgit or something?"

"Yeah, yeah, I better call Birgit. And Rudi." He backed out with a distracted frown.

Seconds later, a round-faced blond doctor entered. Julia slipped to the side, but he barely noticed her. The pale, sleepy woman occupied all his attention. His broad back stretched ripples in his coat, and his voice flowed in gentle waves. Its deep warmth and light consonants brought to mind a beach on a summer afternoon.

"Frau Kunz!" The doctor took Astrid's hand. From his warm tone, Julia knew it must be Dr. Kowalski. "Frau Kunz! What have you done to yourself? I said try and see! You were supposed to take it easy at first!"

A faint pulse of irony stirred Astrid's voice. "That job center, they don't do 'take it easy.' They just do 'all or nothin'.'"

"Well, from now on, it's going to be nothing." Dr. Kowalski drew Astrid's hand to his lips and kissed it. "Let these people clean their own houses. Your housecleaning days are over."

His bearlike body moved surprisingly fast as he glanced at the monitors and took notes.

"You shouldn't have left us like that," he said sternly, but sorrow mellowed his tone. "From now on, you've got to take better care of yourself. I want to see you on a regular basis."

"Of course, *Herr Doktor*," whispered Astrid.

The big doctor left as quickly as he had come. Light flashed off his gold-rimmed glasses, and a trail of warm cologne marked his wake. Astrid inhaled deeply, as though trying to drink his scent. Tears flowed from the corners of her eyes, but on her face was a look of bliss.

———————————— ■ ————————————

Within hours, Astrid was out of the ICU. Her heart attack had been serious, and it might have been fatal, but she soon recovered her passion to talk.

"I had a bad feelin' about that place," she told Julia. "Right from the first time I saw it. It was dark in there—like nobody was livin' there. A guy in a suit let me in, but I could tell it wasn't his house. Musta belonged to someone who died."

Astrid's dried-out blond hair clung together in clumps. Color warmed her face, but she looked battered.

"Yeah." Julia nodded. "So they were fixing it up—what, to sell?"

"Yeah, yeah," muttered Astrid. "That musta been it. It was just—there was so much of it. Dead plants—I musta carried fifteen plants out to the back porch. I was all alone in that place. Somethin' in that house gave me the creeps." She shuddered.

"So you started to feel sick?" asked Julia.

Astrid frowned, trying to recall. "I did the dustin' first," she said. "You know—so if somethin' gets knocked down, you can suck it up later."

"Yeah, that's right." Julia nodded. On the monitor, Astrid's heart beat a recurring melody.

"I was thinkin' about Diana," she said, "and how those people decided nobody higher up was involved. 'Gutless,' I was thinkin'. 'Friggin' gutless.' And then I started to feel sick. Musta been somethin' I ate, I thought. Somethin' was makin' me wanna puke. So I reach up for this vase—this beautiful glass vase, with a lot of dried flowers in it—and I get this terrible pain in my arm."

"Wow," said Julia. "Good thing you weren't up on a ladder."

On the monitor, Astrid's melody increased its tempo.

"Yeah, no kiddin.' I grabbed hold of the bookcase. I was sweatin' like a pig. I kept tryin' to breathe, an' I couldn't. It was so dark in there—I felt like the walls were closin' in. That's when I called the *Feuerwehr*. We ain't supposed to use the phone, but—" Astrid's voice wavered, and her eyes reddened. "I was so scared. I think I was cryin'. After I asked 'em to come, I ran to the door. I had to get outa there. I couldn't breathe. On the porch I fell down, and I couldn't get back up. I felt like somebody was standin' on my chest. I lay there lookin' up at the railing, at this spider's web in the corner. I thought that was it. I couldn't stand it, lyin' there all alone like that. That's when I heard the siren."

Julia took her hand and squeezed it. Astrid stared with the same tiger's eyes as Basti.

"You did everything right," said Julia. "It wasn't your time."

"You're damned right it wasn't." Astrid snuffed. She raked her free hand through her hair and wriggled her fingers to fluff it.

Astrid wanted to see Bettina, so every day after day care, Julia brought her by. Since the *St. John Passion*, her daughter had grown livelier than ever. She chattered in a style few people could follow and shrieked when she lost her listeners' attention. Julia feared Bettina would cause more heart attacks, but she was a hit on the recovery ward. Astrid's roommate, old Frau Torgauer, beamed with pleasure when the noisy, self-important girl stomped in.

At two, Bettina was fearless, energetic, and proud, with dark eyes, full features, and reddish-brown curls. Longing to be taken seriously, she stormed when grown-ups laughed at her frowns and grinned delightedly when they joined in her laughter. She had an insatiable hunger for sweets and could eat cookies until she cried from the bellyache. Her favorite companion was Knuti, her old white bear, whose fur had grown gray and matted. Her prattle careened between speaking and singing and interwove her own phrases with Basti's and Astrid's. The pat of her searching hands made Julia smile with pleasure, and she shuddered to think that she had wished her away.

Today some game from day care had set her off. "Lookit my hiney!" she crowed.

Frau Torgauer, who had been lying lost in her thoughts, burst into uncontrolled laughter.

Astrid chuckled. "I've gotta get outa here. This kid's gettin' outa hand."

Julia stopped Bettina from pulling down her pants, but the little girl quickly squirmed free. She scampered up and down between the beds, singing her way through the new game. Trying to calm her, Julia grew impatient since she had eaten almost nothing since breakfast.

"C'mon," she said sharply. "Let's go get something to eat."

"No!" Bettina relished her favorite word.

"Oh, let her stay here," growled Astrid.

"Are you sure you can handle her?" asked Julia. "What if she runs off?"

"Are you kiddin' me?" Astrid sniffed. "She's got a captive audience. C'mon, kid. What else can you show us?"

"Show us your kneecaps!" said Frau Torgauer.

Bettina grinned and yanked down her pants, revealing a white puff of diaper.

———————————————— ■ ————————————————

In the cafeteria, Julia watched gratefully as a woman dished up Wiener schnitzel and pale peas. At a table near the window, Basti and Rudi were talking intently. They must have decided to meet before visiting Astrid. The voltage of their gazes made Julia hesitate, but when Rudi smiled and waved, she approached.

"The schnitzel's good," said Basti, meeting her eyes warmly.

He had a calm, measured look that Julia hadn't seen since Astrid's collapse. It had fallen on Rudi to separate Basti and Kowalski, a task he had accepted with resignation. Rudi specialized in calming raging bulls, and from the sound of things, he was still at it.

Rudi and Basti slipped back into their talk, and as Julia chewed the rich meat, she tried to follow. It was something about computers—Dreamweaver and posting digital pictures. With a felt-tipped pen, Rudi sketched a rough-edged design on a napkin. Basti grasped an imaginary picture and rotated it with a twist of his hand.

"No, no, up top!"

Full of food, Basti was flushed and cheerful. He seemed relaxed after his scare that morning. Basti draped his arm over the back of Julia's chair and fingered her hair as he studied the drawing.

"Once we have the pictures," said Rudi, "I can get this up in a few days."

Due to a lack of photos, the website had been temporarily postponed. Basti sold everything he refinished, and to show what he could do, he needed before and after shots. He would have to craft a few more pieces before they could launch the site.

"Good." Basti frowned reflectively.

Rudi's eyes shone so that he looked like a silver-haired boy. Since the two had been working together, Basti had seemed to mature, and Rudi, to get younger, until they met in the middle like a grown-up businessman and his eager consultant.

Julia swallowed the last of her peas and washed them down with a swallow of chocolate milk.

Basti patted her shoulder. "Pretty good, huh? You musta been hungry."

"Yeah." She crossed her knife and fork on the empty plate.

Glancing from Basti to Julia, Rudi glowed with pleasure. A spark of naughtiness snapped in his brown eyes.

"So he's safe then—this resplendent Polish doctor? I won't be doing a website for the Moabit Correctional Facility?"

"Oh, yeah, I guess so," growled Basti. "But geez—if it was your mother—"

"What's bothering you?" asked Rudi. "That he misjudged her condition, or that she—"

"Both!" exclaimed Basti. "Shit—both! Oh, excuse me." He glanced at Julia and blushed deep red.

Julia laid her arm on Basti's and laughed low in her throat. She wondered at Rudi's daring. No one in the neighborhood spoke to Basti this way, at least no one who wanted to stay out of the hospital.

Basti drew a deep breath and struggled for words. "It's both!" he spluttered. "Geez! I mean, come on! He tells her to go back to work when she's got this aortic valve thing—the guy oughta lose his license. And then I've been hearin' about this guy for years. 'He's got magic hands,' she says. Jesus! 'Why are you tellin' me this?' I ask. 'You're tellin' me this *why?*'"

Rudi smiled sadly. "She likes him." He shrugged.

"Likes him! Geez! It's friggin' ridiculous!" cried Basti.

"I think you've got your hand on the problem," said Rudi. "When it comes to mating, we're all ridiculous."

"Just—don't—" Basti warned him.

"It's okay." Rudi grinned. "We won't talk about your mother's passion for an inept Polish doctor."

Basti pretended to punch him, then playfully grabbed his shoulders. Rudi whooped with a tenor version of Bettina's squeals.

"Hey! Hey, guys!" hissed Julia.

A group of nearby nurses glowered.

"All right!" Julia laughed. "I can see I'm going to have to separate you. Somebody go upstairs. You know, to check on the patient? The one we're supposedly here to see?"

"Yeah, get up there." Rudi grinned. "Who knows what she's doing. Probably she needs a chaperone."

Basti whacked him good-naturedly on the shoulder, then gathered their trays and walked off. Rudi's long, thin face quivered with pleasure, and his dark eyes sparkled with mischief.

"I can't believe you said that to him," said Julia. "Nobody talks like that to Basti."

"Oh, he may surprise you." Rudi laughed.

Julia raised her eyebrows.

"No, no, not like that." Rudi waved his hand. "But he's deep …" His smile faded.

"Oh, no," said Julia.

"Yeah." Rudi sighed and looked down, half-amused. "I'm a masochist, I guess. But I'll die happy."

Julia shook her head and smiled, glad to see Rudi so animated. She still feared a hideous crash. For the moment, Rudi seemed happy without Arno, whom he hadn't mentioned in days. She wondered what the conductor was doing and pictured Arno's slow, ironic smile. With little effort, Rudi followed her thoughts.

"So the big meeting went well, from what I hear. Nobody's dead."

Julia laughed deeply, enjoying the warmth in her belly. "So Handshaw's okay? All that frizzy hair's still on his head? His nose is still on straight?"

"Far as I know." Rudi smiled. His eyes darkened, and Julia wasn't sure why. "Handshaw wants to do the piece. Next year, in a special series on new German composers."

"Wow, that's wonderful!" cried Julia. Her face glowed with warmth. "So he pulled it off! That must have been some meeting."

"Oh, the music speaks for itself," said Rudi. He frowned at some trash on a nearby table. As a woman passed, a napkin fluttered like a wounded swan. "It's a beautiful thing. D minor, A major, D minor, A minor ... all roundness, swirling ..." He began to hum a winding melody, his voice fading as his inner pains awoke. "He's brilliant," said Rudi. "The piece is brilliant." Sound barely tinctured his breath.

"So Handshaw liked it?" asked Julia.

"Yeah." Rudi sighed. "They spent the whole time talking about schedules. Handshaw must have wanted to do the piece as soon as he heard the music."

"Wow," Julia breathed. "The Philharmonie—so who's going to conduct?"

"Handshaw."

She gasped. "Arno agreed to that?"

Rudi nodded with a strange half smile. Julia wondered what was happening to Arno. To trust his music to a man he had been insulting for years—just like that. Once again, Rudi read her thoughts.

"He's always known how good Handshaw is. He knows his piece is in safe hands. Just now, for the first time, he's got to act on it."

Julia breathed out in a long, slow stream, and her cells settled like stirred leaves. Inside she felt peaceful but old. A tightness that had troubled her was dissolving.

"And *Messiah*?" she asked. "Does he talk about that? Does he talk about *Messiah* in New York?"

"All the time." Rudi smiled. "Linda found us a place. It's all set."

"All set!" exclaimed Julia. "When? Where? With who?"

The skin around Rudi's eyes crinkled. "Second week of December, a year from this Christmas. Not Lincoln Center, not one of the famous halls, but someplace nice. Linda, Michael, Markus—that's all he'll say."

"So he hasn't said who's going to sing alto?"

Rudi's front teeth formed a rabbit grin. "I think he'd rather talk about his mother's sex life."

Julia's heart accelerated, and her jaw set. "Well, tell him it's me," she said. "Tell him I'm doing it. He doesn't have to talk about it, because it's going to be me."

"I thought you had an audition in Frankfurt." Rudi leaned back and raised his brows.

Julia nodded, frustrated. "Two of them," she said. "First week in July. They called me right after I applied."

"So you'd really go down there?" Rudi's face darkened.

"Hell yeah!" she exclaimed. "I don't want to, but if I can't sing here ... And Erik's mother could watch Bettina ..."

"I thought you didn't trust her," said Rudi.

"Oh, I don't know." Julia shook her head. "She does so much for her educationally. And Erik's so good with her—it's good for her to have a dad. You get boxed in—you get boxed in …" Tears softened the ground under her voice. "If it weren't for Bettina, everything would be so easy. I wish …"

"Oh, come on," said Rudi. "She's wonderful. You made the right choice."

"Huh—that's easy for you to say." Julia laughed. "You don't have to live with her. You can go home at night."

"Come on." Rudi stroked her hair gently. "Let's go up and see that sexy doctor."

After his blunder, Kowalski kept Astrid in the clinic and carefully monitored her progress. When her heart behaved well, he cautiously released her but warned her not to exert herself. For a woman in a fifth-floor walk-up, this was easier said than done. Once Astrid had climbed the four flights, Basti ordered her to stay put. He brought food and magazines, but she squirmed with boredom and shouted out the window to her neighbors. As the heat increased, the house opened itself to breathe. The temperature topped eighty, then ninety. Stifling in her kitchen, Astrid listened glumly to the meals, fights, and trysts underway in fourteen other apartments.

With Astrid's condition, the Kunzes couldn't stay on the fifth floor, but Basti refused to leave the building. He and Astrid needed to switch with someone else, and they couldn't afford the Vorderhaus. The obvious candidate was Frau Riemann, on the ground floor above Basti's workshop. As he began to court her, Astrid taunted him, but Julia urged her to ease off. Since his mother's heart attack, Basti had been on edge. He was seeing less of Birgit, since she worked late and was pulling shifts at Pinkies all over Berlin.

"What? What am I supposed to do with her?" yelled Basti when wiry Frau Riemann declined his offer.

"If you don't know, I can't help you," snapped Astrid.

Frau Riemann continued to resist Basti's plan. Four flights were nothing to the stringy, ageless woman, but she insisted she had to think of her own heart. The real issue was her fear of change, her inherent suspicion of any deal. Seasoned by years of bargaining, Basti slowly upped the ante. He offered a month's free rent, then a year of free repairs. Trusting his instincts, he saved his best cards for last, trying not to think of her bony fingers and greasy hair. Rudi approached her with different tactics and listened attentively to her descriptions of romantic movies.

After a month, Frau Riemann was still holding out, and Astrid was trapped on the fifth floor. As her nearest neighbor, Julia became her favorite conversation partner, and each morning, she leaned out over her plants to greet Astrid. In the heat, four flights up and down became unbearable, and her open window promised the world. Astrid and Julia exchanged thoughts that zoomed like flies between their stifling apartments.

In eighty-five-degree heat, Julia's body swelled until its boundaries blurred. She clipped up her hair and padded around in a limp bra and panties. With a sopping-wet washcloth, she sponged herself down and shivered as wetness kissed her back. On her flushed, dripping face, the warm drops pooled in the hollow over her smile. Bettina squirmed and fussed when Julia wiped her down with playful pats. She laughed delightedly as Julia fanned her wet body, spreading her arms to catch the breeze.

Bettina had grown so heavy that Julia could barely lift her. Each day she hoisted her with a martyred grunt so that she could talk to Astrid. The fearless girl befriended everyone she met, but the blonde woman next door remained her favorite. Through adjacent windows, the two grimaced and waved, compared what they had eaten and how it had tasted, and shared fantasies about their next meal. When Julia washed dishes or paid her bills, Bettina cried, "Assi!" Grudgingly, she led the girl to the window, where she clamored until Astrid appeared.

As Julia prepared for her Frankfurt auditions, she felt a new inner power. Until now, her musical energy had flowed through Arno, gaining strength as it spiraled through his circuits. Now, as he refused to connect with Julia, she vibrated with a desire to move. The directors in Frankfurt wanted her voice, and their distant music beckoned. She imagined herself soaring free, singing out as her own will guided her. And then Bettina fell, and Julia crashed with her back to earth.

◼

Bettina's fall crushed Julia's voice as though the ground had slammed her own chest. On her cell phone, she canceled the Frankfurt auditions in empty tones that barely stirred the hospital courtyard. As Bettina's breast rose and fell, her own breath skulked, ashamed of its persistent flow. Her daughter breathed on in a gray void, without a ripple stirring her marble face. Bandages masked the red crust on her arms, where stones had torn her pink skin. With a survivor's instinct, she had reached out to fend off the approaching ground.

With her index finger, Julia stroked some soft flesh surrounded by plastic strips. Was she imagining it, or had Bettina's breath lost its rhythm? The white squares of the hospital blanket refused to rise. No—there they went. A tiny mountain asserted its outline. Bettina's eyes remained closed, their red-brown lashes spread like fairy brooms.

If only those eyes would open! No look could sting like those silent lids. If they rose, what questions would those brown eyes ask? Julia's own breath lost its pattern. She had let this accident happen. It was all her fault. Under that sharp refrain, a dark string section was making a more ominous sound. In some way, had she *wanted* this to happen? She had never stilled her inner cries for freedom, her wish to move unencumbered by clinging hands. Julia raked her memory. What had she imagined? What had she dreamed? She suspected her mind of composing songs that had never reached her inner ear. "Out the window"—that phrase lurked in all of them, a wish that the hindrance would fly away. Out into the air it would soar, rushing off to a distant place.

With her thumb and finger, Julia circled Bettina's wrist. She couldn't remember a time before that warmth had met her seeking touch. A tiny pulse stirred her grip, and she felt the throb as she did the beat of her own blood. She couldn't let Bettina glide off, and no one could cut her daughter from her life.

Since Julia's interrogation, she had learned more about Renate's suit, which moved forward like a row of cutting scythes. The child welfare office was handling the case since Julia hadn't been charged with criminal negligence. The pale young lawyer appointed to represent Julia described the accusations pending. In her fitted pants suit, she spoke in flat, gray tones that she must have thought sounded professional. Julia was denying Bettina's father the chance to raise his child, although he had formally declared paternity. Instead, she had let her daughter languish in day care or left her with people unqualified to supervise her. Not only was Julia withholding education during the most vital period of Bettina's growth, but the child had nearly died because she'd refused to move a table after she had been warned of its dangers. This was not the first time the neglected girl had risked death in her care. Caught up in her singing, Julia had allowed her to become so dehydrated from the flu that only a trauma team could save her.

Julia listened with parted lips, her nails digging into her salty palms. The story had the awful coherence of a propaganda film. Its word-driven turns sounded so much like truth that she hardly knew how to block them. The spinning phrases resembled the real, yet the path of their motion was false. Her own arguments heaved with hot, wet power that didn't cohere into spoken words. Touching, pulsing warmth stood so little chance against these bright-edged claims. How did Renate know about the virus? Her case stood on more than angry phrases. Her charges whirled in harmony like the blades of a slicing machine.

Julia scanned her store of conversations. In her memory, spoken phrases hung like melodic lines. Who had she told about Bettina's illness? Astrid and Basti knew, as did Arno and Rudi. None of them would have revealed it to Renate, but the question was, Who had they talked to? Astrid swore she hadn't told a soul, but Julia had doubts about Basti.

"It's the Princess," muttered Astrid. "That's gotta be it. Who knows what she gets out of him."

Julia reeled as her remembered phrases formed a neat, progressive fugue. The inner melodies brought pictures—Birgit's blue eyes searching her, Basti's sideward glance. Her face must have betrayed shock, since Astrid grasped her arm.

"It ain't his fault. He needs it, and she's there. She knows he wants somethin' better."

Astrid's eyes had the heat of strong black coffee.

"You think I don't know my own kid? I know what he wants. You can't get what you want, sometimes you settle for trash."

"I can't believe she would do that," said Julia, but she heard the words even as she spoke. Birgit's bright tones merged with Renate's hungry alto in a clear, plausible duet.

Astrid sighed. "Surprises me too. I never knew she was that bad. She's always wanted you out of the picture. Guess she saw her chance, and she took it."

Julia hardened. "They're not going to do this," she said. "They can't. I won't let them."

Astrid's front teeth caught her lower lip in a bitter grin of approval.

Julia's case came together with the apparent ease of a well-practiced string quartet. Renate's guiding hands shaped each turn of her suit, but Julia's defenders followed an inner pulse. Her witnesses sensed each other's truths through their keen, open ears. She learned who had testified after the fact, through vague, uneasy references. Basti and Rudi were summoned first, as the two who had found Bettina in the Hof. Marga complained about the bureaucrats' idiocy, but Astrid noted their efficiency. Her trip to the child welfare office was her first solo excursion since her attack, and she returned exhausted but impressed.

"When they try to take your kid," she said, "they move a hell of a lot faster than the job center."

Only Rudi seemed nervous, which worried Julia because of his fine ear. Custody of Bettina could turn on a tone, and Rudi's tension revealed the keen arguments he was hearing. Above all, Rudi felt anxious about Arno, who had agreed to speak on her behalf. No ensemble player, he might perform a crashing solo that would alienate any bureaucrat.

Julia smiled to herself. She could hear Arno fulminate, and his roars provoked a laugh. Since he had started working with William Handshaw, his rage had settled to a suffusing glow. The Philharmonie conductor had chosen Arno's piece to open his new series on young composers. That October, Arno's music would thrill four thousand ears drinking sound from a vibrant stage. The orchestra had begun rehearsing Arno's piece, and Rudi described the drama. Arno glowered in a plush seat, his thumbnail cleaving his lower lip. When Handshaw's fine gestures altered his music, Arno jumped to his feet. The Australian conductor met his protests with a good-natured smile. "Let's just try it this way, shall we?" he asked. And Arno relented—a little faster each time. As he listened, his frown cleared. His face fell blank, as though viewing a wondrous sculpture for the first time. His smile spread as he saw resonances in a shape that he hadn't heard in his head.

Rudi's phrases recreated Arno's music with a passion that electrified his thin frame. Finding that words couldn't do it justice, he hummed the melody in clear tones. The piece began in brown D minor like a December morning, cold and hard but pregnant with joys to come. The shift to bright, tense A major promised change, and when D minor returned, its somber face beamed. Julia sank with the sad retreat into A minor and stroked Bettina's lonely wrist. The warm, reflective wisdom of B-flat major spread its honeyed delights. Then A major pushed forward again, demanding change and growth.

Under the force of Arno's melody, Rudi's hum opened to an "ah." His voice flowed into the indented white squares of the hospital blanket. D minor. The dancing theme began a new round, and the blanket moved. Its heaves missed the beat, and Julia stood, her hand seeking Bettina's red curls. One small arm raked the other and tried to free it of its clinging strips. A major. Her daughter's chin rose, and her dry lips parted. Her brown eyes opened.

"Mama!"

14

And He Shall Purify

Bettina rode like a triumphing conqueror into the Hof of cheering friends. The neighbors' applause made Julia feel a rush of gratitude, but she kept her eyes on her daughter. Still in her cast, with rusty scrapes on her arms, the little girl beamed with joy. Craving fresh air, she had thrashed in her hospital bed and cried angrily until she was exhausted. Only in the past week, when Julia had sat with her constantly, had she begun to smile. On the spot where she had landed stood a glazed chocolate cake, toward which her eyes turned greedily.

Since the interrogation, Julia had refused to leave Bettina and had spent each day and night at the hospital. Only Basti had persuaded her to wash and dress.

"C'mon," he muttered. "You gotta look good for that social worker. You stay like this, she's gonna think you're nuts."

That had been the condition: Julia retained full custody of Bettina, but her home would be inspected each week. Frau Krieger, a fierce, dark-eyed little woman, confronted Julia as soon as she was assigned to her case. In her loose-fitting black dress with popcorn-shaped flowers, the social worker buzzed like a threatening bee. Sick with humiliation, Julia listened to her warnings about how to care for a two-year-old girl. She wanted to shout at the domineering woman, but she knew that she couldn't protest. Because of her mistake, the girl squirming to see the gooey cake might not have been here today. She resigned herself to Frau Krieger's visits and told herself she would have to endure. Probably the woman had become a bully from handling girls who really *had* killed their kids.

A tight warmth stretched Julia's face, and she realized she was smiling. After those dark weeks, happiness surged up from below like water from a forgotten spring. Raked and groomed, the Mehringstrasse Hof had never looked so fine. With loving fingers, the bushes had been watered and trimmed, and the blue and yellow recycling bins shone from scrubbing. Neighbors Julia barely knew waited shyly around the softening cake. A stocky Czech man from the ground floor was fighting sleep after a long night on guard. Even Frau Riemann had turned out for Bettina, looking bonier than ever in a red dress. Overwhelmed, Julia embraced them all, and she felt no blame in their touch.

In the last week, as she had sat in the hospital, there had been a breakthrough in the housing negotiations. Rudi had offered to sublet his Steglitz apartment for half price, and Frau Riemann was leaving the house after thirty-two years. When Julia told Astrid about Frau Krieger, her neighbor refused to move downstairs.

"You take the place," Astrid insisted. "What if the kid tries flyin' again? What am I gonna do down there anyway? The place stinks."

Sure enough, the ground floor apartment reeked of Frau Riemann, a mix of cologne, soft vegetables, and sweaty sheets. When Julia scrubbed the place down a few days later, regret slowed her strokes. The close rooms smelled of unfulfilled longing, and once she had scoured them, no trace would remain of its throbs.

In early August, Basti and Rudi turned the Mehringstrasse house upside down. To accommodate Astrid, the Czech guard offered his ground floor flat in the side wing and moved up into Julia's old place. Four flights of stairs were nothing to him, as long as people would let him sleep. Grumbling, Astrid left her high perch, but she savored the smoky man-smell of her new space. In a rental truck, Basti and Rudi fetched the books from Steglitz and hauled them up to Astrid's old place. Where Astrid had shouted from her kitchen window, Rudi now appeared with friendly dark eyes.

Overnight, Astrid stopped moaning about the stairs, but she quickly found a new complaint. Down in the shadows, she couldn't call to her neighbors, let alone track their movements. With her window open, she leafed glumly through magazines and yelled to people as they crossed the Hof. Once again, she found herself next to Julia and waved to Bettina from her nearby window.

Julia's own windows now faced south, but few rays reached the ground floor. If her plants were going to live, they would have to drink the weak light like gallons of underbrewed tea. Her only hope was to put them directly under the living room window, but from the start, she knew that she couldn't. Sadly, she fingered the shining, heart-shaped leaves begging her for sustenance. Renate had been right. Someday she could have her plants again, a living, breathing tangle. For now, she settled for some violets on the sills and passed her mass of green on to Rudi. She polished and oiled Basti's table, but she moved it as far from the window as she could. Instead of plants, it now held magazines, spread to cover the lingering water spots.

Bettina adapted more quickly than Julia to the sensations of the ground floor. Although there was less light, there was a feast of noise. From the Hof came slams, footsteps, and raucous duets, but Julia focused on scrapes from the shop below. She listened to Basti's tools coax reluctant wood as though she were hearing the house's heart beat. On those aimless days, nothing comforted her more than the rhythm of Basti's work.

A pause in the continuo meant he was up with Rudi, whose apartment served mainly as an office. With Rudi as manager, Basti's business was thriving. He boasted to Julia that someday he would buy his own building, and she could live in his finest apartment.

When Basti wasn't working, he spent most of his time with Julia since he had cut his weakening bond with Birgit. When he learned she had been passing information to Renate, he left her with searing disgust. Birgit protested in a bitter scene that Astrid described with glee. She had caught gusts of it blowing through the basement gratings—like two cats screaming in a whirl of fur. Basti's wrath had ejected Birgit from the house in a stream of sulfurous shame. She and her mother had landed well, in an apartment financed by her boss—Szczemanski, Szczepanski, something like that. The hapless middle-aged Pole was smitten with Birgit. In return for her favors, he had transferred her to a store on the teeming, fashionable Ku'damm.

"He's off the hook!" Astrid grinned. "He's safe! He's free!"

"How's he doing?" asked Julia.

"Aw, he's fine," she scoffed. "I don't think he even cares— 'cept maybe for bein' relieved."

Julia doubted that, but she let Astrid savor her delight.

"Maybe he's gay." She giggled. "Maybe I'll luck out. That friend of yours is the best thing that ever happened to him."

"Oh, I don't think he's gay," said Julia quietly.

"Oh, no?" Astrid's eyes dug into her. "You got evidence to the contrary?"

"No, no." Julia smiled. "I just don't think he is."

That August, she enjoyed the slow mornings when sleep withdrew instead of being snatched away. With little desire to go out, she spent all her time with Bettina and relished the ripples of her daughter's voice. Grudgingly, Frau Krieger noted Julia's clean apartment, which she dusted and swept out each day. After her third visit, the social worker softened since she could see no defiance on Julia's part.

In daily calls, Marga urged Julia to come back to work, and the last week of August, she consented. She deferred the return as long as she could since it terrified her to leave Bettina. Anxiously, she delivered her daughter to the women at Kinderfreude. They swore that without their strongest voice, they had been going gray with boredom.

Sensing Julia's fear, Basti walked with her to work. She cherished their soft early-morning talks in the delicate air. With Basti's arm around her, she passed the Turkish fruit seller, who frowned at her confusedly.

At the doughnut shop, Marga embraced her hungrily and told of squabbles in the band. The Inter Alia gig hadn't brought them an agent, and she and Kevin were fighting the guitarist, who wanted to try their luck in the provinces. Julia stacked soft, powdery doughnuts and smiled as Marga turned irreverent. She balked only when Marga urged her to sing again, as everyone else had been doing.

Since that terrible day, Julia hadn't been able to sing a note. She had tried a few times, but all that emerged was a choked whisper. Her speaking voice flowed, but she couldn't make music. A dam was blocking the river that ran from her belly to the world beyond her lips. Rudi told her to be patient and promised that the music would return. If she just kept on living, someday it would surprise her.

"When'll that be?" Julia asked.

Although Rudi had his own apartment, he often stayed the night. Maybe he wanted to watch Julia, or maybe he was lonely.

The tracks under his eyes spoke of battering nights. The day of Bettina's fall, he had been working with Basti, and he had quickly followed him up the steps. Since Rudi had found Bettina lying in the Hof, he had taken her fall harder than anyone. He wouldn't talk about it, but the memory throbbed behind his eyes. If only she could scrub away that picture of a still, outstretched little hand against the dirt. In the weeks since the accident, Julia had drawn Rudi in, sensing that he needed comfort as much as she did.

Since Rudi had left Steglitz, the longer ride to the lab had been tiring him, and Julia urged him to eat and rest. Only work sustained him, and he took his drug liberally. In the lab each day from eight until six, he helped physicists and planned the choir's *Messiah* trip. When he got home, he went straight to his computer and started his third job as Basti's manager. When Julia spent the evening with Basti and Rudi, Rudi drooped as Basti raved about his new projects. With a quiet smile, Rudi struggled to listen and told him which were realizable and which weren't. Sometimes Julia cooked dinner for Rudi since with Basti, he never relaxed.

Tonight he had eaten some spaghetti and salad, and the food had made him sleepy. Julia hoped he would stay. Alone, he couldn't defend himself against the night's tortures. Every hour and a half he awoke, thinking of ticket prices or whether the liquid helium valve would freeze. At least that was what he said. She suspected he was whipped by a storm of memories, swirling around an image he shouldn't have seen. Rudi faded beside her in his blue-gray shirt, his thin leg warming her thigh.

"Your voice will come back," he murmured. "This is normal. Who could sing after something like this?"

"Mm-hmm." Julia's voice caught, and Rudi turned to face her.

"Are you all right? Do you want to go to bed? Don't worry about cleaning up. We can do that tomorrow."

Rudi's concern made Julia smile, and his long, thin face warmed. It pleased her to see him smiling back.

"Have you heard from him?" she asked.

Rudi looked down and sighed. "Yeah. He asks about you a lot."

Julia's heart thumped. "But he hasn't called—he hasn't come. I thought—"

"He doesn't have the guts," said Rudi.

Julia stared at him, shocked, but no irony enlivened his face. It was the worst thing Rudi had ever said about Arno. In the soft light, his gray shirt deepened the shadows under his eyes.

"He doesn't—" Julia faltered.

"He's a human being. He's afraid." Rudi flexed his knuckles. "But he did talk to that policewoman. I think he helped you there."

Julia froze. She hadn't wanted to think about it, but she was starting to realize how many people had talked to the *Kommissarin*. She hated having her life turned into other people's stories, then interpreted by a stranger. Rudi watched Julia silently, hoping she could escape her thoughts.

"He is who he is." He sighed. "Neither one of us can change him. But he does want you for *Messiah*."

Julia spluttered. "He thinks I can sing."

"He's not a singer." Rudi frowned. "There are things he doesn't understand." He floated into a memory, half smiling at her weathered coffee table.

"Do you see him much?" she asked.

Rudi smiled ruefully. "When would I see him?"

Julia laughed, and Rudi squeezed her hand.

"Well—I talk to him—" He hesitated. "But he's been hard to reach. He's been spending time with William Handshaw."

"Oh …" Julia breathed.

"But it's okay—it's okay." Rudi's voice gained strength. "Since London—things have been different. It feels different now."

"Yeah?" Julia wished Rudi would raise his eyes, but he kept them fixed on the table. "What happened in London?" she asked.

"Just what I told you," he said slowly. "When he came back that night, I felt so happy. We went out to dinner, and he told me this crazy story about some Jamaicans he met."

"Oh," said Julia. She tried to find the spot that was holding Rudi's eyes.

Immersed in his memory, he smiled dreamily, and she waited for him to go on.

"He ate a lot—drank a lot." He laughed. "This great big steak and a whole lot of beer. I can still see him there with the fork in his hand—the patterns of light shooting off it. Then when we got back—when we got back—" Rudi raised his eyes. He smiled at an African violet that was drinking the day's last glimmers. "I went to brush my teeth, and when I came out, there he was in bed—fast asleep, taking up the whole thing, like he forgot I was there."

"That sounds like him." Julia laughed. "So what'd you do?"

"I got right in with him." Rudi's face glowed. "There wasn't any couch—no place else I could go. There was nothing else to do—so I got right in with him. I couldn't move him, so I went to the far side."

"Yeah?" Julia's stomach tightened.

"I got in with my back to him, on the edge of the bed. From the way he was breathing, I thought he was asleep." His smile faded. "But—he wasn't." He stared straight ahead, trying to press his thoughts into words. "He wasn't. He reached for me—the way a little kid reaches for a teddy bear."

A thud in the Hof broke the silence as a bag of wet trash hit a bin.

"He pulled me against him, and he said, 'Thanks. Thanks for waiting for me. Thanks.' Half-asleep. Just like that. I think he really meant it."

"Of course he did," said Julia.

"And then—and then—"

"You don't have to tell me this," she murmured.

"Oh, don't worry." Rudi glanced at her playfully. He hesitated, his memory stream slowing.

"He—he just held on to me. All night. We lay there side by side—after a while we were breathing together. I stayed awake as long as I could."

"That's nice," whispered Julia.

Rudi stared at her shelves as though he had forgotten her presence. Rapture washed his thin features. For the first time, Julia sensed what kept him going.

"But I did fall asleep—I must have fallen asleep. Because when I woke up, I didn't know who I was, where I was, who *he* was." Rudi laughed softly in the embrace of memory. "But I had this feeling of peace. I've never known anything like it. I've never slept like that … I knew I … *belonged*—that I had a place in the world and I was with the person I was meant to be with." He turned to her, his dark eyes shining. "After that—no matter what he does—I know it's going to be all right. I think if you're honest about who you are and what you feel, nothing can ever hurt you."

Tears welled up in Julia's eyes, and Rudi looked at her guiltily.

"I want to sing again." Julia's voice broke. "I want to sing, and I can't."

Rudi wrapped his arms around her. "You will," he whispered. "You will."

■

Despite Rudi's claims of understanding, he and Arno clashed about Julia. Rudi wanted to wait and believed her voice would return as she healed. Arno wanted action—therapy, voice lessons, relentless practice. Julia was a singer, and nothing would help her but singing. When Rudi spoke to her, he softened their conflict as an ocean smoothes stones, but Julia could imagine the smashing breakers.

"Do you want to help her, or do you want an alto for your *Messiah*?" Rudi had yelled at Arno one night. Julia could hear subdued aftershocks of anger as Rudi relayed the conversation to her. "She's a person, you know! We're all people! It takes people to make music!"

"What do you want, for me to pamper her for years?" Arno had roared. "While her voice goes to shit? Fuck that! She's a singer! She should be singing!"

"And that's in whose interest?" Rudi had snapped.

Arno had grinned at that, to Rudi's surprise. "Hers. It's in hers."

Rudi had ridden home in a passionate rage, but to his dismay, Basti backed Arno. Julia felt surprised by that until Rudi told her Basti's reasoning. "If she can do it, it'll make her feel better," Basti had said. "Sometimes people just need a little push."

That night Rudi thought of a compromise. He later told Julia it was so simple and obvious it had left him laughing in the dark. At two he called Arno, who liked the idea. Julia could sing with the Bartholdy Choir. She had left Arno's Friedrichskirche group soon after she started at the Hans Breithaus Academy, partly for lack of time, but mainly for her voice. Despite all her efforts to control her sound, she flooded most alto sections. Remembering her as a geyser among fountains, Arno and Rudi had forgotten she had been a choral singer. Now, with fifteen strong voices as camouflage, she could blend without worrying how she sounded. Julia in the choir—it was perfect.

———————————————■———————————————

Next Monday night, Julia joined the Bartholdy Choir altos. Arno placed her in the middle, where singers surrounded her like warm water. On one side was Carola, who had returned at last, having convinced her husband to watch their son Monday nights. On the other sat Sabine Buchholz, undaunted by her failure in London. On the edge of her seat, holding her score with skinny arms, Sabine tracked Arno's moves through rimless glasses. With a voice a little like the one Julia had lost, she made each entrance precisely. Carola didn't sing as cleanly, but her sound was fuller and enriched the notes Sabine offered.

Even floating among so many voices, Julia found that she couldn't sing. Only breath with a hint of a tone emerged, like a drop of syrup in a glass of water. She felt her throat waiting to shape the note, but the driving force in her belly had died. As Sabine guided her, Julia sensed the musicians listening, especially the sharp ears up front. That was the worst—watching Arno strain to hear her voice and frown as he failed to find it. The rehearsals reminded her of nightmares in which she tried to scream but her throat was shut.

It didn't help that the singers around her saw her as a fallen goddess. Any choir was a kettle of gossip, and Julia sensed the hissing she never heard. Julia Martens in a choir! Julia Martens, who had lost her voice! Julia Martens, who had inexplicably gotten pregnant, then let her baby fall out a window! When the singers spoke to Julia, she began to realize how her mother must have felt with cancer. When they asked about Bettina, she felt a jolt, and when they didn't, the air curdled. Anja's high voice expressed understanding, but most people's supportiveness rang false. Julia preferred the looks of the younger singers, whose curious stares at least seemed honest. In the choir that Christmas, Julia watched Sascha Neumann's back sway as she performed the alto solos. Except for Rudi and Anja, most people avoided Julia. Her affliction pained them as much as it did her.

When the new year began, Arno overpowered Rudi, saying that there was no more time to lose. He called Nigel Hunt and begged him for the best voice therapist he knew. Remembering Julia from her audition, the RBB Choir conductor found a top vocal coach. Both he and Arno offered to pay for any sessions that Julia's health insurance wouldn't cover.

Twice a week for an hour, Julia worked with Herr Hahn, a tall, serious man with a bird's face. Behind his glasses, his hazel eyes sought a spark like those of a cold man starting a fire. Their stinging flashes of pity revealed that he knew about Bettina's fall. But practical and encouraging, Herr Hahn stuck to mechanics and never asked about what had silenced Julia. For weeks he demanded nothing but breaths, deep breaths that began in her core. Doggedly, Julia exhaled with an open throat and produced a low, toneless "ah." Like a broken machine, she wasn't engaging. Her driving force was turning, and her controls stood ready, but they didn't connect. Damping his frustration, Herr Hahn urged Julia to keep trying.

When Bettina turned three, the little girl's voice overpowered her mother's. Most of the neighbors came to her party, which also marked the departure of Frau Krieger. Convinced of Julia's competence, the social worker told the *Jugendamt* of her clean apartment, abundant food, and musical talent. Julia's scrubbing and dusting had ceased to be a performance. She took comfort in anything physical, gripping potatoes and fondling soft, plump doughnuts. Most of all she loved to caress Bettina, who squirmed and giggled delightedly. Her wriggling warmth drove Julia's pulse, and she vowed not to lose Bettina again.

With nowhere to go but rehearsals and work, Julia savored the rhythm of her days. Erik's calls sometimes broke the pattern because he wanted to visit. Since the accident, Julia had shunned Renate, whose exploitation she couldn't forgive. It was one thing to criticize but another to take a woman's child, and when Julia thought of her, her fingers curled. For the first time, however, Erik seemed to be acting alone. Another mind's cadences no longer shaped his voice. He didn't mention Renate, and his interest in Bettina seemed real. More than anything, he wanted to know about Julia's voice, and he asked what he could do to help.

When practice resumed after the summer break, Julia's whisper had condensed to a pleasant rill. With liquid sweetness, she could glide through any melody, but her voice lacked strength and fullness. Nurturing its flow, she sang with Arno's altos as they began their work on *Messiah*. The New York concert was set for December 12, the date chosen by Arno and Linda over a year ago.

One night at practice in October, Handel's runs flowed easily after a warm, sweet day of dry leaves. At Kinderfreude, Bettina had drawn a startled red cat with a bushy fox tail. That weekend, Erik had come up to visit and delighted Bettina with new games. He'd said nothing of Renate but talked for hours about old times at the Imbiss. Late at night, Julia had laughed deep and hard as she remembered her father's old tricks, like how whenever the skinny health inspector came around, he would offer her a bratwurst and say, "I don't think she's seen one of these in a while."

Tonight, a warm platter of potato pancakes lay comfortably in Julia's stomach. Handel's English collapsed in her mouth like soft vegetables, but she liked "And the Glory of the Lord." In bright A major, Handel had set the alto line in the heart of her range. The opening notes were sweet juice on her tongue. The altos led, and after their third try at their entrance, Carola glanced at Julia and smiled. Something in those first low notes made Julia resonate like an organ pipe. She imagined Handel writing them and picturing a great, big, hearty alto. As Julia held a clean A, Sabine glanced at her sharply, but Julia barely noticed. Up front, Arno started, but he kept up the beat. Julia wondered what was bothering him. "And all flesh shall see it together!" she sang, relishing the 3/4 tempo. In the front row, Rudi turned his head, so that his startled dark eyes pricked her. As she approached the last phrase, Julia felt herself rising: "For the mouth of the Lord hath spoken it!" The final A was a living pillar around which she wrapped her soul. Before the choir reached the final cadence, Arno stopped them, producing anguished groans.

"Hold it!" he called. "Hold it! Julia, you're too loud. You're going to have to hold back."

As the first sad chords of *Messiah* sounded, Julia drew a deep breath. Herr Hahn had offered her beta-blockers, but he'd smiled when she refused and said that he never took them either. Since that crucial rehearsal, Julia's voice had returned in surges and bursts. Only in the past few weeks had it reclaimed its original power.

Facing a full house of fifteen hundred, Julia wished she knew someone in the red seats. Except for Michael's wife and girls in the balcony, she recognized no one and would have loved to see Astrid or Basti. Both of them had wanted to come, but for different reasons, they had declined. Kowalski had forbidden Astrid to make the long flight, so she'd settled for buying Julia a new dress. For the first time ever, Julia was singing in a fresh gown chosen especially for her. The stretchy, close-fitting black velvet looked a lot like Linda's, except that it was cleft by a tasteful décolletage.

"That looks real professional," Basti had said. "You're going to look nice."

By now Basti could have afforded the New York trip, but he couldn't leave his work. Out of nowhere, he had landed an apprenticeship. In early November, he had gone to see Herr Seidemann about a tool and found the old man dead on his couch. Since summer, the sick carpenter had been seen less and less in the neighborhood, except for regular trips to Getränke Gillmann. For a week, Basti and Rudi stopped work to arrange his funeral, clean his apartment, and find his family. They had little luck, and after calling every number in his phone, they rounded up only some carpentry friends. One of them was a craftsman from Wilmersdorf who had worked with Herr Seidemann in the 1980s. Hearing of Basti's predicament, he offered to deal with the job center, knowing he would get a skilled carpenter as his apprentice.

With his apprenticeship letter, Basti would be able to open his own shop in a year. He and Rudi were already checking locations in Wilmersdorf, where they hoped to colonize a building. They would set up shop on the ground floor and do the heavy work in the back rooms and basement. Up above, they were planning to rent two apartments, one for each of them, and they urged Astrid and Julia to join them.

Astrid balked, refusing to leave her Kiez for the Wilmersdorf widows and their fat dogs. Since Birgit and her mother had moved out, the house's atmosphere had improved.

"Why give up a good thing?" demanded Astrid. Her hand swept the Hof in a possessive wave. "The Kiez management association needs me. What would I do way off down there?"

Her real reason for refusal was the distance from Kowalski, whom she still saw every two weeks. He had convinced her to have surgery, which he was going to do personally.

"He's gonna have his hands on my heart," she murmured. "Just think of that!"

Julia ran her finger over Basti's necklace, which she was wearing for the first time since the *St. John Passion*. She followed its fine links up toward her shoulder, where he had rested his hand yesterday at the airport.

"I'd come with you if I could," he'd said. "If I could, I'd always be with you. I want to take care of you and Bettina. And I will—as long as you'll let me. But we both know you play in a different league. You're gonna be a big-time singer."

A grunt from Arno interrupted their hug. Basti glared a warning as the conductor ushered Julia toward the security gate. When she glanced back at Basti, he smiled and waved. He'd stayed pressed against the glass until she, Arno, and Rudi had disappeared into the jet bridge.

The E minor chords of Handel's overture stirred sadness in Julia's blood. Their slow cadences fell like the steps of refugees trudging down an endless road. She smiled when Udo straightened for the fugue and showed his string section the energy they would need. With crisp gestures and parted lips, Arno led them into the fugue, and Handel's clean melody filled the hall. Both Udo and Jakob had sought Julia out to say how pleased they were to work with her again.

"You're the only one who can do justice to this music," Udo had murmured. "Thank God you're here. I wasn't sure he could get you."

Jakob had asked her to slip out with him into Manhattan's throbbing pockets of life. Julia was sure he and Udo knew of the accident, but they showed none of the awkwardness that had stiffened people last summer. With his head full of Handel, Udo seemed to have forgotten. He swayed tranquilly as he played. Glancing from Arno to his musicians, he guided the exchanges among the strings.

Udo's look reminded Julia of Erik, who had called a few hours before. Although it was ten at night in Frankfurt, he had put Bettina on. "Mama!" she'd crowed. Thrilled to be up past her bedtime, she had piped on until Erik retook the phone by force. She had a new doll who sang different notes depending on how you tilted her. As she swooped through the air in chaotic loops, "Lola" could sing entire melodies. Bettina had been throwing her as far as she could and echoing her cries as she crashed. Lola had been a special get-well gift from her *Oma*, Renate.

After months of searing, murderous thoughts, Julia had begun to relent. She had never known her grandparents, and having an *Oma* opened a rich world to Bettina. Renate's voice still knotted Julia's stomach, but the grandmother offered Bettina a fan of glowing paths. Julia pressed her fingertips into Basti's chain as she sensed that Bettina would never be hers alone. The warm, wanting child brought together everyone who had made her, and though they moved to different rhythms, they would have to dance. If Julia was going to sing, she couldn't control Bettina's care. She couldn't perform without Erik's help, and with Erik came Renate. As Julia watched the sea of soft, dark heads, she wondered what bonds held them in place. It seemed there was no love without humiliation—at least, none that was worth living for.

A sudden flash pulled her eyes to Arno, whose face was aglow with passion. Seized by the music, he had merged with the sound, his movements sculpting its shape. As the melody gained force, his gestures broadened and drew together the instrumental lines. With their eyes on the conductor, the players slowed through their last cascade and settled into a solemn E minor chord. Markus stood.

In the three and a half years since the *St. Matthew Passion*, he seemed to have grown a decade. Like his voice, his body had rounded out, yet neither one seemed heavy. Score in hand, he stood straight and serious and directed himself to the audience.

"Comfort ye ..."

Warm and full, his opening notes throbbed with compassion.

"Comfort ye ..."

His high E was a living force. The audience leaned back with parted lips. Knowing what his tenor could do, Arno gave most of his attention to the orchestra. He encouraged Markus only with his sparkling eyes.

"The voice of him that crieth in the wilderness!"

Markus's clean F-sharp resounded from every surface. Next to Julia, Linda smiled and studied his rounded lips.

The audience stirred as the first chorus started. For too long they had sat perfectly still. This was what they had come for—even the *New York Times* music critic, whom William Handshaw had called a few days before.

"And the glory, the glory of the Lord!"

With one voice, the Bartholdy Choir altos sang out, rich and powerful. Stretching his fingers, Arno led them with a joyful smile.

"And the glory, the glory of the Lord!"

The choir came to life. Unable to resist, Julia turned. On a high E, Anja was singing with her mouth open wide. An octave lower, Rudi was straining passionately. With Arno's hands urging them, sixty voices created living beauty, a pulsing, ever-changing shape. Listening to the music, Julia forgot everything she knew and thought only of what the sound would do next.

Her breath brought her back when A major darkened to D minor and Michael rose to sing. She was next. She had to keep the music alive, and if she faltered, she would kill it.

Deep and daunting, Michael's rich voice filled the hall. "Thus saith the Lord!"

With a sharp glance, Arno signaled him to give full power.

"I will shake …"

Storming through rapid turns, Michael's voice rocked every atom, so that the audience lived God's threat rather than hearing it. With limitless force, Michael warned of divine wrath. Under him, Udo and his strings played rapid chords, led by Arno's dramatic strokes. The music moved so quickly there was no time to breathe. Oh, God. She was next. Why didn't Michael keep singing? No one conveyed God's wrath better than he did. Could she create Handel's fire? Julia listened for Herr Hahn telling her how to breathe. Instead, she got Frau Glintenkamp.

"From all the way down. From your center. That's a good girl."

Julia rose. Linda smiled as she passed, and Michael winked on the way back to his seat. Julia held up her score and squared her shoulders, so that her bra bit her breasts. With his arms raised, Arno met her eyes.

Minutes ago, he had held her at arm's length and smiled down after a crushing hug. "Are you ready?"

"Yeah." Her voice had flowed out from a dark place.

"*Dann los geht's.* Let's go."

Behind her, Julia felt Rudi's presence, but she could no longer turn. With a sharp movement, Arno started the orchestra. Julia inhaled. The breath felt right.

"And who may abide the day of his coming?"

Her voice emerged in a warm wave.

"And who shall stand when he appeareth?"

Julia spun the high D, and an inner force took hold. She wasn't making the music; it was already alive, drawing its strength from her. Slowing the pace, Arno restrained her, but his eyes shone. The audience leaned back.

"When he appeareth ..."

Julia sustained her last note, knowing she could hold it as long as he asked. Arno's arms snapped down, and Udo and Jakob burst into action. With strokes too fast to see, they built the refiner's fire, the terrifying sea of flame. Udo's fear turned to exhilaration as his strings matched Arno's pace. With a furious look, Arno drove them on.

"For he is like a refiner's fire ..."

Julia glided through her first cascade, her voice rising over the orchestra. In her core where the breaths began, the music made sense. She met Arno's eyes and felt herself join him. Effortlessly she soared through Paul, George, and Ringo, hitting every note despite the fast pace. She pummeled the audience with her arpeggios, then raced down through Motherfucker. "Who shall stand when he appeareth?" she demanded, evoking a collective gasp. Handel's music belonged in her body. When someone who produced life warned of never-ending death, the threat became so much more real. With fierce concentration, Arno cut Julia off to prepare her for the larghetto section.

"And who may abide the day of his coming?" she sang to his restraining eyes. As they held a long chord, she and the strings watched Arno intently, waiting for what they knew was coming.

With one sharp stroke, Arno touched off the last section. Over the orchestra, Julia's voice broke free.

"For he is like a refiner's fire!"

Udo smiled as his arm shot back and forth, but no sound of his players could match Julia. Like a lightning bolt, her highest note sliced the hall. Pulsing, alive, she soared up with the music.

How easy it was! Bouncing through her last arpeggios, she looked up playfully at Arno. He frowned a warning and ordered her to slow as they approached the final measures. After Julia's last note, she felt keen disappointment and wished that she could go on singing. But following Arno, she waited through the frenzied measures as the orchestra brought back the flames. Just one more chorus until she could sing again. She met Arno's eyes and found sheer joy. An instant later, Arno shifted his gaze to the sopranos and cued them to begin "And He Shall Purify."

Acknowledgments

I would like to thank all the people who gave generously of their time to advise me as I wrote *Refiner's Fire*, offering thoughts that have helped bring the novel to life. I am grateful to the conductors, Kilian Nauhaus, Eric Nelson, and Achim Zimmermann; to the voice teachers, Marina Gilman and Rainer Schnös; to the singers, Joseph Curtis, Judith Engel, Shawn Kirchner, Ulrich Stern, and Barbara Zettel; and to the mothers and mothers-to-be, Rachel Bowser, Hyo Yoon Kang, Nuria Monn, Antje Radeck, Edna Suárez Díaz, and Kelley Wilder. I thank Susanne Krusche and Krish Sathian for their medical advice, and Ulrich Haase and Thomas Sieberz for their pointers on carpentry. For their information about Berlin life, I thank Safia Azzouni, Sabine Bremer, Uljana Feest, and Britta Lange, and I am grateful to Sabine Seip and Jan Krusche for their tips on the German judicial system. None of these generous souls are responsible for any errors I may have made in interpreting their advice or for the liberties I have taken in applying it.

Refiner's Fire benefited greatly from the advice of faculty and students at the 2008 and 2011 Squaw Valley Writers Workshops. I am especially indebted to Randal K. Jackson, whose suggestion for restructuring the novel brought it to life in a new way, and to Diana Richmond, whose encouragement in 2008 affirmed my faith in the story. I would also like to thank workshop leader Sands Hall, faculty member Elise Blackwell, and fellow students Ilana DeBare, Danielle Farrell, Ruth Halpern, Robert Hunting,

Joe Heinrich, Kristin Kearns, Beverly Parayno, Erin Striff, Alia Voltz, and Andrew Wiener for their comments on the novel. I am also grateful to my friends who read and commented on *Refiner's Fire* as general readers, especially Lorraine Daston, Sander Gilman, Diego Luis, Jesse Moskowitz, Lynna Williams, and Hubert Zapf. Most of all, I want to thank my colleague and trusted friend Jim Grimsley, who has helped me learn how I can turn the worlds in my head into worlds that can be seen, felt, and heard by other people.

I am indebted to my conscientious, brilliant copy-editor at iUniverse, Kelsey Adams, and to Editorial Services Associate Cynthia Wolfe; Publishing Services Associates Reed Samuel, Flynn Sarte, and Robin Sawyer; and Check-In Coordinators Vinnia Alvarez and Christine Colborne.

Textual quotations of the musical pieces described in this novel come from the following editions: Johann Sebastian Bach, cantata 72, *Alles, nur nach Gottes Willen*, © Breitkopf & Härtel [1726]; Johann Sebastian Bach, *Johannes-Passion*, edited by Walter Heinz Bernstein, © Bärenreiter-Verlag, 1981 [1724]; Johann Sebastian Bach, *Matthäus-Passion*, edited by Alfred Dürr, © Bärenreiter-Verlag, 1974 [1727]; Johann Sebastian Bach, *Weihnachts-Oratorium*, edited by Alfred Dürr, © Bärenreiter-Verlag, 1989 [1734]; and Georg Friedrich Händel, *Messiah*, edited by Kurt Soldan, © C. F. Peters [1741]. The dates in brackets indicate the original dates of composition and performance. All translations of the German texts are my own. For information about Georg Friedrich Handel's *Messiah*, I have relied on Donald Burrows' *Handel: Messiah*, Cambridge University Press, 1991; and Calvin A. Stapert, *Handel's Messiah: Comfort for God's People*, William B. Eerdman, 2010.

Printed in the United States
By Bookmasters